PRAISE FOR OLIVIA KIERNAN
AND *TOO CLOSE TO BREATHE*

"Dublin makes a formidable background for a tense police procedural that introduces a strong heroine in *Too Close to Breathe*. Irish author Olivia Kiernan imbues Detective Chief Superintendent Frankie Sheehan with intelligence and unusual sleuthing skills in the exciting debut.... Kiernan's insights into Frankie's emotional and physical recovery are skillfully woven into the plot.... While the serial killer is often overused, Kiernan finds a unique twist to this trope, where Dublin's streets and neighborhoods receive a fresh view. *Too Close to Breathe* excels with realistic characters, from Frankie and her police colleagues to the surprising villain."   —Associated Press

"Olivia Kiernan pulls no punches in the tense, atmospheric *Too Close to Breathe*. . . . In a setup that's equal parts Fiona Barton and Gillian Flynn . . . A crime thriller extraordinaire."   —*Providence Journal*

"As much a procedural as a character study of coming to terms with one's own capacity for perseverance in the face of tragedy, this will hopefully not be the last time readers encounter Kiernan's tough heroine."
                                                        —*Kirkus Reviews*

"[A] sure-footed, perfectly constructed mystery . . . One cannot read *Too Close to Breathe* without wishing and hoping for much more, and sooner rather than later."   —*Booklist*

"Olivia Kiernan is a formidable storyteller. She is a welcome voice in the world of crime fiction. The plot of *Too Close to Breathe* is tight and the story moves in an intricate way that makes it captivating and thrilling. The characters are meticulously crafted and will remain stuck in your memory for some time. *Too Close to Breathe* is an assured debut."
                                                —*Washington Book Review*

"One can only hope that this is the first of many to feature Kiernan's strong heroine."   —CrimeReads.com

"Solid debut . . . likable characters, strong pacing, and the appealing Dublin locale bode well for any sequel."   —*Publishers Weekly*

"Mesmerizing. Olivia Kiernan carefully unspools a complex riddle of murder, betrayal, and secret lives, layering on the menace even as she builds her tough-as-nails chief detective for the climactic finale. Clever plot. Brilliant characters. Everything you need in a great thriller."
                    —*#1 New York Times* bestselling author Lisa Gardner

"*Too Close to Breathe* welcomes a thrilling new voice to crime fiction. Taut and gritty, smart and dark, and with a brilliantly crafted detective in Frankie Sheehan, Olivia Kieran plots twists and turns that will keep you in knots to the very end."
                    —*New York Times* bestselling author Linda Fairstein

"A really slick, dynamic-paced police procedural, very much in the vein of Tana French. A proper page-turner, lovely, accomplished writing."
                    —Internationally bestselling author Jo Spain

"*Too Close to Breathe* is a fearless, fast-paced debut that drops you into the world of Dublin detective Frankie Sheehan—who is a perfect mix of frailty, ferocity, and guts. Add to this flashes of deft, dark humor and a compelling city setting and you have a must for fans of Irish crime fiction. Olivia Kiernan is a writer you'll read with your breath held."
                    —Jess Kidd, author of *Himself* and others

"Gritty, cynical, and haunting, this is crime writing of the highest order and the product of a darkly fascinating mind. First class."
                    —Internationally bestselling author David Mark

THE KILLER IN ME

THE KILLER IN ME

A NOVEL

OLIVIA KIERNAN

DUTTON

DUTTON

An imprint of Penguin Random House LLC
penguinrandomhouse.com

LIBRARY OF CONGRESS CATALOGING-IN-PUBLICATION DATA
Names: Kiernan, Olivia, author.
Title: The killer in me: a novel / Olivia Kiernan.
Description: New York: Dutton, [2019]
Identifiers: LCCN 2018047187 (print) | LCCN 2018050321 (ebook) |
ISBN 9781524742652 (ebook) | ISBN 9781524742669 (paperback)
Subjects: LCSH: Murder—Investigation—Fiction. | BISAC: FICTION / Mystery &
Detective / Women Sleuths. | FICTION / Suspense. | FICTION / Literary. |
GSAFD: Suspense fiction.
Classification: LCC PR6111.I43 (ebook) | LCC PR6111.I43 K55 2019 (print) |
DDC 823/.92—dc23
LC record available at https://lccn.loc.gov/2018047187

Printed in the United States of America
1 3 5 7 9 10 8 6 4 2

For Ann

THE KILLER IN ME

You might not look like a murderer but stay in prison long enough and time carves evil's face onto yours until you walk and talk like the devil himself. Inside, you're still the same man but no one sees that fella anymore. No, all they see is a killer.

—Seán Hennessy,
Fifteen Years a Murderer
Courtesy of Blackthorn Films © 2012

CHAPTER 1

THERE ARE TIMES in my line of work when I have to sit down with a known killer. Shake their hand. Talk to them. Where I have to let them think we're on a level, that their mind isn't so far from my own. It's a fine balance of control and you want them to believe they have it, even when they don't but especially if they do. You'll get the odd detective, wet behind the ears, who'll talk about building trust, a knowing glint in their eye because they think if a murderer chats with them, they've won them over, that their perp will peel off their mask and spill all.

But I've been doing this long enough to know that when a killer smiles at me, it's not me who's doing the indulging but them doing the tolerating. Thing is, no one really knows what a person is capable of, despite the smile on their face, the firmness of their handshake, or whether they look you in the eye as they lie to you.

I watch him make his way through the bar, trainers soft, heels sure. He is almost unrecognizable. Another bloke looking for a pint on a Sunday evening. He finds me at the back of the pub, holds out a hand. Fingers flex, shape around mine; calluses, a ridge along the top of his palm. Neat nails clipped back. The muscles bundle in his forearm as he squeezes my hand.

"It's good to meet you, Detective," he says, smiling. I feel his eyes take in the measure of me and I hope for his sake he's seeing more than a blonde in a suit.

A man free of his sentence. I watch him put his smile away, pull out a chair, lean strong hands on the table as he sits down. He's tall but I almost match him for height. Overall, he's a good-looking guy. Blue-eyed. A slim build, hair cut short, a fine shade of gold. A man who murdered his parents, tried to murder his younger sister. And the question is not whether he's a murderer but whether fifteen years inside is enough to change a person.

Tanya West is also sitting at the table. She's keeping it casual. A black T-shirt over blue jeans that could've come from the teens department. Dark hair pulled back into a high bun, large silver hoops dangling to her shoulders, a silver stud in her nose. I can feel her quick, dark eyes watching the interaction between Hennessy and myself. Tanya is a lawyer. The pain-in-the-backside kind: a defense lawyer. No detective working this side of murder likes defense lawyers. How many times have I watched serious criminals walk because of a crafty defense team? Not to mention that their job is to show up our stupidities, where we've fucked up, spoken to a suspect at the wrong time, or where the wrong procedure has invalidated solid bloody evidence.

Defense is the line we have to push our cases across. And Tanya's good at her job. You could catch a perp in the act, elbow deep in the entrails of their victim, and Tanya could convince a court that he'd only tripped over the body and landed hands down in the victim's guts. But I can't dislike Tanya. Her aim is not to trick or fool the law but to ask justice to bring its best game. Besides, she's my sister-in-law and I guess family counts for something because there are not many who could persuade me to sit across from a convicted murderer and listen to what he has to say, but Tanya can and has. Although, she was cute enough to keep the fact it was Seán Hennessy to herself.

"Good to see you again, Seán," she says. "Well"—she slants me a grin—"now we've got that warm greeting out of the way. Let's get started."

I rest back against my seat, unable to move my eyes from Seán Hennessy. Unable to shake the image of his crimes from my head. The furious mess of murder. The happy spree of knife wounds over his mother's body, his father's. His sister's.

Tanya places a file on the table and lays her hands on it with a kind of reverence. "Seán, we're very lucky that Frankie is willing to consider your case." She turns, smiles at me. "She's one of the best."

"Of course, of course," he murmurs. Lips dry. His tongue clacks in his mouth. Along his hairline, the wet gleam of moisture. He wipes it away with quick fingers. "I'm very grateful, Detective."

Looking at Hennessy is enough to make me doubt the point of my own career. Where's the remorse? Not sitting across from me. He took two lives, almost a third. He's served his time and now here he is. "I didn't do it," he says.

I rub the base of my neck. "I can't stay long."

He glances at Tanya then to me, leans back, and runs his

hands over his pockets. "Well, let me get you a drink. What'll you have?"

"No thanks. I'm on call."

He stops. "Tanya?"

"Thanks, Seán. A sav blanc, please. Small," she answers.

He looks to me again, as if he's about to ask me if I'm sure, but he thinks better of it. "Grand. Grand."

He gets up, steps away from the table, back through the Sunday punters, head turning from side to side as he works his way to the bar, eyes stalking the room. The pub we're in was a favorite of mine when I still lived at home. It used to be a one-room treasure, where you could fall in the door to a row of bar stools, and that was it. At some point in the last few years, it's been gutted out and extended but the owners have tried to capture that old-bar feel—dark wood booths, low ceilings, and dull wooden floors. I watch Seán step up to order, rest his foot casually on the shining brass footrest that runs along the base of the bar. The barman looks up from the other end of the room, finishes wrapping a set of cutlery in a paper napkin, then approaches Seán with a nod.

I lean toward my sister-in-law. "Christ, Tanya, you never told me it was Seán fucking Hennessy you were working with."

She gives a tiny shrug. The thin hoops of her earrings bounce off her shoulders. "You never asked." She fixes her attention on the file. "Does it matter who it is? He has a good case for appeal."

"He murdered his bloody parents."

"There's room for doubt." She throws a quick glance at Seán across the bar, keeps her voice low. "We've been approached by a production company called Blackthorn Films. They're doing a documentary on Seán's case. It's due to air in the next week. This could do wonders for our charity's profile."

Tanya's charity, Justice Meets Justice, works on new evidence or overlooked avenues of investigation on cases where they believe there might have been a miscarriage of justice. An innocent person convicted for a crime they didn't commit.

I'm busy but since the Costello case a few months back, nothing has broken my stride on the murder front. The Bureau for Serious Crime is doing its job. Set up three years ago to keep a focus on complex investigations in Ireland in a world where increasingly our law enforcement must look outwards, the aim of the Bureau is to remain a bastion of defense against our own criminals. Four districts of the gardaí's finest detectives with a central hub in Dublin, run by me. We are a flexible, well-oiled machine that can step in where local resources are scant, or conversely handle those cases of national concern that feed the media. And the last few months have seen me on a roll. Three cases slapped down and filed away as if I'd been working on a kids' crossword.

I sigh. "What do you need me for?"

"It would help to have a detective chief superintendent on board. Even if not in an official capacity. We don't have anyone with your skill set. You're good at reading people, Frankie."

I look across the bar at Hennessy. I could make short work of this, run a few interviews, get to the real truth of why he thinks his conviction should be scrubbed out. I'm curious as to what it is that has Tanya so worked up about his case. She knows I can't resist a puzzle. Even one I know already has an answer.

"This isn't about money?" I check.

She flushes but keeps a lid on whatever emotion is behind her reaction. "This is a big risk for us. With the media interest, if we come out looking like mugs, we'll not survive it. But if we're right, this will make us."

I watch Hennessy as he waits for the drinks. The barman reaches for glasses. He laughs at something Hennessy says, his thin shoulders shaking in response. And I can see how the public will be seduced by Hennessy if a documentary airs. He's not hard on the eyes. He appears kind. He seems normal. Like one of us. He wears his sheep's clothing with ease.

I think of the constant reports of serious crime that pass our desks daily and the careful designation of energy and money to each one. Even looking at Hennessy's case in the hours around my work, it would be hard to justify the time.

I hear the regret in my voice when I speak. "Tanya, I'm sorry but I don't think I'm the right person for this. The law served up the right sentence that day, and I don't believe society owes Seán Hennessy one further moment of thought. From what I can re-member, there was a crate-load of evidence, as well as witnesses."

"But what if the evidence was wrong?"

"Tanya—"

"Wait!" She holds up a palm. "Bríd and Cara Hennessy's blood was found beneath Seán's fingernails and on his shirt. What if I told you that the first paramedic on the scene assessed both Bríd and Cara"—she counts off both of the victims on her fingers as she speaks—"but then treated Seán for shock?"

I sigh.

"Come on, Frankie. It's cross contamination. This was one of the major pieces of evidence submitted by the prosecution. What if there were more errors?" She gives me an intense look and pulls the file back across the table. Opens it. "Blackthorn Films. They've won awards. This is going to be big. The charity can't pass it up. Yes, we need the funding, but more importantly, I believe him."

The memories I have of the Hennessy murders come drenched in an incongruous golden sunshine. It had been a scorcher of a summer. Heat drives up crime rates, with August being the time when families are most at risk of turning on one another. You could say that working on the force we were expecting something like it to happen but to be honest no one truly expects a person to murder his family. Even when you're standing over the bodies it's hard to believe.

"I don't," I say to her.

"And that's okay," she says quickly. "I only want your opinion. We just need an objective voice. Your expertise in profiling, at compiling cases, would be invaluable to us." She slides the file across the table. "There's documentary footage in the folder. One-on-one interviews with Seán. Three hours of unedited material in total. I'll send it to your email too but you'll need the password to access it."

Hennessy returns to the table. "Here you are." He places a glass of wine in front of Tanya then sits down, a pint of lager safe in his hands.

Somehow, I make myself speak to him. "Why do you want to do this, Mr. Hennessy?" I know the answer. Money. Always. But sometimes, with killers of this nature, it's simply attention. The narcissist can't resist indulging his own reflection.

He lifts the pint to his mouth, takes a drink. Blue eyes flash at me. Meek. The right touch of sadness and regret. Perfectly measured. "My sister." He says it quiet, and I think there's some shame in him after all.

"Your sister?"

"The way things are, I'll never see her again."

"That's probably for the best. Don't you think? Shouldn't she be allowed to live her life in peace? To move on?"

There's a slight rise to his shoulders; the gray neck of his hoodie bunches. His hands stiffen round his drink. He looks down. "I don't think it does anyone any good to live a lie."

"I doubt your sister believes she's living a lie. Out of everyone, she knows exactly what happened. She was there. And if she'd wanted to contact you, she would have done so already, right?"

He nods as if he was anticipating my response then says with a stubborn note of determination, "If Cara doesn't want to see me, there's nothing I can do about that. But she should know the truth."

A thick kind of anger closes round my neck. I feel it redden my face. I look to Tanya, but she's avoiding my eyes, her face a pale slate of neutrality.

"She already knows the truth," I say. And the confidence stumbles on his face. "Mr. Hennessy, I believe you slaughtered your parents and almost managed to kill your sister." He flinches but I continue. "I believe justice has been served and its only fault is that you are free to sit here, across from me, and discuss how you can rescind that sentence."

He slides a hand over his face, squeezes his eyes with his fingertips. Tanya gives me a look that could work as a slap in the mouth but I want him to know whose side I'm on. Always, victims first.

Finally he speaks. "I get it. I was convicted. Now I'm guilty until proven innocent." And when he looks at me again, there are tears watering in his eyes. "But I swear to you, I didn't do it." The last comes out between tight lips, an urgent rasping whisper.

There's a clatter of cutlery from behind the bar and I glance over in time to see the barman bend to collect whatever's fallen to the wooden floor. When he straightens, he wipes a knife on the cloth at his shoulder then resumes wrapping the cutlery in a paper napkin.

I turn to Tanya. The thin lines of her eyebrows are raised in an expression of hope and encouragement. I suspect she knows as well as I do what the answer will be. I sigh. "I'll look at the footage. But that's all."

"That's great, Frankie." She smiles her enthusiasm.

Seán nods and for a moment, it looks like he might grip my hands. His slide across the table but he stops halfway. "Thank you."

Tanya is already retrieving more documents from her bag. More homework for me. "Here's a summary of our approach. We've a new office in the city, off the quays." She places a business card in front of me. "But it should be easy to touch base. As you know, I'm doing most of my work from home."

Home translates into my parents' house on Conquer Hill in Clontarf. I picture my folks' spare bedroom turned into an incident room. Justin, my brother, and Tanya are waiting to move into their new home. Justin, a real estate lawyer, is laid-back to the point of horizontal and has somehow managed to mistime the chain in the purchase of their new home and now he finds himself back at our parents' at the age of thirty-seven. I wonder how my mum is coping with Tanya running a criminal review from their house.

She passes me the documents. "You can keep those. They're copies."

I take them, slide them into my bag, and she tells me that I can take my time with the report but perhaps it would be helpful to have it in the next month. My phone breaks through her instructions and I have never been more grateful for the interruption.

"Excuse me." I stand, move away to the back of the room. Press a finger over my ear. "Sheehan."

"Frankie, it's Clancy. Looks like we'll be seeing you tonight after all." Jack Clancy, the assistant commissioner, my boss, friend, and in a lot of ways persecutor.

"Trust me when I say the interruption is a welcome one," I reply.

The sound of the sea crashes down the line. The wind buffets against the speaker. He raises his voice. "Where are you?"

"Near my folks'." I check my watch. It's seven forty-five. "What is it?"

"We've two bodies. At the church. St. Catherine's."

"Here?" I walk out of the pub, turn, face into the wind that's sweeping in across the water. Clontarf is a suburb along the coast, a stone's throw from Dublin's center. Its name is synonymous with battles and victory. A streak of pride that once upon a time we rose up and conquered Vikings. Clontarf, the making of me, my home.

"Yeah. This one's a headliner; you'd better get down here," Clancy says.

I look down the street, back toward the city, where Dublin's lights are just awakening in the distance, then out to sea, where the sun is low on the horizon, hidden behind thick clouds. The path of the promenade is picked out in amber streetlight. A few walkers are striding along the path, coats done up to the neck, arms beating steady rhythms along the seawall.

"I'll be fifteen minutes," I say then hang up. I picture the church, St. Catherine's, at the mouth of Clontarf, dark and brooding in her iron cage. I pocket my phone and head back into the pub.

Tanya stands. "You have to go?"

"Yeah."

"Right." She stands, one hand against the table, the other pitched against her hip. "I'll call you tomorrow then?"

I take a deep breath. "Sure."

She smiles. "Thank you."

I collect my coat from the back of the seat and face Seán Hennessy. I'm about to throw out the usual platitude—it was nice speaking with you, or meeting you—but I can't. Instead I hear myself saying: "Enjoy your freedom, Mr. Hennessy."

And he frowns. "Thank you for your help, Detective."

Out on the street, I listen for sirens, search for blue lights. Already I'm at a run in my head. I should be disturbed by the drive in my blood, a sick kind of curiosity that all detectives house in the darkest corners of themselves. A little kick of excitement stitched up with a fearless kind of hope.

I **WALK DOWN** the street. The wind, full of the stink of seaweed and salt, rushes at my face. The summer has been one rainfall after the next, and if not that, the days are so cold you couldn't tell which arse-end of the year it is. I grip the edges of my coat together and quicken my pace. By the time I get to St. Catherine's, my hands and face are numb. I shake out my fingers and peer in at the church. The building crouches beneath a few thick elms that creak in the turning air. It's set well back from the road. Uniforms walk the grounds, marking out the scene with blue-and-white tape. There are three cars pulled up nearby. I spot Clancy's among them. I duck under the tape and one of the officers approaches with the log-in book.

"Evening, Detective Sheehan."

I sign the book. Add the time. "The coroner here?"

"She's inside. Forensics got here twenty minutes ago."

"Thanks." I move toward the entrance. Large oak doors pushed back into the dim shadow of the church. I step inside, and the sound of my footsteps comes back to me from the arched ceiling. Clancy, a couple scene of crime officers, and a woman I recognize as the coroner have congregated at the center of the main aisle. I take out my torch, switch it on, cast the beam around the entrance. Mass leaflets stacked in a cardboard box to the right. A sprinkle of confetti, forgotten, beneath the first pew. A tower of wicker baskets leaning to a topple behind the door. There's a box of foot protectors and plastic gloves nearby. I slip them on and walk slowly up the aisle.

The woman's body appears first, a foot, bare sole, milky white in the shadows She's naked from the waist up, a pair of dark jeans belted around her hips. She's on her front, arms bent, cheek turned. You could think her sleeping but for the injuries down her back and at her throat. Her eyes and mouth are open, the startle of death on her face. Beside her, a second victim, a man. Dead. Dead as can be. Days, by the looks of it. Death mottle over his hands, his face. He's clothed, a priest. Black suit. The collar, white as angels shielding his throat. In his palm, a knife. Not gripped. Not grasped. But sleeping there in cold flesh. Cold metal, cold blade.

CHAPTER 2

LOOKING DOWN at the bodies, I feel a sinking sadness. It's such a fucking shame. The magnitude. The finality of death. It comes at me, full blow.

Clancy turns to me, offers a palm out to the woman at his side. "Frankie, you know Judith?" The coroner. A petite woman with a giant reputation. Officious. Serious, with a posture so straight it would make you wonder whether rigor mortis was contagious.

"Good to see you again, Dr. Magee."

"I'm almost done here," she replies. "Then scene of crime can take over."

I turn to the coroner. "The sooner the better."

"Agreed."

At the altar Keith Hickey, our lead scene of crime officer, is directing his team. Keith is eagle-eyed but big-mouthed. His voice booms down the church. "If it so much as looks out of place," he tells his team, "you tag it, photograph it, and write it down."

Magee adds some notes to a clipboard in her hand. Signs it and hands it to a nearby officer then looks down at the victims. "Not that anyone would argue with this, but I'm ruling manner of death as homicide." She waits to the side to answer any questions we might have, her face tight with answers she doesn't want to give. Not yet, anyway, not until our victims are on the pathologist's table. The autopsy is our only hope to get our victims to speak. All confessions out under the cut of her scalpel. The pathologist in Dublin's mortuary at Whitehall, Dr. Abigail James, has a busy couple of days ahead.

"Who found the bodies?" I ask.

"A Mrs. Berry," Clancy answers. "She's outside with paramedics. Works in the parochial house. She came in to do the flowers." He's staring at the female victim's back, stab wounds like a constellation of dark stars over her skin. Eleven knife wounds, a puddle of blood gathered in each one, small bursts of blood spatter speckled over the skin. He points. "Not much blood from them. They postmortem?"

"I would agree with that," the coroner says.

I take a step back, survey the scene, look as the killer would want me to look. *Let me see what you have to say.* The slick mass of blood beneath the woman's body. The man on his side, curled round his middle. Under the woman's right arm, the blood is smeared across the floor, as if at some point she'd dragged her limbs inwards, folded herself up in preparation for a long sleep. Between the thick fall of her dark hair, her scalp gleams red, a tidemark of blood neat along her temple. Dried blood around her ear. There's a deep, angry gash across her throat.

"Is there a head wound?" I ask.

"None visible," Dr. Magee answers. "I'm confident cause of death was exsanguination: bled out from the throat wound."

"The male? He's been dead longer."

"A few days. Maybe more," Magee answers.

"But the woman died here?"

"Undoubtedly." She points to the pews at my left. I turn, follow the arc of the victim's blood across the pale, varnished wood, a stream of dark spots. Projection spatter. Arterial blood from where the killer slit her throat. There's a lot of rage here.

I look down at the knife in the priest's open hand. Six-inch blade, inch and a half wide. Four deep indentations along the handle. "Is that the murder weapon?"

"I can't say," she replies.

I rephrase. "*Could* it be the murder weapon?"

She tips her head, studies the knife as if there could be another possibility. "We can check for DNA. Compare the wound width and depth to the knife. If we can match those elements to the wounds on her back and neck, then you'll be the first to know."

I hear the tartness in her voice and look back down at the body to hide my irritation but I can understand her caution. In her role, she owns this scene until she gives the nod, then it belongs to CSI and only then are detectives like us allowed to come sauntering through it. In her eyes, we are contaminants. Imprecise and careless. And her watchful eyes track my every movement to make sure I don't so much as move a hair on the victims' heads.

I squat down to get a closer look at the weapon. The blade is pointing at the woman's back. It's sheathed in blood, a thin skin of brown and orange. But beneath the blood, along the blade, I can make out letters. A word.

"There's something carved into the blade," I say, aiming the torch at the knife.

Clancy bends over my shoulder. "Looks like a W and an E."

The tips of the deceased man's fingers are bent inwards, the nail beds blue-black, the lines on his palm picked out in deep red.

"Weapon. It says WEAPON," I say. I crouch lower and hear Magee's intake of breath. "It's been inscribed onto the knife. Badly." I get up and look back at Clancy.

"Clearly this guy, whoever he is, doesn't think we need an autopsy to tell us that this is the murder weapon," Clancy says, and Magee shoots him a sharp look.

"Time of death?" I ask.

Magee looks down at her notes. "Rigor has begun in the jaw and neck of the female victim but it's not advanced. I estimate her time of death to be in the last couple of hours." She checks her watch. "Seeing as the bodies were discovered at seven, I'd make that between five and six P.M. this evening. It will be more difficult to estimate the male victim's time of death."

I walk around the bodies to where the blood spatter crosses the church pews. It reaches right over the length of one of the benches. The blood, at first a congealed mess, fades into a fine sprinkle of droplets. I reach for my torch again. Shine it over the area and see that halfway through the spatter the pattern is interrupted.

"We have a void in the blood spatter, here." The void is well demarcated, about six inches in width, the edges defined apart from the end nearest to us, which is smeared as if an object has been dragged away.

"Oh?" Dr. Magee turns and looks across the pews.

Clancy waves at a tall, thin scene of crime officer. The SOCO approaches. Skinny face disappearing into the hood of her suit, hooked nose red at the tip and shining. The smell of menthol from the gel she's smeared under it floats out around us.

"Mark that up, will ye." Clancy points toward the bench and the SOCO nods. Then, to me, "What do you think? Some item taken? Or a hand smear?"

Dr. Magee has come to my side. "It's too clean at the center to be the perp's handprint. Whatever was there was removed after the victim was killed."

"Which means it would have her blood on it," Clancy provides. Clearly on a roll. "An item the killer put down then remembered he needed and took with him?"

I raise my hand, illuminate the bodies: the woman, the priest. There's something about how the bodies are laid out that suggests a purposeful hand. That everything here is exactly how it should be in the killer's eyes. The void doesn't fit. "This killer's too careful for the usual mistakes."

"He could have been disturbed? Hurried, maybe?" Clancy suggests.

"It would have to be something like that." I shine the torch over the floor around me. "The blood spatter hasn't extended this far. No chance of a footprint?"

"No such fucking luck." Clancy says. "We've had the black light out already. A few stray droplets near the exit on the east side of the church there but minimal. It's like whoever this fecker is floated in like a bloody ghost." He nods down at the blood spatter. "What do you think?"

"I'd say her wallet. Or her bag was here. It's about the right size and shape."

The hook-nosed SOCO reappears. "Excuse me," she says apologetically, moving around me. More photos, more labels.

"When was the last service?" I ask Clancy.

"Mrs. Berry says the congregation left at one."

"Six hours." I look down. "He's worked hard on this," I murmur. "Any ID on the victims?"

"Nothing yet. Mrs. Berry didn't get too close. Saw them from the altar there then left to get help."

I move the beam of the torch over the woman's back. The stab wounds are clean. There's no dragging from the blade along the edges that I can see. The knife stained with her blood placed in the male victim's hand. Both victims early forties, maybe late thirties.

And I see him. The killer. Moving over the bodies, flexing bloodied limbs into position. He stands back, surveys his work. I feel him behind me, as close as the skin on the back of my neck. He's watching. Watching me seeing his handiwork, his breath still lingering in the stale church air.

I look out over the church, beyond the bodies to the shining pews where, as a child, I sat, fidgeting against the hard wood, my polished shoes pressed into the maroon kneelers, counting the white flakes of dandruff on the shoulders of the men and women in front of me. The priest's low drone, drugging my eyelids, lulling me into a bored stupor.

Then a final look down at the victims. Down at this killer's crime scene, and I'm thinking again of how the bodies have been positioned. How it must have taken some planning. These are the types of cases that keep detectives awake at night. Not only because of how appallingly terrible they are but because the first thought I have when I look at this scene is: There's going to be more.

The SOCOs continue around us, bagging, labeling, collecting, and photographing evidence so that we can reconstruct the scene later. I turn away, move back down the aisle toward the exit, Clancy beside me. "I'll talk to Mrs. Berry," I say. "Get a statement if she's up for it. Who took the call?"

He frowns and looks down at his feet as he moves through the church, the blue plastic of his foot protectors rustling against the parquet floor. "Switchboard took it up and Harcourt Street passed it on."

"Harcourt Street throwing us a bone?"

"A fucking anvil and the side of a cliff," he says. "Say the sergeant heard the sorry tale, knew there'd be a media frenzy, and decided this was just about dirty enough for our mitts."

"It would have ended up on our table in the end. Best we get it fresh before there's any fuckups."

We emerge out into the fading light. The sky is closing over. Clouds thick. More rain on the way. Already media vans have gathered. On the road, cars slow, windows down, drivers stare out at the unlikely view of a crime scene at a church. The uniforms stationed at the outer cordon are watchful, urging people to move on, but two white-haired women remain, stubborn, their faces screwed tight with worry and bent over shopping carts. I imagine the morbid curiosity alive in their eyes.

I find Mrs. Berry sitting in a garda car. The door is open and when I approach she steps out, pulls the edges of her cardigan together, and clasps shaking hands over her stomach. Thin, neatly buttoned, with a crucifix glinting over the collar of her blouse. A church mouse, if ever I saw one.

"Mrs. Berry," Clancy says. "This is Detective Chief Superintendent Frankie Sheehan."

She gives me a tiny nod of her chin. "Hello."

I take out my notebook. "Mrs. Berry, do you think you could answer a few questions?"

"I suppose so."

"What time did you come to check on the flowers?"

"Seven. I said seven."

"And you'd not been in the church since the last service, at one? Is that correct?"

"Yes, maybe a couple minutes here or there of that."

Clancy steps back, nods his good-bye over Mrs. Berry's shoulder. He turns and walks toward his car, leaving the blood trail to me.

"Did you come in the side door or the front?"

She twists her head round, a cautious look back at the church. Her arms tighten around her waist. "The side, 'tis easier from the house, you know."

"So the door at the front stayed locked?"

"Until youse arrived."

"There was no one else here when you discovered the bodies; you hadn't noticed anyone around the church before then?" I ask.

"If I had, I woulda said."

I glance back at the slow trawl of traffic heading into Clontarf, the walkers, the families, the cyclists, and think how quiet a Sunday evening could really be around the church. Then look back at the cold, unwelcoming sight of St. Catherine's sitting in her gloomy spot, back from the road and under her black canopy of elms. The rest of Clontarf is enjoying the last of the miserable light left to the day, but around the church, night has already fallen.

There's a small two-story redbrick house close to the church.

I know it's likely the priest's residence. "You live at the parochial house?"

"Yes."

"And up until returning to the church, you'd been there?"

"Yes. I do the carpets in the vestry every Sunday. It's a day of rest and all, but not for everyone."

"Only the house overlooks the churchyard here."

"I don't be paying mind to all the comings and goings of everyone," she says with a firm nod. "I've me own business to be getting on with." For some reason that prompts her to bless herself.

"Can you take me through exactly what you did and what you saw?"

Her mouth sets into a taut little pout then she nods toward the side of the church. "I went in the side door and to the altar to collect up the flowers from the day's service. I saw them almost straightaway." She snatches a breath. "It took me a moment to cotton on to what I was seeing. And I might have taken a step or two from the altar down to the aisle but as soon as I was sure, I left to phone someone."

"And what were you seeing?"

"A man, a priest by the looks of it, and a woman. Dead."

"You phoned someone. Who?"

"I tried Father Healy first. Then when he didn't answer I phoned the guards."

"Father Healy?"

"Our priest."

"So, that's not your priest in there?"

She shakes her head, a small movement; soft gray hair drifts over her forehead. "No."

"You're sure? It doesn't sound like you got too close to the bodies."

"Father Healy is a bit more padded around the middle, grayer in the head."

"How about the woman?"

"I didn't see."

"Where is Father Healy now?"

"He goes on house calls every Sunday. I left a message on his mobile. But he sometimes turns it off so as not to be disturbed now."

She says the last with a slightly defensive edge to her voice, as if she's saying he shouldn't be disturbed by us lot either. "I see," I reply. "Clontarf is a large area for one man to cover; did he mention north, south, a street, even?"

The skin on her forehead wrinkles, gathers like tissue paper over her brows. "He could have mentioned Sybil Hill, it's often around there, sure I do be only half listening to him."

I hear a car pull up behind me and Mrs. Berry's features fall with relief. "Ah sure, here he is now. Father!" she shouts.

Father Healy is a tall man, his face the only narrow part to him; his body widens steadily toward his abdomen, his chin and neck funneling into the collar at his throat.

"Mrs. Berry, what's this about?" he says, tripping his way across the yard.

I don't recognize him, not that I should, having stopped attending any sort of church as soon as I understood that praying often got in the way of doing. But even so, in a community like Clontarf you'd not move far without someone name-dropping the local priest into their conversation.

He stops before us, his expression an arrangement of concern and fear. His drooping eyes wide in his face, cheeks pinkening slowly.

Mrs. Berry's arms loosen from her waist. "There's people dead inside, Father. I only went in to do the flowers."

He rests a hand softly on the housekeeper's shoulder and she seems to calm immediately, her hands moving into a prayerful clasp at the base of her throat.

"Father Healy," he says as an introduction then moves his hand from Mrs. Berry and takes mine. He gives it a light squeeze, pats my knuckles, then lets go.

"DCS Frankie Sheehan."

He stands uncomfortably close. His eyes level with the top of my head so that he looks down on me, his breath warm in the cool evening air.

I take a small step back. "Father Healy, I'm afraid the church and surrounding area are now a crime scene. You might want to make provisions to stay elsewhere tonight."

He looks over my shoulder, craning his neck so that I can see the patches of inflamed skin where his collar rubs along the follicles of his beard. "We have to leave the parochial house?"

"You don't have to but it might be for the best."

He reaches out, beckons Mrs. Berry to his side. She moves next to him, her eyes directed meekly to the ground. "We'll cope," he says. "Who is it, Detective?"

"I was hoping you might be able to help us with that. The deceased are one male and one female. The male is dressed in priest's vestments."

His eyes widen. "A priest? Who would do such a thing?"

"That's what we aim to find out." And his face pales a little. I see the meat of his chin tremble against the rigid band of his collar. "Do you think you might be able to ID the victims?"

He nods. "Sure, sure, I can take a look."

"Thanks. This way." I hold out a palm, wait for him to lead us inside.

He hesitates, shares a look of concern with Mrs. Berry, a brief moment of withdrawal. Then, with a pat to the older woman's forearm, he pulls himself up and moves ahead of me toward the church.

I can tell the moment he sees the bodies. His gait slows; the shuffling rhythm of his step breaks. His arm flexes as he brings his hand up to cover his mouth.

I move beside him, watch the patches of pink on his face disappear, the skin around his eyes pale. Listen to the draw of his breath against his palm.

"Do you recognize either of them?" I ask.

"Good lord," he says. "Good lord." He nods. His hand drops from his mouth. "Geraldine, Ger Shine. She, erm . . . nice lady. Good lord." His eyes flick between the two victims then settle on the woman. Gray brows drawn down. "Oh, Geraldine," he whispers. His tone full of regret, as if he'd lost some sort of battle. "She was a weekly regular, I guess. But occasionally she came to talk about things that were troubling her."

"What things?"

It seems to take a huge effort but eventually he pulls his eyes away from the woman's face, angles his shoulders toward me as if he can't bear to look down again. "I'm not really able to say; she spoke to me in confidence."

"She's dead."

He lengthens his neck. "I can see that, Detective."

"What about the male victim? The priest. Do you know him?"

The briefest of glances at the man's body. "Yes. But he's not a priest."

"You're sure?"

"Yes. That's Alan Shine. Geraldine's husband."

CHAPTER 3

I **SHRUG OUT** of my coat, close the door on the office noise. The photos of the crime scene are laid out on my desk. I stand over them, peer down at the victims. We are our behaviors, our actions, and a killer is no different. A crime scene can tell us a lot about an offender. A messy murder scene, a weapon of convenience picked up quickly in a struggle, an abundance of evidence left behind all point to a killer who's disorganized. These scenes are often careless, poorly executed, and frequently bloody, the killer acting impulsively, aggressively, focusing only on the moment and on the kill. They are usually male, have poor social skills, are loners and of low intelligence.

I rest my fingers on Alan Shine's bloated face. The Shine killer is different. This is an organized killer, the type of killer they make movies about, that writers stir into the plots of their novels. Usually in their late twenties or thirties, male with average to high IQ, their crime scenes leave little behind in the way of evidence. Generally, they are psychopaths. But what sets a killer like this apart is their ability to mimic the appropriate social cues. He's a chameleon. A shape-shifter. And he'll delight in getting close to the horror he's created.

I pick up the photo of Alan Shine. He was maybe a little thin, a rounded bloat to his abdomen but a good height. It's not easy to strangle someone and it couldn't have been easy to subdue Alan Shine. I lay the photo back down. Father Healy suggested Alan had a drinking problem but wouldn't elaborate much more. Only that Alan still turned up for mass and had been a lay minister with St. Catherine's for years. In response to my confusion around what that meant, he said that Alan gave out Communion at the church and participated in other church-related activities. He'd said it with a strange mixture of bitterness and defensive pride that I couldn't quite understand. It was as if Healy was at odds with Alan Shine but also careful not to have me judge the man. For what, I couldn't get out of him.

I look down at the image of the woman; disposed of in one grand stroke across the neck. I close my eyes, try to get into the killer's mind, imagine it, the release, the relief he must have felt, when her body weakened, sank into his own. Down she goes, limp and heavy to the floor. His breath washes over hers, churns out his desire. Finally, it was really happening. He watches the life dial down in her eyes, waits until she's still. Then her shoes tugged off, her top, her bra. It's odd that he does this but leaves her trousers. A token of respect? Or a message that this is not a sexually motivated kill. Then he stands, panting, admiring the ghostly sheen of her skin against the dark

shadow of the church. Eager then to draw out the image, to reconstruct what has lived in his head, he leaves to get the husband. And then, how long does he linger? It must have been
difficult to walk away from this scene, the end point of so much
planning.

I think of my meeting with Tanya earlier. Of Seán Hennessy.
A killer. Of a different nature. A disorganized killer, someone
who acts on emotion, in the moment, however callously. He
doesn't match the profile but I can't help holding him up against
the puzzle to see if he fits. Maybe time has shaped him. Changed
him. I make a note to check his whereabouts in the run-up to our
meeting. It would be an audacious move to meet with a chief
super and a defense lawyer minutes after leaving a murder scene.
But there are killers who would.

I sit back, my eyes still pinned to the photo. The husband and
wife. The male victim threatening, knife in hand. No outward
sign of injury, his posture in death a display of dominance. I can
just about make out the inscription on the knife, the crooked
scratch marks spelling out the word WEAPON. My eyes move to
Geraldine Shine's postmortem injuries, the stab wounds down
her back. I get the sense the killer is building his story. A dark
narrative. And again I have the feeling that I'm witnessing a
beginning rather than an end.

There's a knock on the door and my partner, Baz, steps inside. His sleeves are pushed up to his elbows, the shoulders of his
shirt wet. After working up through the ranks of the gardaí sans
partner, I got delivered one a year ago in the form of Barry Harwood, a detective who, after a shaky start, vacated the Bureau in
favor of Ballistics. Then realizing that Ballistics was boring as

fuck, returned at a time when the powers that be thought I needed a leash. And seeing as a leash would never work, they tied me to another detective instead. And that might've worked if they hadn't chosen Baz.

Baz will play by the rules, sure, but he's not one to court authority either. His caution only apparent when safety is an issue, mention to him that if you walk into this danger you'll get your man, and Baz will throw on a stab vest with the best of them and ask you to point the way. Often that's what's needed in this job; sometimes the obstacles in your path don't give you the time to ask permission or to fill out a form. That drive to get the man above all else is what makes you work through the night with or without the extra paycheck. Get it done. Find our perp and take him in. Sometimes there's a cost to that. And I have the scars to prove it.

It helps that Baz is not bad to look at in a slightly off-kilter kind of way. He's tall, a little angular; his shirt with or without a tie always hangs too loosely around the neck. But a small upward drift around the left side of his mouth and clear gray eyes give him a boyish kind of charm that comes in handy during interviews. He lives about an hour's drive from the city center, in Blanchardstown, in a two-bed flat-share with an uptight French teacher called Arielle, or it could be Adriane, who Baz reports has their accommodation divided firmly in two. Separate cupboards for food, labeled shelves in the fridge, and a schedule for cleaning that could be enforceable by law, it's that prescriptive. Needless to say there are often times when you'll find him on my sofa after a late night or a long day at the office being that peering into crime scenes and talking murder feel more appealing to him than battling the Dublin traffic home to then negotiate the invisible lines drawn up by his flatmate.

All in all, and I did try to resist this at first, Baz has become a close friend. I don't think even he's sure about how that happened. But he's shown he's got my back. Both of us with the same goal, like ticks on a dog, neither lets go until we're ready to drop off, full and fat with the answers to whatever we're working on. Our work is every waking and every sleeping hour. That's a rare thing to find replicated in a partner and it's true of Baz. As long as you remember to feed him often, he's as dogged on a case as I am.

"Howya," he says, and throws himself into the seat across from me, pushing his hair back. "This bleedin' weather. Wouldn't mind the cold if the fuckin' rain would let up."

"You been out to the scene?"

"Yeah. They've moved the bodies now. Cleanup is under way. A right lock of reporters filling up the street now though."

Baz has more than a spring in his step. It's been a few months since we've been dealt a murder case of this nature and in the interim we've been stuck to desks, on paperwork, laying out procedure, setting out protocol; I see the spark in his eyes now. Excitement wouldn't be too far off the mark but determination certainly.

I slide the crime scene photos toward him. "Not your usual Dublin fare."

He leans forward, takes up the pictures. "Been a while since I seen something like that, if ever."

We're on the right side of this case. Everything neat and tidy, waiting for us. No mistakes yet. We can work under the illusion that if we follow the rules, the answer will drop into our waiting hands. It's a nice feeling and Baz is fizzing with it. I'm not so naïve but for the moment, I'm happy to be pulled along by hope.

"Keith still there?" I ask.

"Just caught him before he left. Not a fucking print got? How's that? How's this fella come in, left carnage, and not a trace of himself behind?"

I reach up, pin copies of the photos to the corkboard above my desk. "There's always a trace; give it an hour, will ye."

"There was a fair pong beginning to rise off the male victim by the time I got there."

"So we know we're looking for someone who can store a body for days. A fridge or freezer large enough. Storage unit, warehouses, basements."

"If the perp's local, that might narrow it down."

"I'm thinking we start with sheds, outbuildings. Somewhere the killer would have felt safe in storing a body. Not his house. Too risky."

"You think this guy's a loner?"

"Not necessarily. He's extra careful, maybe even a little nervous. He wanted this to work out, needed it to. This may have been his first kill, so he's made it good. Thought it through well. He feels he's had to do this to make us see." I look back down at the crime scene photos. "We must see."

Baz gets up, goes to the watercooler in my office, fills a plastic cup, sits again, and takes a drink.

"Ger and Alan Shine. Husband and wife," Baz says. "Do we have a motive?"

"Nothing apparent yet. We're still gathering family info." I take up my pen, make a note to contact the family liaison officer. "The priest's uniform, what do you think that means?"

"I think they're called vestments," Baz corrects.

"Right. I forgot about your altar boy days. Any idea?"

He spins the photo of Alan Shine round, considers the image for a while. "A satirical attack, maybe? Do they kill for that kind of thing?"

"Any theme is game." I've seen cases where killers have murdered partners then in some strange remorseful or controlling act have eaten with, slept with, even watched TV with the body for days before the smell alerted neighbors that something was wrong. It's all there, a kaleidoscope of possibility. If you can imagine it, a killer can too.

"Could be just the killer got creative or maybe it's simpler: a jealous lover? Money trouble?" he suggests.

"Money? I'd be surprised but we can't rule it out." I reach out, pass him a close-up of the knife, point to the word WEAPON etched along the blade. "These murders are fulfilling a deep psychological need in our killer. He wants us to hear him. He's left us a message."

Baz holds up the photo, turns it about. "Not much of a message." He lets out a long breath. "Christ. Whatever happened to just killing your enemies? Fuck, my life, your life hasn't been a bed of roses at the best of times. But you say, life dumps its load, sometimes right down the back of your neck, that doesn't mean you wake one morning, slit someone's throat open, and stick a man's body in your freezer along with the fish fingers."

"I'm glad to hear it." I wait for his shoulders to unwind from his neck then drop the photos into the file, hand it to him. A day's work, threading through the lattice of these murders. "Let's get to debrief."

———

DETECTIVE STEVE GARVIN has gathered the room around. Steve doesn't walk a crime scene the way the rest of us do, preferring a desk and the blue glare of his computer. He's our very own fifth dimension, traversing the virtual worlds of our victims and suspects, an eye on both planes. Technology, infrared analysis, the little life contained in a mobile phone, all never fail to bring color to his narrow face. Two rows of chairs are positioned in a semicircle under the bright lights of the office.

He sits at the front. Ginger hair a shock against his skin, a thick silver chain visible at the base of his neck, his angular body over itself like an awkward teen, his feet hooked behind the metal legs of the chair. He's wearing a thin white shirt but beneath it a black T-shirt, the Metallica logo standing out in sharp letters across his chest. I notice he's shaved his goatee but he's acquired a new quirk: a black disk of plastic in his right ear. His long fingers rattle a pen against his notebook as if he doesn't know quite what to do with his hands without a keyboard in front of him.

The rest of the team are slopped into their seats, but their eyes are sharp and eager. Behind them, Detective Inspector Paul Collins is still at his desk, finishing up a call. Paul is in his mid-forties or maybe younger, chubby or fat, whichever way your sensitivities might allow you to describe him. He long ago shrank away from the notion of fieldwork, preferring to fill out his role on the other side of a desk. He's a quiet man. However, put a phone line between him and whoever he's talking to and he's full of banter. Or at least more than he throws out to the office. He lives alone as far as I can tell, still prefers to make his lunch at home, unpacking his sandwiches and biscuits from a Tupperware box at the allotted time. The only suggestion of a significant other in his life, a framed picture of a tabby cat looking out from behind his computer. His size or maybe his social awkwardness wins him a certain kind of patronizing affection from the rest of the team. Plenty of shoulder digs and back pats accompanied by indulgent smiles.

He is bent over his wide middle, shirt straining, dark patches leaking out from beneath his arms. He hangs up the phone, throwing me a worried glance as he does so; then, wiping his forehead, he joins the rest of the room in front of the incident board.

I check my watch. It's coming up on one A.M. but our work is only starting. We've got a tight window now to get things right. Fuckups in the first twenty-four hours after a crime scene won't be forgiven down the line.

I throw out an encouraging smile. "I hope you've all had your coffee. It's going to be a long one." A few of the team return my smile, others sag a little, reach for phones, maybe to send a text to a partner or spouse, let them know they won't be having sight nor sound from them until we have this killer on our radar. I wait for all eyes to return to me, until the room quiets, stills with hungry concentration.

The victims' photos, smiling profile pictures, grin out over my shoulder. A snap of before. I feel that pressure, the weight of life across my back, valid, asking questions: Why? Who? The heat in the office breathes over my skin, settles damp and sticky around my neck.

"Right," I say. "Let's get started. The victims." I clear my throat, step aside, introduce them. "Geraldine and Alan Shine. Wife and husband. No children. Geraldine worked from home, selling makeup samples online. Alan was an electrician. Money was tight, but they met their bills, no debt that we can find presently. Have family been notified?"

Helen, Detective Flood, stands up, clears her throat. Helen wears her stripes proudly. Her preferred work uniform: blouse done up to the neck; practical, well-wearing trousers with those Velcro-topped pockets sewed on the leg; and hair pulled back into a bun, as tight as her hair follicles and scalp allow. She's a persistent detective, insightful and dogged. A little on the overeager side, which can veer into neediness at times.

She tugs at the knees of her trousers as she stands. "Yes. Alan Shine's siblings, five older brothers, immigrated to Australia some years ago. His mother's deceased." She nods as if to say, small mercy. "His father lives in Cork. Geraldine's parents, Aileen and Ken Garry, are both alive and living in Louth, Drogheda. Geraldine had one sister, Fiona. Older by two years, unmarried and living with her parents. According to Fiona, Geraldine hadn't been in touch in any regular sense for about two years. Though they met up last Christmas for a family meal."

"Any reason for not being in touch?"

"She said they had their differences. But I suspect some conflict on the side of the Shine marriage. Door-to-door are picking up a lot of reports that the marriage was an abusive one. Lots of shouts heard through the walls. Screams. Crying."

"Any callouts? Did anyone visit, check that Mrs. Shine was okay?"

Helen presses her lips together, a look of guilt on her face as if she was responsible. "I'll check."

I sigh. "Okay. What else?"

"That's it so far. The family liaison officer has just gone out to Geraldine's parents and sister."

"We'll get to them as soon as we can. Find out what those differences between Geraldine and her family were."

I turn. Point to a picture of the church, the inside, the crime scene laid out. I'd taken the photo standing on one of the pews.

"Initial assessments tell us that Alan Shine was strangled. From the front. By hand. The rate of decomposition strongly suggests he was stored in some kind of refrigeration unit. Possibly for days. So he must have been gone during this time. Did anyone miss him? If not, why not? There's not been a missing person's report and Geraldine Shine was active online, selling products up until the day she was murdered. Any concern she had for her husband's disappearance did not extend to contacting the gardaí.

"Geraldine Shine had her throat cut at the scene, from behind. Cast-off blood spatter from the weapon was found here." I indicate slightly to the right of the bodies. "A line of blood spatter that reaches beyond Alan Shine's body, although none over Mr. Shine himself. This indicates she was killed and posed first. The killer then positioned Mr. Shine's body after."

I give the team a moment, wait for questions, frowns, hesitations, additions.

"For those of you unfamiliar with the area, the church is situated at the far west of Clontarf. Congregation dwindling, on a Sunday the housekeeper says the average number of attendees might be as low as twenty. The last service was at midday; the church was cleared by one P.M. The parochial house, in which both the priest and the housekeeper reside, is situated to the left of the building, not more than fifty yards away."

Helen raises a hand. "Is there a back or side entrance to the church?"

"There's one entrance on each side of the church. The front is routinely locked when not in use, but for ease of movement between the parochial house and the church the closest entrance is kept unlocked except for at night."

Baz leans against the wall on the other side of the case board. "The killer will have had, at a stretch, six hours to murder Geraldine Shine and then lay out her husband's body," he says. "We're assuming he or she used a vehicle of sorts to transport Alan Shine's body. There are two points of vehicle access to the church grounds, the public access at the front, which would allow a car to draw up close. This access is very open. There's a bus stop almost directly outside and it's in full view of the parochial house.

"The second access point is at the rear of the church, a low metal fence and a narrow pathway that slopes down toward a wooded area. To the further west of this there is a car park, which is in use most of the week. This would have been a considerable challenge to our killer but we think it's most likely the route he took."

Helen's hand flicks in the air. "So Geraldine Shine was already in the church when she was attacked? She was brought there by her killer?"

I glance back at a satellite photo of the area. The Shine house is circled in red, the church in yellow. Neither can be more than a quarter mile from the other. "She'd been known to visit the church often and sometimes spoke with the priest there, Father

Healy. He said she often slipped in the side door to reflect or pray in quiet. So, I suspect she was already at the church. And if that's the case, it means the killer likely knew her movements."

Baz takes over. "This guy's done his research. Probably stalked his victims for days, if not longer. Knew that Geraldine Shine wouldn't report her husband missing."

Ryan Toomey sits front and center. Ryan, thirties, gym built, and well-sculpted. He wears his pressed suit as if he runs the Bureau and I know he thinks there'll come a day he will. He works hard when he's here but he's not one for pushing himself beyond the demands of his wage. And that won't get you far in this job. Still, there's never a more useful detective than one who's always on the lookout for a promotion. He's had it easy over the last few months and I can see he's almost salivating at the chance to prove himself on this case. He taps his pen on his notebook; his foot waggles over and back. Patent leather shoes have an irritating gleam under the white office lights. "So we're not thinking the priest is a suspect?"

"We've not named any suspects yet," Baz says. He spreads his hands. "The priest says he was out in the hours that led up to the discovery of the bodies but so far he's no alibi."

"My money's on the priest, then," Ryan replies. He clicks the top of his pen, closes his notebook.

"We're keeping an eye on Healy," I say. "We certainly want to close down on his activities over the past twelve hours. Ryan, you're on Cell Site Analysis, track his phone, see if you can get a list of the visitations Healy was due to make yesterday."

He nods, happy.

I point up at the images on the case board, a close-up of the pews. "There was a void located in the projection spatter from the injury sustained to Geraldine Shine's neck. An unknown item was removed from the scene. CSI at the Shine house have yet to locate Geraldine Shine's or Alan Shine's phones, a wallet, credit cards, money. So we're going on the assumption the void in blood spatter was caused by Geraldine's handbag or wallet. Either she set it down on the pew when she arrived, before she was attacked, or dropped it there."

I pull the blouse away from my back, feel a welcome stir of air over my skin, stand and look out at our team.

"Our killer," I say, "will be male. Most likely early to mid-thirties. He's intelligent but may not be educated. He's had an abusive past, not necessarily sexual. He may have spent time inside, for petty crime, possibly assault. He's probably well-spoken. He's organized. He likes routine. He's probably unmarried. No children. He could have a girlfriend. He feels society has never given him a break, his childhood: failed by social services, by his parents, by school, so he invents his own rules"—I look to Baz—"his own morality."

"The arrangement of the stab wounds on Geraldine Shine's body are significant. They are well thought out. Inflicted postmortem. Do they stand for something? Betrayal? A person stabbed in the back?"

Baz speaks out again. "It may be Geraldine knew her attacker. We need to look into anyone who's done work on the house, new and old friends that the Shines might have met up with recently. Keep in touch with door-to-door about her neighbors." He passes round the photograph of Geraldine Shine in a clear folder. I recognize the image from her Facebook page. A mirror selfie, her phone held up over half her face. A glittering cover over the back, adhesive diamanté. "This is her phone," Baz says. "We've uniforms on the embankment at the back of the church but need a search team to go wider. The sea might be an obvious dumping point. Ryan, can you add that to your list?"

"Spot on, Detective," he answers, as if Baz was one of the lads down at the pub on a Friday night. I see Helen slide a glance of reprimand at him but it's lost on Ryan.

I tap my pen over Geraldine Shine's face. "The female victim was naked to the waist and footwear had been removed. These items could have been dumped along with the bag, or the killer might have kept them as a trophy."

"Whoever it is must've been pretty sizable, yeah?" Helen says, pen to her lips. The comment wins a short snicker from Ryan but she ignores him. "I mean, Alan was not a small man, was he?" She looks pointedly at Ryan when she says this and the grin on his face turns to confusion.

"No, he wasn't," Baz says, looking at the wounds on Alan Shine's neck. Deep purple finger marks, most likely from the assailant's thumbs, sit on either side of the throat, dark scratches and deep nail impressions penetrating the skin. "It would have taken some strength to squeeze the life out of Alan Shine."

"That's true but the right amount of anger can make a beast out of anyone," I say, then I turn to Steve. "Geraldine Shine worked from home as a beauty rep. She had an online business. When Tech delivers her computer, make a list of her customers. What kind of sites had she been visiting, chat rooms, articles she was reading, her most recent social media posts."

"Actually"—Steve holds up his phone—"I might have something on that."

I wait and he moves toward me, shows me his phone. "This is a photo she posted yesterday morning on her beauty blog."

His screen is filled with Geraldine Shine's face. A neat pout at the camera, her face angled to show a light glimmer of makeup along her cheekbone. Dark hair, poker straight, is swept over her left shoulder.

New product, ladies. Come and get it, is written below the image. The edge of a white blouse begins at the tops of her arms.

"Is there any way to get that on the screen?" I indicate a projector screen to the side of the case board.

"Sure." He goes to his desk, retrieves a long black cord, connects the phone, and in moments the image looks down on us.

Yesterday morning's date appears in light gray letters below the image.

Steve taps the phone and the image widens, sets itself on a black background. Geraldine has taken the photograph near the window in her kitchen. Behind her, an orchid rains pink blossoms over the tiles. And tucked in the far right, a digital calendar, yesterday's date in stark white on the small black cube.

Helen points at the screen. "It's called a Bardot top," Helen says. "My nieces, they're into fashion," she adds quickly. She glances round at her colleagues, redness creeping over her face to her hairline.

"Okay, so we know what she was wearing. Let's find it. Good work, Steve, Helen." I pause, look out at the room. Take a deep breath. "Any questions?"

Blank.

"Find the phones, update me on the CCTV, any dashcams in the area."

"Yes, Chief," a few voices sound out from the seats. The others are silent but focused on the case board, making notes or taking in the faces of our victims.

"Keep in mind," I add, "a killer has always, *always* got more work to do than us. A killer must carry out his crime undetected, unwitnessed. He must then leave his crime scene and the run-up to it without a fragment of himself behind, something we know, in this life, history never allows. There is always a footprint. Always. Find it."

Ryan is first out of his seat. He takes up his chair and sets it against the wall where the others will soon be stacked. Steve stretches a kink out of his spine, his neck, his joints pop.

He removes his phone from the projector. "I'll get a printout of this up straightaway."

"Thanks."

Finally, Paul approaches. "That was Assistant Commissioner Jack Clancy on the phone before, Chief. He says you've a meeting in the morning at Garda HQ with the commissioner."

I go to Helen's desk to sign the warrant request for Geraldine Shine's phone records. He follows. "He'll have to do without me, Paul. I can't leave this."

"He says it's vital."

"Send this to the district court immediately, please, Helen." And I hand her the warrant request.

"Yes, Chief," she replies.

I straighten. Face Paul. He lifts his chins, runs a finger beneath them. "What'll I tell him, Chief?"

"What time?"

"Eleven A.M. He says the commissioner won't budge."

I divide up the hours ahead of us, weigh the inevitable backlash if I ignore a request to meet with Phoenix Park against the cost in time. The bloody headache I'll get from Jack Clancy afterward might be more than it's worth not to show up.

I give Paul a nod. "Fuck it. Right. Yeah. Okay, I'll be there."

"Thanks, Chief."

Baz is at the door, shrugging into his sodden coat. "I'm heading back out to the scene. Check on door-to-door."

"The autopsies are scheduled for ten thirty A.M. You okay to oversee them?"

"You're not going to be there?"

"I've a meeting in Phoenix Park."

He snorts. "Not like you to loosen your grip on a case once it's sucking diesel. I thought you'd be pushing for a front-row seat?"

I throw him a grin. "You need someone to hold your hand?"

He slides me a teasing look. "Just know how you hate to take your eye off the ball."

"Just because I'm not there doesn't mean I can't sense when prey hits the web."

He laughs. "Fuck me for asking." He glances across the office toward the window then flicks up the collar of his coat. "I don't like the look of this case at all. It's got follow-up written all over it. Clontarf certainly won't be sleeping easy with a killer prowling the streets."

And I can feel the chill of his words ring through my bones. I think of another killer, Seán Hennessy, already walking those streets. "I met up with Tanya yesterday evening before the call."

He runs a hand over the sides of his coat until he hears the jingle of his keys. "Oh? What crook is she pulling off the hook now?"

"Seán Hennessy."

"Should I know who he is?"

"Convicted for murdering his parents and attempting to murder his sister. He was released four months ago, wants to challenge the charges made against him. " I glance back at the case board, look pointedly at the photos of the Shines.

Baz fixes his gaze on me. I've got his attention now. "Is that so?" He's still for a moment as he takes this in then, "Would he have had the time? To kill then get to you and Tanya?"

"Judith says Geraldine Shine could have been dead for as long as two hours."

He looks doubtful but his eyes don't leave mine. He knows better than to dismiss the unlikely. "We bring him in then."

"On what? Guilty once, therefore again? That won't go down well. Tanya says there's TV involved."

Baz puts his hand on the door, shrugs. "Fuck TV. Get a uniform out to him. We're only trying to rule him out." He pulls the door open. "Along with the rest of the bleedin' city it looks like; you know as well as I do that there's more than one man in this country capable of evil."

I nod. "You're right. Autopsy should give us something."

"Hope to fuck it does, 'cause lord knows there's little in the way of evidence at the scene."

"Call me with anything new."

He leaves and I go to the coffee machine. It's going to be a long morning.

CHAPTER 4

I **TURN DOWN** the road, through the grand pillars of Phoenix Park. A fine, persistent drizzle falls across the windshield. The trees are shapeless dark figures in the surrounding mist. In the green, beyond a cast-iron fence, a personal trainer charges over and back in a series of short sprints; his client, soaked and heaving, stumbles after him. I slow down in anticipation of a speed bump, reach out to the note Paul gave me on the meeting.

Review of mission statement, is all the note says. I feel the tug of apprehension. I'm not a fan of being unprepared and definitely not when meeting the woman who could pull the plug on our operations. Or even, the Bureau.

Séamus Barrett, the commissioner who set up the Bureau, retired this year. His replacement is an ex-financier with sod-all law experience. Donna Hegarty. And now this, what is it, an assessment? A checkup. In some ways, a change in commissioner could be a good thing. But generally, when it comes to the gardaí, I've found change is a motherfucker. And meetings to discuss that change an even bigger one.

Through the trees, the main garda HQ appears. I turn through the gate, pull up at the security barrier. Flash my badge and the barrier lifts. I park. Check the time. A quarter past eleven. I'm late. I sit for a few moments, enjoying a further few seconds in the warmth of the car. Beyond the headquarters, the clouds are thickening, darkening.

Taking my bag, I step out of the car and slip into my raincoat. I pull my hood up against the swirling damp breeze, squint through the drizzle at the building, and sigh at what's waiting for me inside. I lock the car, tuck my head against the rain, and walk quickly toward the entrance.

Johnny Byrnes looks up when I enter. Johnny was once a detective working Murder for breakfast, lunch, dinner, and beyond. Five years ago, three years before he would have made chief super, he was moved to Gangs and a knife through the abdomen saw him impaled to a desk job for the remainder of his working life. His move to HQ made room for me. I felt bad but at the same time didn't. Everyone wants to work Murder, everyone wants to lead Murder, but there are only so many spaces at the top. I was sad he'd been injured. But it was an opportunity made for me and I stepped into those ruby slippers without hesitation.

"Detective Sheehan," he says. The browns of his eyes are surrounded by a network of thin blood vessels, the bottom lids slack and watering. His nose wears the signs of a drinker.

I push back my hood. "Johnny. Hi. I'm here to see the commissioner."

He nods and I see the tremble in his hand as he picks up the phone. "Detective Chief Superintendent Sheehan here to see you, ma'am."

The reception desk is curved, positioned against a wall to the right; portraits of the significant men of the garda look down on the room. Johnny hangs up the phone, takes a lanyard from a box on the desk. A printer behind him spits out a square card with my name and title on it. He slides the card into the lanyard, passes it over the desk. Stands and points down the hall.

"If you go up the stairs there, Mrs. Hegarty is in meeting room two with the assistant commissioner." And I think in that moment he's glad he's not in my shoes.

I unzip my wet coat, hang it on a rack near the entrance then, nodding my thanks to Johnny, I head for the stairs.

When I get to the meeting room, I find Clancy and Donna Hegarty at the far side of the boardroom table. Clancy stands, supports himself against the desk with his fingertips, the pad of his index finger taps an impatient beat against the surface.

"Detective Sheehan." He lifts his hand and makes a show of checking his watch. "Nice of you to make the effort." He gives me a hard glare, his mouth compressed against his teeth. He might as well have roared, *What fucking time do you call this?*

"If it saved the commissioner a trip into town in early-morning traffic, then I'm glad to oblige," I answer and watch the edges of Clancy's mouth disappear further into his face.

"Nice to finally meet you, Detective Sheehan." The commissioner doesn't get up but acknowledges me with a curt tip of her head. I've only seen photos of her in the newspaper or the little news flier on the force I delete from my inbox once a quarter.

In her photo, she appears younger, less stooped, less like

someone's granny. She's hitting mid-sixties at least, not unusual for anyone of seniority in this occupation, but her attire is bundled, a cardigan stretched over her chest, pale-yellow blouse, loose and layered over the waist of the pink floral pattern on her pencil skirt. But it's in her eyes that I look for the woman and they have it: the patient gleam of authority. *Don't look at how I am; look at who I am*, they say.

"Yes, ma'am. Thank you," I answer, placing my bag on the table.

"Call me Donna, please. We're all friends here," she says, spreading her hands. Never was there a phrase that meant the opposite more. "All on the same team."

Clancy moves a palm roughly over his cheek. "Yes, yes."

I sit. My leg aches. Old scars from old cases tightening along my thigh. Donna Hegarty is already rubbing me the wrong way. "My caseload is particularly full today," I say, looking straight at her. "We've had a double murder on the north side. It needs my full attention."

"I'm aware of that." She settles back against her seat. "A tragedy. Have we a motive yet?"

We? The woman has never set foot in a crime scene. "The layout of the bodies suggests a particular signature."

"A signature?"

"A pattern the killer will feel compelled, for want of a better word, to act out. A ritual, if you like."

She looks up, meets my eyes, holds me in her milky gray gaze, her mouth a firm line. "It's so clear to you?"

Clancy interjects. "Frankie is used to working out these things; she's had a lot of training in profiling, built up a lot of experience. She's yet to fire off base."

Donna frowns. "Is that so?"

"As the sky is blue," he says. Beyond the window at his back, the sky continues to darken.

I look at him and wonder what it is he's afraid of. There's a threat here, in this room; I feel it but I'm not sure where it's coming from.

Then as if to answer that question, Hegarty replies, "We all remember Ivan Neary, Mr. Clancy. Or at least, I do."

I feel the vertebrae in my back lock straight. "We got our man in the end."

"Hardly a case to be touting around as your best work."

I draw a stream of air in through my teeth. A hiss and I don't care if she hears it.

Clancy, sensing the room closing in, clears his throat. "We're not here to talk about the past though, are we? The important thing about that case is that there was good work done and the end reflected that."

I want to ask him if he's dropped his balls in the car park outside.

"But that's not what the public hears. It's not the lingering memory," Hegarty replies.

I open my mouth to speak but she silences me with a hand. She takes up a couple of pages from a stack at her side, pushes one to each of us. The first line. Mission statement, it reads:

To provide the highest level of expertise on cases of public interest.

She points down at the statement. "This is what the Bureau is about. This is why we selected you." She takes the time to look at each of us in turn. "You're supposed to be the killer whale here. Nothing should get by you."

"Nothing has," I say.

She lets her shoulders drop a little. It looks like she's conceded something but I've a strong feeling she's softening us up for something bigger.

My eyes stray to a clock on the wall. Time is seeping away. Our window around the crime and our killer closing fast.

In an attempt to push things along, I ask, "Is that what this is about? You don't think we're meeting our goals? Some words on paper?"

Her eyes widen. "As meek as words on paper are, Frankie, they are a good guidance for us. A reminder of what we're about." She opens a file on the desk. I can just about make out the images of Geraldine and Alan Shine in the church. "The Shine case—from what I've read, there's a whiff of domestic violence about it, would you say?"

There's only one other person in the room who could have given her those images so quickly. I glance at Clancy. He has the sense to look ashamed.

"So we've got an unhappy marriage," she continues. "An abusive husband? I heard there'd been some reports of that nature? But he was dead before she was?"

"Yes. For some time."

"So it couldn't have been a murder-suicide then? Perhaps a jilted or jealous lover?"

I check my phone, try to hide the annoyance in my voice. "If I knew that I wouldn't be here; I'd be charging someone right now."

She pulls herself up, her round chest swelling beneath her blouse, and I know we're getting to the heart of the matter. "You're aware of the move to have Seán Hennessy's conviction overturned?"

My head snaps up at the change of subject and I feel a jolt of panic. Normally a callout to HQ and a meeting with the commissioner is to discuss our lack of loose change, the press, or new policy and how we might have broken it. Dull, dusty conversations that feel a mile away from the heat and hit of crime on the ground. My face grows hot under Hegarty's expectant gaze and I wonder what the fuck she knows about my meeting with Seán Hennessy.

"Yes," I reply. I feel Clancy watching me and I choose my words carefully. "The papers are already running his story."

"So the timing for these fresh murders is not ideal."

"No." I shift in my seat, the reason for the commissioner's callout becoming clear. Cover our arse because we're about to take a hit.

She passes us both a photocopy from a newspaper. The headline from the front page pops in shouty black capitals: SON WHO MURDERED PARENTS RELEASED.

"Seán Hennessy was released four months ago. How familiar are you with the case?"

My head is shaking. "As familiar as the next person. I didn't work it. I was still in uniform at the time, stationed elsewhere."

"But the murders happened where you grew up, right?"

I'm silent.

She pushes on. "Did you know the family back then?"

Flashes of the case take turns in my head. Grainy photos from newspapers, images of the house taken from a distance, white suits ducking under garda tape.

"No." Even as the words leave my mouth I remember. A memory that shouldn't be important but feels important. It crawls out of the gray fog and plays in my head. Bríd Hennessy, the mother, passing me on the street. The swiftest of meetings.

And not even that. It stirs in me a tiny well of discomfort. "I didn't know them personally," I say.

"He murdered the mother and father and attempted to kill his sister. She was ten at the time. Fifteen he was, when he committed these crimes. The judge sentenced him to fifteen years to be served on top of the two he'd already spent in custody up to that point. A harsh sentence for a minor and something that will not reflect favorably on any of us in hindsight if the conviction is overturned."

I wait for Hegarty to elaborate, look over at Clancy, check for signs he knew the direction of this meeting. He's focused on Hegarty, hanging on every word. Or pretending to.

"Mr. Hennessy has signed a contract with a production company called Blackthorn Films. They've been filming a tell-all documentary on the case."

"I heard."

Clancy shoots me a dark look.

"Oh?" Hegarty raises a thin eyebrow.

"My sister-in-law, Tanya West, works for Justice Meets Justice. She's asked me to look at the files. But I haven't got to them yet."

Hegarty tips her head to the side. "Do you think that's the best idea?"

"It's in my own time. I'm providing a background. Nothing official. My name or the Bureau won't be mentioned."

She makes a sharp clicking noise of disapproval then taps the image of Seán Hennessy. Her finger hits the smooth angle of his chin. "At the time, Mr. Hennessy made a verbal confession during interview but later retracted it. He hasn't shown one jot of remorse throughout his incarceration. Make no mistake, he's

arranging the PR stunt of the century right now. Public sympa-
thies are easily lost but just as easily won. For him to look good,
we'll have to look bad. If we don't counter this with something,
we'll end up looking like the villains."

That's what she says. What I hear is: *If Seán Hennessy's conviction is overturned, the gardaí will face litigation.* The payout in
compensation could easily stroll into the millions.

She turns her laptop around and the screen lights up. "The
trailer is already titillating viewers and setting tongues wagging.
In case you missed it, here's what they're running with. I'll let it
do the talking, but I think it gives a glimpse of the cliff we're
about to drop off."

The trailer plays, the screen opening from darkness to a man
sitting on a stool against a gray background. Seán Hennessy. He
wears light blue jeans that look soft to touch. A loose, dark green
T-shirt. His shoulders and hands suggest outdoor work or someone not afraid to shovel the shit if he needs to. His face is strong-
boned, aged enough to give him an attractive rougher edge. A
small scar under his right eye looks like a dimple when he smiles
or frowns. He looks kind. Patient. And I know exactly how viewers will perceive him when the documentary airs: vulnerable,
victimized, and tragic.

His eyes are cast to the floor. His head is shorn, but you can
see the stubble of golden hair glint under the camera light. He
rubs his hands, one over the other, and the round caps of his
shoulders flex, unflex.

Then he looks up, and his gaze reaches out, beyond the lens,
settles on me. And I listen. Never able to resist a killer's story.
Never able to resist a glance into a black soul, just to see. To

check that they're different. That their blood runs darker, their heart beats slower.

"When I stepped round the side of that house. My home," he says, "I thought I was walking into a dream. A nightmare. The sun bleaching everything, a haze of horror. I closed my eyes. Waited. But when I opened them the same scene in front of me. My ma. I knew she was dead. Even though I was a ways away I could see the wide openness of her eyes. Unblinking. My da could've tripped over, fell down. I'd seen the same posture on him after a heavy night; I might've thought he was sleeping off a binge but for the blood."

His eyes fall again for a moment. He swallows, then he's there again, a look of something in his eyes, a soreness, and despite myself I almost wince on his behalf. He continues, his voice down low, rolling over the ground like a stone.

"There were people everywhere, a garda car and those crime folk you see on TV. And she was right there. My sister. Closest to me. There were people around her, in a little huddle. Paramedics, I think. They were shouting things. For help or drugs. And between their legs, I could make out her thin, small body. The paleness of her skin. Feet tucked up. I thought she was dead. But then her foot moved, just a fraction. A twitch of her toes. And I remember the breath rushing out of me. Thank God. Thank God.

"*Cara!* I called out. And one of the paramedics looked up. He waved a hand and they must have moved me. Brought me away. I can't remember."

The title rolls up, *Fifteen Years a Murderer,* Blackthorn Films. Then the screen goes black.

Silence spreads out between us; I'm half-expecting Seán

Hennessy to walk in, pull up a chair, lick his lips as we flap about like chickens.

"Why *Fifteen Years a Murderer?*" I ask. "His sentence covered seventeen."

Hegarty throws me an impatient glance; her lips bunch into a tight wrinkled knot before she replies. "Facts don't bother these people. Soundbites and ratings are all that matter." She closes the laptop. "It's due to air toward the end of next week."

"JMJ will have to disclose the evidence before then, surely?" Clancy says.

"No." Hegarty doesn't look at either of us as she speaks. "This is not a trial. They'll wait for public support, newspapers, then submit their appeal."

I'm still not sure what she's asking of the Bureau. "Sorry, maybe I'm not following. But what has this got to do with our work?"

She laughs, throaty and hollow. "This"—she points to the computer—"is going to be lighting up every newspaper for the next year and with it, anything with a waft of familial violence, like the Shine case, will follow. Our reaction to those cases will be linked directly to any failure the public believes has resulted in Seán Hennessy's arrest."

"All eyes are on us. What's new?"

"What's new is, I was brought in to keep the Bureau focused. To keep our eyes on what we're about. If I fail"—she shrugs— "I'm out and the Bureau will have lost its last champion." She presses her meaning down my throat with a hard look. "I'm on your side. And I need you on ours."

"I've never been otherwise."

She closes the computer with a snap. "He wants to overturn his conviction. For many reasons, that can't happen."

She means for one reason: money.

Clancy nods. "What do you want us to do?"

She arranges the paper neatly before her, picks it up, taps it on the table, and sets it down again. "The Shine murders: I know it's hard to keep a case in a straight line, but do it. Seán Hennessy"— she pulls the edges of her cardigan together and throws another look in my direction—"if you're not familiar, get familiar. Maybe this relationship you've got with JMJ will be a good thing, Detective. If we can get a preview of where it is exactly they think we've messed up, we can remain one step ahead."

I feel a prickle over my scalp. "I'm not sure I'm comfortable with that."

Her face hardens. "Are you comfortable in your job, Chief Superintendent?"

I blink at the threatening tone in her voice, draw in a long breath, and try to control my reaction. "With all due respect, I'm up to my neck in a double murder investigation. I don't have the time."

She sets both hands on the table, calm, soft movements; the glint of pearlescent pink over her nails. "I have every faith you'll find the time," she says, and it's not a vote of confidence she's giving me, a supportive slap on the back. It's an order.

I leave the office, my shoulders like strips of lead. Clancy walks ahead, his hands in his pockets, his posture hunched against the light drizzle. He hurries to his car and I follow after him. I wait until he's settled himself into the driver's seat, then get in beside him.

"Don't," he says. He runs a hand over his forehead and through his hair. "Just don't fucking start." He turns the key and the Mondeo gives a chesty rumble; then he fiddles angrily with the heater, directing warm air to the windshield.

"What do you know of this old case?"

He pauses, sighs, then: "Feck all. It's done and dusted. Just go through the motions, that's all she wants. Fucking paper pushing."

"Well, what's up with you then? Thought you were going to piss down your fucking leg up there."

"Go way to fuck, I was. I'm tired, tired of that shite. A bloody nobody telling us how to do things. We've a fucking double murder to be working on. This isn't a bleedin' TV show. This is real life."

He's a lying shitbag sometimes, Clancy, and a pretty bad one at that. At least to me, anyway. He barely met my eyes in Hegarty's office.

"You're not sure Hennessy did it?"

"He fucking did it, all right."

I dig about in my memories. "You worked it?"

"No. It breezed by my desk in the first hours, I passed it on to Murder. Never saw the shitbag and never want to. That's it."

"As far as you know then, everything's clean our side?"

His face turns sour. "As I said, I didn't work it. I wish to fuck I had now, there'd be no questioning his guilt at all. He would have clamped the fucking manacles round his ankles himself."

"So you know nothing?" I ask, to make sure.

He shuffles in the driver's seat, turns toward me. "Why am I in the hot seat here? You're the one with all the inside info. Why don't you ask your sister-in-law?"

"I will. And eventually, I'll get to the truth. But I don't want to put my finger on a trigger only to find out later my boss is at the wrong end of the gun."

His hand goes to the ignition, a signal for me to get out. "I didn't have the cushy number you have now, Frankie. Assigned to a specific team, with only the juicy crimes coming my way. The area I was over had anything from some snot-nosed kid committing arson to the fucking IRA dumping bodies in the Wicklow Mountains. What was one more bleedin' murder?" He huffs. "Get on that Shine case. That's our priority. Not some whistle-blowing documentary."

I get out of the car. It takes two goes to slam the door closed. Then Clancy settles himself into the seat and drives away. I sit in my own car for some time, staring up at the HQ building and thinking about Donna Hegarty's not-so-veiled warning. Seán Hennessy's voice echoes in my ear. *When I stepped round the side of that house . . . I thought I was walking into a dream.* I take up my phone, search for the Hennessy murders on the internet and the screen fills with photos. I recognize one that was used with some frequency by the press at the time. John and Bríd Hennessy standing outside the front door of their home. John's arms out, one hand on Seán's shoulder, the other round his wife's waist, Cara, a slip of smiles, sandwiched between them.

For weeks after, I remember looking at this photo for signs, for hesitancy or nerves in Bríd's smiling eyes or a petulant gleam in their children's faces. But there was nothing that hinted at the family's fate. I remember tracing Bríd's jaw, as if I could waken her from the image. I remember the feeling of guilt that we'd crossed paths. A transient brush of shoulders as we passed each other outside my parents' home. Bríd hot, heavy, and flustered, and me too preoccupied with a fresh homicide on the other side of the city to notice. A young detective in my twenties, my head too full of witness statements, blood, and murder to ask my mam who the woman in the blue floral dress was. And then, after, once Bríd Hennessy looked out from every newspaper, it didn't seem important to ask why she'd been there. Another woman my mam tried to help but where help came too late.

I reach for my phone, the Hennessy trailer and my meeting with Tanya lingering in my mind, and I reckon Baz is right—it might be a good thing to draw a line through Hennessy's name when it comes to these murders. I call the office, tell Ryan to get Seán Hennessy's alibi for the hours leading up to Geraldine Shine's death.

CHAPTER 5

THE FIRST FAT DROPS of heavy rain hit the windshield as I pull up along the pavement. The Shine house sits on a corner. The building is two stories and perched high on a short, steep garden. Curved bay windows capture the gray-blue light from the sea. The premises is closed off by a redbrick wall, which extends low on the road side, leveling as the street inclines. CSI have erected a cordon around the house. But rubberneckers have gathered. Neighbors in their gardens, mugs of tea in hands, arms folded, necks craned. A couple of teens have stopped on their bikes on the far side of the street, iPhones trained like weapons on the scene.

I get out, walk toward the house, duck under the garda tape. I step into the tent, greet the first officer, and sign the logbook.

"How we doing?"

"Nothing startling as yet. Pretty tidy scene by the looks of it."

I look back out to the street. A sharp breeze rises up and I can feel the atmosphere coiling back, ready to strike. The rain patters against the roof of the tent. It might drive the neighbors indoors, but the kids have that stance, narrow-lipped and thick-skinned. They won't be shoved indoors by a flash of poor weather.

I nod toward the gawkers. "Any of them get too close, get a uniform on it."

"Yes, ma'am."

I pull on a suit, foot covers. Prepare to peel back the secrets of the Shines' life. My mobile rings and I fish it out of my pocket.

Helen's voice comes down the line. "Chief, I've followed up on Geraldine Shine and possible domestic violence callouts."

I step to the side, let a SOCO pass, his arms full with a plastic box of envelopes, marked and tagged.

"Go on."

"She made three calls to the local station over the last year. There were two callouts. The first call was made to the station in February of this year. A domestic dispute. Gardaí were sent to the house but Alan Shine had left. They took a statement. In the end, she didn't press charges. The second call came two months ago, at 3:23 A.M. on June 14. She reported her husband smashing through the back door. He was threatening to kill her. She was too frightened to let him in. Her call was patched through to the garda on beat but was not followed up."

"No one checked on her?"

"No."

"A statement?"

"No." Voice tight as guitar wire. She takes a breath. "On Wednesday, August 8, at 6:17 P.M. there was another call. This time she phoned emergency services. She was sure someone had broken into her home. There's a recording."

The eighth of August, eleven days before her murder. Another

SOCO passes. Hands another box labeled EVIDENCE to his colleague, turns, and goes back into the house.

"You have it there?"

"Yes. Hold on." I hear a slight scuffle on the other end of the line then, "Okay, playing it now."

The voice is as clear as a bell, as if the operator is speaking to me. *What's your emergency?*

Geraldine Shine's voice is remarkably steady. There's no sing-song warble of terror, no tremble. But she keeps it low, as if she's hiding. Not moving. "I think someone's been in my home."

I see Geraldine Shine sitting on the floor, next to the bed. Knees drawn up, one arm around her legs, the phone against the small curl of her ear. Dark hair swept back from her face into a ponytail. The lines that over the last few years have only begun to deepen on her forehead are stitched tight between her brows.

Could we have your name and address, please, ma'am?

"Geraldine Shine. One Kincora Drive, Clontarf."

What makes you think someone has been in your home?

"In my bedroom. It looks like someone has laid down on the bed. There's a dent in the pillows."

Are there any signs of breaking and entering? Are there any windows broken? Was your door locked?

"No and yes, the door was locked but"—her voice lowers further—"my husband, we split up recently. I asked him to leave. I've not seen him in a few days. He can be violent. He's threatened me before."

Does your husband still have a key?

"Yes."

Mrs. Shine, is it possible your husband could be on the premises?

"No. I checked."

Mrs. Shine, we are sending someone over. Please stay on the line until you see the garda car.

"Okay."

There is a click. Helen is back on the line and Geraldine Shine dissolves into the past. "That's it. Or nearly it; gardaí arrive, and the call ends."

"Any report on what they found when they got there?"

"Yes, there'd been no evidence of a break-in. Nothing had been taken from the house. In her statement she mentioned she'd a sense someone had been at the back of the house a few times in that week. The back gate, which she usually kept closed, she'd found it open on occasion. And that's it. No follow-up and no further calls."

My hand is tight on the phone. There is no worse feeling than knowing your victim sensed their murder, reached out, and no one listened. "Thanks, Helen. At least we're clear on the state of their marriage. This could be either-or, the killer stalking or the husband. Could you ask for reports of a similar nature around the neighborhood? Could be it's a prowler caught in the midst of all this."

"Yes, ma'am."

I step through the front door in search of our lead SOCO, Keith. He's laid down squares of cardboard over the hallway but beneath them lies a worn black-and-white cork tile that at one time probably looked the part but along the baseboard, the edges are swollen and chunks have broken away. The house has a stale, damp smell; the cloud outside has turned the hallway to shadow. Behind the radiator, a bloom of mildew has loosened wallpaper from the wall. Beyond the dampness is the faint, sweet smell of garlic and the tang of rosemary. I keep to the cardboard and follow the scent to the kitchen at the end of the hall.

Keith's standing in the middle of the kitchen, a small man with small-man habits, never quite able to get his heels on the ground, chin overly high to stretch out his height, chest raised up around his short neck.

Currently his arms are extended, holding back two SOCOs. "Get the luminol, Gerry, Christ's sake."

I stop in the doorway. Gerry, the recipient of Keith's order, keeps his head down and ducks out of the room in search of the luminol. Another scene of crime officer stands in the corner, pointing a camera toward the floor. Keith hasn't noticed me. His arm's are still out, protecting whatever fragment of evidence he's discovered.

"Nick," he says, calling the other SOCO forward. "Tape this off." For a moment Nick appears stricken but he corrects himself quickly, takes a roll of tape from his arm, and steps toward the patch of floor Keith is standing over.

Then Keith changes his mind. "No. No, wait. Wait until we see what we're dealing with. Just wait!"

Studying the area, I look for what's got him so agitated. On the floor. A tiny speck, easily missed, easily mistaken for a fleck in the grain, a dent in the wood, or a piece of dirt.

"Is that blood?" I ask.

Keith lifts his head. His black hair falls into his eyes, his forehead red from looking downwards, a glow of sweat across his cheeks. He swallows. "I think so."

The rain is coming down outside, the thrum of it hitting the pavement that runs around the house. A low growl of thunder trembles off in the distance. Both of us look up to the window. It's open. Not wide, the long metal latch lies flat on the sill. The breeze lifts and the window swings outward then back against its frame.

I look back to Keith. "Did you open it?"

"No. No. Sorry, I checked, thought it was closed."

There's a tiny brown leaf curled on the draining board, where, now it dawns on us, hours before a foot found purchase.

I move quickly. "You." I point to Nick. "We need to cover the area outside the kitchen window." Even as I say the words, I know we're too late.

I hurry outside but by the time we have the window sealed off, the scene extended, there are rivulets running down the pathway. The sill has been washed clean of debris. I stare at the ledge, rain beating down against the hood of my suit. Nick hovers behind me, waiting for further instruction.

When nothing comes, he clears his throat. "What should we do, ma'am?"

I sigh. "See what you can get from it."

He nods, his expression doubtful.

I change into fresh overalls and return to the kitchen. Keith is spraying the floor with luminol. He takes out the black light, switches it on, and the speck lights up. A star of blue. Blood. And next to it, the edge of a footprint.

Keith meets my eyes. "Well, look at that," he says. "Mark it up, boys."

For all our caution, none of us expected the bloody crime scene at the church to extend to the Shine house. The question is whether it was before or after Geraldine Shine's death. The thought brings new angles to the shape of the investigation. There's one reason someone would've come here before the killing: to pursue their victim. And many reasons for coming back to the house afterward: to steal money, drugs, some secret document, or to destroy evidence that could lead to their arrest. And the presence of blood here suggests the killer returned after the scene at the church.

"Why would he come back here?" I say, mostly to myself but Keith rocks on the balls of his toes and gives out a puff of air.

"I just collect the deets, Detective. This might be his own blood or even a droplet that fell from his clothing; when he came through the window. That was a pretty vicious scene at the church; I'd be surprised if he came away clean or unmarked."

I'd be surprised if he got a single scratch on him. His attack on Geraldine Shine was sudden. He came at her from behind. His hands would have been covered, his sleeves likely taped down. He's too organized for this. I recall Geraldine's complaint of stalking, the phone call to the local station that she believed someone had been in her home.

"Was the gate at the side open?"

He pulls himself upright. "No. We had to use the bolt-cutters. Nice new brass lock. It's in the tent there if you want a look at it."

"Thanks." But I remain in the kitchen, transfixed by the path picked out from window to floor.

In the oven there's what could be a roast, burned. The oven is off.

Keith follows my line of vision. "A nice Sunday roast on the go? I'd thought she'd put it on early, forgot about it. It burned and she turned it off before she left but now . . ."

"He turned it off."

Keith shrugs. "Might suggest he knew the routine. Knew she might have had a meal on, needed to turn that oven off. Maybe why he returned. Why the bleedin' hell he'd be worried about a burned dinner now is beyond me. Or a burned house, for that matter. Lord only knows how the minds of these fuckers work."

"I agree. This has cost him," I say, smiling down at the speck of blood.

"I wouldn't get too excited yet." He nods to the tiny drop of blood. "I break wind that leaves more of a mark."

"Undoubtedly true."

But there is a footprint. It's barely more than a smudge but the arc of the sole is visible, the impression suggesting a heavy boot or a thick-soled trainer. I look across the kitchen. Two strides and anyone could get across it. A SOCO appears in the doorway.

Keith turns to her, his expression softening so much it looks likely to drip onto the floor: "What is it, Lisa?"

"I think we found a piece of her clothing." She flushes, holds up a clear plastic bag, a white top, blood in dark smears over the fabric.

I take it, turn it about. The frilled edge and wide shoulders look identical to the top worn by Geraldine Shine on her Facebook page yesterday morning.

"Where was it?"

"Hanging in her wardrobe among the party frocks." She doesn't add, *what the actual fuck,* but I can hear it in her voice.

"Show me." I turn to Keith. "Get a photo of the footprint back to the Bureau as soon as you can with a note to Steve Garvin."

He gives me a salute and I follow Lisa out of the kitchen.

Geraldine and Alan Shine's room is depressingly pink. Pink sheets, dark pink curtains, a creamy pink carpet. An overdose of chalk paint on every piece of furniture, the headboard, dresser. Plain wooden drawer handles have been replaced with shining knobs of glass. Nothing has escaped the pseudo vintage effect.

The SOCO leads me to the wardrobe. "The rest of the clothes were pushed back so that the blouse was clearly visible," Lisa says. "We've taken them from the wardrobe. And we're going through the laundry now."

I see the marker placed where the blouse was found. There's a row of footwear slotted neatly onto shelves on the floor of the closet.

"You should take them too," I say, and she nods. I look in at the wardrobe, stripped bare of its contents. There are many reasons a perp might return to a house after offing someone, but I can't recall a single case where someone comes back to deliberately leave a whopping piece of evidence behind. I look at where the blouse had been, try to think why the killer would risk getting caught for this. The thrill? Or maybe the fantasy he was trying to replicate required an item from his victim to be returned to the house. He would've had to move quickly after he'd finished at the church, a quick search of the rooms to find Geraldine's. Although there's a good chance he knew already where her bedroom was, and if that's the case it could play nicely for us. We can deduce one of two things from it: Either he was her stalker or he'd been here before.

Hoping for the latter, I ask Lisa, "You got many prints?"

Lisa turns from the bed, looks to the door handle and the light switch, which are covered in black dust. "A good sample, yes."

I take a deep breath of hope. "I don't see the husband's clothes in here," I say, pointing at the wardrobe. I remember the call to the gardaí, where Geraldine said he'd left only a week ago. Had he actually left the marital home? Or had he not come back because he was already dead?

"There's a spare room, down the hallway. Most of his stuff's in there. A right mess and that's before we got to it," Lisa adds.

She goes to the bed, unhooks the sheet from the mattress, folds the corners inwards to capture every particle that remains of Geraldine.

I move to the window, look out on the street. The room points to the houses across the road. A mirror image. To the left the gray slab of the sea, to the right the tips of the Poolbeg chimneys are just visible against the rain-streaked sky. My phone beeps from my pocket and I remove it. Helen has sent through the summaries of the witness statements. Pictures painted of the Shines' lives. I scroll through the reports, add shade to the victims; color, depth, detail. The uniforms have been busy this morning. Door-to-door, collecting words and memories from neighbors. A dismal summary of the marriage. Geraldine a shy but friendly face on the street. She liked to run in the mornings. She was spotted at about eight yesterday morning, Windbreaker on and heading off toward the promenade. She returned an hour later, her movements slow, muscles cooling down, no sense of urgency in her gait. No outward signs of distress.

One woman neighbor, from across the street, reported a delivery at about ten A.M. Geraldine spent a lot of time sending out and accepting deliveries for her business, but the aged Nancy Drew noticed this one. *Who gets a delivery on a Sunday?* she asked. That was odd. The deliveryman didn't arrive in a vehicle either, but walked up to the house. The woman saw Mrs. Shine sign and the deliveryman went off down the street.

Her description of the man could be any Tom, Dick, or Harry within a thirty-mile radius. Above average height, hood up, possibly white. She'd spotted the exchange from a top window but her eyes weren't the sharpest any longer. Although she'd thought it odd at the time, there were odder things about and she wouldn't be mentioning it if it weren't for been asked.

I catch sight of Keith, below, exiting the tent. He ducks down against the rain and trots to his van on the other side of the cordon. I put away my phone and peer down at the front of the house. Ger Shine would have had to press her face against the glass to see who was at the door or to see up the street. I look out over the road, across the rooftops, off in the direction of the church.

I leave the bedroom, walk down the stairs and out through the tent. We've got what we were supposed to find from this house. I retrieve my raincoat from the car. Throw it on, pull up the hood. The teens have taken shelter under one of the trees across the street. One of them gobs spit at the ground when he sees me looking. I start the walk toward the church. I move slowly, taking the same route Geraldine Shine would have walked yesterday afternoon.

Cars pass, wheels spinning water out over the pavement. People rush toward their vehicles, umbrellas down over shoulders, weaving through the puddles filling up the path. A bus heaves by, the number 50. I look up, count four dark shapes behind the condensation of the window. Make a mental note to check if it runs the same time on Sundays. I wait at a pedestrian crossing, watch for more potential witnesses of Geraldine's last movements. The traffic stops and I step onto the road. I glance in at the drivers; windshield wipers tip over and back at full speed.

I hurry to the other side of the street and the church is there. The roof a pointed shadow through the gray curtain of rain. The area is still cordoned off. Garda cars stationed at all access points, the cleanup van in the churchyard.

It has taken ten minutes, at most. Ten minutes for the killer to pick his pace. Was he in his car at this point? Parked. There are vehicles all along the street. The meter says free on Sundays. I look back, see the rows of houses looking down on me. A curtain shifts in an upstairs window. A child appears; a cuddly toy waves at me through the damp pane. I lift a hand and the curtain falls back.

The rain pours. Sheets of water, waves of it stand against the horizon. The water gathers debris, litter, dirt, a sodden mulch, carries it down the road. Soaked through, I head back to my car. Quicker now. Almost a run. I'm back at my car in seven minutes.

Opening the door, I drop into the driver's seat and peel the raincoat from my body. Throw it onto the backseat. I check my phone. Looking for the next step, my foot already lifted, waiting for a lead. There's nothing yet. Baz is still in Whitehall, overseeing the autopsies. I picture the knife in Alan Shine's hand, the angry puncture wounds down Geraldine Shine's back.

I try to see her, imagine her passing the window of my car. Make her walk those steps toward the church again but instead I see the past, Bríd Hennessy, a frantic shuffle in her step, down the dry, bright road. Hot, hot day. I close my eyes on the image. I'm not sure what it is about Geraldine Shine that calls up Bríd Hennessy's ghost in my mind. A shared history of domestic violence, perhaps, or that I'd met Seán Hennessy the same evening I saw the Shine bodies in the church. Or maybe I'm realizing that both women conjure up another feeling in me, a discomfort, a little knot of guilt.

I rub a fist against my stomach, take a long breath, look out at the garda cordon, the blue tent pitched up against the Shines' front door. Perhaps it's this place: Clontarf. A place that's always been a haven for me but now I've a sour feeling that's akin to betrayal, as if I've been hoodwinked somehow. That my mind has managed to rewrite the past in some way, rewired my memories around the jagged canker of the Hennessy murders, of crimes past. And now, I can see the place for what it is, like everywhere fucking else. Full of creeping evil behind safe houses.

Searching through my emails, I find Seán's files, select a clip at random, and press *play*. Letting my head tip back on the seat, I listen for truth:

"The first few days could well have been sentence enough for any innocent man. And I was not more than a boy. I still had hope, you know. I thought: Any minute now they're going to see, they're going to realize it wasn't me. They'll let me out. Hold on. Hold on. And the anger. Pure frustration. Whoever did this could still be out there. What if it wasn't my da? What if it was some other sicko and no one's looking for them?"

There's a pause and I hear him take a ragged breath before he goes on.

"When the lights went down. Nine sharp, you know, whether you were tired or not. That voice. Boom. It echoed down the hallways like the call of the apocalypse itself. It clanged through that place: Lights out! And there was nothing. Nothing could coax sleep to me.

"I lay there, waiting for my eyes to adjust. Hours staring down the length of my sentence. Hours picking out the patterns between the bricks in the wall. The whole nightmare tumbling round my head, and my mind willing to take always the darkest of thoughts to live in for the night. What if this is it? But it couldn't be; they'd soon see it was someone else. They'd still be looking. But then another day would come by, sauntering up through the fucking window. And on it went. Those first few days, yeah, they were sentence enough."

CHAPTER 6

BAZ FLOPS DOWN at my desk. I pour a glass of water and dump it into the base of my bonsai tree. Its straggling branches are reaching toward the window. The clippers lie unused next to the pot. The tree appears to enjoy rubbing it in, satisfying itself by growing unchecked and wild until I've the nerve to hack it back.

"You know I've taken about three showers this afternoon and I can still smell Alan Shine's corpse on my skin." He pulls back his sleeve, presses his nose to his forearm, inhales, then grimaces.

"Tell me you gleaned something other than a keen sense of smell at the autopsy."

"Freezer burn along his right side. Which, to be fair, is what we'd suspected. A great big fatty liver, which the doc says was near-on cirrhosis. Alcohol in his blood. Cause of death strangulation. The missus, as seen at the church, throat slit, cause of death. Stab wounds down her back, definitely postmortem."

I turn away from the bonsai, sit across from him, check the time. Clancy has yet to grace the office with his presence. "When I went to the house, there was a blackened roast in the oven."

"I heard about the killer's little visit there. A full roast would be a bit much to be eating on your own. Maybe she was expecting someone else?"

I lean back, look to the ceiling. "Her husband? There's no file for separation. His things were still in his bedroom. Perhaps he was due to come home."

"Or she put on a bit of dinner for a date, a lover, say. She knew her husband wouldn't be walking in any time soon for one of two reasons." He makes a fist, sticks up his thumb. "One, she'd kicked him out, or two"—he points his index finger—"she knew he was dead. She could've been involved in his murder or hired someone, didn't pay up, and this is the interest."

"This is too involved for a pro, who'd want to get in and out quickly. If the bodies were found any other way I might go with that but as it is, no."

There's a knock and Helen's face appears round the door. Good news. I can see it's caught in her chest, her breath seized up with it. "Chief, Ryan's fed back on Seán Hennessy's alibi for the Shine murders. He said he went to the chippie at about six fifteen. Ate the takeaway at a bench across the street. Ryan's verified with a witness, the chip-shop owner, said he should be able to get CCTV footage to confirm it."

And I'm not seeing why this should make Helen excited, we're down a subject.

She goes on: "But we have had some success on the CCTV around the Shine house," she adds with a smile. "We've got the delivery guy that the neighbor reported. Approaching the Shine home. Clear as day. I've sent it to your screen."

"Good," I say. Then thinking about Geraldine Shine's blouse, "How about later? Any footage of our perp going to the house after the murders?"

"No. The view from the camera is obscured."

"Obscured?"

"At six thirty a couple of tourist buses pull up to collect holidaymakers. They're stationed at the bottom of the road for about half an hour. But I've notified door-to-door on the street, given a description to see if any of the neighbors saw someone return later."

"Thanks, Helen. How about Geraldine Shine's phone records?"

"Nothing on those yet, Chief."

"Chase them up. See what we can pull from them. If the phone is still on, we might get a location."

Clancy appears behind her, and she keeps her eyes to the floor, as if looking directly at him could scald her retinas. "Right away, Chief," she answers, stepping to the side to let Clancy pass. She reverses away from the door, closing it quietly as she goes.

Clancy moves across the carpet, throws a nod of greeting at Baz, then pulls up another chair and sits himself at my desk with a huff. He tips his head, settles those eyes, busy, blue-bottle blue, on mine.

"Well, where we at then?" He pushes his coat back, choosing to leave it on despite the dry warmth of the office. Clancy as always, on the move, ready to leave before he's even here. We give him the sad summary, the few nibbles we've had from the killer's plate, the initial autopsy reports, the tiny spot of blood on the Shine kitchen floor, the partial footprint, and the oddity of the blouse. And now the footage of the deliveryman approaching the Shine house. He nods, his tongue working behind his cheek, rolling over the bitter offering.

He flicks his eyes at my computer. "Spark her up then, let's have a gander at this fucker."

Baz reaches out, starts the CCTV. The footage is remarkably clear, the first images almost over-bright. Baz adjusts the exposure on the screen. The camera is stationed to the west of the Shine house. Facing the bedroom, you can make out the gray flats of Dublin Bay reflected in the window.

A young woman appears at the lower end of the screen. She powers up the road, one hand pushing a buggy, a toddler housed beneath clear plastic. Her face is buried in her phone. In a blur of time she's gone.

The ticker counts on the minutes, then at 9:55, another figure steps into view. An apparition, a flicker of charcoal grays and blacks. One hand in his pocket. His head held stiffly, like a bird of prey looking for movement. His walk is slow, a slight bounce at the knee with each step. The quirk to his stride gives him the look of someone who's ready to push off, to take off at the first sign of a chase.

The woman with the buggy would have passed him, might've recognized him if she'd looked up from her phone. But she's gone and now I look. Let my eyes feed off his image, pick it apart for any detail that might give him away.

I pause it. Look at Baz, Clancy. "Recognize him?"

Baz pulls back, hooks his hands over the back of his head. "No. No wonder the neighbor couldn't give a description. The guy's better wrapped than a burrito."

Clancy has his hand under his chin, his eyes moving over the screen. "I'd make him, what? Six foot two at least? Maybe a little over, judging by the height of the garden wall there. Pretty lanky lad. I'd say your first analysis was on the mark, Frankie. Mid-twenties, early thirties."

The man is a blurred shadow, paused midstride. "I don't think this guy was there to deliver anything," I add. I hit *play*. The man moves onto the main road away from the house. Gloved hand on the lip of his hood, obscuring his face from the camera. He turns back up the corner, a slight pitch forwards to his posture to compensate for the slope in the road. Then he's out of view.

"He knew about the cameras right enough," Clancy comments. "Not worried we'd work out who he was."

"Or cocksure we wouldn't," Baz says. He pushes the heels of his hands against his eyes. Blinks hard. "Or maybe he wants us to find him."

I give him a look that says he should know better than that, and he shrugs back at me. "I'm going on two days now with no sleep; it's the best I can do."

"I would think he knew about the buses too," I say. "Knew what time they'd be pulling up, when the camera would be obscured."

Baz takes up a pen, taps it on his knee. "It gives us a tighter window to work around. If the killer knew the buses were a regular thing, we know he returned to her house in that half hour. Between six thirty and seven P.M."

"When did Ryan say Hennessy went to the chip shop?"

Baz raises an eyebrow. "You're thinking Hennessy?"

I look to Clancy but he's studying the backs of his hands as if life's answers were written there. "I don't know. No. It's a possibility, isn't it?"

"He said six fifteen. If he went to the bench outside, was seen there for a while afterward, it rules him out."

Clancy is pushing out of his seat.

I look up at him. "You're going?"

He flicks the cuff of his coat, checks the time. "I've a meeting. Get working through the database for anyone who matches this fella then. And keep sifting through CCTV. Can you get that license plate recognition technology on it?"

I glance at Baz. "ANPR?" I reply.

"That's the one. There's no way this fella carted Alan Shine's body to that church without a vehicle. Close down over Clontarf area, maybe stretch into Raheny if there's a no-show. Let's go back six weeks. I want everyone on this team able to memorize what vehicles have come and gone between Clontarf Road and the Shine house. This little shit is coming in." He gives his shoulders a jiggle under his coat as if shaking away his bluster. "And that will be the end of it." He gives us a look that says we're to get the bloody job done and done quickly. He leaves, giving the door a firm slam as he goes.

"What's up with him?" Baz asks. "Wound so tight he squeaks when he walks."

I look over at the closed door, chew the tip of my pen. I need a cigarette. "I don't know."

"We'll have something on this guy soon," Baz offers, throwing a glance at the computer. "Abigail is processing evidence as fast as her team can snap slides into microscopes."

"I know." I replay the video. Look at our suspect. The figure comes up the road. His head tucked in against his chest. I try to fill out his features but fail. The clock ticks on.

Baz is tapping the pen against his leg again, his face drawn down in thought. After a moment the tapping stops and he turns from the desk. "I think we should bring in the priest."

"The priest?"

"Father Healy."

I point to the screen. "You can't tell me that's Father Healy."

"Agreed. But as much as I hate to admit it, Ryan is right. He's looked into it and Father Healy wasn't accounted for all afternoon. He knew the victims. Alan Shine was dressed in priest's vestments. Now, he may not have been a priest but he had been a lay minister."

The queue for confessions at St. Catherine's must've been a long one.

He nods, points the pen at me as if we're both on the same page. "And," he continues, "the most important point: Geraldine Shine might've thought she was meeting him. He said himself that she often stopped by the church to talk to him."

I look at our perp frozen on the CCTV footage, then consider the likelihood of Father Healy carrying out these crimes. I think of Father Healy meeting our victim. She was attractive, vulnerable; perhaps their relationship had begun to take a different shape in the priest's eyes. The answer closest to us is often the one we seek.

"He would have been well-placed, sure," I say. "And maybe there's a motive there. It won't be easy to get information from him though. He doesn't seem like the share-y type."

"What priest does? Expect us all to pour our darkest secrets into their ears but keep their own to themselves." Baz is on his feet. He pushes up the cuff of his shirt, checks the time. "First thing tomorrow, I bring him in," he adds. Then giving me a quick salute, he's gone; a bounce in his step at the thought of putting the priest in the hot seat.

The office quiet, I pull the door-to-door transcripts onto my lap, take up a highlighter pen, scan each statement for anything that might give us more on the shadowy specter on the CCTV. But I can't concentrate, the echo of Clancy's presence around me still. The sense that he's a little too quick to leave. Too eager to push Hegarty's instructions aside. It's not like Jack to avoid diving into a cold case like the Hennessys'; these are the ones he relishes. *It's a grand feeling to tie up a loose end, Frankie. Give families answers. That's what it's all about.* I put the witness statements back on the desk, pick up the phone, and dial an old friend.

Mike Owens answers on the second ring.

"The doghouse," he says, his voice loud against a wave of chatter, shouts, and phone rings.

I imagine the organized chaos of the local station at Harcourt Street. The computers listing on full desks, keyboards smeared in years' worth of greasy, sandwich-eating fingers. Piles of reports and folders on either side. Stab vests thrown over broken-backed chairs. Seventies' law enforcement melded with the modern day.

"Hey, Mike. It's Frankie Sheehan."

"Frankie," he says. "Long time, no speak."

"How's it going down there in the pit?"

"Dirty," he says. "Fucking dregs of society sucking our resources dry. Gang crime up to our eyeballs. Bloody endless. No sooner are you onto one of these fuckers, someone puts a bullet in their head and we've got a whole other heap of dung to shift."

He talks the talk but I hear the hunger in his voice.

"Still sleeping well?"

"Like a clear conscience. Heard you got the big job, eh?" I imagine him pulling at his tie. His neck covered in shadow already. A well-worn look in his eyes, dirty blond hair raked through with over-caffeinated fingers. "Should I call you Chief now?"

"Let's pretend we're both in that lecture hall, staring up at the same ladder."

"Easy for you to say. Anytime I got by the third rung, I'd snakes round my ankles."

I laugh. "I've a job for you."

"You know how I like those. Anything to take me outta the current shithole. Hang on, let me put you on the mobile. Can't hear jack shit in here."

There's a muffled sound, a click on the line, and I imagine him levering away from his desk, escaping the office and out onto the courtyard at the back of the building. There's another click on the line and then, "Right, I'm all ears."

Owens is a walking and talking stereotype. I hear his cigarette lighter pop and the sound of the city beating away in the background. "What can I do for you?"

"I'm reviewing a few old files. And wondered if I could jog your memory."

"Jog away."

"Seán Hennessy. You may have heard of him."

"I'm not deaf, so yeah."

"Off the record, you got anything in the archives? I've his file here but have little in the way of interview transcripts. That kind of thing. I thought I'd pulled everything but maybe there's more somewhere."

He laughs, chesty. "There's some big cracks in the ground all of a sudden?"

"You know how it is."

He doesn't answer right away and I hear the cigarette smack at his mouth. A sigh comes down the line. "Am I looking for any names?"

I hesitate. I've known Owens for so long but trust is not always cast iron. Time can tarnish the hardiest of metals. "Jack Clancy."

There's silence. Then, "I'll check it out." I hear the swoosh of a door and the sounds of the city quiet as he steps back inside. "We should catch up for a drink sometime."

"Yeah," I say. "We should."

He laughs. "I'll be in touch if I find anything."

"Thanks, Mike." I hang up. Collect my bag and coat and set out from the office to meet Geraldine Shine's family.

IT'S EIGHT THIRTY and still light. I stand at the window of my flat, four floors above the bustle of Grafton Street, looking out over Dublin city, armed with a cigarette and a coffee. The other side of the window pane, a beetle, a tiny black bauble, thin limbs reaching up the wall like a mountaineer. Below it, a thick pocket of webs, a little pouch of softness to cushion a fall.

A peachy sunset builds across the Dublin sky, lilac clouds pulled back over the horizon. But the air outside is cloying, stiff. More rain coming. More low pressure.

Geraldine Shine's deliveryman remains unidentified. And the ghost who slipped through her window to leave her bloodied blouse remains faceless. Geraldine's family. I take another drag of the cigarette. Her family was broken and bitter when I visited them. Fiona Garry stayed wedged up against her mother through-out. The smell of polish and baking stuck in the air. Years' worth of it. Pope John Paul II waving a holy hand from prime position above the fireplace. Both women, red-faced, red-eyed, held hands through their grief. The father, Ken Garry, silent on the chair across from them. On the wall a school picture of Fiona, plait over the shoulder, on the cusp of teen-dom, her hand resting on her younger sister's left shoulder. Geraldine Shine, black hair sculpted like a shining cap around her head, a square fringe reaching to her eyebrows, two front teeth missing from her smile.

The family breathed life into Geraldine Shine. Colored in the blanks that only they could fill. Geraldine had slowly dropped out of her family's life or they had eased away. That husband, Fiona spat, finally had her where he wanted her. Every time they thought she would leave, she was pulled back. It's hard to watch a loved one go through that, Fiona said. Like being forced to watch a car crash in slow motion. *We all wanted to look away.* Then came the tears. Shuddering tears. Alan had to be involved in this somehow, she'd said, wiping snot and wetness away with a frayed piece of tissue. There's nobody else who'd want to hurt Ger.

I put out my cigarette, move away from the window, go to the bedroom. I change into a T-shirt and jeans then return to the living room. Seán Hennessy's notes are spread out over the carpet in front of the sofa. On the coffee table the Hennessy documentary footage is paused. Seán's head is down, searching for the right phrase, perhaps. The right sentence to persuade. His case file is fat. Fatter still will be the boxes of evidence and sundry affiliated with court proceedings. Seven folders of court summaries, interview summaries, witness statements, and garda reports. But even then I know some of it is missing. Tabs mark out pages that aren't present. Indexes reference interview transcripts that aren't on file. It doesn't look good. Clancy's reticence about the case has lodged under my skin like a splinter. And I can't help but look, to check there's nothing there.

I sit down. Take a breath and open a folder on the Hennessy crime scene. Photographs taken on the thirteenth of August 1995.

Seventeen years ago. Among the photos a stray picture cut from a newspaper. The headline reads: SON SUSPECTED IN FAMILY MURDER. It's dated the fourteenth of August. The day after the bodies were discovered. The image in the article shows distraught residents gathered as close to the Hennessy home as the gardaí will allow, their expressions caught by the camera: hands covering mouths, a string of rosary beads woven between fingers, tissues pressed to eyes, heads tipped together in communal grief. Behind the neighbors and rubberneckers, all along the street, news vans. Photographers. Cameras. I don't want to remember the grotesque scuffle in the media about who and what had failed so much an entire family had been as good as wiped out. The son turned monster. Transcendence. Is that the word? Becoming.

Taking up the photos from the crime scene, I look down at John Hennessy, his head to chest, propped against the back wall of the family home, as if he'd drifted off in the August sunlight. Ireland was in the midst of a heat wave. A scorcher of a day. Dry as bone. The sun lightens the photo, gives the picture a surreal, sepia quality, makes it dreamlike. Seán's words come back to me, *I thought I was walking into a dream.*

The blood from John's injuries is dirty down his front, around his neck. His hands rest palm-up on the patio. John. Heavy-fisted. That's what they'd said. The lighter version of the truth. Followed by the reassurance that he was a grand man, really. Brought home the bacon. Honest to goodness.

I turn to the next photo. Bríd is facedown on the grass, her head turned to one side. One shoe missing, twisted off in a struggle. And the daughter, Cara Hennessy. Ten years old.

I peer down at the young girl's face. A gentle outward curve to her young cheeks. Peach shorts. White T-shirt. She survived.

Just. But I know she's relived that scene every night, every day, that it's waiting at the end of every heartbeat. Putting down the picture, I search for the papers in her file. Papers that seek to shield her from her past. An attempt to scoop a girl out of what's shaped her. Name her anew. I find it at the bottom of her summary. WSP. Witness Security Program. My eyes bear down on the signature at the bottom of the page; my fingers tighten, hold on. Hold on to what I'm seeing: *Jack Clancy*.

I stare down at the signature for a long time then close my eyes. The stiff letters of his signature float behind my eyelids. I remove the page from the summary, set it down on the farthest edge of the coffee table. There's nothing about Jack Clancy's signature that should make me worry, but seeing his name there, attached to Hennessy's, does make me uneasy. The thought that working on this case, the magnitude of Seán's badness, might have caused good people to make bad choices. It happens. But then our criminals could use the same excuse. Seán could use the same excuse, surely. Exhaustion, a need to escape his family home even if it meant killing his mother and sister. He'd do anything to free himself of his father. That was the wall at Seán's back. We all have one. A place where we find ourselves making unthinkable decisions. A place where we might decide to kill.

In the months leading up to the Hennessy murders, I was still living with my parents and I found my own back inching up against a wall. I was tired, ambitious, probably impatient and too full of my own life and problems to deal with much else. Dad was ill with depression. It lurked in his motionless eyes, in the stiff movement of his face. He'd tried twice to kill himself. Despite medication, he couldn't break free, and every time I stepped into the house I was afraid of what I'd find. And I knew why. I knew he was sick, squirreled back into some dark hole inside himself that I couldn't reach. And I became expert at reading his mood. Just from the back of his head, a little angle to the right, the gray hair that covered the troubled husk of his skull, spread out over his shirt collar. Just by that I could tell where he was, with us or somewhere else.

One day I came home early from work. I didn't think there was anyone in the house. I walked upstairs and saw him, through the open door of my parents' bedroom. Just sitting, staring out the window. But around him on the clean white bed, pills. Lots of pills. Counted out. Ready. All of a sudden I wanted it over. Whatever bad thing was hurtling toward us, I no longer had the strength to keep it back. In that moment, I hated him a little. I stood there and looked. Looked at the back of his head, at that little skirt of hair over his collar, and I willed him to succeed. Willed him to die. Yes, there's badness in all of us. We're all human. That's the fault line, right there.

I swallow, pack away the pain of that day, and angle the laptop toward me. Looking into Seán Hennessy's face, I reach for the keyboard and hit *play* on the next clip.

"It was three days in when I got my first kicking," he says. "The lads, you know, they need to show you who's who, what's what. I was no saint before all that happened. I was a skinny bloke, to be sure, but I knew how to dodge a beating, knew when to fade against a wall, slip behind a corner. And I'd learned to sniff out trouble. Normal folk now, they'd be going along with their lives and trouble found them. Growing up with my da, I wasn't so green as that. I'd learned to look for it, size it up. I knew when to hide and when to throw the first swing. No fist was going to find me looking the other way, you know.

"And I knew it was coming to me. My cell mate, Reece, he was the proverbial shit. Shaved head. You could pick out the marks of every fight he'd won in the white lines that mapped his bulging skull. At first it seemed he'd taken me under his wing, like. Then he heard I'd a sister. That she'd nearly died."

His hands slide over each other, right comforting the left. His eyes water. I lean closer, try to worm out the truth between his words, the workings of his mind between breaths. He swallows.

"Well, he knocked me sixty sheets to the wind. That was the third day. I cried out but no one came. After, I lay curled on the bed and the door banged open. They ordered Reece outta the cell. They checked me over. Not a word out of them. Then I guess they decided I was well enough and left. Reece was packed back into the cell. He pulled himself tall and the look in his eyes as he stood over me. It drove ice needles through my blood. I didn't need to be looking for trouble no more. No. Here it was. Two feet from my life for the next seventeen years."

I close the computer, take up my coffee, return to the window. The beetle is still lurching up the wall but its back leg has caught on a sleeping tendril of the web, ensnared. The leg tugs, and his stiff body rolls. Then he's gone. Falls. Down into the little soft pouch. And there, a tiny spider. Faster than light, it scrabbles over the web, anoints the beetle with some deadly toxin. The spider retreats but I know it's watching. I can see the brown shadow of it beneath the veil of silver. The beetle turns, enmeshing itself more surely. And slowly the poison takes over; its black legs bend, tuck, and fold neatly inwards.

CHAPTER 7

'M PLACING BETS in my head about how long it will take Father Healy to remove his collar. We've cranked up the heat in the interview room. The lights are high. No water on the table. Baz sits relaxed, two buttons open on his shirt, sleeves rolled to the elbow. Every now and then, he lifts the folder and waves it in front of his face. Dark strands of hair lift from his forehead. Each time he does this, the priest shifts in the chair. The heavy, starched black suit he's wearing is enough to make me sweat in sympathy.

Baz checks his notes. "So you're saying that no one can confirm your whereabouts between one fifteen P.M. and when you returned to the church at . . . eight forty-five P.M.?"

"I was out visiting, Detective."

"You sure you can't give us any names?"

Regret turns down his mouth. "Some of it's very sensitive. It wouldn't be right for me to disclose it."

"Patrick, I don't think that's altogether right." Baz lays his palms on the table. The priest's neck winds in at the use of his Christian name. "You told my colleague Geraldine Shine visited you. Why can't you disclose where you were when Geraldine Shine was being slaughtered in your own church?"

Healy's brows, gray thickets of hair, draw downwards. "I shouldn't have admitted that to your colleague. I was shocked. Traumatized. Two people had been murdered."

"We know that." Baz opens the file, takes out the photos of the scene. Places them square on the table. Healy's eyes drop down to the gruesome images. "Talk to us. Help us."

Healy opens his mouth, closes it again. "I can't. I took an oath."

"An oath can't protect you from the law."

"Do you have some water?"

"In a moment. Alan Shine was a lay minister, right?"

"Yes."

"You didn't think it odd when he never showed up for Sunday's service?"

Healy shakes his head. "Lay ministers help out when they can. It's not always set in stone, the timetable, so to speak. And when Mr. Shine did sign up, it was usually for the midweek mass."

Baz nods slowly and waits for a while before asking his next question, but his eyes never leave the priest's. Healy shifts on the seat, his ample stomach pressing up against the table.

"Let's go over your movements again. You finished service at one, right?" Baz asks.

"Yes. I waited at the door, saying good-bye to those who attended. It wasn't a busy service. Most were gone in about fifteen minutes."

"What did you do once the last of your congregation had left?"

"I went into the vestry. Changed out of my clothes. Mrs. Berry had put out a flask of tea and some sandwiches for my visits, which she does every Sunday. I got in the car and started my rounds."

"And you had your phone with you?"

"I did. But it was on silent, which is why I didn't hear Mrs. Berry's calls when she tried to reach me after . . . after finding the bodies." His mouth twists.

Ryan steps into the viewing room behind me, closes the door quiet, as if he is in a library. "So," he whispers, "I drove up to the parochial house like you asked, Chief, and had a nice chat with our Mrs. Berry." He catches his reflection in the viewing window, touches a hand to the front of his hair, held upright by some kind of gel that hardens on contact. I suspect he has hair straighteners at home. It's grating how much he fancies himself rotten but he can bring out the charm when he needs to, and I imagine Mrs. Berry was close to melting by the end of their meeting.

He gives me his best smile, still basking in the warmth of Mrs. Berry's eyes, forgetting that I'm not Mrs. Berry, and I give him a sobering look that smacks that feeling right out of him.

"What've you got?"

"His list of visitations for the Sunday and their numbers, in case there was any sort of emergency. Here." He passes me a list of eight names. "I asked her about a few. There's one or two who may not be the most reliable of witnesses. Addicts. Erm." He leans over, careful not to get too close lest I bite. "That fella, Stuart Power. He'd phoned during the week about a visit; his mother is ill and I think he wanted a blessing. I called him and he said Healy canceled. The rest said they had only seen the priest at service over the past three weeks. No house calls. Mrs. Berry did say he'd missed tea at the parochial house. It felt like that woulda been unusual. A grand life he has there."

I scan down the list. "Can we run Cell Site Analysis on his phone? He said it was on silent, not off."

"Might not be able to get that for a day or so though, Chief."

"Get started on it."

"Sure, sure."

"And thanks."

A glimmer of a smile and he's out the door.

I move back to the mirrored window. To another, Baz might seem still at ease. Hands splayed casually on the table. Feet steady on the floor. But now I can see the red flush creeping up the back of his neck. The way his mouth has closed down when he speaks, his back teeth together. Every now and then he rolls a stiffness out of his right shoulder, rubs his ear before settling back into position with a sigh. He thought Healy would be an easy squeeze. But the priest has years on him when it comes to avoiding confession.

"When was the last time you saw Geraldine Shine alive?"

"Detective, I really—"

Baz gives a frustrated laugh. "Come on, Father. What's the point in not answering our questions? Surely your Lord above would want you to help us find her killer?" He pushes a finger against the images. "Unless you think you've something to hide."

"I've nothing to hide and only God to answer to."

"Lucky you." Baz is getting sloppy. The priest has riled him. He didn't expect a moral tug-of-war when fighting on the good side.

I grab a bottle of water, knock on the door. Walk in. "Father Healy, sorry I'm late."

Baz folds his arms. "Detective chief superintendent entering the interview room at"—he glances at the clock—"oh eight twenty hours. Father, you've met my colleague, Detective Sheehan, at the scene?"

"Forgive me but it is warm in here." He hooks his finger beneath the white band at his throat, flips it free of the collar, and opens the top button.

"It is. Here. Straight from the fridge." I place the water in front of him.

He picks up the bottle, opens it, and takes a long drink. "Thank you."

"You mind if I sit in awhile, Father?"

"Sure," Father Healy says. His eyes light on me. Wary.

I place the information collected on Healy's visits in front of Baz. He turns away to read through it.

"You won't know this," I say to Healy, "but I used to attend St. Catherine's. As a child. I think your predecessor—"

"Father McNamee," he offers.

"He was something of a character. You knew him?"

"Briefly. I knew he liked to, erm, socialize."

I smile. "Not half. He never turned down a wedding reception, that's for sure."

"Ah now, we all know there's more of a party at a funeral." He catches himself. His hand passes swiftly from his forehead, chest, then the tip of each arm in a sign of prayer. "Sorry."

"No, it's true! Nothing wrong with saying so, is there?"

"I guess there's not," he says. He smiles at me. It warms his dull brown eyes.

"Father, we're running through a minefield here. I can only imagine how hard it is to see a couple in your own community die like this. The fear it must ignite in your congregation."

"Yeah. We've had a lot of calls over the last couple of days."

"Communities need to pull together. I've had a call only this morning from the press." I fix my eyes on him. "About you."

"About me? What about me?"

"Your relationship with Geraldine." I hold up my hands. "I mean, I said whoa there. This is a priest. I couldn't comment on that. But obviously, someone's talking to someone." He opens his mouth to speak but I continue. "And as for the church, it'll be very hard on the congregation to return, don't you think? At least until they know we've got whoever did this." I wait a beat, set my eyes on him again, and lower my voice. "Whoever he is."

Healy looks from Baz to me. He turns his finger in on himself, points to his chest. "You think it was me?" He almost squeaks it.

I let the question hang for a moment. "It's not always about what we think. But we could straighten this out quickly, right?"

Baz turns back in his seat. "We know you didn't go to any of your usual visitations on Sunday, Father. In fact, most of those people you normally visit say they haven't had a house call from you in almost three weeks. So I'll ask you again. When was the last time you saw Geraldine Shine?"

I see Healy turning his options over. Eyes down, mouth closed against his reply.

Finally, he looks up. "I'm not sure."

"She text or call you on Sunday?"

"I had a call from her on that Sunday. I can check my phone. It was right before service and I didn't answer it. She sometimes phones to see if I'm available for a chat on a Sunday, especially if she's been having a hard time at home and she can't get down to the church. I tried her when I was out"—he sighs—"but I didn't get a reply."

"Did you ever visit her house?"

He flushes. "No."

Red patches rise on Baz's face. He takes in a tight breath and eyeballs the priest. "What are you going to do if we find your prints or your DNA in Geraldine's home, Father?"

The priest swallows. I see the movement of it down his throat. His eyes lift to mine. "Okay, sometimes I called in."

"Sometimes?"

"In the last few weeks, I'd stop by for a bit of lunch. She was feeling guilty about coming to the church so regularly, taking up my time."

Baz spreads his hands over the table. "That must have been cozy."

"It wasn't like that." Healy's bottom lip turns in over his teeth. He swallows.

"You weren't worried about her husband finding you there?"

His face draws in, his eyes round orbs of weariness. "I'm a priest. Why would her husband mind? Besides, Ger told me they were separated and even so, he was rarely there on a Sunday."

It's always in the details. How regularly he must've visited the house to know Alan was rarely there on Sundays.

"How long had you got this little deal going?"

"Just the last few weeks."

The roast dinner begins to make sense.

"But you didn't go this week?"

An intensity grows in his eyes and I think he might cry. "No. I didn't." He sniffs. "I wish to God I did. But I didn't. Maybe she'd be alive now . . ." He trails off.

Baz remains silent.

I turn the screw. "Father, where were you between the hours of one thirty and seven on Sunday, the nineteenth of August?"

He winds his thumbs, one over the other. "I was in a bar. Drinking. I've a text on my phone from Ger, asking where I was. You can see it, if you need to. But I didn't meet with her. I needed to clear my head. I was beginning to—" His face reddens slightly. Thumbs stop winding. "I was finding it difficult to support her in her marriage."

"You had feelings for her?"

He closes his eyes tight, squeezes them briefly. "My role was to help her find a way to remain in her marriage." He gives me a pleading look. "That's my job. How do you do that? Say to a woman that she should stay with a man like that? I prayed for guidance. I told her to pray too. For her to ask for the strength not to provoke him." He takes a trembling breath. "And now this. Maybe this is God's way. A way out for her."

Anger fills my mouth but I swallow it down.

Baz steps in. "We'll need the name of that bar, Father."

The priest nods. "Of course."

I get up, leave the room, then wait for Baz to join me. "We've got the paler version of the truth but we've got nothing further on him until something else comes in." I look back at Father Healy.

Baz's face falls. He looks longingly in at the priest. "I'm really beginning to work up some hatred for this fucker."

STEVE IS TURNING the footprint retrieved from the Shine house on the screen. He looks pale, more so than usual.

He lifts a spidery hand to the side of his face, wiggles his jaw about, and winces. "I've run it through our database on footwear," he says. I peer down at the computer. He's marked up areas of interest with thin blue arrows. "The impression is the outer toe region of this brand. The manufacturer has sent us copies of the outer sole and their respective molds." He pulls up another image of a black sneaker. "For this product they used twelve different molds, all creating the same shoe. Each will have minor variations. Defects but not incredibly noticeable, to be fair. To Joe Public anyway. But to us, it's helpful."

"So you can narrow it down to where it was distributed?"

"We can try. There's more. We got lucky. There's a specific identifying characteristic here." He hovers the mouse over the print, points to the manufacturer's image of the outer sole. "An area of damage along the outer sole. This will be unique to the print. Probably where a stone or a piece of debris became embedded at one point."

I straighten. "So if we can find this trainer, we can link it conclusively to whoever broke into Geraldine Shine's home?"

"Yes," he says.

"Good, send it out to the rest of the team."

Helen pushes back from her chair. Phone pressed to her ear, her shoulder balancing the handset; one hand scribbling notes on a scrap of paper, the other striking keys on her computer.

A light sheen has broken out across her forehead, brown hair smooth and gleaming under the office lights. "Right, thank you, Dr. James." She ends the call, gets up from the seat, the scrap of paper in hand. "We've recovered fingerprints from the nightstand in the Shine bedroom and the bedroom door. Prints that don't belong to either of the victims."

"You ran them through our database?"

"Yes."

"Who?" The dark, sleek image of the deliveryman walks through my head.

"Robert McDonagh." She passes me the details. "Pretty much the same height and build as the man seen approaching the house in the CCTV footage the morning before the murders."

There's a photo of him. I can smile now, really smile. "Robert McDonagh." It's him.

"Priors include: aggravated assault, burglary, three counts of shoplifting before he was even mid-teens. And here, I think this might be a red flag." Her narrow eyes darken. "Animal cruelty. Killed and mutilated a neighbor's dog. That's a warning sign, right?"

Animal cruelty. An almost certain indicator of a killer's future path.

"We've got his address?"

"A government-subsidized house in Dollymount." She gives me a brief look of concern. "Clontarf. Lives with his mother. The father is a no-show."

"Lucky dad."

"I've stationed a pair of plainclothes at the house."

"Good. Thanks, Helen. I'll go out with Baz and a unit now. We'll collect his footwear. Work with Steve on the trainer and call me as soon as something else comes in."

CHAPTER 8

THE DRIVE FROM THE CITY out to Robert McDonagh's is slow. Morning commuters huddle like cattle beneath the shelter of bus stations. A sea of umbrellas moves down the wet street. When we get to the outskirts of Clontarf, the traffic lightens. The horizon breaks up; the gray sea meets the gray sky in a haze of silver mist. Even in this shitty weather, people have drawn up along the coast. Families and tourists gawping out at the sea, drinking from flasks and eating breakfast muffins. Kids, restless on their summer break, lean through from backseats to glower at the uncooperative sky. A few families are toughing it out. Raincoats on, beating a stride along the brown sand; their children, slapping seaweed at one another, digging moats round tumbling sandcastles. T-shirts soaked, feet bare.

Baz peers out at them. "Fecking nutters. It's Baltic. Is that what you used to do in your spare time?"

"People who live by the sea don't go to the sea." I throw him a grin.

I turn off the engine. The plainclothes are up ahead. Sitting in a blue Escort. I nod through the windshield; they nod back.

"Subtle, aren't they?" Baz remarks. "Look like a pair of bleedin' hit men."

"Let's hope they've kept their eyes peeled and Robert McDonagh hasn't managed to get out from under them."

"Right little thug by the looks of it."

We get out of the car; the wind sweeps rain over my face, stings my eyes. The children squeal cold cries of laughter from the beach, their screeches turn in the rolling air. The plainclothes officers step out of their vehicle and pull on their coats.

"Detective," one of them says by way of greeting. "Where do you want us?"

"Go out back until we've eyes on him. I don't want him running. We've a warrant and a unit with two uniforms on the way; send them straight in for the search on his trainers when they get here. They're to collect anything that looks like it might fit the description." I hand them a plastic folder with a printout of the sneakers, the trousers, and the jacket as seen on the CCTV footage.

"Grand," he says. He nods to his colleague and they disappear up a side lane that leads to the back of the house.

Baz comes to my side, his nose stuck in his phone. He sighs, keeps his voice low. "So, on Healy, it looks like his alibi might check out. The pub he mentioned verified that he was there for a few hours. He reckons from about three but he's going to look back through the receipts for us."

"Not enough time for him to get to the church, kill Geraldine, arrange Alan's body, then leave again."

He looks up at the McDonagh house. "Our suspect pool is growing small."

"Small as in Robbie McDonagh is our only one."

The McDonagh house is tucked at the back of Dollymount Avenue. A row of government houses, similar, predictably dated. Two up, two downs. The garden is a mean, stingy strip of lawn to the right of a wobbling concrete path. Tall ropey weeds reach up where one time someone thought to put in a flowerbed. The door of the house, a dull red, a thin plate of glass on the top half.

I glance at Baz then push the doorbell. It clangs through the house. I can hear a TV grumbling away inside, the drone of a commentator reporting on sport, the rush and rise of a low voice building momentum. A door slams and a shape emerges behind the ridged glass. The door opens.

Rita McDonagh. I know from Helen's background notes that she's not more than forty-eight but time has not been good to her. Lower lids sag down into bloated cheeks, white deposits of fatty tissue have settled in lumps around bulbous eyes. Her stomach strains against the band of her jeans and seems to drop downwards into her thighs. She stands with her knees locked and pressed together, her swollen, slipper-clad feet splayed outwards. She settles a fishy eye on me.

"Hallo," she says, the Dub accent tangling up the greeting. "Ye all right?"

"Mrs. McDonagh, is Robert home?"

"Who's askin'?"

"I'm Detective Sheehan and this is Detective Harwood. We need to speak with your son."

"Detectives?" She scowls. "The fucking shit. I'll lift him off the ground with a bleedin' clatter." And I believe her. "Come in, come in, detectives. The little fucker's still in bed."

Baz gives me a nervous smile and I step into the house. The carpet points the way to the living room, the center displaying worn track marks, hardened with dirt, mud, and wear. I would doubt it's ever seen the nozzle of a vacuum.

"Robbie! Get down here," Rita shouts up the stairs. She turns and gives us a smile. One of her teeth on the bottom row is missing; the rest look fit to topple out on the floor with a gentle sneeze. "Tea?" she asks.

Baz is shaking his head. But I answer for both of us. "Yes, please. One sugar in mine."

"Make yourselves at home." She points to the right, where the hall gives way to a grim-looking living room. "Yis can turn that down if it bothers you."

I remain in the hall. Stand at the bottom of the stairs. Baz moves into the living room. Locates the remote from the deep bowels of the couch then, shaking something quickly from his hand, he turns the TV off.

Upstairs, I can hear movement. A door creaks open and in a few seconds a pair of legs appear. Skinny but muscular with a sparse covering of dark hair.

"What the fuck's wrong now, Ma?" He ducks beneath the stair ledge. Clocks me standing there.

He moves down, lowers each foot slowly. "Who the fuck are you?"

"Robert McDonagh?"

Naked to the waist, boxers, bare feet but he stands as if he's wearing full armor. "Yeah."

He takes a step closer and I can smell the sleep on him. The stench of sweat and some sickening tang of aftershave. He's tall enough. Clancy was right, over six foot. He's using that now, pulling himself into every millimeter of his height. I hear Baz move out behind me and see the brief flash of uncertainty that crosses McDonagh's cocky face. The momentary slip of his shoulders, the sag of his spine.

"Mr. McDonagh, we need to ask you a few questions."

His teeth grind at the front. His jaw bunches. Neck muscles, tense bands wired down to the shoulders. "I don't talk to no pigs without a lawyer."

I wouldn't have thought a woman her size could move so fast. But in a couple of bounds, Rita McDonagh is up the hall.

She delivers a belt so swift and sure to the back of her son's head that both myself and Baz wince. "You stay under my roof, you live by the fucking law. Ye hear me?"

"Yes, Ma."

Robbie keeps his head down, his hands clasped in submission at his groin, but his eyes, his eyes point out from under his brow. Right through me they go and I feel the detective in me falter.

"Go on in," Rita says, and nods again toward the living room. "He gives you any guff, come an' get me. I'll bring yis your tea in a bit." She gives Baz her broken smile.

"Thank you, ma'am," Baz says in return.

Robbie pushes by me, throws himself into an armchair, the arms of which are stained in that particular shade of yellow-brown, a grubby mixture of sweat and dirt. His legs lean outwards, his hands on the sides of the chair like he's lord of the manor. When we sit, he sniffs, reaches for a pack of fags on the coffee table, and taps one from the packet. He jabs the butt between his teeth, pats his chest as if there might be a lighter housed there, then, sighing, heaves upright. He finds one down the side of the chair, where it seems most of the McDonagh necessities are hidden, leans back, and lights the fag.

He blows the smoke right across the room, an arc of rebellion. It washes over my face.

"Yis mind if I smoke?" he says, a corrupt little smile at the corner of his mouth.

"Mr. McDonagh," I begin. He rolls his eyes. "Could you tell us your relationship to Geraldine Shine?"

He takes another drag, shoots the smoke upwards. Then he leans forward, his elbows perched on his skinny knees, his hands dropped casually between them. His eyes glide over my face then track down my body.

"If I have to talk to you cunts, I won't talk to no slit in a suit."

Baz stiffens beside me; I will him to keep it together.

There's a shuffling from the hallway, the sound of the uniformed officers shaking out their jackets, wiping their feet.

One of them sticks his head in through the living room door. "What room, Chief?"

Robbie's head flicks up. It seems to take him a moment to understand what's going on; then he's on his feet. "What yis at, hi?" He points a rigid finger at me. "Stay the fuck outta my stuff."

"We've a warrant, Mr. McDonagh." I turn, look up at the officer. "Rita McDonagh is in the kitchen at the end of the hall. She'll tell you where to go."

The officer disappears down the short hall. I hear Rita's rasping voice reply. In a few moments she passes the door, the guard following, his face twisted in an expression of distaste.

Robbie looks as if he could tear the room up. The muscles on his abdomen flexed, shoulders turned in, arms braced for war. His eyes follow the officer ascending the stairs, trailing the creaking weight of his mother. I watch him struggle, fight down the urge to throttle something, someone.

"Please, sit down, Mr. McDonagh," Baz says.

Robbie drags a deep breath in through flared nostrils and seems to gain some control. Finally his shoulders release and he slouches back into his throne. On the table between us, there's a half-drunk mug of what could have been tea; fat gobs of blue-green mold garnish the surface. He stretches out a thin arm, tips ash into the mug.

"Geraldine Shine. What's your relationship with her?" I continue.

"Never fucking heard of her."

"She was found murdered along with her husband two days ago."

"Nothin' to do with me."

"Where were you on Sunday, the nineteenth of August?"

He laughs and then stops suddenly. His right knee bounces up and down. "At a mate's house."

I take out my notebook. "Whose?"

Hand over shaved head. He rubs the bristle. "Lynch. In Tallaght. He wasn't in though. But I chilled there for a while, thought he might come back."

"Does Lynch have a first name?"

"Jimmy."

"He doesn't mind you staying at his house when he's not in?"

"As long as I bring the cans, Lyncho wouldn't mind if I took a dump on his couch." He keeps his eyes to the floor as he speaks.

"So there's no one who can verify you were there?"

He looks up as if he's got me. "No." He takes another drag of the cigarette, spreads his hands. "But that's where I was. Watched the game, then the races."

I watch his face for signs of lying. "You bet?"

"Yeah, I'd a couple of bob on a tip," he says, deep in his story.

"A tip? That's too good to pass up, right? What horse?"

His mouth tightens. That glare again, knife sharp. "I don't remember."

Rita McDonagh comes into the room, tea on a tray, and sets it down on the table. "I've no milk," she says.

Baz scoops his up. "I prefer mine without anyways."

Another crooked smile. She retrieves a T-shirt and jeans from the back of a radiator and pegs them at her son. "Put some clothes on. Have some respect. There's ladies present."

Robbie McDonagh's fag is knocked from his hand. "There's no fucking ladies in this room."

Rita picks up the dropped fag, deposits it in the mug. Sharp hiss and it's extinguished. She sits down on an easy chair near the window and helps herself to a few of the biscuits she's laid out.

Robbie sniffs. Stands. Feeds his limbs into the jeans then threads his arms and shoulders into the T-shirt. His arms raised, I see a long graze down the inside of his forearm. Still a savage shade of red. I picture the droplet of blood on the Shine kitchen floor. The open window. The wound is just the perfect place for a latch to bite. I glance at Baz, and I see the same realization on his face.

"You cut your arm," I say.

"So?"

"When did you do that?"

I can see Rita McDonagh's head moving from side to side, following the questions and answers like she's watching a tennis match.

"Answer the detective," she barks.

"Don't remember."

"It looks deep. I'd know if I'd cut myself like that, wouldn't you, Harwood?"

"It would've smarted right enough," Baz replies.

"I fell. Broken bottle."

"Nasty. Did it bleed much?"

His face twists. A grin. "Get a kick out of a fella's pain, do ya? Sick fuck."

Rita McDonagh's hand raises.

"Bled a bit, yeah," he says.

I flick back through the pages of my notebook, leave a long bridge of silence between Robbie and our next move. To some suspects, lying is second nature. Deception and alternate stories flow from their lips with the ease of breathing. And sometimes you have to hit them with more, give them the whole picture, or as much as you can, so that they can't wave away their connection with a word or two. Robbie waits patiently through the silence.

"Mr. McDonagh," I say, and he lifts his eyes to mine, sharp arrogance intense in his gaze. "On Sunday morning, you went to Geraldine Shine's home on Kincora Drive at approximately ten A.M. Just before six P.M. you returned to the house, where you gained access to the premises through a back window that led into the kitchen. You cut your arm in the process. Does this sound familiar to you?"

The knuckles of his hands yellow, his fingers biting into the armrests of the chair; his head lowers. Eyes set and cold on my face. I feel heat building under my skin. But he remains quiet.

"You left a footprint at the scene," I say. "Fingerprints. Our officers are collecting your trainers as we speak. We can match them with almost one hundred percent accuracy. We have you on CCTV approaching the Shine house that morning."

Rita McDonagh stops mid-chew, a biscuit halfway to her mouth "Robbie? What ye been at?"

His eyes are still on mine, locked and fierce. "Ma," he says. Voice low. "Get out."

The air in the room closes in, hums. Whatever message vibrates in the tone of his voice, Rita McDonagh pales, levers herself out of the chair, and shuffles out of the room.

He fixes me with a stiff glare. "You arresting me for murder, Detective?"

"We'd like to hear your side of things."

He laughs. The sound like a blade along my nerves. "My side! Stupid cunt." He reaches forward, taps another cigarette from the packet, lights it. His face turns cold. "If my prints were there," he says, "it's because we screwed a couple of times. I barely knew her, just fancied a bit of hole, and she was putting it about. These older ones will give anyone a go." He looks at me. "Am I right?"

Baz stiffens again and I put my hand on his arm, a warning. We need to keep control here.

One of the officers puts his head around the door. "Chief?"

I get up, move out into the hall, away from McDonagh's keen ears. The officer holds up a clear plastic bag containing a pair of trainers.

"Good work. Any of the other clothing?"

"Nothing yet, we're still looking."

"Keep at it."

"Yes, Chief."

I stand at the doorway, lean against the frame.

"When was the last time you saw her?" Baz asks Robbie.

"I dunno. A month or so ago. I don't keep track of these things."

"Lies can't help you now, Robbie."

I feel my phone buzz against my thigh and move back into the hallway.

"Sheehan here."

Steve gets straight to it. "The trainers were in stock in a store in Blanch but they were stolen along with half a delivery two months ago. Got a right ear-bashing from the store owner."

"Stolen? That wouldn't surprise me. Good work, Steve. We got a pair here at McDonagh's house. The same size anyways. Looks like same brand. The team will bring them in shortly."

I glance in through the living room door to where McDonagh is lounging. His fingerprints are at the scene. Now the sneakers to match. "Thanks, Steve."

I move back into the room, take a deep breath, savor the moment. I'm going to enjoy this.

"Robert McDonagh, I'm arresting you on suspicion of the murder of Geraldine Shine on the nineteenth of August 2012. You've a right to a lawyer. You do not have to say anything but anything you do say may be taken in evidence and used against you in a court of law. Do you understand?"

"Fucking bitch," he spits. He throws the cigarette at my chest;

it hits my jacket and falls in a dirty shower of sparks and ash to the grimy carpet.

I push it out with my foot. Baz hands me the cuffs, stands, and pulls McDonagh into a hold, turns him, pinches his wrists together. I tighten the steel around his wrists, make sure the metal chews down on his skin.

A grunt of pain gutters in his throat. "I want a lawyer. Now."

ROBBIE MCDONAGH IS STOWED AWAY in the garda car. One of the officers steps out of the house. He holds two black bags, marked EVIDENCE. He carries them toward us, holds them out.

"Where do you want them, Detective?"

I pop the boot of the garda car and he heaves them inside. "Take him to the Bureau. Contact his lawyer or have one assigned."

"Yes, ma'am." He dips his head to the radio at his shoulder. "Returning to the Bureau. Suspect secured. Over."

Baz leans against the garda car, cigarette moving to and from his mouth.

"We hold him until we've confirmation on the footprint then we interview," I say.

He passes me the fag and I take a long drag. "We could charge on the fingerprints?"

I push damp hair from my face. The rain has stopped and the sky has opened up. Sun spills down onto the slick street. "You know yourself that won't stand up, if he says he was seeing her. But when we've a match on the trainer, we can definitely put him at the crime scene."

"Nothing on the blouse?"

"Only Ger's blood. Not a fiber nor a droplet of blood to be got from anyone else."

"Fucking unbelievable."

"I know. But still, we got him and we'll get this story out in interview." I let my gaze slide to McDonagh's dark silhouette inside the car. His head is pitched back against the headrest. Eyes closed. Not a bother on him. The sight sends a little charge of adrenaline skirting through my blood. "They should have the footprint analysis quickly." I check the time. "I'll follow you back in a couple of hours. No one is to so much as smile in his direction until I get there. You can interview; I'll oversee."

"You want me to leave the car?"

"No, I'll get a lift back." I go to Baz's car, collect my bag from the trunk, then return to him. "I need to drop in at the folks'. See what Tanya has going on the Hennessy case, as per Hegarty's orders."

"I've been reading up on it. The Hennessys. It's a broken kid that'd do that to his parents." He glares through the car window at McDonagh. "It's cases like these ones that make me yearn for the needle."

I look up the street. Already there are neighbors at the window, a couple of lads on bikes circling between the parked cars.

"Justice will do for me," I reply.

The cloud shifts, draws closed over the sun. I put out the cigarette with my heel, pull my coat closed, button up against the breeze.

Baz gives the roof of the garda car a slap and the officer starts up. "I'll phone you," he says, and walks back to his own vehicle. He checks the hubs, gives the tires a gentle kick, then gets in. He starts the engine, pulls out onto the street, lifts one finger from the steering wheel in good-bye, then heads back to the city center.

Beyond the McDonagh house, the lads on the bikes are on their phones, their eyes trained on the business end of the road. When they hang up, they turn away, stand up from saddles, and push off up the hill out of sight.

CHAPTER 9

AFTER **B**AZ LEAVES, I walk toward the promenade, cross over the wooden bridge that leads to Bull Island, a long, narrow island running parallel to the coast. The wind runs off-land, against my back, my hair thrashing in stringy strands over my face as I move across the damp wooden slats. A car rumbles up behind me; I stand to the side and let it pass. It moves on toward the small nest of white buildings, buried in the stiff grasses, on the other side of the bridge.

I look back across the coast, inhale the salty air.

Clontarf beach has filled with walkers and children but the tide is turning. Already, water is creeping in over the strand, collecting in silver ridges and pools between the dark mounds of seaweed. Along the promenade, a thin black spaniel clears the seawall, barks sharp warnings at a flock of seagulls. They rise into the air in a squawking scatter of madness. The dog hunts back up the lip of the bay, head bobbing and low, body stretched out, a tiny black target in the distance. My eyes lift, rove over the familiar outline of the Poolbeg Stacks, then the low line of Dublin city in the distance. Finally, I let my gaze drift over the Clontarf coastline and then on, inland before settling on the upward curve of the street toward my family home on Conquer Hill.

Seventeen years past and Bríd Hennessy would have walked these streets, not knowing the grisly end that waited for her . . . or maybe she did. The wind stills and I can almost feel the heat of that day on my skin. I imagine I see her, heading out, away from her home toward mine. Looking for help.

She pushes the thick nest of her hair behind her ears. It immediately bounces back, curls cling to her damp forehead. She's carrying a shopping bag, a prop. There are no groceries in it, only her wallet, which is fat with money-off coupons. She tells herself she must remember to pick up milk on her return home or John will ask questions.

Her throat does that squeezing thing, a mixture of anxiety and fear. A feeling of dread chasing her every step. She's had it for months now. Like Indiana Jones in that tunnel, a great round ball of catastrophe rolling after her. She has to keep moving. She has to try. She thinks of how she left Cara alone in her room, only the thin pine of the door between her and her father's aimless anger. Seán sullen and quiet in front of the TV in their living room. John hazy-eyed with drink in his battered recliner. Both of them watching the match but not watching it.

Lately, when Bríd passed by the door and they were like this it felt like they were both listening. Like dogs. One ear cocked, keeping track of breathing changes, sniffing out shifts in mood. Seán, tall and skinny, his elastic muscles coiled tight down his arms. John, belligerent, sending out waves of fury, like a grenade without a pin.

She pushes on down the street, against the surprising scorch of the Irish sun, bald and hot on the back of her neck. Her dress a tangle around her legs; her feet swollen in her sandals. At the bottom of Conquer Hill, she pauses to catch her breath, her hand going to her chest, her heart a rapid thump under her fingers.

When had she become so fat? So unfit? Before she was married she'd walked everywhere. For miles! People used to comment on it all the time: *Seen you pounding the roads again, fair play to you, Bríd. Fit as a fiddle.* But after Cara she'd let everything slip. Her working hours, her mind, her body. She'd become an expert at avoiding herself in the hope that everyone else would avoid her too. Don't look too closely. That had been the plan. Maybe a bad one.

And now she couldn't remember who she was. She found herself doubting simple things about herself. How do I take my tea? I'm not sure. One sugar? None? Did it matter? She dressed blindly, looked blindly, and felt blindly. Life had eclipsed her thoroughly. Only two emotions took turns in her: fear and relief. And the relief had almost trickled to a stop.

She keeps moving, makes herself walk fast up the hill. Now that she's nearly there, she needs to keep her nerve. She checks her hand where she's scribbled the address. She'd got it from the phonebook. The woman, Mrs. Sheehan, seemed nice. Like she would help. Bríd didn't know where else to go. She knew the woman worked in social care. She helped kids. Like hers, right? She'd take them, wouldn't she? And the husband, he was a guard. Couldn't go far wrong there.

Things were coming to a head. She could feel it. Her son, he

was a man now. Only fifteen, but tall and strong. Sometimes
Bríd saw a look in his eye when he watched his father. A dark
look. Like he was biding his time. What would happen when he
eventually struck back? She pressed her lips together, felt the bite
of teeth at the back of her mouth. It wasn't fair on him. Christ, it
wasn't fair on any of them. She thought of the bag she had hidden away, packed and ready for the right time. But she couldn't
go until she knew her two babies would be safe. She couldn't take
them with her, not yet. John wasn't one to let a possession slip
away. She'd no doubt he'd come after her. And she couldn't have
her children with her when he did.

She stops at the small garden gate. A crown of iron swirls
decorates the top. She puts her hand on it, pushes the gate inwards, and walks up the short garden path.

I take a sharp breath and pull myself away from Bríd Hennessy's hot face on a hot day, a huge sadness moored in my chest.
The wind cuts over my shoulder, spins out over the misty grays
of the sea toward the East Wall, where beneath the dark waters,
Clontarf Island lies drowned and dead. Its single residence long
ripped from its body, picked up and thrown against the main-
land like a discarded toy.

I retrace my steps back over the wooden bridge and find a
bench facing the sea. I sit, tucking my coat beneath me to protect my trousers from the damp rungs of the seat. The wind is at
my back but over the horizon there are patches of blue beginning to show again in the sky. Pulling my bag onto my knee, I
locate my headphones, put them in my ears, and search through
the interview clips on my phone.

Seán Hennessy smiles into the camera. His eyes hold that

faraway look. He runs his hand over the short shave of his fair hair.

"When I turned fifteen, I decided to let my hair grow. Kurt Cobain. He was a god to me. His music, his words, his look. I wanted to be him. My hair, it grew quickly, straggly bands of blond. The trend then was all about saying you were deeper than image. Which is ironic, you know. You think you're rebelling but really you're conforming.

"I worked so fucking hard on that hair. My girlfriend, she loved it. Fancied herself my Courtney, bleached her hair, wore it in those layered spikes, deep red lipstick, the works. She was fierce, a roar like a lion if you pressed the wrong buttons and a purr like a cat if you played her right. All the lads wanted a piece of her but she only had eyes for me."

He pauses; the pads of his fingers rest on his mouth, a smile drifting at the corners in remembrance. The hand drops and he goes on:

"I felt lucky, you know. With her, I could forget the hassle at home. When she looked at me, there was no scorn in her eyes, no distrust or pity. I was younger than her, only over a year, and at the time it didn't seem to matter. I knew she loved me as much as I did her.

"The fourth day after my parents were murdered, my lawyer came to see me. He didn't look like the lawyers I'd seen on TV. This guy, his shirt was so thin I could see the curling sprawl of his chest hair, almost down to his navel. His jacket, open loose at his sides, was worn and shiny at the cuffs.

"He sat down and I saw him seeing me: a boy, the cuts on my face, my eye half-shut, my lip, sliced right through from the beating I'd taken the day before. He looked for a minute like he might ask me about my injuries, what had happened, but he didn't. Just took a notepad out of his suitcase and a pen, set them on the table in front of him.

"He said: *Seán, I'm not the guards; you can tell me everything. You must tell me everything that happened. The truth. So I can advise you and help you. You understand?*

" 'Yes, sir,' I said. Ready.

"*Take me through it. Start from the morning of the thirteenth of August. Sunday.*

"I tell him. Tell him how me and my girlfriend had met up and gone to the cinema, how we'd smoked a spliff round the back of the castle. Then went back to her house, got drunk on cider. I told him that we were together. I told him we fell asleep on top of the covers listening to Nirvana's 'Come As You Are' on repeat. The next day, we did more of the same. We went downstairs in the late afternoon. Her parents were away. We made sandwiches. Didn't get dressed for most of the day. We stayed holed up in her room, having sex, drinking, smoking, laughing. Being young, you know."

He swallows. His face darkens. "It was coming up on four by the time I decided I should show my face at home. I was walking up the road, the heat so fierce the tarmacadam was bubbling underfoot. And I saw the cars. Neighbors were out on the lawns. No one stopped me. No one held me back. I could hear voices in the garden. There was a bad feeling around the joint. A hushed kind of panic, like a grand shock had thrown my home into some kind of time warp. Frozen, like.

"I bent under the tape, walked in a kind of daze, a stupid curiosity, round the side of the house. Saw them there on the lawn, me ma, my sister. And him. Me da like a broken king slumped against the back wall. Too late, an officer saw me. I felt like an apparition, like I'd somehow walked through time to a preventable future and I could fade back again were someone to only pinch my arm." He takes a wedge of flesh from his forearm between thumb and finger, gives it a hard squeeze.

"As I spoke, the lawyer, I watched the changes in his expression, which at first seemed open, the easy ear of the law ready to listen. His pen moved frantically across his legal pad, keeping pace with me, but as I went on, there were little things that I noticed. His eyes met mine less and less. His mouth began to twitch on occasion, a sigh, barely there. Eventually, the movement of his pen slowed. Then stopped. Stopped taking notes. He placed his pen down, gentle as a baby.

"You need to tell me the truth, Seán, or I can't help you.

"I am, I said. That is the truth. My girlfriend, if you talk to her, she'll tell you. I wasn't even at home.

*"She denies that you were with her at all. She says—*he flipped through the pages of his notebook—*you are infatuated with her and that she's never been with you. Would never be with you.*

"And it was like an exorcism, like someone had come along and waved over me some unholy benediction. Sucked the last living ember of hope right from my body. I finally got it. I was alone. A lone tree out on a cold desert, the last leaf loosed from my body pulled away from me on a twist of air.

"All those times we'd said to ourselves that the age gap didn't matter. And it hadn't to her and me. Truly. But the law, oh the law. Yes, it thought differently. She was seventeen; I was fifteen. Yes, it mattered a lot. Fear makes cowards. Even of lions."

———

MAM IS ALONE when I get to the house.

"Your dad's been dragged into town. New curtains," she says in reference to Justin and Tanya's new house. "Bit of telly and a cup of tea for me this afternoon." She drops the kettle onto its stand and flicks it on.

"That's nice," I say.

Mam is laid-back, or at least likes to pretend she is. At seventy-two, age has not yet stooped her, her hair whitening now and helped along with a few highlights. She's a trousers and V-neck kind of woman, soft well-soled shoes meant for being on your feet all day. A castoff from her work. Her favorite phrase: "Ah sure, what've we to worry about?" The tight twitch of her eye the only thing that suggests plenty. Years of working with troubled teens and traumatized children, navigating the suffocating whirlpool of social work left the words eternally on the tip of her tongue, as if someone had pulled a string at her back and out it came no matter the weight of despair. Even after Dad had his breakdown, even after he had to retire at fifty. Even after he tried to kill himself.

An old friend used to say to me, "That phrase is the death of the Irish. Fucking inertia. There never seems to be a problem that can't be whitewashed over with an old, *Ah sure!*"

"Actually, I was hoping to chat with you," I say.

She gives me a warm smile but I see the tiny lift of her shoulders, up and rounding inwards. On the outside, Mam isn't the warmest: She stiffens when hugged, her hand patting your back from the get-go, her face never quite able to hide an expression of relief when you release her. There's always some small fear under her skin that stretches taut around her eyes, pulls her away when you get too close. But she's clever, inquisitive, and one of the most quietly generous people I know. Charity events, fundraisers, soup kitchens, shelters for the homeless, you name it, my mam has organized it. A one-woman show, desperately trying to scratch back gold points for humanity's shittiness.

She makes two mugs of tea, adds too much milk, and carries them both into the living room. I follow. Sit down on the sofa, the cushion lopsided on one side where Dad usually sits, newspaper spread out over the remainder of the seat. I balance my weight against the armrest and try to look comfortable. I want to know about Bríd Hennessy. Want to know what it was that brought her to our door all those years ago. Get a feel for the mother of the son. The mother of a killer.

I start softly. "Tanya's really busy with this case then, huh?"

Mam lifts the mug from the coffee table. "She's doing too much but sure, I know what it's like. That kind of thing. Think you'll change the world, then more comes. You know it too."

"True." We sit for a while. I hedge around the questions in my head, wanting to find a way under the lid. I slide a cautious glance toward her. "Did you know Bríd Hennessy?"

She makes a slow slurping noise at the milky tea but doesn't balk at the change in subject. "Not much."

"But you'd have recognized her?"

She gives me a testy look. She knows when she's being interrogated. "I knew her from Mass really. Nothing more than that. She was younger than me, not my crowd."

I take another sip of lukewarm tea, look at her over the rim of the mug. "I'm sure I saw her here once."

The shoulders come up again; her eyes drop. She gives a

shake of her head. Too quick. "I don't think so, now, Frankie love."

"I was coming back from work. I don't think it was long before . . . before it all happened." I reach over, place the tea on the table. "She passed me on the path on the way out. I remember thinking it was strange. She barely looked at me. Just shoved past and went. I didn't clock who she was until after."

Mam sighs, looks at me. It's the first time she's looked at me properly since I came through the door. Her eyes rove over my face, take in the changes. But she doesn't remark on them.

"There was always a detective in you, all right," she says, then waits a moment before saying more. I can see her working down some emotion: guilt, fear, regret. "I guess I would rather've forgotten the whole thing. When the murders happened, when I read about it in the papers I felt rotten. We were running an event through the church"—she throws me a tired smile—"for Crumlin. So we were lingering by the door after Mass a few weeks or so before it all happened. We were trying to get signatures to fund-raise and she went to move by. Her daughter was there, the little one, but she shooed her on, asked her to wait by the church gate. I thought she wanted to sign up, so I smiled and went to hand her the clipboard.

"She shook her head and asked me, quiet, her lips barely moved a millimeter: Could she talk to me. And it was then I saw the bruise. She'd tried to hide it with makeup but she'd missed the edges." Mam raises a hand to her face, lets it hover over her cheekbone. "It was yellowing already. I passed the clipboard to one of the other ladies and led her to the side.

"And then she wouldn't talk. I'd lost something in those moments, the fear had won out. I tried. *Do you have something you want to talk to me about?* I says. And her eyes darted about the place, her feet lifting one to the other as if something was about to snap her ankles. *Mrs. Hennessy, right?* She nodded but still nothing. *Are you in trouble?* It was as if there was a hand over her mouth. I could see the words wanting to work themselves out but they wouldn't come. Tears began to gather in her eyes. Finally she pressed her lips together, shook her head, and left."

I wait. Mam lost in the past now. Bríd Hennessy's back, summer dress flowing from hips, feet in thick sandals, the sun beating down on the tarmacadam of the church car park. Cara Hennessy, skinny and small, running along the church gate, a broken twig in her outstretched hand, hitting each of the iron railings as she went. Bríd calling to her. The twig thrown down and Cara Hennessy tucked into her mother's side for the walk back to that house.

"I wasn't expecting her to turn up here. I'm not even sure how she knew my address but I guess in those days you couldn't have an extra egg for breakfast without the entire neighborhood knowing about it." She takes up her tea again.

My mouth has dried. I take a sip of the tea. "What did she come here for?"

"She had the idea that I might know somewhere. He was knocking her about and she was worried for the kids. She wanted to leave him. I don't think it was easy for her to come here. She was a quiet woman but I could see she knew things were escalating." She looks down again. "She seemed desperate. She'd heard that I worked in social care, wanted to know that if she did go to a refuge could the kids go with her. Wanted to know if I knew somewhere that he wouldn't be able to find her. And sure, I didn't, you know. I didn't work with women's refuges. I said I could send out a worker for a chat, an assessment, but I could see the idea terrified her, I guess in case he found out. Then she asked if they could come here. That with Martin being a guard and all, it'd keep them safe. That I could at least get her out. I didn't know what to say, really. We couldn't be taking in an entire family. So I said I'd talk to Martin about it."

"Then she left?"

"She left and I spoke to your father, who didn't want us to get involved."

I pull back.

"Don't judge too harshly, Frankie. It was just after all that business. We'd enough on our plates and he was only beginning to find a bit of balance. His opinion was that we should leave well enough alone. The next week at Mass, I gave her a pamphlet. One for a women's center. A refuge in the city that had a good rep and would sort her out, help her with the kids until she felt ready to stand on her own two feet. And that was that."

"That was that?"

"What more could I do? I'd my own family to think about."

I take a deep breath. "So you think the husband, the father, killed them?"

She pauses for a moment, sadness creeping over her features. "To be honest, I don't know. It all made sense when it came out. Or it seemed to. The son. Growing up in that kind of environment, sure haven't I only worked with kids like that all my whole life and through no fault of their own, the apple doesn't fall far from the tree and sure isn't it the same ground that feeds them."

She pushes out of the sofa. Conversation over. She puts a hand out for my mug and I pass it over. "They should be back any minute now and I've the dinner to get on."

I follow her out to the kitchen. "If you remember anything else, Mam—"

"That was it now," she says quickly.

I step out into the backyard, light a cigarette. The day is a mess of past and present in my head. Bríd Hennessy's plea for help. Robbie McDonagh's arrest. I look out on my childhood garden, small now when once it felt like a rolling meadow. The old swing-set crooked and rusting beneath a craggy apple tree. It's become part of the unseen view from my parents' kitchen window. If it disappeared I'm not sure I'd know it, only have a vague sense that something was missing. The last time I sat on it, I was twenty-five and it moaned under the burden of all my adult heaviness.

After I saw my dad in the bedroom that day, I left him to it. I was angry at him. At myself. At the illness that was swallowing him up. So I crept away, out here, sat on the washed-out plastic of the swing and waited. Waited for it to be over.

I finish the cigarette, push it out on a saucer on the kitchen windowsill, then check my phone.

Two missed calls. Baz and a voice message from Owens at Harcourt Street. I dial Baz first and he answers on the third ring.

"Frankie, I was just about to phone."

"News?"

"It's not good."

I take a breath. "Go on."

"McDonagh's trainers don't match the shoe print."

My hand tightens around my phone. "Fuck."

"There's more. The results of the blood droplet found in the house." He sighs. "It's Geraldine's. So no link there."

I tip my head back, look up at the flat gray of the sky. "What's going on here?"

"We knew it was a possibility."

I see him, the killer, coming through the Shine window like a cloud of darkness, the deep orange of a raging sunset behind him. His foot lands heavy in the middle of the floor; the sole squeaks through the quiet house. He puts a hand out for balance and from his sleeve the smallest of drops, a spot of her blood, shakes loose. Geraldine Shine working her way back home.

"We can hold him," Baz is saying. "I know he said he was sleeping with her but we do have his fingerprints at the scene. We've charged on less."

"It's weak. We didn't find any of his prints in the kitchen, only the bedroom."

"He could have worn gloves in the kitchen then taken them off in the room?" I can hear the hollow sound of defeat in his voice. He knows it's not enough.

"Ugh. We're going to have to let him go," I say.

There's silence. Both of us trying to find another route into this case. Both of us failing.

"We can hold him until tomorrow afternoon," Baz says. "I can interview. Push him a bit more."

"You can try but I doubt we'll get anything else from him. Fuck." I pace up and down the small stretch of patio. I remember the kids on the bikes, circling like gulls waiting for a chip to fall. Phones to their ears. "He could be working with someone, for someone. There was a bit of an audience when we brought him out. When we release him, put eyes on him. If there is someone else behind this, they won't want Robbie here sharing their secrets." I look back down the garden, my eyes resting on the swing-set. "If anything comes in on McDonagh's movements after release, let me know."

"Will do. You talk to Tanya?"

"Not yet. She's out."

"Okay, well, I'll see you tomorrow."

I hang up, stand in the yard for a moment. I walk down the garden. The lawn is soft from too much rain; the damp soaks through my shoes to my socks. I get to the swing-set, sit down. The frame sags a little and gives a weary squeak. I wrap my fingers around the stiff chain, look back at my family home.

Eventually, I returned to the bedroom that day. Sat with my dad. I wanted to cry. That I'd allowed my sense of powerlessness to weaken me so much I wished him gone. I placed my hand over his, stared out at the blank white of the sky beyond the window. And the hatred I felt soured like milk left in the sun and turned toward myself, where it'd really been all along.

I dial my voicemail and Owens's rough voice comes down the line.

"Frankie, I've managed to retrieve Seán's arrest papers from archives. His statement, unsigned. Filed under S here, fucking admin numpties. It's a wonder it went walkies, ha?" I can hear the cynicism in his voice. "Anyway, the confession is interesting enough. A recording of it too. And the deets for WSP. I'll courier it all to your place. I think that'd be best, all round, rather than the Bureau? Send me your address and I'll get it there first thing. Catch you for that drink soon?"

The line goes dead.

Mam is over a magazine on the kitchen table, pen in hand,

attacking a crossword puzzle. I give her shoulder a squeeze and she pats my hand.

"I might hang around, wait for Tanya."

"Sure, stay over, your dad'll be pleased to see you." She aims the pen at the kitchen counter to a bag of potatoes. "Come on then, make yourself useful. There's spuds to be peeled."

CHAPTER 10

CLEAR AWAY THE DINNER PLATES. Dad and Justin are settled into the sofa. Mam is reading on the armchair in the living room. Tanya follows me into the kitchen. The curls of her hair loose, earrings tipping against her shoulders. She leans up against the counter, watches me rinse the plates and load them in the dishwasher.

"How you getting on with the Hennessy footage?" she asks, the question rising at the end as if she was only prompting me about something I might've forgotten.

I've watched Tanya in action in court, seen her nudging a playful elbow into a family member's side during recess and minutes later systematically tearing down a prosecutor's case, brick by brick; every word a delicately handled but firm hammer. She's usually good at hitting whatever tone she's aiming for. In this case, she's going for casual but she doesn't quite achieve the right note and instead of the question feeling conversational, it sounds loaded with expectation.

I turn from the sink, give her a slow smile. "I've made some notes. I'm maybe halfway through."

She nods, studies my face for a while, then turns, pulls a bottle of red across the counter. She opens a few of the kitchen drawers, pushes her hand through cutlery. I reach behind her to a large ceramic pot where the kitchen utensils are crammed. I find the corkscrew and hold it out. "Here."

"Can never find anything in this house." She throws me a look of feigned exasperation, holds up the corkscrew. "Anything of any use anyways. Thanks."

I take two glasses down from the cupboard and set them out in anticipation. "You'll be in your own house soon."

She unwinds the foil from the neck of the bottle. "Not soon enough," she says, then pushes her hair back behind her ear. She stops, rests her hands on the counter, looks at me. "Sorry, that came out wrong. Your parents have been great, you know, but it gets a little cramped sometimes, time wise."

I give a short laugh of acknowledgment, remembering only too well Mam's persistent manipulation of your time, her inability to hear you when you said you were working late. Her absolute commitment to impose the house schedule on your life, whether you are five or thirty years old, it doesn't matter. House rules. "You having to check in for dinner every evening?" I ask.

"Oh yeah," she says as she winds the corkscrew down. She angles the bottle between her hands and removes the cork with a clean pop. She doesn't waste time filling the glasses, exchanging bottle for wineglass as soon as they're full. I dry off my hands and she passes me one.

"Cheers," she says, and clinks hers to mine.

"I suppose it doesn't help that Justin becomes a lazy fuck

when he's here," I say, nodding my head in the direction of the living room.

"Jesus, tell me about it. What is that? I feel if I don't get out of here soon, my husband will have morphed into a dinosaur from the fifties."

We're alike, my brother and I, in coloring and looks, but he stole all the calmer genes. Those that existed in our family anyway.

I laugh. "Justin always takes the easy road if it's offered to him."

She takes a mouthful of wine. "Don't know what he was thinking the day he met me then."

"That was one of his better decisions," I say with a smile.

She flushes, then after a moment she says, "I bumped into a mate of yours today, well, an old friend, I guess."

"Oh?"

"Yeah, Mike Owens, the sergeant down at Harcourt Street."

I swallow, wait a second before I allow his name to register on my face. "Mike, that's right. We were students together. How is he?"

She shrugs as if to say how would she know, then says: "I was inquiring after Cara. Cara Hennessy. I wanted to see if they would release her WSP forms so I could contact her." She shrugs again. "It was a long shot."

I look down into my glass. "He couldn't give them to you?"

"Said I'd need a warrant, which we won't be granted. I knew as much but you don't ask, you don't get, right?"

I give her a half-smile, relieved. It's not that I don't want Tanya knowing Clancy was involved in the case. I just don't want her to know before I understand the extent of his involvement. "How's it all going? You have anything new?"

Her face brightens, a twitch at her mouth. "The team met

today; we had a retired wound specialist come in, a pathologist. Really highly regarded in his day." She takes another sip of her wine. "He made some interesting observations. Come on," she says, turning and taking up the bottle. "I'll show you."

The sounds of the TV rumble from inside the living room. I hear Mam laughing at something, the echo of mirth from a studio audience.

Tanya leads the way up the stairs. "Mike had some damning anecdotes about you from your uni days," she says over her shoulder.

"I'll bet he did. It's all lies."

She laughs and opens the door to Justin's old room, steps aside to let me pass. "Your mam let me set up here, although I'm not sure she knew what she let herself in for."

The room looks smaller. The bed has been removed. The wall covered in corkboard. Images of the Hennessys look out at me, headlines from newspapers. A rough timeline is stretched across one wall, cataloging the trial, witness statements, and highlighting important moments in the media. Two laptops are open on a desk and on either side, plastic boxes are stacked, filling any other available space in the room.

Tanya picks her way to the desk. "Sorry, find space where you can."

"I'm liking the homey touches," I say, moving into the room.

She sits at the desk. "You should see our office in town. You can barely see the floor. Standing room only." She blows out a long breath. "We have some apprentices coming in next week to go through most of the paperwork. It should help."

In some ways, Tanya is not so different from me, willing to work to the point of breaking. A dogged determination in the set

of her jaw. Eyes pinned on whatever case has caught her attention. That's where it ends though. Her face is enviably quick to
smile; even with the odds threatening to suffocate her, she'll
wriggle hope free. Tenacity has a new meaning on her shoulders. And she needs it. My role is to set a ball rolling; hers is to
stop it then push in the other direction. Physics will tell you
which is more difficult.

I check my phone, look for any messages on McDonagh,
on the Shine case. But it's frustratingly quiet at the Bureau. I pull
a couple of the boxes forward, sit down. "Have you spoken to
Hennessy since Sunday?"

"We update every couple of days." She pauses, pulls at a loose
thread on her jeans. "He's been getting some harassment. Shit-
heads on the street shouting abuse, graffiti on the door of his flat,
that kind of thing. It's shaken him up a bit."

"That's too bad. You don't think it will make him back out of
all this?"

A shadow of something crosses her face and suddenly she
looks tired. She reaches for the wineglass. "No. If anything it's
made him more determined to prove his innocence." She looks
at me. "He told me he was asked for an alibi. For the Shine
murders?"

I shift my position on the box, try to keep the defensiveness
out of my voice when I answer. "We needed to clear him." The
moment I speak, I hear just how ridiculous that sounds, especially to a defense lawyer; hundreds of convicts in the Dublin
area with a history of violence and murder but Seán is the one
we ask for an alibi. I feel my face growing hot.

But fair play to Tanya. She doesn't argue with me but moves
on to the case at hand. "The reason I wanted to contact Cara

Hennessy is because her statement says that Seán did not attempt to kill her until he had already disposed of both John and Bríd. That she was conscious during the attacks and witnessed Seán killing them."

I remember. It was a key part of the prosecution's case—doubtless in Tanya's hands something that will become their Achilles' heel.

Despite the rising defensiveness I feel on behalf of Cara, I'm intrigued. "Go on."

"After reviewing the evidence, I think, regardless of who murdered them, Cara was attacked first and therefore there's a good chance she was already unconscious and couldn't have seen her parents' attacker. Or maybe even her own if he came from behind."

"What evidence?"

"Blood transfer. There wasn't one droplet of Bríd Hennessy's or John's blood on Cara's clothing or around her wounds. A bit of an oddity, don't you think, if they'd been knifed so viciously beforehand and with the same knife."

I take a steadying drink of wine. "No blood transfer at all?"

She keeps her eyes on mine. "None."

For the first time the Hennessy murders play out differently in my head. Cara sitting cross-legged in the garden, her mother kneeling at the flowerbed, the baking sun on her neck and John, angry and glowering, watching them from the kitchen window, the knife waiting in his hand.

"Why would she lie?" I ask.

Tanya's eyes darken. "Fear, trauma, memory loss, and let's not forget coercion. The guards thought they had their man, didn't they? He'd confessed. They needed a witness, so they made sure they had one."

"But she's not a child anymore, Tanya. Surely if she knows the truth she'd have come forward by now."

She reaches across her desk to a pile of papers and files, begins sifting through them. "I guess if you tell yourself something for long enough, you begin to believe it, right?" She pauses in her search for a moment. "You know, I can't help feeling she's the real victim in all of this. She loses her entire family in one day and nearly her own life, then she has to testify against her brother. It must have felt like she was losing them all over again."

I think of Owens's message, the WSP form that secreted Cara Hennessy away, and think of how she's lost more than her family; she lost herself.

I refill my wineglass. "John, the dad, you're saying he killed himself then? That he managed to stab himself in the neck?"

Finally, she unearths from the pile what she's been searching for and opens up a cardboard folder. She passes me a photo.

She taps the folder with a long nail. "This is John Hennessy's autopsy."

I look down at the photo, a close-up of John's throat, the image extending to just above his mouth; the square tips of his teeth are just visible through stiff parted lips; his skin is covered in light brown stubble.

Tanya leans forward in her chair, reaches out, and points to a one-inch gash in his neck. "We know from the report that it's likely the knife was angled in such a way that the direction of the attack came from his right side." I look down at the wound, open on his skin like a taut red mouth. "So here's the first serious injury, it hit the carotid. And this one"—she moves her finger to another gash just above the collarbone—"would have been afterward as it went through the subclavian artery and the brachial plexus, severing the nerve supply and ultimately leaving the arm paralyzed." She moves her hand across the photo. "But it's this that's got us excited."

She points to a number of smaller wounds around the throat. Four tiny breaks in the skin, triangular cuts where the knife entered but didn't fully penetrate the deeper structures of the neck. "The original postmortem said they were partial stab wounds sustained during a struggle but we don't agree with that. There were no other defensive wounds on John Hennessy, none on his hands or up his arms."

She lays out the other photos in the folder, showing John Hennessy's swollen abdomen, thick hands and arms still covered in dried blood and spatter. I look from one image to the next, knowing what's coming.

Tanya taps the image of John's neck again, her finger hovering over the tiny nicks in his skin. "Our guy says these are—"

"—hesitation marks," I finish.

Leaning back, she spreads her hands. "Exactly."

She has my attention and she knows it. She goes on; excitement speeds through her voice. "The father was a complete tyrant. Even Cara admitted that. A drunk, abusive, unpredictable, angry, and vengeful."

"Agreed."

"So you might ask, what upset the status quo? What could have clicked in him, made him graduate from potential killer to killer?"

I know the answer to this one. It happens all the time. A manipulative narcissist is threatened by desertion. He'd rather kill his entire family than let go of that control. And Bríd Hennessy's hot, flustered face rushes by me on that path. So long ago and I want to reach out. Stop her.

"I've done a little digging around Bríd Hennessy's past." She reaches over the paper at her side and removes a file from the back of the desk. "Turns out she visited a women's refuge in the south side about a week before this kicked off."

I find myself feeling a stupid kind of hope that Bríd Hennessy could make it, that she might pull free of her fate.

Tanya hands me a form. "I think she was planning on leaving him."

In the file, a transcript from a phone call from a women's refuge, dated a couple of weeks after the murders. Bríd Hennessy had visited on the third of August 1995.

"This isn't in the record?"

"It is! But the lead detective at the time discounted it. Just over a week later she was murdered. By the time the report came in, gardaí would've had Seán nice and neat where they wanted him. It's no surprise this was swept to the side. An intentional oversight if ever I saw one."

I look down at the print on the page, a helplessness stealing through me. "A few weeks before the murders, she asked Mam to help her leave."

Tanya's not able to hide the tinny sound of betrayal in her voice. "Your mum told you this?"

"Don't take it personally. Mam's a hard nut to crack."

She makes a snorting sound. "Must run in the family."

I sigh. "It was a hard time for my parents. Dad was very ill. Mam doesn't know anything really, just that Bríd came here. Mam gave her a pamphlet for a women's refuge shortly afterward and that was it."

Tanya doesn't push it further. She knows the ins and outs of my family well, how we're held together only by our silences.

I change the subject before she can ask more questions. "If he's found innocent, we're looking at a huge financial strain on the force."

"The man's been convicted for a crime he didn't commit. Served seventeen years. Someone should pay," she says a little tartly.

I hand her back Bríd Hennessy's call for help and she takes it, places it on top of the other papers gently, stroking down the corners as if she could wipe away Bríd's concerns.

"From what you've shown me, you've a strong case."

She glances at me, nods. "Yes, we do but Cara's testimony is a problem."

"The law does like a firsthand witness."

I take a deep breath. "The commissioner wants me to feed back what you've got. Your angle, so to speak."

Her head snaps up. "And?"

"I'll have to tell her something. I mean, you'll be submitting this soon, I imagine."

She wakes her computer screen, moves the cursor to shut it down. The hard drive makes a short whirring noise, and then the screen drops to black. "I bet she's dying to sweep all this under the carpet."

Tanya leans back in the chair, her eyes lift, move around the room, circle the narrative of the Hennessy murders stuck to the walls. Finally she comes back to me. "But I know that no matter how uncomfortable the consequences, you'll do the right thing. That's why I asked you to help."

Heat spreads over my skin.

"Besides"—she smiles—"you'll want to be able to sleep at night."

I push my fingertips against my eyes, drive away gritty exhaustion. "Well, we all know what a pipe dream that is." The sound of the kettle boiling below comes up through the ceiling, the deep murmur of Justin's voice, Mam's quick reply, the sound of Dad's step on the stairs on his way to bed. I ease up from the box and rub at the tightening scar tissue along my leg. "If the Bureau is under threat I don't want it to go down while I'm resting on my backside," I say. "When the time comes, you'll have my full report on Seán Hennessy, I promise." And I feel Donna Hegarty standing behind me, her arms folded across her soft middle, her mouth tighter than a cat's arse.

I STUFF A SECOND PILLOW under my head. Try to balance myself in the worn hollow of the single bed. The springs jabbing into my shoulder blades, the wool blankets scratching my skin. The room is dark, small, and overly hot. The radiator at my leg on full tilt. Storage heater. Takes half the day to crank up, then it's hot as lava and you can do nothing to turn it down. I hold my phone on its side, search through Seán Hennessy's files, and play the next clip.

"On my twelfth birthday, my da bought me a dog. *A man should have a dog,* he said. A mongrel. Russet stripe down one side of her face, black speckles over her back. A white tail that waved like a flag when she was happy. She was an outdoor dog, Da told me. Never to cross the threshold of our home. So I built her a kennel in the backyard, got some old felt, nailed it to the roof, and lined out the inside with coats I had grown out of, old duvets and pillows. Inside, it was as dry and warm as a summer's day when I'd finished. I spent hours teaching her to sit. To fetch. She had the softest mouth. That dog could've carried a live chick across mountains and deposit it at your feet unharmed.

"She was friendly to a fault. Always running up to strangers on the beach, sticking her wet nose into closed palms. But with my da, she knew. When he was around, she knew to make herself scarce. I'd watch her in the morning from my bedroom window, him making his way round the side, heading for work, and her eyes following his every move. If he did call her to him, she approached slowly, that white tail couched between her legs, her belly as low as her legs would allow.

"One morning she didn't come to the back door for her morning feed. I thought she was ill, so took up the bowl and went to her. Squatted next to the kennel, reached out to stroke her head. Her eyes haunted, loaded with wondrous exhaustion; three fat little bodies nestled in the long fur along her middle. Pups. I was elated. I reached out, scooped one up, Lola's nose followed the movement, nuzzled the back of my hand. *Be careful*, it said. The pup was snow white, a tip of black on the tail. His eyes were closed but I could make out miniature lashes, a tiny row of white spikes. His paws a newborn pink, so pure and soft. Unmarked.

"All day at school, I willed the time to pass so that I could get home to them. And when I did, myself and Cara sat under an umbrella in the rain, just staring at them, occasionally reaching out to stroke their trembling coats.

"My da, he came home from work. Found us at the kennel. Lola curled tight around her young, her nose counting each beating bundle of flesh. He stood over us, hands on hips, lips tight. I followed him back into the kitchen. They were already going at it, Ma and Da. *Can't they at least keep them for a while, John? We don't have room for more fucking dogs; we've enough of them in the house already.* Ma's face, I saw her retreating into that place. Drawing herself low, just like Lola did. I felt helpless. I could sense something dark approaching, as deeply as you feel the shift in the air before a storm.

"I stayed in the kitchen, stood by the back door, watched as my da went to the garage, Cara yabbering after him, her chat full of puppy-dog tails and all things nice. He appeared then, one of those deep black buckets in his hands. He went to the garden tap, filled it. The water twisting out in a cold rope. Bucket full he carried it to the side of the house, laid it down.

"It wasn't until I saw him stride for the kennel that I began to move after him. Lola, sensing the same threat, began to bare her teeth, her tongue darting out, smacking against her muzzle, a trembling growl in her throat. But my da was master of all in our small home, and a growling dog was no match for him. He hauled her out by the collar, the fat pups rolling from her stomach like feathers dropping from a bird.

"*Fucking mutt*, he said.

"'Da, don't hurt her,' I yelled.

"*I'm only getting her outta the bloody way.*

"He pitched her into the garage, locked the door. I went to the pups, gathered them up, folded them into my sweater. Me da, when he approached, looked down at the squirming nest in my arms, lifted his hand, and rested it on my shoulder.

"*A man should do what needs to be done*, he said.

"He pointed to the bucket.

"*Get rid of them*, he said.

"'No.' I was crying then, really sobbing. But I don't think he noticed. He squeezed down on my shoulder and I swear to you I can still feel that now, as if my very bones were bending under his weight.

"*Get fucking rid of them*, he said again.

"He let me go, turned, and went into the kitchen. I knew he'd be watching. If I failed, he'd be waiting. Card marked. The garage door rattled. Lola crying, barking. I couldn't stand it. And I guess I wanted it over too. I couldn't win against him. If I didn't do what he asked, he would take it out on me or my ma, and he'd kill the pups anyway, probably even Lola. I carried the little bundle to the bucket. Knelt down beside it. My hands shaking, I lifted out the first pup, little black tail curled in along its pink belly, tiny paws threading the air. A lump in my throat the size of a fist.

"I put my hand and the pup in the water. I don't know how long I held it there. How long does it take to break a heart?"

I **WAKE AT TWO** A.M. Nightshirt stuck to my chest, sheets damp against my neck. My phone is trembling across the bedside table. I sit up, pull the shirt from my neck, and reach for the phone. The screen flashes Paul's name.

"Chief, we've got another body," he says. "I think."

My heart hits fast thumps against my ears. "You think?"

"I've called the local station." His words come at a rush. "They're sending a car there but we've nothing yet. I wasn't sure what to do, to be honest. I didn't think I should leave the Bureau. There's no one else here to pick up calls."

"Slow down. What's happened?"

"I got a call about fifteen minutes ago. Saying there was an-other body in Clontarf."

"From?"

"I'm running a location, nothing yet. A male caller. Just said there was another body in Clontarf along the strand and hung up." A sagging feeling of dread pulls through me. Another victim.

"It could be a prank call," he continues. "We've had a few but I don't know. This sounded . . . different."

I push back the covers, pull my limbs free, and reach for my clothes. "Get Steve on voice recognition as soon as he gets back. Call Baz; have the coroner alerted and a forensics team on standby. Feed back to the officers you've sent out that they should begin their search at the city end and work down. I'll begin along the promenade. If they find anything they're to stay back and alert me immediately."

"Yes, Chief," he replies and ends the call.

The forensic team and the coroner might be excessive and I can hear well enough Clancy's lecture on money wasted on prank calls but we were expecting this. More murder. More death.

The radiators click and hiss from every corner of the house. The air, fragile, brittle as time, dries in my mouth. I get dressed then go to the window, peel back the curtains. The street is empty. Cars parked along the pavement, windshields covered in cool condensation. And the moon, wide and full, throws cold light across the black sky. I let the curtain fall then turn to pull on my shoes. I unplug my phone, make my way quietly downstairs. In the kitchen, I search the drawers. Finding my dad's torchlight, I flick the beam on and off to check the batteries. The light is yellow and weak but it will have to do. I tuck it inside my coat pocket, the weight pulling the fabric down, then I go to the front door, ease it open, and leave the rest of the house to sleep.

THE NIGHT BREEZE curls around my throat. The beach is empty. The air damp and chill. I want to reach up, tighten the collar of my coat, but I can't make my arms move. He's slumped against the seawall, legs out like a doll, left foot turned in, hands folded neatly over his stomach. Dead. I know it from the unnatural tip of his head, his neck stretched out to his left shoulder. The torch remains unused in my hand; the batteries died within moments of turning it on. In the dim light, I cast my eyes around the area to and from the body. He's dressed in a dark suit, a white shirt luminous in the shadows. And the smell, the breeze pushes the stench at me. I can taste it, the rot of decaying flesh. Just like Alan Shine.

Up along the promenade, the road is quiet. Thin clouds of mist twirl in the orange streetlight. Beyond the silence, the occasional drunken shout as people tumble out of the local yacht club. Behind me, the fat moon rolls on the shining black sea and the beach glows blue in its wake. The waves splash and drop behind, beginning their slow climb back up the beach; the tide is turning. In a few hours, he'll be underwater. The realization shoves my mind into gear and with stiff fingers I remove my phone from my pocket and make the call.

CHAPTER 11

IT'S NOT LONG before the cars draw up along the roadside. Doors slam; instructions are delivered and fall down from the promenade to my ears. Baz is first to emerge out of the darkness onto the beach. I force myself straight, step back, away from the body, my hands clenched in my pockets.

"Frankie," he calls. His long frame a slice of shadow.

I wait until he's next to me, breath clouding the air between us. He looks like shit. Whatever night he's been dragged from was born of the same nightmare as mine.

"Baz. Hi," I say. "The coroner?"

He catches his breath, turns. "She was just behind me."

I move my gaze away, over his shoulder. Judith Magee steps down off the slipway onto the narrow beach. She picks her way across the damp sand, her case cradled in her arms. Her short hair is already held fast in a net, headlamp in place and casting bright white beams over the shale.

"Detectives." She gives us a tight smile.

"Judy," Baz says. The doc's face draws inwards. Too familiar.
"The body?"

I turn toward the wall and death rushes up my nose.

"Fuck. That's ripe," Baz mutters and lifts a hand to his face.

Judith is already stretching her small hands into gloves. She
slips a mask over her face, retrieves her case, and moves forward.
I follow in her wake, breathing through my mouth. She crouches
down, gets close. She moves quickly over the body, deft and sure.
Eyelids peeled upward. Hands searching for obvious trauma, fingers pressing down over the bloated abdomen. In one brave
movement she pulls down her mask and sniffs the area around
the victim's mouth.

"No alcohol," she says. "But I think it's fair to say he's not recently deceased." She pauses, looks up but can't quite meet my
eyes. "You found him like this? You didn't touch him?"

"Of course not."

She stands, moves away, ushering us with her. She pulls her
gloves off one by one, then slides them into an evidence bag.
Preserving any clues clinging to the surface.

"Murder," she states. She nods toward the forensics van
parked on the street. "Call your guys down. Full CSI. There's
enough here to knock the rear end out of the commissioner's
budget."

Baz and I share a glance. "She'll like that," Baz murmurs.

Magee continues. "There's some freezer burn under the hair,
on the right side of his head. Possibly a wound near the occiput
but I can't be sure until we move him. I would say this is definitely related to our current case. And . . ." She pauses, turns her
headlamp toward the body. "There's that."

We follow the silver path of light. It picks out the ground between the man's legs. Written into the sand is one word: KILLER.

WHEN THE LIGHTS GO UP, the man's hair gleams black, shadows stretch from his eyes, his nose. Baz is circling the body, eyes on the victim's face.

"I reckon the doc's on the ball. It's not unlike the Alan Shine case, I mean the extent of decomposition."

"McDonagh still in custody?"

"We released him at five this evening. Plainclothes report that he's not moved from his house since. I don't think we can pin this one on him. Not unless he's perfected astral projection."

"No," I reply. I tip my head back, try to get a lungful of air that's not tainted by death, and I feel the grip of frustration around my chest. No suspects. Not one. Around me is the hiss and clunk of cameras, the scatter and crunch of shale underfoot, and the crackle of plastic moving over the crime scene, yellow markers pushed into the sand indicating possible evidence.

"We might want to get a list of missing persons from the Dublin area."

"Maybe it's the male thing, you know," Baz says from behind his hand. "The way the two men were held for a while. A fetish."

Gloves on, I lean across the body, reach over the man's head, follow the same path as Dr. Magee. "There were no signs of sexual abuse on Alan Shine's body."

He sighs, lifts his hand from his nose to push his hair back. "So not sexually motivated."

My palms press down the victim's suit, lift the lapels, squeeze the lining. Nothing. No ID, no wallet. But there's a familiarity to the victim's face that I can't quite place.

"Was there anyone else on the prom? When you came down here?" Baz asks.

I stand. "No one. What do you make of his appearance?"

He lets out a whistle of air. "Dressed well? The guy's suit looks newly pressed almost. A bit wet, obviously. But barely a stain on it. I guess Alan Shine was dressed well too. In a way."

The victim's mouth is sunken inwards, lips trapped against teeth. Sealed shut. Unable to speak. KILLER. One word. An entire sentence, an accusation at his feet. Straightening, I move back to take in the position of the body, my eyes on the man's bloated face.

"The victim could represent the killer himself?" He points at the word KILLER in the sand.

Although I've known killers who've chosen victims because they saw something in their victims they despised about themselves, knowing that this body is related to the Shine murders throws that theory away. The Shines were different from this lone figure. I let my gaze linger on the man's thick dark hair, the long sweep of his nose and think what it is that's made this man deserve the title KILLER. He's got a type of clichéd good looks. Even with the bloat, I can see an adequate jawline and I have a sudden memory that I know him. I see him, a teen standing in a photo for his Gaelic football team.

"I think I know who he is. He played Gaelic football with my brother when they were kids. Teenagers. He played for the team above Justin." It doesn't take much to recall his name. "Sheridan. Conor Sheridan."

"Fuck." Baz looks at me as if testing whether he should be concerned. "I'm sorry?"

"I recognize him but I didn't know him. Not really," I reply. I take out my phone, flick on the torchlight, scan the ground again, then up the wall behind the man, toward the promenade to street level.

I move up the beach; the smell of Sheridan's corpse lessens and I allow myself a few good breaths. I let my eyes follow the prom all the way down to the beach. It would've been a struggle to haul the body down here.

Nearby, a SOCO is photographing something in the sand.

"Any sign yet of how he got down here?" I ask.

She stands, glances at the image on the screen of her camera. "Detective, hi. No, nothing." She plucks a clamshell from the ground. "Thought maybe the edge of a bootprint but no, a shell upturned, flipped by the tide." She straightens. "He could have come down the slipway? The sea's out."

Turning, I follow her gaze to the slipway, a short pier-like structure where the yacht club launch their boats. The victim is heavy, not overweight heavy, but dead-weight heavy. There should be drag marks at least or the scattering of sand. But there are no grooves to and from the access points to the beach, no footprints, guilty and hurried, pressed into the ground, apart from our own.

I make my way back to Baz, my eyes over the sea. The tide is, in fact, not climbing back up the beach as I'd originally thought.

"When's the next tide in?" I ask him.

"Is it on the way out? Four hours, maybe."

"Our perp lays out their victim, labels him as a killer, then doesn't worry that we might not get to him before an incoming wave wipes out half his handiwork, wipes out what he wrote in the sand?"

"So he knows about tides."

I swallow and face the dark beach. I know that when the tide comes in on Clontarf, hundreds of years of man-made seawalls and reclaimed coastline guide the water first into a shallow canal that slowly widens. It's deceptive. The area we're standing on is one of the last places the sea engulfs. Turning, I scan the scene. Again, the killer has taken time over this. He's done his homework, planned all the details of his crime, this wondrous achievement, for it to look a certain way.

The techs move around us, setting up a tent, metal poles hammered into the ground. A uniform walks between them, a roll of tape spinning out in her hands, closing off the beach. A yellow-gray light is bleeding out over the horizon, an early sunrise making promises an Irish summer should never make.

The van arrives; the techs carry down the stretcher. "We're ready to go now," one of them says.

"Okay." I walk to Baz. "Will you oversee the removal of the victim to Whitehall? I'll be there in under an hour. I need to collect my things from my folks'."

"Sure," he says.

"Try to get the body off before the dog walkers get their slippers on. We want to keep the media back for as long as possible, and we don't need any Snapchats with a body bag in the background."

"Door-to-door?"

"As soon as you can rouse people. We'll need a formal ID. I think his parents, if they're still alive, are in Clontarf somewhere."

"Wife?"

I shrug. "Possibly. He's been gone a few days at least. Someone must've missed him."

A small twist of distaste on Baz's face. Always more victims than the dead when it comes to murder.

THE SQUAD CAR leaves me at my parents' house. I let myself in through the back. The kitchen is warm with peaceful silence. The tick of the clock over the sink, soothing. Quiet clunks, the hand moving over the seconds, casting off time like it's nothing. I stand against the sink, look over at the kitchen table. Justin, Conor Sheridan head-to-head in a drinking game. Our parents out for the evening. Me looking on, shy glances from the sofa by the far wall, wanting desperately to join in and reveling every time Conor threw me a smile, a wink. Tingling starts up in my fingers and I release my grip on the drainboard, shake my hands out.

There's a creak on the stairs, second from the top. A callback to early school mornings, Mam padding down to the kitchen ahead of us waking to get breakfast on the go. She appears in the doorway, her eyes blinking, her hair in mad tufts over her forehead.

"Frankie. What are ye doing up?" She looks at the clock. "Jesus, sure it's practically the middle of the night still." She frowns, takes a few steps toward me, worry deepening the lines at her mouth. "Is everything all right?"

"I've got to work, Ma." I nod at the window to the gradually lightening sky. "I just came back to get my things."

"Okay, love, if you've got to go, you've got to go." She doesn't prod for details, relief that it's work and nothing else that has me up in the small hours. That whatever tragedy has fallen in the middle of the night, it has fallen on someone else.

Upstairs, I pull the sheets over the bed, tuck them in tight at the corners. Position the pillows, the cushions the way that Mam likes. In less than a few minutes the room looks like I've never stepped foot in it.

Downstairs, I give a kiss to Mam's cheek, apologize once more, then I'm out the door and back in the squad car. I dial the office, let them know I'm coming in.

Helen is quick to the phone. "Chief. Baz filled me in. Same killer. Clontarf again."

"It doesn't like to be left out of the action. We have a tentative ID, Conor Sheridan. His parents lived in Clontarf. You'll need to send someone out there. There could be a wife, a family. Can you get the address for me?"

I can hear a rustle of paper, her scribbling down the victim's name. "Sure, Chief."

CHAPTER 12

THE UNIFORM TAKES the North Strand Road back to Dublin. The streets are quiet as a graveyard; the odd bus moves sleepily out in front of us, pulling up at empty stops where the driver can have a crafty fag before continuing on his lone voyage. We turn into the underground car park at the Bureau. I get out and stop sharp when I see Clancy getting out of his car.

"Jack."

He gives me a nod. "Well, Frankie. You're like the pied piper of murders. Baz said the corpse stank like a rancid old fish."

"Yeah, this one's been a keeper for a while."

"Like Alan Shine."

"Undoubtedly the same killer."

"McDonagh?"

"We have his fingerprints in the Shine house but he says he was intimate with Geraldine Shine. The trainers we seized from him did not match the print from the Shine house. So we released him yesterday afternoon. Plainclothes say he's not moved from his home since." We enter the lift, select the fourth floor. "If we can get a time of death quickly on Conor Sheridan then it will give us a window to work with at least."

We step onto the floor. There are five occupied desks in the room, gray faces under the sharp fluorescence. Helen looks up when she sees us enter.

"The parents are on their way to Whitehall, Chief," she says over the partition. "We'll get statements from them but the visiting officer says so far they seem as clueless as we are as to why their son would've been murdered. I have the wife's address, or ex-wife. Jane Sheridan now Brennan: Bay Road. Number 29."

I drop my coat, bag inside the door and hold out my hand.

"The victim, Mr. Sheridan," she continues, "lived in the south of the city. I've noted his address also"—she flicks over her notebook—"in Tallaght. Subsidized flat, one housemate, long-standing, a Mr. James Lynch."

"Lynch?" I ask, not quite believing I've heard her right.

"Yes, Chief."

I let out a long sigh of relief. There's such a sweet feeling of victory when a name crops up twice in an investigation, makes you more aware of the ground beneath your feet, drives away that feeling that your legs are pedaling the air before you drop into nothing. Robbie McDonagh, in an attempt to save his own ass, has given us a foothold.

Clancy turns to me. "He on the roster too?"

"McDonagh mentioned a Jimmy Lynch during interview. Said he was a friend and that he was at his place when the Shine murders happened."

Clancy nods toward the information on Conor Sheridan in my hand. "When did Sheridan's marriage go tits up?"

"Five years ago," Helen replies. "Nothing untoward on the papers filed, no reports of domestic violence and Conor was on top of his child support."

My stomach tightens at the mention of kids. "Alimony?"

"Not any longer. Jane Sheridan has since remarried."

I feel a familiar mix of frustration and excitement, not uncommon in the early hours of a murder investigation when time is tight and there are too many doors to knock on and no one can say which will lead to the all-you-can-eat buffet of evidence. I think through the hours ahead, whether I can spare Helen from the floor so that she and Ryan can take the ex-wife. But Jane Sheridan's personal connection to our most recent victim is too much for me to give up. It could be that she's able to give us a sense of the relationship between Conor and his flatmate, something we could use during Lynch's interrogation.

I turn to Clancy. "Best send some eyes to Sheridan's flat, keep tabs on Lynch until I can get out there. I'll talk to the ex first then see what Lynch can tell us. Helen, how about the husband?"

"A David Brennan. We're still looking into him. For the moment all we got is that he works at the port. A crane driver."

Clancy nods. "When you go out to that flat, I want you to take Baz with you."

"I'm fine on my own."

"Until we know what kind of fuckers we're dealing with, we stay with our partners." His voice shakes with barely restrained force.

"Briefing in two minutes," I say to Helen.

I walk Clancy to the coffee machine. My stomach is clenching with hunger; acid works its way up my throat. I pour a coffee, take a couple of cellophane-wrapped biscuits from a basket at the side of the machine.

"Well, Hegarty will have to cool her heels now," Clancy remarks. "Our resources are stretched enough with this." He jabs a button on the machine, curses when it spits out creamy latte. "You got to the scene prompt."

"I was in the area, at my folks'. Spent the evening running over the Hennessy case with Tanya before bed."

He shakes a packet of sugar loose, rips the top, and dumps it into his coffee, then reaches for another. "She sucked in by Hennessy's tall tales?"

"She's raised a few worrying flags. Possible cross-contamination of the scene. A question of the validity of Cara Hennessy's testimony."

"Validity? Cara Hennessy was an absolute trouper during an event that would have broken many an older person."

I narrow my gaze on his face. "You're remembering a lot nowadays."

He dumps the second sugar into the coffee. White, plastic stick stirring at speed. "Not because I want to, I'll fucking tell you that."

I think of Owens's message. "What about Hennessy's confession?"

His selective memory returns with a shrug. "Never heard or seen it."

"It must've lit a fire, right? Made him seem guilty at first."

He stops stirring his coffee, faces me. "His guilt made him seem guilty."

I take up my coffee, give up playing tic-tac-toe with Clancy. I move toward the case board and wait for the room to settle. Clancy stands near the back. I don't meet his eyes.

"A body was found at approximately two A.M. on the beach at Clontarf. Time of death is still to be decided but we're looking in the last week. The victim, a male in his forties, believed to be Conor Sheridan, Tallaght, formally of Clontarf. There are major tie-ins with the Shine case. The victim's body was in the early stages of decomposition. The word KILLER was etched into the sand at his feet. The body is undergoing autopsy at Whitehall under Dr. Abigail James. Steve, anything on who called it in?"

Steve is folded into a chair at the front, red head bent over his notebook. Pale, narrow face still on his notes. "Nothing. The voice was disguised, I think."

"What about our victim? What else do we know about him? Have we got his last movements? Or those that led up to his disappearance?"

"Helen's been looking at the vic's background, his work, I think laboring, mostly," he replies. "Scaffolding, steel-fixing since his divorce."

"Girlfriend?"

"Nothing yet. I guess his housemate would have a good idea."

"So Jimmy Lynch's name came up when we interviewed Robbie McDonagh. It could be a coincidence but you all know how I feel about those. Also, Robbie McDonagh, by his own admission, was sleeping or had slept with Geraldine Shine. So we have a very loose link, suspect wise, between our victims. It may be a couple of degrees wide but it's there. When sorting through door-to-door and the evidence, keep it in mind. We need to build on it."

Clancy smacks his hands, rubs his palms together. "Right. Let's get on the chase, lads. This fella looks like he'll have the juice for more of the same, and we don't want to find ourselves with a queue of messed-up corpses to deal with."

I nod. "Paul?"

Paul looks up from the side of the office, his rounded chin rolling over his collar. "Yes, Chief?"

"Make the usual statement for media, please. We've yet to make a formal ID." Then I look out at the room. "Where are we with the Shine case? Helen? Phones?"

Helen makes a show of examining her notes before she speaks. "Yes, we have something. I've chased down both of the Shines' phone locations with Cell Site. Alan Shine's hit a mast near his home on the fourteenth of August."

There are fourteen masts in the two-mile radius around the Shine home. It would be fair game for his phone to hit any of them during a normal day.

Helen continues, the volume of her voice raising slightly. "But I've just got Geraldine's phone details in," she says slowly. "It hit masts as far out as Howth Head even after she'd been murdered. The last feedback coming at 7:01 P.M. Site 2195 near Cliff Walk in Howth."

Twelve kilometers from our crime scene. Twenty minutes of driving. I smile. The phone is no doubt in the Irish Sea now. Lost. But it's done the job. Given us another small glimpse at the killer's movements in the wake of this murder. He deposits the blouse in Ger Shine's house then drives out to Cliff Walk to dispose of the phone. That would bring us up to approximately seven thirty P.M. We have traffic cams on that route. And where we've traffic cams, we have license plate recognition.

"Ryan."

"Yes, Chief?"

"How's ANPR going?"

"Nothing really sticking out, I'm afraid."

"Get on the traffic cams out to Cliff Walk and Howth Head. Cross-reference the findings with those vehicles passing by and parking near the church on the Sunday."

"Yes, Chief."

I turn back to Helen. "This is great work. We now have a shot at finding Geraldine's bag and phone. Let's get a team out there."

"Yes, ma'am," she says, pleased.

I can see Clancy is eager to leave, and as he's never been one to miss an opportunity to breathe down my neck, it makes me anxious. He walks toward a chair at the front of the room, where he's thrown his coat. He has it half on when I step up behind him.

"My office?"

His cheeks pull inward and he hoists his coat up over his shoulders. "Thought you'd never ask."

Clancy settles down into the chair at my desk, stretches out his legs, crosses them at the ankles, his hands gripping the seat like it's about to take off. His eyes cast downwards, searching for more questions to keep the real ones at bay.

"Have you spoken to Hegarty again?" I ask before he has time to think of one.

"Not heard a fucking peep from her. I won't be the one to invite that headache in." He laughs.

I sit across from him. The desk between us. "What happened with the Seán Hennessy case?"

His hand goes to his forehead and he pushes it through his hair. "Fuck sake."

"I don't understand why he would confess then retract it?"

"If that's surprising you after all these years then I don't know what to say. These fuckers do it all the time."

"Was he beaten?"

Eyes harden. "I'll pretend you didn't ask that."

"You said yourself, it was different back then."

"Is that some fucking shitty way to get me to open up, huh?"

"No."

"It fucking sounds like it. It fucking sounds like you think I'm going to step into that one, lie on my back and let you tickle me bits."

"Jack, come on. It's me you're talking to. You told me you barely touched this case. That it breezed by your desk, in the early hours. You know I'll get to the bottom of this; it would be easier if you just told me what's going on."

He stands but leans over the desk; his face grows heated, crimson patches light up over his neck. "I've never laid into any of the inmates in my charge. Although, if there was one I woulda happily sent into a corner with my right boot, Seán Hennessy would have been it." He runs a hand over his face. "That fucker murdered his parents, tried to kill his own sister. He's fucking darkness itself."

I blow air through my lips. "Okay. Sorry."

"Fuck it." He takes a juddering breath. He walks toward the door, opens it, but turns at the last moment. "Be careful with this, Frankie. Sometimes when you look into the mouth of that kind of evil, it's hard to look away. You think, give it another few moments, your eyes will adjust, you'll see the bottom of that darkness, understand it. It's alluring. Addictive. And whilst you're standing there rooted to the spot, you're not noticing that the fucking shadow is closing over you and you're disappearing."

He walks out. Closes the door. I sit there for a long moment, wondering at the spiky shoots of distrust that are pushing up inside me when I think of Clancy. Maybe I shouldn't, like he suggests, indulge the past too much. I look up to the pin board above my desk. A miniature of our case board, so our current investigation is always standing over me, never out of my peripheral vision. I study Geraldine Shine's white corpse. The red wounds down her back.

I unpin the photo from the board, hold it in my hands. Along the edge of the photo, the camera has caught Alan Shine's hand open, the murder weapon, the knife, cold and spent in his palm. The skin over the palm a deep purple, the creases at his wrists a creamy yellow where after death his hands were flexed in on themselves.

I can just about make out the edge of the black shirt, part of the vestments the killer dressed him in. The sight brings Father Healy to my mind. I think of Geraldine Shine's phone, Healy's reluctance to talk, and the ease with which he would've been able to move to and from the church. I dial Helen. It takes her only a few moments to do a location analysis on the path Healy's phone took on the evening of the Shine murders and compare it with Geraldine's.

"His phone hit tower 2195 on Cliff Walk, Howth; 7:01 P.M. on the evening of Ger Shine's murder," she says.

"That's the same tower?"

"The same."

The void in the blood spatter at the church stands out in my mind. I lean back into the seat. I should feel jubilant, but instead I feel confused. I think through the day, interviews with those closest to Conor Sheridan, his autopsy, and any possible connections between Healy and Conor Sheridan. "Get out to him immediately. Bring him in and make him comfortable for a few hours. Secure the parochial house; send Keith out there if you can."

"You think he did it?" She sounds doubtful.

"I don't think so. He knew the Shines but where's the connection to Conor Sheridan? Reckon this fecker is just about selfish enough to fuck up a murder investigation to protect his own rep. I think he took the bag because there's something on that phone he doesn't want coming out."

"Oh."

"A killer this organized does not lay out his masterpiece only to leave a great big smear on the canvas and a handy little techno trail to where he dumped the victim's phone."

She sighs. "No, I guess not."

"Let's get Healy in and see what he has to say, and can you send Jane Sheridan's address to my phone? I want to get out there before Abigail's finished with the autopsy of Conor Sheridan."

CHAPTER 13

CONOR **S**HERIDAN'S **EX-WIFE** lives on a nice street in Clontarf: wide-open drives, windows all turned to the morning sun. Her house detached but identical to its neighbor. Two floors and a loft conversion. Stucco-clad front. Pebble-filled drive. She answers the door in a breathless rush, a dog barking at her heels. Her blond hair looks unwashed, unbrushed, piled high in a clip at the back of her head. Fake tan is caked along her hairline, around the small lobes of her ears. Behind her is the sound of spoons against cereal bowls, children crying. She glances at me then grabs hold of the dog's collar.

"Hang on," she says, turns, then shouts, "Jax, give it up or it'll be straight home after school." Immediate silence slams down over the house. She lets go of the dog and he lumbers out into the wet garden, flops down under a rosebush. "Sorry about that," she says. She takes a step back. Her thin face pinches over her eyes as if she's seeing me for the first time. "How can I help you?"

"Mrs. Sheridan?"

"No. That's my old married name. I'm Mrs. Brennan now." She waves a diamond ring at me. "What's Conor gone and done this time?"

"Mrs. Brennan, I'm Detective Chief Superintendent Frankie Sheehan. Would you mind if I came in?"

She frowns, glances back down the hallway as if anticipating another outbreak of noise. "I've to get the kids to school. We're late as it is."

"Is there someone who could help you out? It's important I speak with you."

Her blue eyes narrow; black mascara flakes onto her cheek. "Is Conor okay?"

"I'll give you a few minutes to get the kids organized. I'm in that car there." I point back toward the street. "Tap the window when you're ready."

She looks out over my shoulder. "Okay."

I walk back to the car. As I open the door, I hear her shout. "Jax!"

I watch the commotion from the driver's seat. Helen's background check tells me that Jane divorced Conor five years ago, citing irreconcilable differences. Childhood sweethearts broken by the reality of adulthood and the confinement of white picket fences. She has no criminal record. Worked as a hairdresser from her teens but no steady employment recently.

I send Helen an email, see if she's got anything on the new husband yet, although I can't see jealousy being the problem here. Only Jane's reaction when she answered the door, *What's Conor gone and done this time*, makes me consider it. And if Conor was making a nuisance of himself around Jane, there could be a motive for murder here. But even as I send the email, the Shine case nags away at the back of my head, unable to marry any motive Brennan could have against Sheridan to the Shines.

I phone Baz, look for some feedback on Sheridan's autopsy.

"Well, when the clothes came off, this fella's death wasn't as clean as we thought," he says down the line.

"You've a cause of death?"

"Sheridan was shot. Right through the chest. The wound was cleaned out thoroughly. Abigail here thinks she has a couple of fragments, no bullet. It went through him."

"So the killer shot him, cleaned him up, dressed him, then dumped him?"

"Yep. As we thought, he's been stored for a few days. Lividity over his right side, through the scalp. None at the backs of the knees or across his middle. Wherever he's been held, he was curled up on his side."

Three murders in the space of weeks, my stomach turns.

"Abigail's still got a lot of work to do," he adds. "Where are you?"

"I'm at his ex-wife's house."

"I thought I had it bad here."

No one likes breaking bad news to a victim's family. It's been years since I've knocked on someone's door and fractured their life into before and after. I almost always send a uniform. But beyond Jane Brennan's grief there's information on her ex-husband and I'll do almost anything to get to it.

Jane Brennan appears at the door of her house, throwing sharp orders over her shoulder. She's changed out of her tracksuit, into white jeans and a peach blouse. Her hair is still piled at the back of her head but her face is freshly painted. I think between them,

Conor Sheridan and her must have been quite the couple once upon a time. She stands on the doorstep and looks expectantly up the street then folds her arms and disappears back inside.

"I'll be over as soon as I can," I say into the phone. "I gotta go. Let Clancy know we may need to assign firearms if we're dealing with a gunshot wound."

"Already done," he says.

I glance out the window at the dirty gray sky, the swirling misty air. A little way down the street, a dark car pulls up. The door opens and a man gets out. I watch him approach and enter the Brennan house. In a couple of moments, he exits again, Jane Brennan close behind, her hands on the backs of her kids, pushing them out the door.

I hang up. Get out of the car and walk toward them. Jane folds her arms when she sees me.

"Mr. Brennan?" I ask.

He turns and I hold up my badge. He directs the kids toward the car and I wait for them to clamber inside.

"Howya," he says sharply. His expression one of controlled tolerance. "Is everything okay, officer?" His accent is broad and he makes the most of it, every word a punch out of his mouth. There's a stud in his right ear, could be a diamond but I'm thinking zirconia at best. He's wearing a pink shirt, two buttons open to show off a chunky silver chain and a gray nest of chest hair. White trainers, white jeans; a brave move by any stretch, braver still if you live in Ireland.

"I need to speak with your wife, Mr. Brennan."

He nods, seems a little too okay with that. "I'll get the kids off to school then." He leans across and plants an awkward kiss on Jane's cheek. "Phone me if you need anything."

She nods but doesn't say anything in reply.

David Brennan gives me a final glance. "Well then," he says, "I've work to be doing." He walks to the car, gets in without a backward glance, and slams the door shut. I watch him pull away.

"He doesn't like to be disturbed from work. You'd better come in," she says to me, irritation thick in her voice. She turns on her heel and heads back to the house without waiting.

"Thank you," I say, and follow her up the short drive.

She opens the door, waves me inside. The hallway is cool, tiled floor, white, white walls.

She flicks a glance at me. "Coffee?"

"Sure."

The white continues into the kitchen. My shoe hits a football; it rolls beneath a chair. Jane Brennan scoops up the kids' cereal bowls, uses a tea towel to wipe down the table, mopping up soggy Cheerios and milk, breadcrumbs and spilled orange juice. She indicates a high stool.

"Take a seat, there."

I sit. She pours water onto instant coffee, fishes an ashtray out of one of the cupboards, lights a cigarette, takes a drag, then turns, places two mugs on the table between us. I smile my thanks.

She sits across from me, cigarette pinched between her fingers, the end hanging over the ashtray. "Well?"

I clear my throat. "Mrs. Brennan, early this morning a body was found on the beach. We know it to be the body of your ex-husband, Conor Sheridan."

I watch her face; the skin drops, muscles sag along her jaw, lips thin, pale. She blinks but her gaze holds mine, waiting for more. I can see her eyes darken, fear, misunderstanding, confusion taking turns like clouds over a blue sky.

"Conor?" A thin line of smoke draws up from her cigarette. "Yes."

A head shake followed by a sure smile. "No. You got the wrong fella there. He doesn't live round here anymore. He's beyond in Tallaght." She reaches for her phone, as if to contact him.

"When was the last time you saw him? Spoke to him?"

She leaves the phone where it is, brings the cigarette to her mouth. Fingers shake. Ash floats then sinks into her coffee. "I don't know. He took the kids out for a day, maybe a fortnight ago. Sure, he wouldn't be stopping in; he'd just wait by the door." She looks down, mascara heavy on her lashes. "To be honest, Dave is not all that fond of him being round the house."

"Oh?"

She reaches back, scratches a fake nail beneath the mass of hair on her head. "He gets a bit possessive sometimes. You know yourself." A brief flash of pride crosses her face, then she seems to remember again why I'm here. "How did he . . . how did he die?"

"We're still in the process of ascertaining that but it appears he was murdered."

"Murdered?" A squeak of a word. Hysteria on the edge of her voice. "Who'd want to harm Conor? I mean, he was harmless." Her hand leaves the mug, and her arms snake around her stomach. Her eyes water.

"Sorry if this is a personal question, Mrs. Brennan, but we're trying to build a picture of Conor's life. Could you tell me why you divorced?"

She closes her eyes briefly, as if she doesn't want to look back, and when she speaks, she focuses on the ashtray rather than me. "We were young when we got together. Maybe had kids too quickly. Conor did all the laboring jobs he could get even though his heart wasn't in it and really, he wanted to write." She throws me a glance, sighs. "And I think that was it, really. He was unhappy with his lot. Frustrated, I guess.

"He started drinking. Couldn't stop, you know. It broke him. It broke us. Whatever shattered bloody dreams he had, at the end of the day, we'd two kids that needed looking after. And he was still acting the lad and he in his thirties; spending money like our mattress was stuffed with it and coming in at all hours. I couldn't do it anymore." There's more than a hint of bitterness in her voice. "Are you sure? I mean, you're sure it's him?"

"When I arrived, you seemed to think he might have been in trouble. Why was that?"

She shrugs, a sad little smile turning down her mouth. "Only I thought maybe a drunken fight or something, drink-driving maybe." She gets up, pulls a chunk of paper towel from a holder over the counter, dabs under her eyes, sits down again.

"Did Conor have any enemies that you know of?"

"No. I mean, I wouldn't know now. We kept our distance, really, since the divorce. We only communicated when there was something that needed organizing for the kids."

"Girlfriend?"

That wins a small cynical grin. "I'd be the last one he'd tell."

"Was he still doing construction jobs for work?"

"Yes. And there seemed to be more of it lately, taking up his weekends and that, less time for the kids, you know. It upset them."

"The last time you saw him, how did he seem to you?"

She shrugs. "The usual. I don't know."

"Stressed? Happy?"

She purses her lips. "He might've been a bit stressed, sure."

When she sees me frown, she continues. "He wrote a thing. A long time ago now. For a paper. It was controversial at the time. Although, who knows why, everyone was thinking it. It caused a bit of trouble for us."

I feel the ache across my forehead. "Why would that make him stressed now?"

"It was a local piece on a murder case." Tears gather along the rims of her eyes. She wipes the wad of paper towel under her nose, sniffs.

Unease prickles across the back of my neck. "A murder case?"

"Yeah. A young fella slaughtered his family. Here! In little old Clontarf. Conor wrote it, the local newspaper published it, and then the nationals took up the thread. It went big." She reaches back to the counter, tears off another sheet of paper towel, blows her nose. "The guy who did it, he's been released. They're doing some shitty documentary about the whole thing. Conor texted me when he found out. I didn't want anything to do with it. I've moved on from all that."

The bright kitchen darkens. I can feel it, the past walking out the story in heavy footsteps down my back.

"Seán Hennessy," I say, more to myself than anything. To hear the connection spoken out loud.

Her face clears. Eyes widen. "Do you think? It couldn't be that, could it? It was a lifetime ago." She punches out the cigarette on the ashtray.

I manage to keep my voice steady. "Can you remember anything else about the article? What he wrote, for example?"

She pulls herself straight. "It was good, you know. Finally, a real story he could sink his teeth into. And when you're writing these kinds of things, you need an angle, you know. You set your

stall out, pick a camp to sit in. It went well for him. But, I think
in time, he was sorry. He began to think he got things wrong.
Hindsight being twenty-twenty and all that. But he'd known the
dad, John Hennessy. I knew him. John Hennessy was a good
man. Everyone thought so." She looks me in the eye. "He was a
bank manager, you know. Sponsored the local kids' football
teams with the jerseys, the lot." She stops. "Fuck. It must be,
what, ten years ago?"

"Seventeen." I give her a thin smile.

She removes another cigarette, lights it. "The pressure got to
him, you know. He wasn't sure whether the lad had done it after
all." She takes a sharp drag. "Don't know why it bothered him,
really. I mean, he got a shedload of freelance work out of it; what
did it matter to him? It's up to you lot to charge the right bloke,
isn't it? Anyway, he wallowed about for months in the house,
drinking, under my feet. Not working. He wouldn't go down to
the local pub, he felt ashamed, you know."

The tears have settled. Her hand is steady as she brings the
cigarette to her lips. I look at the flat slope of her forehead, unmoving despite her grief. I think for a moment that she's not all
that sad about the death of her ex-husband, that she may enjoy
the notoriety of it. Either that or she's got enough Botox fed into
her skin to fell a small animal.

A quick sip of coffee then she looks up from under her lashes.
"Do you think whoever did this might come after us? Are we in
danger?"

I think of Geraldine Shine, cold and vulnerable on the church
floor. I think of her dead husband next to her. I glance over at the
kids' football, beneath the chair across the room. And I know I'm
about to lie because I've no idea where this case will end up or if

there'll be more victims but I do know that Jane Brennan will have enough nightmares to deal with over the coming weeks without adding a murderous phantom to her worries. So I offer her a weak smile and say: "There's no reason to think so, Mrs. Brennan."

She pulls a face. "No reason to think so! My husband's just been murdered!" She looks down, sniffs again.

I swallow down the urge to correct her, to remind her that Conor was her ex-husband. Instead, I change the subject, attempt to seek out a connection between Sheridan and Healy. "Mrs. Brennan, do you go to church at all?"

She frowns. "No. Maybe for the odd wedding."

"Do you know the priest there?"

"I'd see him about but I wouldn't be able to name him. Why?"

"How about Conor?"

She gives a short laugh. "I don't think Conor's been to Mass since his First Communion."

I nod, get to the final question on my list. "And did he ever talk about his flatmate, Jimmy Lynch?"

Her head drops a little, her expression slowly closing over, fatigue and the reality of Conor's death drawing down her features. "No," she says, "he never mentioned him." She looks up, tears tipping over onto her cheeks, running tracks through her makeup. "I never asked."

I retrieve my card from my pocket, leave it on the table between us. "I've contacted the family liaison officer," I say quietly. "Her name's Joanne; she'll be in touch shortly. She'll answer any other questions you have, how to break the news to the children—"

She crumples forward, her hands over her face. "Oh God."

I stand, put my hand on her shoulder. "If there's anything else you can tell us about Conor that may help our investigation, anything at all, please phone. No matter how trivial it may seem to you. Once we know more, I'll be in touch again."

She nods into her hands.

"I'm sorry for your loss. Thank you for the coffee."

Back in the car, I pull the door shut and sit for a while. The connection to the Seán Hennessy case is perched in my chest, sharp claws closed tight. Jane Brennan's face appears briefly in an upstairs window, phone pressed to her ear, then she's gone again. I look out at the quiet street, smooth, freshly surfaced road, the sweeping redbrick driveways. I imagine Conor Sheridan shaking hands with a neighbor, talking about the weekend's match. The Dub colors beating in the wind from the gate. Or his work boots scuffing unsteadily up the pathway, each drunken footfall hitting its mark just in time to stop him from crashing into the road.

I wipe exhaustion from my face and take a steadying breath. Mid-morning and the day ahead is long.

OUR PLAINCLOTHES HAVE found their way to Conor Sheridan's place. Jimmy Lynch is secure. On my way to Whitehall, I take a detour by my flat to step under a hot shower. Drive tiredness from my eyes, the dead from my skin. The image of Conor Sheridan on the beach lives under my eyelids. Dark hair glowing in the moonlight. The stench catches my breath anew, as if I was still standing on that beach. I dry off, go to my bedroom. It's a mistake to sit down. Exhaustion wraps its thick arms around my chest. I force myself up, go to the wardrobe. Another pair of work trousers, the same as before, another sweater to fend off the wind.

Then it's food. Fuel, tasteless. A frozen meal of some sticky chicken curry. Not breakfast fare, but the mornings, days, and nights have melded into one. I eat the meal like it's meant to be eaten, without thinking, without sitting. Standing over the kitchen counter. I throw the container in the bin, take up my bag to leave.

But on the breakfast bar, a white envelope that I found in my postbox. The package from Owens. I take it up, sit on the sofa, and tear it open. As promised, the remainder of Hennessy's file. A cassette tape and another C4 envelope marked *WSP* in Owens's stiff handwriting.

I flick through the thin folder. There's not much. Maybe ten to fifteen pages, transcripts of the confession interview. I think of Conor Sheridan, whose words written for a local rag so many years ago are reaching out again. Linking his name to Hennessy's. The past unfurling.

Taking up the cassette, I turn it over, read *Interview with Seán Hennessy 13 August 1995* on yellowing tape across the back. I get up, go back to my bedroom. In the bottom of the wardrobe, I find a cassette player. Bringing it back to the living room, I put it on the coffee table, blow dust from the buttons, and plug it in. I set my phone to record and press *play.*

The tape squeals to a start then with a deep warble I make out the sound of crying.

A voice speaks out. The senior investigating officer at the time, Derek Ríordan.

Seán, you know why you're here? We talked about it in the car?

A cough, a jagged breath. "Yes."

It's okay, it will be okay.

There's a garbled sound then another choking cry. "I don't know what happened. I wasn't there."

Okay. Okay. We're just going to have a chat.

A sniff. "Okay."

We need to ask you some questions, all right?

"Yes."

And you've already agreed to that?

"Yes."

Seán, so we've spoken about how you can have a lawyer, if you'd like one?

"I don't know anyone."

We can assign one for you, if you'd like, but you've said you are happy to talk to us without one, right?

"I think so."

You know that at any time you can stop and we can get you a lawyer, right?

The voice calms. "Yes."

Okay. Interview with Seán Hennessy on 13 August 1995, conducted by Detective Derek Ríordan. Interview started at 9:17 P.M. Seán, can you tell me what happened to your family?

"They were killed. I don't know."

Who killed them?

"I don't know."

We have evidence that strongly suggests you murdered your father, your mother, and tried to murder your sister.

"I didn't. I didn't. I wasn't there."

Did you see it happening?

"No."

Who killed them?

"I don't know. When I came back they were all dead."

You turned up and they were already dead?

"Yes."

What did you see?

"Mam, on the lawn, Cara, my dad."

How did you know they were dead?

"I don't know. There was a lot of blood. They weren't moving. But maybe Cara . . ." Another choking cry.

What happened to your family?

"Someone killed them."

Who?

"I don't know."

So you came home, found them already dead on the back lawn. Gardaí everywhere?

"Yes."

Seán, we found your mother's blood and your sister's under your nails, all over your clothes. All the evidence suggests you murdered them.

"I didn't."

Seán, I understand why you'd want to do this. You didn't do badly. I know your dad was a violent man. I know how hard that is, living with someone like that. And you didn't do badly. You held off. You got to fifteen. That's a lot of pressure on your young shoulders. You've a few minors, yes, but nothing major. You've done well, living with the family you had. The situation as it was in your home. It was hard, right?

"Yes."

But you're not like your dad. I know that. This is not who you are; you didn't plan for this to happen, right?

"No."

But your dad, he was pushing you around. Anyone would snap living with that.

"I didn't do it."

Seán, no one understands what it's like to grow up in a home like yours. It was you or him, right? And your mam, why did she put up with him? Something had to give, to change. Your sister, she was too young. That leaves only one person to save things, right? That leaves only you. But you didn't plan this?

"No." [sound of crying]

It wasn't planned. Your dad, he must have come at you. Provoked you or went for your mam again. He did that sometimes?

"Yes."

So he went for your mam and you had to protect her.

"Yes."

So it was in the heat of the moment. You were protecting your mam. And maybe she got in the way a bit. Things got out of hand. The heat of the moment. So you struck out. But I need you to tell me: You didn't plan this, did you?

"No. I didn't."

Where did you get the knife, Seán? We found your collection under the bed. Was it one of your collection?

"Yes."

You're doing great. You're doing great. That's all I'm here to do is to help you let it out. Get your side of things. So you took the knife from your collection because you heard your dad start up?

"I guess."

You need to say it. For the tape, Seán.

"Yes. I took the knife."

And because you were frightened. Because your mam and sister

*were calling for help, you had to stop your dad, right? You
killed him.*

Another tremble of tears.

"I don't remember."

Okay. Okay. Take me through it. You had the knife?

"Yes."

*Your dad was at your mam again. You were scared. Wanted it
to stop, right?*

"Yes. Yes, I wanted it to stop."

Then what happened?

"I hit him." The words come out angry. Petulant.

With the knife?

"Yes."

Where?

There's a shuffle of noise and I imagine Seán's shaking hand,
still childlike, still thin with youth, reach up and act out the kill.

"Here and here."

His chest?

"Yes."

Did you hit him again? With the knife?

"I kept stabbing him." More energy to his voice, a fearful kind
of anger. "His chest, his arms."

Then what happened?

"He fell."

I stop the interview. Rewind the tape and eject it. There are
so many problems with his confession, I don't know where to
begin. No caution. Inducement and the promise the suspect will
"be okay." It's no surprise it was buried, but not before the damage was done. And physically, surely Ríordan should have noted
there wasn't a single wound, superficial or otherwise, found on

Seán Hennessy's body. With such a violent attack, that should have been a red flag.

I go to my laptop, open a search engine, and key in "Conor Sheridan" and "Seán Hennessy." There are only three results, all leading to the same page. I click on it. The article is with the *Clontarf Gazette*, the title reading:

CLONTARF STRUCK BY TRAGEDY.
TROUBLED SON MURDERS PARENTS.

I scan down the page.

Sunday evening brought the most heinous of crimes to Clontarf's quiet sunny doorstep. Much-loved banker John Hennessy and his wife, Bríd, were brutally attacked by their son, Seán Hennessy, 15, in the backyard of their home on Sunday afternoon. Their young daughter, Cara Hennessy, 10, was also grievously injured and remains in critical condition at Dublin's Mater hospital. Residents of Clontarf will remember John Hennessy's generous persona in relation to community.

I lean back from the screen. It's a story that I've heard countless times before. The tyrant husband, angel on the street, devil at home. The article goes on and Bríd disappears into the narrative completely, as does Cara.

Seán Hennessy, who is not a stranger to the hand of the law, is said to have murdered both his parents with a knife taken from a personal collection. A source close to the investigation reports that he remains in custody after confessing to the murders.

I tear open the white envelope from Owens. Remove Cara Hennessy's details. I've a twinge of guilt, like I'm looking at something I shouldn't. Her new identity, or not so new any longer; she has been Eva Moran for the majority of her life. Twenty-seven years old. She's a receptionist at a dental surgery. Nine to five. Her address, 130 kilometers west of Dublin in Athlone town.

I check the time. Work out the logistics of the day. Conor Sheridan's grisly death is heavy in my gut. The empty net of the Shine case. And now a fine, silken thread between the Hennessy conviction and these murders.

CHAPTER 14

ABIGAIL IS PICKING her way over Conor Sheridan's body. A surgical mask shields her mouth. Perspex goggles protect her eyes. Baz is white-faced, his lips pale and sealed shut. We're in the viewing area that overlooks the postmortem examination room.

I offer Baz a coffee and he shakes his head. "I can almost smell him from up here," he says. More color drops from his face. The case is eating hollows beneath his eyes, a fine dark stubble over his jaw. "Almost as bad as poor Alan Shine. Whoever is doing this killing has a strong stomach, all right. Can't imagine it was a bloody bed of roses, laying him out on the beach."

"No."

Abigail comes round the body, places a ruler along Conor Sheridan's chest, measures the wound from the bullet. The center of the wound is dark; a purple web of bruising fans outwards over pale pink skin.

"Why through the heart?" I say, thinking aloud.

It takes Baz a moment but he follows my eyes to the hole in Conor Sheridan's chest. "Why not?"

"It's a little soft, isn't it? You truss your victim up like a turkey, tie his wrists behind his back, strip him naked, to the waist at least. Kneel him before you execution style and then you go for the chest shot?"

"Could be personal, you know, like those victims you find slaughtered with a blanket over them, placed there by their killers in a sick act of kindness or some shit. It would make sense being that he was dressed up in his Sunday finest. A fucked-up gesture of respect or something."

"But if you hated someone that much, were eaten up by so much anger you stored their body in your home or wherever for days just so that you could lord it over their corpse, why wouldn't you spatter their brains all over the floor if you were going to shoot them?"

Baz is staring at me, his eyebrows high. He breathes out slowly. "You go dark sometimes, Sheehan. Too dark. Anyway, to blow his victim's brains out? Where would be the grace in that? I mean, thinking from the killer's perspective, you know."

It surprises me how much he's picked up on the mind of our killer. He returns his attention to the autopsy.

"He wrote an article, years ago, on the Hennessy case," I say.

Baz lifts his gaze away from the window, tilts his head to the side. "Oh?" And I hear it in his voice. A quiet little note of suspicion.

I rub my hands over my arms, try to warm the chill that's sweeping through my body. "Sheridan came down pretty heavy on Seán Hennessy. I think we might need to look at him again."

Baz draws in a long breath, his chest expanding under his suit. "Where's the motive?"

"Some people need nothing other than their own desire to kill."

"He has an alibi for the Shine murders. And we know this is the same killer." He turns to look at me. "The Shine murders took place somewhere between five and six on that Sunday. He took Geraldine's blouse back to her house around six thirty, when Hennessy says he was having his tea by the promenade and then also managed to be down the road at the pub with you by seven?" He lets out a puff of air. "He'd need to split himself in two to accomplish that."

I nod. "Maybe he could give us some more background on that article. On Conor."

"We need all we can get on this one." He stands, rubs the base of his back, straightens his spine. "Abigail has retrieved a synthetic fiber from an abrasion on Sheridan's cheek; could be from when he fell after being shot."

"Dare I ask if we've a time of death?"

"She can't give us anything specific. She reckons a few days prior to discovery, taking into account the rate of decomp and refrigeration." He pauses, then, "When was the last time you discharged a weapon?"

I let my hand drop from my face. "Could do with a visit to the shooting range."

He moves to the door, signs out. "So what's next? Our lovely Father Healy?"

"I wish, but we need to get to Conor Sheridan's flatmate before this gets into the press."

"Jimmy Lynch it is then so," he says, and heads for the exit.

I follow him outside, head to my car, open the door.

"I'm not going in that bone-rattler," he says, opening the passenger side of his own car. He gets in. "But you can drive. I'm wrecked," he says before he shuts the door.

I sigh, lock mine, and send a message to Helen to have it picked up. When I open the driver's side of Baz's car, the smell of pine hits me. I start the engine and put my hands on the steering wheel, my fingers squeaking over the leather cover. "Your car is way too clean for this job."

"Got it reworked," he says, his eyes closed. "Nice new hubs, valet, the lot."

"The smell is nose-strippingly fresh."

"I'm enjoying it while it lasts."

WE TAKE M50 SOUTH, come off on the N81, where the city buzz turns to a shifting kind of quiet, cranes and blocks of flats divide up the cool, gray sky. Baz is scrunched in a ball in the passenger seat, getting his forty winks while he can. It's hitting six and news of Conor Sheridan's murder will be trickling out.

"You awake?" I say to Baz.

He opens his eyes, glances at the clock in the car. "We're here?" He scrambles to check his phone.

"Almost." I slow for a traffic light, come to a stop.

A young fella, sweatpants riding low on his hips, a gray hoodie, a baseball cap perched like a trilby on the side of his head, stops at the edge of the road to give us the finger. Baz reaches out and pushes down the central locking.

"I hope the SOCO team have the sense to stay in the van until we get there," I say.

"You'd think so."

The light changes and I pull away. A small precinct opens up ahead of us. Boxy shop-fronts, peeling fascias, empty windows smeared in graffiti and swirls of white paint, a couple of cars tucked nose to pavement, glinting in the weak sunlight.

"We asking Lynch about McDonagh?"

I see the turnoff for Sheridan's flat to the left. I indicate, turn sharply. "Let's see how it plays out. It might be good not to make a big deal out of it yet. See if he trips himself up."

"I'll follow your lead."

"Gracious of you."

His phone buzzes. "It's Helen." He puts her on speaker and Helen's voice spills out between us.

"Right. So we've been trying to trace Conor Sheridan's last movements. We've got his car stopping at a garage just north of Tallaght. He parks and uses an ATM at the Square."

Hope stretches through me; it might be easy after all.

Helen continues. "We lost him then for a bit and thought we could run a later search at the same cameras, maybe catch him returning home. But no sign of him. Because he was found in Clontarf and his kids and family live there, we ran another search of his car in the Clontarf area and, bingo, we got him pulling into a car park in Fairview one week ago. Wednesday, the fifteenth of August. It was hitting ten P.M. on the cameras."

"It fits with Abigail's estimations on time of death. Is there a visual on him leaving?"

"No return journey for this fella. His car is still here. I'm out now with the forensics lads. The retrieval truck has arrived to take it in."

I check the GPS; we're almost at Sheridan's place. I pull down a one-way street. The buildings crowd over the car, a vacuum of concrete and wet, humid air. The SOCOs' humpback van is parked in the shadows a little bit down the way. No sign of Keith's van. His lot still processing Sheridan's scene. I pull up outside the apartment block, turn off the engine.

"He left midday and didn't get to Clontarf until ten at night?" I say. "He definitely stopped off somewhere. Can you keep working on CCTV, get some more sightings of his journey, maybe? We need to fill in those hours."

"Yes, Chief."

"Any phone? In the car?"

"No. Nothing on Cell Site. Wherever it is, it's turned off. The car was locked up, alarm activated. Quite tidy, the body of the car still smelled of wax, not even a half-drunk water bottle or an old parking ticket on the floor."

"Keep looking. Clancy phone?"

"No."

Everyone playing their own game here.

"We're about to enter Sheridan's place," I tell her. "Update on the car as soon as you can."

"Right you are, Chief."

Baz ends the call and I push open the car door. "Come on, let's get on this."

CONOR SHERIDAN'S FLAT is on the third floor of a five-story building. The façade a dirty cream, greening at the corners, paint peeling around the row of doorbells, Sheridan's name in faded blue ink on a slip of paper. I glance over the other names. There's no one who looks familiar. I push the button next to Sheridan's name. The intercom crackles after two rings.

"Hello?"

"Gardaí. May we come up?"

A stiff silence, then: "What the fuck do youse want?"

I look to Baz. Déjà fucking vu.

"We need to speak to you about Conor Sheridan."

The door buzzes, and we enter the building. There's no lift; the stairwell has that smell: piss, sweat, some stomach-churning chemical floral scent. There's a small disk of pink in the corner of the hallway where someone's thrown down a toilet freshener in an attempt to combat the pong of the joint. The mix is potent and in the humidity it grabs at the back of my throat. I head quickly up the stairs, hear a door unlock, open above us.

Two SOCOs, already suited, follow behind myself and Baz. On the final few steps, I extend a hand to one of them and she passes me two pairs of foot covers and gloves.

"Thanks," I say, and pocket them. "Hold back here for a moment; let us introduce ourselves. I'll call you in when we're ready."

The SOCO looks back down the stairwell, shares a worried look with her colleagues, holds her kit a little closer.

"Yes, ma'am," she says.

Baz and I move up the last few steps.

"You've probably condemned them to death," he mutters. "Stand still for long enough in this place, someone will steal the legs from under you."

"If anything's getting stolen, it's your car outside."

He laughs but there's a shot of alarm about it.

CHAPTER 15

LEANING OVER THE BANISTER is a heavy bloke, tattooed up his neck, white undershirt, stained, the works. His head, round as a bowling ball and almost as smooth, is glistening with sweat.

When I get level, I meet his eyes, a shifting brown, narrow gaze, his forehead a ledge of thick flesh.

"Detective Sheehan and this is Detective Harwood," I say. "Jimmy Lynch?"

He looks over Baz in a way that seems like he might throttle him just because he could. "Yeah."

Baz clears his throat. "It's about your flatmate, Conor Sheridan."

"Conor? What's happened then?" I watch the man, the wee cogs turning like a drugged clock in his head.

"I'm afraid we don't have good news, Mr. Lynch. Conor Sheridan was found dead this morning," Baz says. He waits for Lynch's reaction but the man continues to stare at him as if Baz had only informed him that the weather was lousy.

Baz spreads his hands. "We're up to our neck in it," he says, like he's talking to a friend. "We've nothing. Nothing. We were relying on you, ye see, to give us a bit of background, something for us to work on."

As he speaks I see the effect on the bull-neck in front of me, his frame slowly straightening, his body language loosening. This is a man who wants to be the front-runner. He won't have anyone tell him he has to talk, even if it's only about the fucking weather. He'll be the one making the decisions here.

He looks at me, his eyes gliding down my front then back again. "I suppose youse 'ill want to come in then?"

Baz smacks his hands together. "That'd be a great help, Jimmy."

Jimmy Lynch turns, ducks his considerable size into the flat, indicating we should follow. The door opens into a small kitchenette, shabby with less of the chic; the bin overflowing with pizza boxes, beer cans stacked up around it like beaten sentries.

Jimmy sets his large body into a La-Z-Boy with a huff. "I suppose yis can sit there," he says, motioning to a grubby white sofa.

"Thanks," I say, but remain standing.

Baz sinks down into the fabric, sits forward, his hands loosely clasped between his knees.

"Mr. Lynch," I begin, and he turns, gives me a wary look. "Conor Sheridan's body was found on Clontarf beach early this morning. We believe he was murdered and we've a warrant to search his room."

He doesn't budge. Not one stinking millimeter, not a flicker of shock registers on his face, but I see his hands tighten on his legs. "Nothing to do with me."

Baz holds up a palm. "No, no. But if you felt able to answer a few questions about him, so we can get a feel for where he was at, that'd be great. You know yourself how these things go?"

His dark eyes narrow. "Why would I know that?"

"Right so. Why would ye? Could you tell us when was the last time you saw him?"

"A week, a few days, more. I can't remember the exact time. I work night shift at the Aldi depot, sleep or chill most of the day. Ships in the night, both of us. By the time I'm up and going, sure Conor's only in the door from his job."

"Were you working last night?" Baz asks.

"I was, yeah."

Baz nods. "What was he like as a housemate? Did yis get on?"

"Private."

"Private?"

"Yeah, like his room there now. He locked it, whether he was in or out. Like fucking Fort Knox that place, more metal on the inside of that door than a Swiss bank vault."

I step closer, lean against the breakfast bar. Something crunches under my elbow and I straighten quickly. "Do you have a key?"

"No, I don't. I reckon if he wanted all and sundry going in an' out of that room, he woulda left it open."

Baz laughs. "Good one."

Jimmy looks down to hide a half-smile, pleased with himself for making Baz laugh.

Baz continues. "He must have had something in there he wanted to keep quiet, like. A secret."

"Or out," Jimmy says.

"Out?"

"Well, I lock me fucking front door not because I've got a

fucking secret"—he gives a wave around the room—"but because I don't want every Tom, Dick, or Harry getting in, bothering me."

"You think he was feeling threatened."

He shrugs. "Don't fucking know. He started up with that when he got clean a few months ago. He liked his drink, you know, Conor did. He was grand on the sauce; reckon the detox made him paranoid. Or opened his fucking eyes. The world's a happier fucking place when you're bat-eyed drunk, isn't it?"

"Don't I know it," Baz says.

I lean back, peer down the little annex behind me, see three rooms, the door at the end open, I can see the edge of a bath, a charming shade of vomit green. Another door, open, daylight pouring out into the hallway, and a door opposite, sealed tight. I send a quick text to the lead SOCO, *Bring the enforcer, door locked.*

"You said Conor got clean. His ex-wife said he was still drinking heavily."

"I've yet to meet an ex-wife who doesn't love caking her rejects in shite, have you? Don't listen to that nasty piece of work. Fucking ruined Conor, if you ask me. Took his kids, his money, then shacked up in his house like a fucking cuckoo with some ponce." His face is reddening and he takes a moment, his nostrils flare, his eyes fix on the window. Then:

"When I first met Conor, he was the life and soul, 'tis why I moved in with him. Work kept us kinda busy but on the occasional day we'd be free together, we'd head to the pub there on the corner, go on a bender. It was grand.

"He was lonely though. The type of man that needed a woman, you know. Not that he wasn't up to his groin in bitches any time we went out but he needed a partner. He missed that.

So a while back he signed up to some fucking online yoke. He was always trying to get me to go on there, meet the woman of my dreams. But I got that woman right here." He flexes his right hand, smiles, then throws me a quick glance. "No offense like, but I don't need no fucking headache, you know."

"Did he meet someone online?" I ask.

"Yeah, sure, isn't that what I'm telling ye. Grand little thing from the look of her picture but you never can tell with these yokes, I said that to him. He eased off the drinking soon after that, every fucking minute he'd be in his room, I'd hear the tap and beep of his computer. Thought he was in love, poor fucker."

I think of the crime scene investigators, waiting in the damp stink of the stairwell. "When was this?"

He pats the arm of the chair. "Dunno. Maybe about five months or so ago."

"And that's when he bought the locks. For his room?" Baz asks.

"Yeah. Soon after that. Stopped everything that was any craic really. Took to running, out most evenings after work, eating better. But private, like I say."

Meaning he stopped going on the piss with his mate. The resentment for it chimes in his voice.

"How long have you been flatmates?"

He tips his head then after a few moments answers. "Probably near on five years now. From after the divorce. Yeah."

"That's a long time."

"Suppose it is."

"And in that five years, he never had any visitors?"

"Not that I know of. Could have been shimmying up the drainpipe unbeknown to me."

"How about family? Did they visit?"

"Do you need me to write it down for you? He had no fucking visitors. Ever."

I wait for him to catch his breath, then: "Mr. Lynch, we need to look at his room. It shouldn't take any more than a couple of hours."

He loops his hands over the back of his head, settles further into the recliner. "Not much I can do about it, by the sounds of it. Just keep outta my fucking room; make that clear to your people. I'm not under investigation here for nothing."

You can tell when people have been inside; there's a brazen kind of defense about them. They know their rights and then some. Jimmy Lynch has that in spades.

"No, you're not." I turn, open the door, and wave in the crew. The two SOCOs enter and I point down the short hallway. "The door on the right."

They go at it with the enforcer, make short work of Conor Sheridan's door.

"The fuck?" Jimmy Lynch is on his feet.

"We'll talk to your landlord, get it fixed," I say, my hands out.

He swears again then sits, one eye on the business end of the flat, tracking the SOCOs as they move into Conor Sheridan's room.

"Do you know whether anyone would have wanted to harm Conor?" Baz directs Jimmy's attention back to the matter at hand.

"Not one."

"How about how he was, you know, did he seem stressed or frightened to you?"

He laughs. "A man like Conor doesn't show that kind of side now, does he? He coulda been pissing his bedsheets in fear every night and you'd be none the wiser. He withdrew a bit is all I'm saying but it didn't feel like he was fucking scared, only he'd met this bird and was trying to get himself on the straight and narrow, rise above the bullshit that his ex was throwing at him."

"Did he mention the last time he saw Jane Brennan?"

"That's where he was off to, wasn't it? Last time I saw, he got into his car to take the kids to the cinema or some such."

"It didn't seem strange to you that he didn't come back?"

He rubs a hand over his face and there is a flash of something in his eyes, a brief haunted look. "No. It didn't."

"Really?"

He holds up a hand, examines something on his knuckles. "Just thought he'd fallen off the wagon, gone on a bender, you know. That woman knew how to push his buttons. If anyone could ha' driven him to drink, it was her. I assumed he got there, plans had changed, and she stopped him seeing the kids. It happened often enough when the fit took her, manipulative bitch."

I give Baz that look. He stands. "Mr. Lynch, thank you so much for your time. We're going to have a look at the room now. It might be easier if you had somewhere else to be."

Jimmy lets out a laugh that could be a snarl. "You want me to leave me own home. I don't think so." He puts his feet up, crosses them at the ankles, and Baz sits back down.

I'm already moving away. The door to Conor Sheridan's room is smashed at the lock, splinters, slices of wood are scattered over the thin carpet.

The thing that strikes me most as I look into the room is the neatness of it. The bed is wide, crisp white sheets taut over the double mattress, clean dove-gray walls, the desk and bedside table, the wardrobe all a deep walnut, the dark carpet, thick and plush, looks new. I can't help noticing similarities to Jane Brennan's house. As if she'd decorated it herself or maybe Conor was attempting to re-create one little piece of his past in the small flat.

The SOCOs are dusting, taping, photographing. One of them pulls the sheets and bedcovers back in a confident sweep. Another is emptying pieces of laundry into a bag. Bank statements, letters, passport, scraps of paper removed. His computer, keyboard, hard drive are checked, sealed, and carted out of the room. His life, like his body, disassembled, broken down, so that we can find his killer.

The lead SOCO turns to me. "Is there anything in particular we're looking for, Chief?"

"If you can find a trace of a girlfriend, name or otherwise." I look around the room, check the electric sockets. A phone charger still plugged in next to the bed. "His phone if you can get it but that'd be the dream, all right. And"—I take a deep breath— "any details pertaining to an old case, the name of Hennessy."

The SOCO nods; the hood of her suit rustles. She pulls the paper mask at her throat over her mouth and slides open Conor Sheridan's wardrobe.

I step back out into the hallway. Phone the local station, request a uniform for the door so the SOCOs can work without Jimmy Lynch breathing his hot dog–breath down their backs. When I hang up, I return to the kitchen–living room.

Baz is still on the grease-marked sofa. The words *All-Ireland* come to me, and I know he's setting up a little bromance with our man Jimmy, bonding over Gaelic football. It's all good. If we need to talk to Jimmy again, it helps to have him think Baz gets him. Sees beyond the tattooed neck, the puffy cheeks, the flat nose, and swollen hands broken in the wee hours after a rowdy day on the booze, probably on some other yobo's face.

When he sees me, Baz stands, holds out a hand to Lynch. "Jimmy, thanks a million, all right."

The man puts his hand in Baz's, gives it a reluctant shake, his face set in a grimace, not wanting to touch the hand of any law enforcement officers unless it's to snap their fingers from their wrists. "Sure, it's no bother, I suppose," he mutters.

Baz holds out his card and Jimmy takes it gingerly between his fingers, as if it were a bomb about to go off.

"Anything else come into your head about Conor, even if it seems like it's nothing, gives us a call, right?" Baz says.

"Right you are," Jimmy replies with a good deal of awkwardness.

"Grand. See ya."

"There's an officer on the way to help out with the investigation. He should be here in a couple of minutes," I say. Lynch's mouth twists, and I can see the objection forming on his lips. Before he can speak I say, "Thank you, Mr. Lynch," then walk out of the flat into the sickly stink of the stairwell.

Down on the street, Baz folds himself into the car. "He says he has an alibi for the fifteenth and nineteenth of August. He's given me his time sheet. I'll check with his work. But he gave it up easily enough."

"Fuck." I chew the tip of my nail. "He's given us the economy seats on his flatmate though, lots of filler. He seems way too calm about the amount of locks on Conor's door. They'd been living together for half a decade then suddenly your roomie has enough metal on the inside of his room door to sink the *Titanic*?

I don't think he would have been all, it's your room, mate, each to his own?"

Baz pulls on his seatbelt. "So they might have had it out a bit, so what?"

"Not that they had it out. But maybe it wasn't just anyone Conor Sheridan wanted to keep out of his room—maybe it was Jimmy himself? It would explain why Conor locked it during the day. Why the heavy locks on his room but a flimsy bolt on the front door? Whatever happened or whatever the reason, it only started five months ago." I turn the key in the ignition; I don't need to add that five months would've been just before Seán Hennessy got out.

CHAPTER 16

BY THE TIME I get back to the office, it's knocking on six P.M. On the way back from Lynch's, I left Baz off at his flat for food, a shower, and a change of clothes, then I took a taxi back to town. The team at the office look harassed and tired but the air in the room is filled with an intense concentration. Someone has added Hennessy's case to the board, establishing a possible link. I wince when I see it; Clancy is not going to be a fan of that. The windows have been cranked open, and the buzz and holler of Dublin city is whistling through the heat of the room. Keith Hickey is leaning against the partition at Helen's desk, mouthing off about the big box of nothing they scraped from Sheridan's car.

Conor Sheridan's computer and hard drive have arrived ahead of me and are wrapped in plastic next to Steve's station. But there's no Steve. Emer Kelly sits at his desk, pale but bright-eyed and huffing at whatever mess he's left her with. Emer is our assistant forensic computing expert. Although we try not to use the title "assistant" to her face.

"Steve had an emergency." She makes air quotes around the word *emergency.*

"Emergency?"

"Toothache." She turns back to the desk, scans the debris of his work, picks up a half-drunk energy drink with two fingers and drops it into a nearby bin.

She glances up. "You look like the dead."

Emer's not one to let authority get in the way of an opinion. I like her.

"Thanks. It's been a day. Anything new on the CCTV from the car park and Sheridan's movements?"

She flicks a few keys and brings up a hazy shot of Fairview car park. It's dark. Two streetlamps throw dull yellow light on the scene. Wide puddles shine across the dark tarmacadam. There's a couple of vehicles parked in the spaces closest to the shop but one car sits alone off to the side. Impossible to tell the color, maybe blue, certainly dark.

"This is Sheridan's car," she says. "No movement in the past week, a Nissan Sunny, old, like, '94 reg."

She rewinds the footage then plays it. Conor Sheridan gets out of his car. He keeps his head low, shoulders high, a protective posture against thin rainfall. He's dressed in dark trousers, possibly jeans, a pale or gray sweater, black T-shirt poking out at the neck and down over his jeans. Trainers on his feet. No suit.

"Go back," I say, and she rewinds the recording.

Conor Sheridan pulls into the car park. Slowly. No rush. He gets out. Pats down his pockets, finds his wallet. He locks the car. Then turns and heads into the shop. The clock in the corner ticks on. Emer speeds up the film and after ten minutes he exits, a shopping bag in his hand.

"You can't get any closer on the bag?"

"We tried and no. It pixelates. Helen is working with the staff to see if we can get the contents. A receipt or something. So far, nothing."

Halfway on his return to the car, Conor Sheridan stops. He takes out his phone. Holds it to his ear. He looks out over the car park, his elbow high, his face partially illuminated by the light of the phone.

The call finishes. He turns away from the car, walks, more speed this time, toward the car park exit, the bag hitting his legs, twisting at the handles as he goes. He turns right and disappears out of the frame. I remain glued to the screen, but nothing else comes. He doesn't return. People come and go from the shop, get into cars, drive away, not knowing that a dead man walking has breezed by them.

"That's it?"

"The store has CCTV here." She indicates one of the lamp-posts. "It points toward the shop door. Steve was working on it to see if he could pick up a reflection perhaps, but apart from him exiting the shop, he got nothing. However, I had a closer look." She throws me her best patronizing smile.

She keys in more instructions and another field of vision appears on the computer. The shop-front lit up. The automatic doors slide closed and she pauses the recording. She waits. Waits for me to see what she's seeing. Sheridan's reflection in the shop window. Less than a silhouette but it's there; the white of Sheridan's shopping bag first, then his shadow. His arm is up, as if he's waving to someone. A car, a blur of golden light and darkness, captured on the glass front of the store. Another fragment of Conor Sheridan's last moments.

I study the shape of the car. There's no way to tell who's driving; all that's visible to my eye is a slumping shadow.

Emer is studying my face. "If I zoom in and improve the quality of the image, I might be able to get the make of the car." She shrugs. Tiny shoulders shift beneath her sweater. No promises but likely. "I can run some measurements around the image. Wheel hub height. The angle of the front lights"—then pointing to the rear of the car—"the back." She returns to the mouse, clicks *play*. "Watch him," she says, and she means Conor Sheridan's reflection.

She plays the video, staggers the frames. They jump forward slowly and again I focus on the glass front of the shop. My eyes pick up the image quicker than they did before, now that I know what I'm looking for, and I see Conor Sheridan raise his arm, the shopping bag like a white flag in his hand. The car slows briefly then speeds off again. I feel a stirring of excitement. Whoever is driving that car could be Conor Sheridan's killer.

"You think you'll be able to get a car make from that?"

She replays it, her face intent. "Maybe."

I frown down at the screen. "Keep at it; if you need other resources then let me know."

"Why would I need other resources?" she asks.

"Right," I say. "Good. Also, I want to know who Sheridan phoned before he went into the shop. I'm going to work from home this evening. I'm on my mobile."

She gives a gentle tip of her head in acknowledgment then turns back to her screen.

I PUSH OPEN THE DOOR of my flat. Drop my bag on the floor inside the door. It's cold but quiet and empty, and I've never felt more grateful. I kick off my shoes, shrug out of my coat, then fold it over the back of one of the chairs at the breakfast bar. I move to the kitchen, flick on the kettle, and check the fridge. The date on the milk says last week sometime but it looks okay. I unscrew the top, sniff it, then regret it. I carry it to the sink and empty the carton down the drain then turn off the kettle. I eye the wine rack. Two cheap bottles of red and a nice Sauvignon. I put the white in the freezer then check the heating, swearing silently at the fact that it's August and I need to turn up the thermostat.

It takes a half hour or so for the flat to warm, and I spend my time under a throw on the sofa, the TV murmuring quietly across the room, some tame crime drama playing out. The on-screen detectives dour and serious, stringing together their cases with outrageous budgets and tech and a killer that anyone in an armchair could pick out from the get-go.

I take up my phone, scroll through my last message from Baz. Jimmy Lynch's alibi is solid. His time sheets verified; three different colleagues attested to his presence at work. The sensation of this case sliding out of my grasp is sickening. Every lead turns to dust before we can get a hold. I sigh, throw down my phone, then reach out to the coffee table where a printout of the *Clontarf Gazette* displays Conor Sheridan's article on the Hennessys. The date on the newspaper, August 14, 1995. There's a small thumbnail picture of Conor next to his name. The image—a half-profile shot, eyes downcast as if he's contemplating something serious—is a little too staged. I wonder did Jane take the picture for him, direct him into a pose that seemed right for a journalist.

I put down the paper again and let my eyes close. The sound of traffic on the street outside is a soothing, gentle thrum and I can feel sleep reaching through my body. Conor Sheridan's face plays on my closed lids, at first smiling then stiff and cold. Dead.

I wake to the buzz of the doorbell, my neck aching, my heart jumping in my chest. I straighten and look down at my phone but the screen is blank. I get up, go to the intercom, press the answer button.

"It's me," Baz's voice comes through the speaker. "Let me in."

I push the button and unlatch the door then remembering the wine in the freezer, I go to the kitchen to retrieve it.

He comes in, a bag of takeaway in one hand and another bottle of wine in the other. He closes the door with his foot then joins me in the kitchen, setting the takeaway on the breakfast bar.

"Chinese?"

I reach up to the cupboard, remove two glasses. "How do you know I haven't eaten?"

He snorts, reaches across me to the fridge, and opens the door, nods at the barren shelves. "Thought so. You manage to find a recipe that makes a meal out of nothing yet?"

"Very funny."

He returns to the bag, removes what looks like enough takeaway to feed the entire Bureau, and sets about opening them. "Even got fortune cookies."

"Please, no."

We move to the coffee table. I pour the cold white then throwing a cushion down, I sit cross-legged on the floor. Baz passes me a plate then helps himself to noodles and beef and tucks in happily.

"So, Healy's in custody," he says between mouthfuls. "Thought I'd let him sit awhile inside."

"He say anything when you picked him up?"

"Nope, quiet as a church but I'm not making the same mistake I did last time, letting him think he's got the control here. Let him sweat it out in a cell overnight and see if he's still up for picking and choosing what he tells us tomorrow."

"Healy definitely knows more than he's let on but I still feel he's managed to walk into this drama rather than being the orchestrator of it." I scoop up a spoonful of rice; it's sweet, mixed through with egg, peas, and onion. I hadn't realized how hungry I was until I started eating. I load more of it onto my plate then take a drink of wine.

"Until we get more from him, we can't say that for certain and I'm not having some self-righteous priest thinking he's above the law; those days are gone," he says and pauses, refills his glass. "But I know what you mean. It's all a bit obvious, isn't it?"

I nod, my mouth full. After a moment I say, "One of the victims dressed in priest's vestments. The scene at the church. If I were Healy and had murdered the Shines, I wouldn't lay out my victims in my own church, a few hundred feet from where I live."

Baz wipes his mouth with a paper napkin, takes up his wineglass. "Well, I've done a little digging on our man Healy."

"This sounds good."

"As he says, he's been with St. Catherine's a couple of years. He was moved on from his last diocese, which was in Limerick, would you believe? And I thought, that's a bit of a shift, isn't it?"

"It happens."

"Yeah, especially when there's a concern about the priest in question. Turns out our Healy is not as celibate as the church likes their priests. Turns out he'd been seeing a few of the women in his last parish; husbands found out and he was pulled out of there before he could even get his zipper up."

I push my plate away. Lean up against the wall and stretch out my right leg. The muscles tighten and I massage the stiffness away then take another drink of wine, feel it warm my limbs.

Baz watches the movement but doesn't say anything.

"Well that certainly fits in with the character we know. Cultivating relationships with married women."

"Exactly," he says.

Sheridan's newspaper article is lying on the floor beneath the coffee table.

He picks it up and holds it out. "How are we doing on the Hennessy connection?" He carries on before I can answer. "A guy writes an article about the Hennessys and seventeen years later, he's murdered for it?"

I sigh. "Perhaps I wouldn't be so fixated on it if I wasn't looking through the files for Tanya."

"Or if it wasn't for Hegarty's pushing. Or Clancy's sidestepping?"

Despite the wine, I feel a prickle of defensiveness on Clancy's behalf. "He's under a lot of pressure."

"We all are," Baz replies, a sulk in his voice.

"Seán Hennessy might not have killed his parents," I say suddenly.

Baz sets his plate to the side, looks across the table at me. "Oh?"

"Mistakes were made."

Understanding widens in his eyes. "So, John Hennessy killed his wife after all. Tried to kill his daughter. They put away an innocent man. Not even a man, a child!"

I shrug, swirl the wine in my glass, throw the remainder down my throat. "The sister's testimony is the only thing left that says otherwise." I feel the past swell behind me, Bríd Hennessy, Seán, and the inevitable terror that awaits them. I search for a change of subject so the dead aren't walking around our conversation. "How's the lodger? Adrianne?"

"Driving me nuts. We now have a group fund. In my own flat. She says it's for household necessities, like dish soap."

I laugh and feel the case lift a little from my shoulders. "That's organized."

"I barely even use the stuff."

"That might explain a lot." He snorts at that. "She's attractive," I tease.

He shoots me a hard look then, "If ever there was a time when the phrase 'looks aren't everything' applied, this is it."

I look at the empty bottle of wine and contemplate the hangover that awaits me tomorrow. Neither of us speak for a while; my eyes drift to the window, where I've neglected to pull the curtains and the winking lights of the city play out in the distance. I get up, collect the empty meal cartons, and take them to the kitchen.

"She's not my type," Baz says suddenly.

"I don't think detectives get to have a type."

He nods, finishes off his wine. "You mind if I crash here? I shouldn't drive."

"I'll get the spare sheets."

RYAN WALKS THROUGH the office door. He unhooks a leather satchel from over his head.

"Got not one but two angles of footage from your man down at the chippie. Tony," he announces.

He comes across the room, throws his bag under his desk, and faces me, his hands on his hips. I straighten from Helen's computer, wait for him to tell me what he's got, because he's got something, he just wants to make sure we're all listening.

Helen looks back at her screen, pulls her chair in. I think I hear a small grunt of disgust come from her throat.

Ryan continues. "They'd a camera over the counter that takes in the door from the inside and another over the exit of the shop facing the seawall that takes in the street immediately outside and as far as the promenade. And"—he wags a finger in the air to no one in particular—"they worked. Hennessy enters the venue at ten to six, gets his order of chips, and out he goes. Another camera at the front of the shop shows him heading across the street to a bench on the prom where he stays stuffing his trap for forty minutes or so and then we pick him up heading back up the street. I imagine to meet youse," he says to me.

He holds up a USB.

There's something satisfying about ruling out a suspect. You might think it should be otherwise, but every path followed and eliminated is one step closer to the truth. We're not blinded or immobilized by choice. Every name crossed off leaves only the guilty behind. And I'm not going to lie: To be able to put Seán Hennessy to one side in this case feels great.

"Good work, Ryan. Set it up and send the footage to my computer." My eyes now firmly on Father Patrick Healy, I take up his background info from Helen's desk and smile my thanks.

"Where's Baz?"

"He's in room one with the priest," she replies.

"Thanks." I head for the interview room.

I open the door and settle down on the other side of the glass.

Baz, fresh-faced, clean shaven, ready to challenge Father Healy on how his phone managed to follow the same track as Geraldine Shine's directly after her murder.

Baz gives the priest a reassuring smile. An interview has its own psychology. We want witnesses and suspects like Healy to trust us, want them to believe we're on their side. We rely on a man's capacity to always think the worst couldn't happen. That no matter what they tell us, they will be okay. And because humans want to believe that, eventually they do begin to talk. And when they do, a tongue-tied perp can morph into a grand orator.

"Father, here we are again. Good to see you."

Baz's voice is a boom of energy. The priest gives him a nervous smile.

"So, now. What we got." Baz opens up a folder. "Ho-ho. Right, yes." He becomes serious. "We're going to ask a few questions. Just like the last time."

The priest nods then remembers he needs to speak up. "Yes."

Baz presses the recorder and a red light appears. "We're recording this interview and also, you'll see"—he turns in his seat and points to a camera in the corner of the ceiling—"we have the ol' video going now too. Very high-tech. You okay with that?"

"Yes. Yes."

"Interview between Father Patrick Healy and Detective Barry Harwood, conducted at 6:06 on Thursday the twenty-third of August 2012. Father Healy has declined the offer of legal representation at this time."

He gifts Healy with a wide smile. "You understand you're not under arrest but that information collected during this interview may be used against you in a court of law?"

The priest glances about the room, eyes flitting to the camera. When he answers, he leans forward a bit as if speaking into a microphone. "Yes."

"When we interviewed you last, you said"—he pulls the folder toward him, reads his notes—"you left the church at approximately one fifteen and did not return until gardaí were already at the scene for the murders of Ger and Alan Shine, on Sunday, the nineteenth of August 2012. Is that correct?"

Healy swallows. He opens his mouth then closes it, resting a fingertip across his lips as if silencing himself. After a short pause he says, "That's correct."

"So you were not in the church between the hours of two and seven P.M.?"

"No."

"In our last interview you said that you had been doing your rounds, or visiting parishioners, but later retracted that and said that you had, in fact, been in a pub near Howth. Is that correct?"

"Yes." Confident. "I was in the Anchor."

"Thanks. Yes, the barman verified that you arrived at the Anchor at two thirty and you had a pint of lager shandy and a fish and chips."

"Yes." He nods along with his answer, content with himself.

"What time did you leave the pub?"

"I'm not sure. I took my time."

Baz spreads his hands. "Roughly."

"I guess shortly before I arrived back at the church."

"You arrived at the crime scene at eight forty-five P.M., according to my colleague."

"Yes."

"That's a long drink."

The priest smiles, sheepish. "Maybe I had more than one. I know I shouldn't, driving and all."

Baz looks down at the folder again. He removes a receipt and passes it across the table. "This is your order and receipt from the Anchor pub. It states the time as 2:40 P.M. One lager shandy and one portion of fish and chips. Paid for by card at 3:47. The barman said you left shortly afterward."

Father Healy rubs his head; his fingers brush his ear. It reddens. "Oh wait. Maybe I did. That's it. I took a drive."

"You took a drive?"

"Yes."

"Okay. Where?"

There's a knock on the door behind me and I turn away from the viewing window.

"Sorry, ma'am," Helen says. "The commissioner, Mrs. Hegarty, is here and wants to speak with you."

I look back through the open door. Donna Hegarty stands at the top of the room, her face turned up on the case board. Every eye in the office is focused on the back of her pale blue cardigan.

"Christ. What's she doing here?"

"Jane Brennan's gone to the press. She's mentioned the article Conor Sheridan wrote against Seán Hennessy."

"Fuck's sake." I turn back to the window. "Tell her I'll be out in five." I feel Helen's hesitation, torn between whose orders to follow. Mine or Hegarty's. No one wants to return to the commissioner empty-handed but short of laying my decapitated head in Helen's hands, nothing we do will make Donna Hegarty happy. She's on the career move of the century. Eventually, I hear the door behind me click closed.

"Did you return to the church?" Baz is asking.

Healy can't meet Baz's eyes. Fingers meshed on the table, thumb turning over thumb. "No."

The ground is falling away beneath Healy's feet, and as if sensing it, he draws them further beneath his chair.

"You said Geraldine contacted you on the day she died. What did her message say?"

"Just that she needed to meet up. She thought I could come over for some lunch."

"Lunch?"

The priest nods.

"We're going to need to seize your phone, Father," Baz says, and the priest nods again. "Apart from arranging these weekly meet-ups, were you in touch with her for any other reason?"

The color in Healy's face deepens. "No."

Baz stretches his arms back over his head. "You know mobile phones make it so easy for us nowadays. If a phone is on, we can actually follow its whereabouts, you know. As you travel"—he walks his fingers through the air—"as a mobile phone travels, it hits off masts and sends out signals so we can work out its location. Pretty handy for us, right?"

Healy swallows.

"Are you hearing me, Father?"

The priest looks down. He's not going to give up until he knows he's beaten.

"After she was murdered, Geraldine's phone continued to travel," Baz says. "Without her! Her phone went from the area of the church all the way out to Cliff Walk. And you know whose phone also traveled the same path at the exact same time?"

I see the priest's chin dimple; his mouth turns down. "Yes," he whispers, shame laced through his voice.

"How was that?"

Tiny, tiny voice. "I took it."

"You took her phone?"

I can see Healy's lips moving. Clenched hands rise to his chest. He's praying. After a moment he sniffs, tugs the handkerchief out of his breast pocket, wipes his face, his nose. "I . . . I came back probably around six thirty. I went into the church . . ." He clears his throat, his fist over his mouth, and the skin wobbles over his collar. His lips whiten, disappear into his face. "I didn't see them at first. I walked into the vestry to check it was set for the morning. When I came out again, something felt off. I couldn't put my finger on it but then it hit me. The smell . . ." His hand flutters to his nose. "Something rotten, and blood. That's when I saw them in the middle of the aisle."

"What did you do next?"

"When I saw who it was, I panicked. I know how it would have looked. The message from her phone to me. There really wasn't anything else on the phone but I panicked. I was supposed to meet with her. I didn't want to be connected with this at all. It was stupid but I was scared. I got some gloves from the vestry. I tried to just take the phone but when I removed it there was a message on the screen."

"A message? From you?"

"No. From her own number, like she'd sent it to herself. It was just one word."

"What did it say?"

"Victim."

His hands are shaking on the table. He curls his fingers in on his palms. "The blood, it was still warm," he says, tears in his voice.

"You took her bag?"

"Yes."

"What did you do with it?"

"I drove out to Cliff Walk, like you said, and threw the lot into the sea."

"Can you be more specific? Where?"

"I'm not sure." Then, "Oh wait, there was a trash bin. I was going to just drop it in there but in the end I thought it might be found, so I threw it over the cliff face."

"Can you describe the bag?"

"Erm, black, PVC. It was shiny. Not big. A clutch, I think they call it."

I pick up the phone, dial Ryan's desk.

"Chief?"

"Tell the team at Cliff Walk that we're looking for a black PVC clutch bag. Dropped in the sea below. There's a trash bin next to where it was dropped. Check the bin too."

"Copy that, Chief."

Baz steps out of the interview room. Less buoyant. He shakes his head at me, and we walk the short hallway to my office.

"Victim!" he says when he closes the door. "Could have done with that little nugget four days ago. What do you think?"

"I think he's just about stupid enough to be telling the truth."

"Yeah. What a piece of work. How could he feck off leaving his housekeeper fifty yards away when he knew there was a murderer in the area?" His face lights up. "We can charge him with obstruction."

"And have the media saying we messed up when we release

him. No." And his face falls. "Hegarty is literally breathing down our necks. She's on the case room floor."

"What the fuck's she doing here?"

"She owns our backsides, remember?" I sit at the computer. "Jane Brennan has sold out to the press. We need our ducks in a row on Hennessy." I open up the footage that Ryan secured.

"At least the alibi will make her happy," Baz says, leaning out the door to watch Hegarty.

The first piece of footage is slightly obscured by dull weather, rain clouding up the lens of the camera. But I can see a tall figure, fit, dark jacket pulled up around his neck, baseball cap over his head. It could be Hennessy. His back is to the camera. In his hand, a brown bag. White trainers, jeans, similar clothing to Hennessy's when he met Tanya and me at Smith's bar. He steps off the pavement. I lean closer, try to get a better view through the haze of misty rain. He crosses the street to a bench on the green looking out on the promenade and the sea. The scope of the footage barely covers the bench. But I can make out that he sits. I fast-forward the film, watch the minutes count out to 6:46, obliterating our killer's window for entering the Shine house.

Baz is looking over my shoulder. "That him? Not a particularly comfortable day to be eating chips on the seafront."

"It looks like it's him. Wait a moment." I click the second piece of footage. It's much clearer. Seán Hennessy's face clear as day at the counter of the chip shop.

I sigh. "That's definitely him." I look at Hennessy's face for a while. The front of his hat casts his face in shadow but there's no mistaking his identity.

I sink away from the computer. "Finish up with Healy; I'll deal with Hegarty."

"Thanks."

Baz goes back into the room. I sit for a moment. I take out my phone, find the next short clip of the documentary footage, and press *play.*

Seán Hennessy stretches out his fingers. When he speaks, his eyes don't quite meet the camera. They lift and then slide to the floor, dipping in and out of memory.

"Hope is a four-walled cell with a heavy metal door. After five years pushing against nothing, I began to see my life anew. I was twenty. It was a gift. Here I was, inside Pandora's box. And no one was going to lift the lid. I began to accept that. And I relished the safety. No more accusations. Whatever I was guilty of, time was eroding away my sins. Making me again. I applied to college to study. Philosophy. I exercised. I was fitter, healthier in mind and body than I'd ever been. I joined the library. Filled my cell with books. And I read. Read. Read.

"Inside I'd created a whole other place to be. And no one could take it from me. I began to feel at peace. I saw my old life. The before. I saw a young thug who would have ended up dead on a street corner, marks tracking up my arms before I hit twenty. I experienced a rebirth of sorts. I knew I wasn't guilty and therefore I walked that cell with my innocence filling up my chest. In a lot of ways I was free."

The interviewer steps in. *But you weren't free.*

"Freedom means different things to different people."

CHAPTER 17

HELEN'S HEAD IS THROWN BACK in laughter. A strand of hair has come away from the flat sweep of her bun. It lies straight and long over her cheek but she doesn't seem to mind. She lifts a jug of milk from the mini fridge, laughter still shaking across her shoulders. Donna Hegarty gestures "a small amount" with her thumb and forefinger and Helen lets a little milk drop into a mug of coffee. She gives it a quick stir then holds it out to Hegarty with a smile.

When I walk toward her, Helen's hand reaches up and pushes the hair from her face. "Ma'am," she says.

Hegarty smiles, all teeth. "Detective Sheehan. Glad you could join us." She glances around. "I was just getting to know some of our staff better." She glances at Helen, who is standing between us, her chest high, red blotches appearing over her neck. She'll pass out in a minute if she doesn't take a breath.

"Thanks, Helen," I say. And she looks like she might dissolve with relief.

"Helen was saying you have someone in custody now?"

"We've just finished interviewing a witness."

"No arrest?"

"Not this time."

She frowns. Then points in the direction of my office. "Shall we?"

I'm not above having my place pointed out to me, but there's something about the commissioner's air that gets right under my skin, drawing across my nerves like sandpaper.

I lead her to my office and close the door behind us.

She speaks before I get to my seat. "I'm calling a press conference in a couple of hours. I want you to attend."

"About Jane Brennan spilling to the press?"

"Partly. I spoke to your guy out there, Paul. Jane Brennan insists she didn't sell out to the media. But whatever the situation, it's out there now and of course the media could go one way or the other."

"They'll go one way."

Her face brightens. "It could work in our favor. She reminded them of Hennessy's past. That he's a convicted killer. They may even begin to suspect him of Sheridan's murder."

There's a tinge of glee to her voice. And now I see what's playing out here. That faced with Hennessy's potential innocence for the murder of his parents, the next best thing to ensure the public stay on Hegarty's side would be if he was guilty of more murders. I had thought she wouldn't want Hennessy within a kilometer of these murders, should it look like we were hounding him. But maybe it might look better for the gardaí this way. Maybe it will look better for Hegarty.

"I'm not sure why we'd want that," I reply.

"A man attempting to overturn his previous murder conviction is now facing charges for another. Of course we want that." The skin around her eyes tightens; her lips harden against her teeth. She leans toward me, her voice low. "Hennessy thinks he has us, that he has the media and the public eating from his hands. We'll see how well he does when the public begin to think he's killed again."

I pull back a little, straighten. Comprehension is clear as daylight. Jane Brennan did not leak this story to the press. Donna Hegarty did. I take a drink of coffee. It burns my tongue. "Here was me thinking we wanted the truth."

"He could be behind these new murders."

"His alibi is strong. We have CCTV footage to back it."

She swats away my statement as if it were nothing but an irritating fly and pushes her tongue against her cheek. "I've been doing my own digging around this case. And there's something else that we will need to talk about," she says, and there's a quiet threat in her voice.

I wait for her to give up more. And when I don't prompt her, she pulls back, her lips give a little purse before she speaks. "Rona O'Sullivan."

I swallow. "Rona O'Sullivan?"

"Yes. Jack Clancy's daughter."

THE PRESS WAIT like piranhas in a hot swamp. Their mouths open on mics, Dictaphones thrust forward. Donna Hegarty stands at the lectern, looking out at the room. Jack Clancy has been suspended. In a way it feels like a relief to know what he's been hiding. His daughter's name next to Hennessy's. She'd been the girlfriend he mentioned. His Courtney. They'd met at an interschool football tournament. She'd played. He'd watched. They started up. Hanging out, then more. Paths leading up to that day, to when he said he was with her and couldn't have murdered his parents. To when she'd said otherwise. And her dad, a respected detective at the time, Jack Clancy. Jack Clancy, who kept her name away from papers and reports with a court injunction. Kept Seán Hennessy's alibi hidden.

Hegarty is pleased, I think. She has someone to pin the blame on if Seán's conviction is overturned. She's throwing Clancy to the wolves, so to speak. And with him, his daughter. How Clancy thought Hegarty wouldn't find out eventually is beyond me. She could've found out at any time. But something tells me Donna Hegarty knew all along and it suited her at the time for it to remain beneath the carpet and now it suits her better to scoop it out and shovel it into the mouths of the media.

Hegarty sweet-talks the press into submission. Or she thinks she does. She presents our investigation as if we're in control. But I'm not so naïve to think the press buy into any of it. Not that it matters. Seán Hennessy's innocence is selling papers, filling news channels. The debate over our failure to see it was the father that wrought destruction on his own family speaks out from every station. And with that, a wagging finger at us for trying to link him to these new cases.

Hegarty steps down with a firm "no further questions." She's happy; she thinks it's settled. Her position lulls her into the belief that she'll get her own way but I know better. And when the evening news opens with the line: *Gardaí desperate to take Seán*

Hennessy down in the midst of compensation claim, I feel a sad sort of vindication.

MAYBE IT'S CURIOSITY that has me sitting outside her house but it feels like guilt, a little weight of regret that I've been carrying around since I last spoke to Tanya, that Seán was punished for a crime he didn't commit, and I have a desire to unpick the errors that were made.

It only took a quick call to Athlone Dental to give me a brief sense of Eva Moran's schedule. She has the day off and I've followed her: from her cream cottage, down the wet pavements, across the rail bridge toward a sprawling outlet mall. She's shopping. Dressed casually in jeans and a light blue hoodie. She walks with quick short steps, head down, her handbag tucked beneath her arm. She weaves in and out of pedestrians like a mouse stalked. I stroll behind her, keep my distance. A takeaway coffee ready at the mouth should she turn.

I wait outside a grocery store, check my phone, my back to the shop entrance. After a few moments she emerges with what looks like a bottle of wine in a paper bag twisted at the neck. She stops on the pavement, so close I can smell the peachy fragrance of her shampoo. She lifts her arm, pushes the bottle and a newspaper into her handbag. She looks around the other shops in the outlet, taking her time, as if she's debating whether the crowds are too much, or whether she can be bothered sifting through rows of clothing on her day off. Then she turns, her head down, steps lightly round me, and walks quickly away.

Back at her house, I wait until she's let herself in then find my car on the street. I get in, check myself. I tell myself, I'm not pulling away pieces of Cara Hennessy, only putting them together. In my mind's eye, I see Geraldine Shine huddled on the floor of her bedroom, the door bolted against her husband. Bríd Hennessy waddling away, walking back to the darkest of houses. Conor Sheridan, alone in his room. Searching for a way to cut free of the past. I put my hand on the door, get out of the car. Cross the road. Walk up the short drive.

Cara Hennessy opens the door cautiously. She peers out round my body, as if searching for where I've come from. Her face is half-turned away, ready to retreat.

"Eva Moran?"

"Yes," she says. Her lips don't move when she speaks; the reply whistles between small teeth. "Can I help you?"

I smile. "I hope so." I remove my ID, hold it out. "I'm Detective Frankie Sheehan. I have some questions for you."

She looks at me then, full. Small, round blue eyes. "I have work to do." Her hand tightens on the door latch.

I step closer, hold the door. "Please. It won't take long."

Her chest rises and falls beneath her hoodie. The small thumb-shaped declivity at the base of her throat deepens. Her tongue moistens dry lips.

She studies my ID then looks back up at my face. Nods, a whisper of a movement. A signal that I can come in. She steps aside and I move into a narrow hallway. She closes the door, throwing another slanting glance into the driveway before she lets down the latch.

"The kitchen is through here," she says.

She leads me into a room on the right. A simple counter,

two-ring stove. Dull, yellow Formica covering. She moves to the kettle, flicks it on. One mug. One teabag. In case I had any ideas of getting comfortable. Then she sits down at the table, places her hands in her lap, and clears her throat.

"What do you want?"

I take a breath, try to arrange my thoughts. Now that I'm here, I don't know where to start. The burnished gleam of Cara Hennessy's testimony and the answers that might be hidden beneath it have left me running blind. I shrug out of my coat and she watches the movement.

"Eva, I'm going to be straight with you. I'm not sure how to approach this, but I guess there's no easy way. No right way."

The kettle bubbles to a stop on the counter; white clouds of vapor settle over the cupboards. She gets up, slips out from beneath the table, quick and easy, without moving the chair. She pours the water. Adds milk. Scoops the teabag out with her fingers, throws it into the sink. Then she she's back in the chair. Small hands curved round the mug.

I begin, "I know who you are. Who you used to be. Cara Hennessy."

Her eyes settle on the smooth, hot surface of the tea. She blows on it.

"Your brother, Seán . . ." The briefest of movements, a twitch in the thin skin under her left eye at the mention of his name. "You may have seen something about the documentary? Around his conviction and the circumstances that led up to it."

She brings the mug to her lips, takes a mouthful. Closes her eyes. Dark lashes on pale skin. She doesn't look at me when she speaks but her voice is steady.

"By 'circumstances,' I suppose you mean the murder of my parents." The round Mayo accent softens the edges but the pointed end of bitterness is sheathed in her voice.

"Yes."

Eyes still down. "Is that why you came? To talk about a documentary?"

I shift in my seat. Rest my hands on the table. "Not only that. Because of the media interest, we've had to look at the case again. Do you recall your testimony?"

"I was ten."

I wait. Hope that she'll fill the space, fill it with the past. She lifts the mug of tea, takes another sip, puts it down, then she lifts her eyes to mine, looks right at me, blue eyes unblinking. Her mouth remains quiet.

"Seán insists he's innocent," I try.

"He's not."

I clear my throat. "Some of the footage suggests your father was a violent man."

"Seán learned from the best."

I nod and there's another taut silence, Cara's body held still, braced for the next question. "Do you remember that day?" I ask quietly.

Something crosses her face, the past's shadow running by, but when she speaks, her voice is clear and strong. "I try not to."

She looks at the scar on my temple and I feel her gaze trace along it.

"I've scars too," she says. She reaches up, draws down the neck of her hoodie. A thick scar, clean and straight, the white skin around it strangely hollow, pulled over a deep wound. A fine gold chain glints over her collarbone; an oval locket rests against her chest. She flicks her head in the direction of my temple. "Do you remember *that* day?"

I feel a familiar ache along my scar. "Yes," I answer.

She lets the hoodie fall back over the old wound, tugs the neck up. "I can smell it." She wrinkles her nose. "Still. All the time. The blood." She brings the mug to her face again. "I told them Dad tried to take the knife, that Mam was already down. I said I hid under the thick bushes that surrounded the lawn. But Seán, he knew all my hiding places." She swallows and I see the narrow column of her throat expand and contract. "I knew it was too late. But I didn't want to leave her." She gives a sneering kind of laugh. "I thought if I cried hard enough, she might come back, lift me away." She gives a little shrug, throws her sadness aside.

"He came to you last?"

"Yes." She remains with her statement that she witnessed everything. But I know it wasn't possible. The evidence tells us that Cara was down before her dad turned on himself.

"Have you ever attempted to get in touch with Seán?"

Her hand tightens against the mug. "What do you think?" The words come out in a spit of anger.

"I think it would be understandable if you did."

"Why?"

It's my turn to shrug. "For answers. Or because he's the only family left to you."

"Something he made sure of."

"In a different light, you might say he was driven to act the way he did. He was backed into a corner by your dad."

And the reply comes smooth as a blade from her mouth. "He

killed my mother. He tried to kill me. And, however much he deserved it, he killed my dad." She stops. Places her hand on the table, her upturned fingers folded inwards. The tips twitch, a strange rhythm like a heartbeat. "His hand," she says. "Dad's hand. I feared it all my life. And then there it was, beaten, fallen down, the life playing its last through his fingers." Her hand stills. After a moment she wraps it back around the mug. "Then he, Seán, came for me."

"Your blood was found on your dad. But none of his was on you."

She shrugs. "What's that got to do with anything?"

I tilt my head. "It's got to do with the fact that you must have been injured first."

Those eyes. Again. Right on me. "I know what happened."

The mind is a fragile being, a vulnerable mesh of soft cells. Malleable. The hard shell of the skull unable to shield it from memory or nightmare, loops both together in the brain's primitive pool for survival making memory unreliable. I know this; I've experienced it. Fear or trauma leaving you unable to tell the difference between what's good or helpful and what's bad and dangerous.

"I'm on your side, Cara. I want to help you."

"I don't need help. Anymore." She's silent, then: "Seán has professed his innocence for years. A documentary won't make any difference to the past. It doesn't change anything for me. I want to make something clear: I want nothing to do with him."

"Okay," I say. "The charity working with your brother, Justice Meets Justice, has asked me to look at his profile. But it's very one-sided as you can imagine. I've a few questions to try and even things out. Would you be happy with that?"

She gets up, deposits her mug in the sink, but she doesn't

return to the table, instead leans against the drainboard. "I guess. I don't know what I can remember."

"What about a dog? Lola? Do you remember her?"

A dimple at the corner of her mouth that could be the beginning of a smile or as easily a struggle against tears. "Yes."

"What happened to her pups?"

Her mouth tightens like a bow. "Seán." The name shoots out. "He killed them. My dad made him do it."

I make a note. "And you agree your dad was violent?"

"He was a monster."

"Did you know your mum was going to leave him?"

Guilt. A flash of fear. It's there and gone in an instant. "She wouldn't have done that."

"She'd looked into a refuge. She'd found a place in the city, just ten days before she was murdered. She planned to leave with you both."

There's a softening in her eyes at the mention of her mother. She'd like to know more.

"I didn't know that." The pain in her voice reduces it to a brittle whisper.

"You were a child. You weren't supposed to notice these things."

I see the muscles along her neck work again. She reaches up, hooks a finger on the chain at her neck, spins the locket with her finger.

I wonder at what secret image is hidden inside the locket. I nod toward the chain. "That's pretty."

Her hand closes over the gold disk. "Thanks."

"Is it of her? Your mum."

Her eyes drop to the floor. Hand tightens.

"May I see?"

She lifts her head and for a moment I think she'll say no but maybe it's a relief to have someone to talk to about her old life. Maybe it's to prove that Cara Hennessy was a ten-year-old girl who did exist because she unclasps the chain, opens the locket, then passes it to me.

Inside, a small picture. Bríd and Cara. Beneath the sycamore in their backyard. I can just make out the collar of Bríd's green coat; the bright color pops against the dull background. Cara is wearing a tiny veil and I realize it's a photo taken on the day of her First Communion. "That's a nice photo," I say, and she smiles.

I close the locket and hand it back to her. She clips it around her neck. Keeps her past close. Safe. "They took everything," she says, referring to the officials who swept her life up and secreted her away in a foster home then to here. "They wouldn't let me have photos even. But my aunt, my mum's sister. She visited me in the hospital before they brought me away. She gave me the photo. Told me to hide it. I guess it was the best she could do for us," she says with some bitterness.

"What was Seán like before? Before that day?"

She shrugs. "Normal. A brother."

"He was never cruel to you? Show any signs of aggression toward you or indication he might be looking for some kind of vengeance?"

"No. He was good. He wasn't like that until . . ." she trails off, not quite able to finish the sentence.

I put my notebook away. Tuck the pen into my pocket. I've got what I came for, a woman who is sticking to her testimony. Who wants to believe the lie her life is built around. And I don't blame her. The truth, hard to hear, is often harder to live with.

I stand, push my hands through my coat. "I'm sorry if this has been an intrusion."

She pushes away from the sink. "You don't think he's behind these new murders?"

I zip up my coat. "Murders?"

"I saw the press conference. The lady, the commissioner? She said there'd been three murders."

I move toward the door, show her a smile. "We're still investigating those murders. Don't worry, your brother won't know where you are unless you want him to."

"What about if his conviction is overturned?"

I swallow. "I don't know. It's not an easy process to achieve that; it could take years if it happens at all."

Her eyes fall to the ground but she nods. I hand her my card. "You can call me anytime. Even if it's just to talk."

She pushes the card back. "I don't want to be rude but I've no interest in any of this. I'd prefer it if you didn't come back here."

I nod, put the card back in my pocket. "I understand."

I move toward the hall but stop at the front door. "One thing," I say. "Wasn't one of Seán's arrests for arson? A teacher who had mocked him at school?"

Her shoulders turn in, arms cross. Folding herself away. "Yes," she says with some effort.

"That's quite vengeful, isn't it?"

"I suppose," she says. Quiet. Quiet, like snowflakes on water. "I'd forgotten about that." But I can see she hadn't.

IT'S LATE. I'm tired and Clancy is already halfway through his pint when I find him in the back of the pub. I glance around, barely a sinner about, only the usual old blokes holding up the bar. Enda, the barman, is standing with his back to the room, remote in hand, flicking between Gaelic football and horse races on the small portable TV behind the bar. I slip free of my coat. Throw my bag down. On the way here, I'd it all worked out. How I would ask him about his daughter, Rona, her relationship with Seán. I thought I'd start from the side, like I'd do in a suspect interview, but Clancy knows the dance too well and won't give unless he wants to.

I sit and he reaches forward, pushes a glass of wine toward me. "'Tis not often you summon me to the pub, Frankie. Although I notice I'm still the one putting me hand in my pocket."

Spit it out, he means. So I do. I twist the sleeve of my sweater between my fingers, wind it tight then let go, take up the glass of wine. "Thanks."

I take a breath. "I need to know about Rona."

He remains back in the chair, his hands clasped at his mouth; his lips purse and pucker behind his knuckles.

"Jack?"

He lifts his face out of his hands. "I don't need to talk about Rona. I'm off the clock now, thanks to Hegarty."

"Jack, please, we're fighting for our lives here, trying to deal with these new murders while keeping the past at bay. It's not only you who's feeling the brunt here. The Bureau could close if it looks like we're less than clean." He swallows. His eyes take on a haunted look. And it makes me scared. Jack Clancy is not one for showing fear. I feel my mouth dry; my teeth clip together. "Talk to me."

He looks down into his drink, his mouth pushed up against what he wants to say. "She was the girlfriend." He throws a cold glance at me. "Or supposed girlfriend. But that fucker lied. He fucking lied. And I wasn't going to have my daughter pay his price. No fucking way."

"Her testimony could've prevented him getting a prison sentence."

He lets out a hard laugh, takes another drink. "You're cold on this one, Frankie. Rona spent the night with that piece of scum, yeah. But he left the next morning. Nothing she said would've changed the fact that Seán Hennessy butchered his parents and attempted to slaughter his sister."

"Then why try to cover it up?"

"I wasn't about to let my daughter's name be dragged through the mud because she was a teenager with hormones. He used her. Used her to try and unhook himself from a mess he made."

"We can't rewrite the past when it suits us then force others to relive every step of their own truth."

"Bollocks to that."

"Jack."

He takes a long, slow drink of his pint. It's empty by the time he emerges for air. "It would have ruined her life."

"It would have been a blip."

"A fucking blip, my hole. She was top of her class, had just got her acceptance into law at Trinity. Statutory rape. How's that for a blip? And not only that but your boyfriend is a fucking murderer. Her contribution to Hennessy's case would not have made a blind bit of difference to how his sentence played out." He leans forward, meets my eyes. "Because he's fucking guilty."

"So you sought a court injunction on having her name mentioned?"

His eyes widen. "You would've done the same."

We sit in silence for a few moments. I drink my wine. He places his empty down on the table; white foam slides down the inside of the glass.

"What are you going to do?" I ask.

"I don't know. It's all out in the open now; there's not much I can do." His face draws down. "Rona is beside herself. I'm surprised it's taken this long to surface, to be honest. She's married now so that'll make her a little harder to find, but it won't take long for those fucking weasels to hunt her out," he says, meaning the press.

"I'm sorry."

"It's not your fault." He meets my eyes. "What about that sister-in-law of yours? I thought she would've dug this little treasure up a long time ago."

I smile. "Yeah, but if there was a court injunction, she'd respect that. She would've found out eventually though."

"Like a pig looking for truffles that one."

"She's only interested in the truth."

"We all know where that gets us. Good luck to her." He waves a hand back at the bar, and Enda picks up another pint glass.

I consider telling him about the rest of Tanya's evidence. The hesitation marks around John's throat, which say John turned the knife on himself. That Seán has been innocent all along. But I look at Jack, see the way his shoulders are curving inwards, how low they are, his elbows pitched on his knees, his head dropped, looking down at his hands. I can see what this has cost him. He looks lost.

"Rona will be fine. She's your daughter. If she's anything like you, she'll get through this."

He makes a grunting noise at that.

"I need to speak to her," I say.

He doesn't say anything for a moment, then, "When?"

"Tomorrow. Morning."

He gives a reluctant nod. "How's the timeline for the Shine murders looking? For Sheridan?"

"We've nothing," I say. And that's the truth. The words slap down onto the table between us; Jack, despite everything, sinks into himself a little more. There's a stiff silence, both of us beyond frustration. I give him the rundown on our killer's latest message. The missing piece of the puzzle that Healy destroyed. The word VICTIM.

"So that's the lot then?"

"That's it."

He shrugs, as if to say, *It's no longer my problem.*

Someone at the bar calls for the TV volume to go up. And the opening notes to Seán Hennessy's documentary strike out across the room. Enda approaches, places down Clancy's drink. He glances at me and I put my hand over the wineglass, shake my head.

Clancy settles back into his seat, looks up at the TV. "Well, what's this fucker got to say for himself."

I turn in my seat. A couple of old blokes, their heads together at the bar, tip back their faces, look up at the small screen.

Seán Hennessy pauses, reaches for a glass of water. Takes a slow drink. Puts down the glass, smiles an apology to an unseen cameraman, and goes on: "Cara, the Irish for *friend*. My sister, my friend. Cara would never be any great beauty, never be confident enough to strive for great things. But to me, she was everything. Is everything."

He stops, struggles against something. Sadness. Regret. His nostrils flare into little white circles, cheeks turn, color. Pain falling over his features. The muscles in his throat work. He coughs. "Sorry. Sorry." He breathes in, his head back. Pushes his palms against his jeans. A sniff. Another breath. He nods. Okay. His eyes approach the camera, cautiously, testing the strength of his emotion.

He coughs again, starts over. "Cara. She was small for her age, thin. She didn't have many friends. Then. On the periphery at school, both academically and socially. Slipping through, or weaving in and out of conflict like a bird through trees. It was a skill she learned early. She was gentle. All those good things moved as easily in her as blood through veins. As young as she was, if you hurt yourself, out of nowhere, she'd materialize, her hand always seeking to comfort. Silent and soft.

"Often I'd come home to find the kitchen empty. Make a sandwich. Sit at the counter. When I finished eating, I'd be clearing up and I'd spot her foot or hear a page turn. And I'd find her, under the table or maybe sitting on a cushion, back pressed against the lukewarm radiator, reading a book.

"My da. Everything and anything lit his temper. Money, respect, the cold, the heat. Cara, as quietly as she moved, she left a trail. The space she occupied might have been small but she left her mark. A book upturned here, a half-glass of milk there. And my da, it would set him off, his anger spilling over, wanting to find her, to teach her respect."

He grimaces at some memory then a gleam comes into his eyes. Remembered victory. "But we always beat him. That son of a bitch never got to her. Whatever it took. I did it. Took the hit. Or pressed her into my wardrobe, stood her in the windowsill, wide-eyed and stiff with fear, drawing the curtains over her small body. Whatever it took. I did it.

"Those first weeks in that cell. All I wanted was to see her. To tell her I loved her. I love her. To say, this time, I'm sorry. So sorry I couldn't stop it. Every day of my sentence, every second, minute, every breath has been filled with her. But I never blamed her for testifying against me. I hope one day I can see her again. I've waited seventeen years. And I miss my friend. *My* protector."

I look away, shrug into my coat.

Clancy watches me gather up my bag. "Get some sleep; you look like shite."

"Charming. Thanks for the drink," I say, and I feel Seán Hennessy's blue eyes reach out from the TV. They follow me all the way across the bar until I step free into the wet night.

CHAPTER 18

I **TUCK THE BOTTLE** of wine under my arm. Another evening, another day slipping by. It's Tanya and Justin's housewarming. With three victims and no suspects our investigation has ground to a halt and I couldn't think of an excuse to dodge it. Crooning over new curtains and kitchen appliances is not high on my list of things to do in the downtime allotted to me. And it's not high on Tanya's or Justin's lists either. I suspect the only reason they're suffering through a housewarming party at all is to appease Mam. I received a blunt reminder text from her this morning, telling me to be here and more texts arrived hourly after that.

I cross the street and walk round the new housing development that has risen up on edge of Clontarf's industrial area. I spot Justin at the front door. Hands on hips looking down the road. Mam is beside him, her face pale, her hand hovering over her lips. A man and a woman move out around them, say some quick good-byes, then walk across the garden to disappear into the house next door. I check my watch. I'm late, but not overly so.

Justin sees me, waves me over. "Sorry, sis," he says when I get there. "We've had to cut our celebrations short."

I kiss his cheek. "What's going on?"

And then I see what the small gathering is about. The front window is smashed. Not completely but a large enough hole, the glass a jagged mess.

The hand drops from Mam's mouth. "Someone pegged a brick through the window."

"Fucking wankers," Justin adds.

"Justin!" Mam says.

I'm aware of Dad, hovering somewhere inside. The clink of glasses and the sound of opening cupboards telling me he's assumed the role of tidying up.

We all—Mam, Justin, and I—look stupidly down the small curved street as if the culprit will appear in front of us.

"From a car?" I ask.

Justin shrugs. "Dunno. We were out back and we heard the crash. Tanya's phoning the guards now." He moves back inside and we traipse after him, Mam muttering, "Fat lot of good that'll do."

In the living room, the brick lies in the middle of the new beige carpet. Glass thrown inwards. Written in black marker along the side of the brick are the words *Justice is a bitch*. Tanya is standing in the corner of the room, staring down at it as if it was about to speak.

She folds her arms across her chest. "Someone's on the way out now," she says, meaning the guards.

"We all know what this is about," Mam says pointedly, throwing a look at Tanya.

"Mam, please," Justin says. He gives me a wary look, pushes his blond hair off his forehead.

Tanya smiles but it doesn't look real. She rubs a hand up and down her own arm. "It's only a few thugs having a pop, Sharon, nothing to worry about really."

It's the first time I've seen Tanya frightened.

"It would've been something to worry about if one of us had been sitting in here though, wouldn't it?" Mam says.

Tanya moves toward her, puts an arm round her shoulders, and gives her a quick squeeze. "But we weren't."

Mam quiets but I know she's thinking: *What about the next time?* Because that's what I'm thinking. I pick my way over the carpet. The wine still wedged under my arm. The brick made it a good way in. Not likely a throw from a car. The windows are double-glazed. This took some force. New floral curtains shift in the incoming breeze; the smell of fresh paint stirs through the room.

I look back at Justin, then to Mam, then hold up the wine. "Let's wait out in the kitchen for the officer to get here?"

"I'll go with that," Justin says. "I'm not standing here looking at a brick for the next hour." He takes the wine from me and makes for the kitchen.

Mam follows him, worrying her hands all the way. I stay back, my eyes to the glass-speckled floor and to the window.

"It's fine," Tanya says. "It's fine. Just some idiots. You get them."

"Who knows you've moved?"

She shrugs. "I guess the neighbors, the decorators. Anyone

who might know my face." She shrugs again, her dark eyes pivot over the floor, don't meet mine.

I turn, call Keith. Tell him to send round a couple of SOCOs. Tanya pulls a curl of hair forward, chews the end. "That's a little much, don't you think?"

"No. I don't."

She nods. And I see her throat working. Finally she lets out a long breath. "Drink?"

WE'RE BACK AT MY FOLKS'. Mam and Dad are in bed after two hours of nothing at the new house. Justin has stayed behind but it took less persuading than I thought to have Tanya leave her new home and return with us.

"I'm not going to let some git push me out of my own house," she'd said.

Eventually, I used the Hennessy case to lure her away. She sits in her dressing gown at the desk in Justin's old room. Legs crossed, bare foot wagging. The Hennessy murders all around us.

"Has anything like this happened before?" I ask.

She purses her lips then answers. "You know how it is; we get a few shitty messages via our Facebook page. But nothing personal. Nothing like this."

"You saw the press conference yesterday?"

She dips her chin. "Yes. Jane Brennan was quick to sell out."

"Isn't everyone nowadays?"

Tanya watches me. I know she's thinking the same thing as me, knows the leak won't have come from Jane Brennan. But she doesn't say anything more about it. Instead she offers, "I heard about Jack. I'm sorry."

I nod. "Thanks." Rona, Jack's daughter, cried when she opened the door to me this morning. It was messy. And messier still was her guilt. I told her that there was nothing to feel guilty about. He still would've had plenty of time to stage an attack on his family. Ultimately, he left her house on the morning of the killings. Not the afternoon like he said. Or so she says. I believe her. I think.

Tanya tucks her head down, nods into her chest. There's silence for a moment. "We're still nowhere on Cara," she says testily, looking up through the veil of her hair. "This whole leak to the press will not induce her to come forward," she adds a little sadly.

"I would think she'd want to be left alone." Nerves and a shitty conscience make it come out a little sharp but Tanya simply nods.

"Sure. Sure. I suppose that's her right. Is there really a connection? Between the cases?"

"You know what it's like. We get a whiff of smoke we have to see if there's fire." I get up, stretch. Move to the window. "There's something there but nothing solid linking Seán to the cases. He has an alibi for the Shine murders, and we're confident it's the same killer for all the victims."

I lift the curtain, look down on the street, imagine Bríd Hennessy's desperate steps striking the hot pavement. Running for her life. I think of Ger Shine, her pleas for help landing on deaf ears. And I'm caught up with a peculiar feeling, a tension tightening round my gut. Two women, years apart, same story, same path, and it sinks through me, pulls me inwards. I swallow down their fear, feel the pulse of their lives thrum against the inside of my skull.

The chair creaks as Tanya gets up. "We're almost ready to submit the appeal," she says. "You've got a struggle on your hands, Frankie. I think your commissioner knows her job is on the line if, or rather, when we win this case. But if she's already sent someone, Jack, to the executioners, then maybe the price has been paid and for the moment she gets to keep her cushy job at Phoenix Park, cutting fucking ribbons and sending out sound bites to the media until she can retire in a few years to a French chateau."

"If I thought it'd be that easy to get rid of her, I'd join Clancy in retirement immediately."

She moves to the door, smiles. "Good night."

I SIT ON THE CARPET, pull my bag forward, and remove the Shine and Sheridan case files. I spread the pictures around me, a collage of murder. I lift the bottle of wine from the floor, top up my glass, take a drink. The glass is half empty by the time I put it down and there's a nice glow of heat spreading through my veins, a balm for a dashed ego.

I lean forward, shuffle through a few of the pages. Find Conor Sheridan's crime scene picture, him propped up against the wall, waiting for the tide to take him out. I place him next to the Shines. Lean against the corner of the desk, take a mental step back, and study the spread of images. I wait for clarity, for my mind to build the connections. The ritual, the motive—I'm searching for both, for the killer's signature. Nothing speaks to me.

I drift back to Geraldine Shine on the church floor. A beaten wife, prone, the wound through her throat silencing her cries for help forever. The text on her phone spelling out VICTIM. Then to Conor Sheridan, a journo, the media. KILLER scratched into the sand next to his body. Eyes trail slowly between the images. Back to the Shines. Alan Shine. An abusive husband, the murder weapon lying in his hand. WEAPON. I frown, feel the ache of frustration grow over my brow.

On the walls around me are the scenes of old. The Hennessys, John Hennessy, his cold body propped up against the back of the house. I look to Conor Sheridan, his body lit up in the darkness, against the seawall. Again, I have the feeling that the solution is in front of me, like one of those optical illusions; a sense that were I to narrow my eyes or adjust my view, the true image would reveal itself.

I pick up Geraldine Shine, trace the numerous wounds down her back, then glance at the Hennessy photos. Bríd Hennessy: facedown, head turned, throat cut. Stab wounds puncturing her back. And then I see it, see how the bodies are laid out. So similar to the old case. Geraldine Shine's postmortem injuries mirror the violent burst of wounds over Bríd's prone back, almost exactly.

I stand, draw closer to the Hennessy crime scene. Step into the past. I can almost smell the sting of blood tainting the air. The heat rippling up from the ground, searing down from the sky. Then back again to the images over the floor: to Alan and Geraldine Shine, to Conor Sheridan. A beaten wife. An abusive husband. Dressed in a priest's vestments. A symbol of the patriarchy, of hypocrisy. Then Conor Sheridan. The media. KILLER. A tickle of adrenaline. I feel it chase the fog from my brain. As if the room were lighting up. I lean over the pictures. There. There! And I feel his anger rising through the room. His roar in my ear. "I hear you. I hear you," I whisper.

I pick up the phone. Dial Baz's number in the hope he's

burning the candle. He answers after the fourth ring, his voice scratchy and low.

"Hey," he says.

I gaze down at the images. "Where are you?"

"Trying to be normal. Pretending to sleep."

"I think I've hit on something."

I hear a rustling, picture him reaching for the light, checking the time. "Go on."

"Ger Shine's injuries are almost identical to Bríd Hennessy's. Conor was laid out like John Hennessy."

A yawn. "And Alan? He was on his side."

"Cara was found on her side."

I hear him draw breath, know that he is seeing the landscape of the killer's world. There's more silence, as if he's waiting to wake up. I imagine him rubbing sleep from his face, massaging blood into his cheeks. "So the blouse then? Him wanting to take some of the crime scene back to the victim's house?"

"I don't know. That's the anomaly. But I'm sure it's part of the ritual," I say. "A further invasion of Ger Shine's life."

"Is it not enough for these guys to murder people?"

I look down at Alan Shine's image, the discoloration of his skin telling me his killer kept his body for days before leaving it in the church. "Anything to prolong the thrill," I answer.

"So we've got a killer checking all the boxes of a crime scene, victim, weapon, and killer, but has some sort of hero worship for Hennessy? Is that it?"

"Or anger on his behalf," I add. "Someone who suffered similarly and needs society to pay attention."

"Whoever it is, they're finished, right? Victim, weapon, killer. There's no more."

I look around the room, a shrine to Hennessy's innocence. "They'll never be finished. Maybe he repeats the pattern, maybe he'll add some new twists but he'll never finish. The hit is too delicious and the frequency of the murders is concerning."

"Escalation," Baz agrees. "So if we're dealing with some sicko who has a fascination with Hennessy or wants in on his glory, it would have to be someone who knows the case, right? Knew how to pose the bodies."

"The crime scene photos are on the internet for anyone to find. Besides, if we're looking in that direction we'd have to include anyone working on the documentary, anyone who worked the case years ago."

A long sigh comes down the line. "If this person is obsessed with the Hennessys, could he be in danger?"

"Seán?"

"Or the sister."

I hadn't even thought about that and with the harassment Tanya said Seán was receiving, the jibes on the street, the graffiti on his flat door, it could be a possibility. But until we've something more definite, an overt threat, there's little the Bureau can do about it. "I can't see the commissioner signing off on protection for Seán Hennessy."

"We should all be working on the same team," Baz says, unconsciously parroting Hegarty.

I think of Clancy, sitting across from me in the pub, his head down with the weight of his secrets and the enormity of his suspension. "We should," I say into the phone. "Doesn't mean we are."

CHAPTER 19

THE GUN IS LIGHT in my hand. I aim, finger-light squeeze. A loud pop and I see the target bounce. Straight through the heart. Easy as that. I see him falling back, the killer, arms, head flung back, shock spreading over his face making his eyes wide, his mouth round.

"Not too rusty," Baz says. He draws the target forward. Examines the bullet hole. "The heart, right through."

I holster the gun. Adjust it at my shoulder. "I hate these."

Baz steps away from the firing platform. Tucks his Sig into his waistband. "You might not hate them so much when one saves your life."

I think of the near misses I've had in the past and I should agree. "In my experience they cause more trouble than they prevent." I check the time. "Have you spoken to Clancy?"

Baz lifts the goggles from his eyes. "That I did. He shouldn't have kept this stuff to himself. Then or now."

"Thing is, it doesn't make much difference to the case. Even with Rona's admission that he'd been with her."

I don't know, it could have helped people see how it happened. Seán probably got home and an argument about him being out all night might have been the match to light the tinder."

I shiver, thinking of Bríd Hennessy's escape route. Planned out, her bags packed, just a little too late. I take up my coat. Go to the desk, sign out the weapon.

"We got press in twenty," I say to Baz.

UP ON THE FLOOR, I stop and study the case board. It has grown into a mighty oak of listing tendrils. The Hennessys and their tragic demise, short summaries on short lives, trail down one side. Wobbling arrows of blue marker drawn between the Shine and Sheridan murders. Outside, down on the street, the sound of demonstrators. Calling for our heads. Or someone's.

I walk to the window, peek out between the blinds. Hennessy's face erected like a messiah on placards. Images of his family on others. And among them our present-day victims. Geraldine Shine's dark glossy hair swept over her bare shoulder, as she was that morning on her Facebook page, unsuspecting of what lay in store only hours later. The cries alternate from "Justice for Hennessy" to "Justice for Victims of Abuse."

The staff have taken to using the fire escape to enter and leave the building. It takes only a shadow passing the front door before the media and crowds close in. The result is an office that sings with pressure. The tension pressing up against the dull gray walls. All morning phones flash, ringtones screeching down the spine of the room.

Another press conference to hold back the baying crowds, and it feels like I've been asked to part the Red Sea. We've been reduced to scraping the bucket. Desperate for a lead, and the public might just give it to us. Hope that the bias in favor of or against Seán Hennessy does not get in our way. We've managed to become the enemy in the public's eye. We're not to be trusted. And the result is anger. Facebook pages have appeared calling on witnesses and armchair detectives to put together their own clues. It's a fucking mess of misinformation and we have to look through it all. Poor Paul spends his day hunched over his screen, his brow drawn in ridges, his mouth a tight pout of panic.

I check the time. The afternoon is twirling away. I swallow down frustration and walk around the office floor, restless. The staff sense it; no one dares look up from their screens in case they draw my eye. I move to Helen's desk.

"Yes, Chief," she says, not looking up from her computer, a quick click of the mouse and she minimizes her screen. She flushes, glances up guiltily.

"We're staying focused here?"

"Yes, Chief."

I give the tab a pointed look and her color deepens, creeping up over the long sweep of her forehead, the tight scrape of her hair. She clicks the minimized tab and a site on boats appears. Inflatable boats, rowboats, small dinghies.

"It's probably nothing but I've been thinking about how the killer got Sheridan's body to the coastline." She throws a quick glance up at me, checks my expression, which must appear encouraging because she continues: "We've been scouring the

CCTV along that area. And there's not much but it would have been risky for him to access via the street, wouldn't it? Even in the middle of the night. You said he'd have this well planned so I thought, maybe, he wouldn't have risked carrying a dead man across the prom and then down the slipway to the beach."

I stare at the array of boats on the computer, feel the claws of this case loosen a little. "He came in by boat."

"This way he wouldn't risk being seen and could get nice and close to the beach. You said he's likely familiar with the area, the tides."

I picture the word KILLER at Conor Sheridan's feet, scratched into the sand. "Yes."

She turns away from the screen, her eyes alight with the idea, words coming fast now. "It would be hard work for him, sure, but I guess if we're looking for someone who has the strength to strangle someone then our killer could manage it, so I'm thinking he hired one or owns one. That way he could come in, hook up to the slipway or somewhere close to it, unload Conor's body onto the strand."

And another curtain pulls back from the killer's window. An extra shadow, the pointed nose of a boat appears. The motor on a low gear, quiet. Nothing big enough to cause a witness to search the dark horizon. The boat bounces slowly toward the coast then drifts up along the slipway.

The killer secures it. Goes about getting his cargo to shore. He pauses only long enough to check the beach. There are no witnesses, an empty coastline. The perfect canvas. It's hard work, but he's fit. He's planned for this. A dead man's lift.

He's chosen an area of the beach where the sea is lazy, where the waves are last to leave and last to come. He lays out the body.

It doesn't take him long. And in a way, that's disappointing. He's held on to this one for longer than he should have. There's an anticlimax of sorts. Already he's longing for another. Another buzz, another victim. One last message, a taunt for the media, a statement of revenge maybe, written into the sand. And then he's gone.

I smile. "This is good work, Helen. Can you feed it out to our uniforms?"

She returns my smile. "Sure."

Baz appears in the doorway, waves for my attention. I look at my watch again.

"Also, it might be worth checking with the coast guard," I say to Helen. "See if they spotted any boats on the water."

"Righto," she replies, then flinches, hearing Ryan in her own voice. "Sorry, I mean, Chief."

The conference room is packed to the gills. Journalists stripped of the usual Irish summer attire, overcoats, sit on the edges of their seats. Notebooks and phones carefully shielded from their neighbors; no one wants to give away their angle. At the front, TV crews train their cameras on the lectern, check their speakers, their focus. The cameramen wait like cats behind their equipment, ready to pounce. Baz stands back, waits for me to step up to the mic, then joins me at my side.

"Thank you for coming," I say. "I'm Detective Chief Superintendent Frankie Sheehan and am acting as the senior investigating officer over these tragic cases." I give a brief summary. Geraldine and Alan Shine in the church, Conor on the beach. Then I make my plea. "We have no suspects as yet but our investigation is still in its early stages. We urge anyone who was in or around the area of St. Catherine's church on the evening of the nineteenth of August to get in touch, or anyone who was on Clontarf promenade in the early hours of the twenty-second of August. We ask the public to report any behavior they might deem suspicious to us.

"Both Alan Shine and Conor Sheridan were missing for some days before their bodies were discovered. Is there someone who recalls seeing them alive in the week before their murders?" I take a steadying breath, leave room for the viewer to think, then using Helen's theory I continue: "We believe there was a boat used to transport Conor Sheridan's remains to Clontarf beach on the morning his body was discovered, the twenty-second of August. Did anyone see a boat? Did someone borrow a boat from you? If you've any information you feel might help our investigation, please call this number." I turn to the placard behind me, where the helpline is printed in large font. Paul will be on the other end, ready to sift through it all in the hope of finding a golden nugget. "Thank you."

The questions fire out from the seats. "Are these random murders?" "What's the relationship between Conor Sheridan and the Shines?" "Will there be more victims?" And finally, the one I've been waiting for, a young female journalist at the front.

She looks up, sets her pen over her notebook. "Patrice Philips with the *Clontarf Gazette*. Are these murders related to the Hennessy killings in 1995?"

I work to keep my face neutral. "We have many lines of inquiry open and are investigating all avenues," I reply. And the room recognizes the answer for what it is, a big fat yes.

"Is Seán Hennessy a suspect?" the journalist goes on. There is a sweep of murmuring throughout the room. The cameraman pulls back from the lens. Blinks then refocuses. He doesn't want to miss a thing.

"Mr. Hennessy is not a suspect at this time."

My hands tighten on the edge of the lectern. I do the best I can to stamp out the embers that are about to set us all alight. "I'm aware of the growing speculation around the Hennessy case. But we're here today to appeal to the public for information and witnesses pertaining to the murders of Alan Shine, Geraldine Shine, and Conor Sheridan. Thank you very much for your time."

I step down and every journo in the room is on their feet. Over the din, I hear the female journo's voice again: "What do you say to the idea that the arrest in 1995 and subsequent conviction of Seán Hennessy were wrongful?"

I smile at the cameras, ignore the voices rising at my back.

We return to my office, close the door.

I sit at my desk, drop my head into my hands. After a few deep breaths, I look up at Baz. "I might pay Seán Hennessy a visit. See how he's taking all this attention."

He blows air through his lips. "The powers that be will like that."

"Nothing official but if I happen to bump into him then what can I do?"

He nods. "He could do with answering some questions. Perhaps he's been talking to someone inside. Someone who also has a thirst to quench when it comes to murder. You need company?"

I stand and pull on my jacket. "No, hold the fort here."

He lifts the holster from the back of my chair. "Forgetting something?"

"Thanks."

Removing my jacket, I hook the holster across my shoulders, check the gun. I remind myself that the weapon is mine to help, to defend. Not to kill.

I PULL A BLANKET off the backseat of the car, throw it around my shoulders, and huddle deeper against the seat. I'm outside Hennessy's flat. Or rather, I've picked a place across the road, another street running perpendicular to his that allows me to sit hidden among a row of parked cars.

It's cold. The wind rages against the car, every now and then an angry spatter of rain hits the windshield. A little draft has worked its way through the elements of the car and I long to start the engine and turn up the heat. I rub my arms and stare up at Hennessy's window. His flat is in a square complex that has seen better days, all windows ignoring the sea view and looking out on the rooftops of the adjacent street. Wisely, the media vans and journos stalking the premises have given up. Gone home for tea and biscuits. Hennessy is holed up on the third floor.

I try to get my head back to where it was a week ago. A place where Seán Hennessy was the one who murdered his parents and his father was innocent. But I've seen enough domestic violence cases to recognize the pattern when it's in front of me. All the evidence that pointed to Seán, even his sister's testimony, is either weak or has crumbled under scrutiny. John Hennessy was a controlling abuser who, when he felt his family was close to escaping his clutches, decided to try to murder them all. But there's something about his son, Seán, that I can't quite shake. The remembered feeling of him as a predator. I'm not sure where it comes from, a castoff from the long-held belief that he'd committed the worst of crimes or an echo chiming in my mind after my meeting with his sister. Whatever it is, I need to exorcise those last remaining ghosts and there's only one person who can do that for me.

In the past four weeks, Seán's called the local garda station four times. Reports of abuse and harassment. Dog shit smeared on his door handle. A bottle pegged at him from a passing car. Verbal attacks in the local newsagents. Eggs flung at his window. He's frightened, he says, and I wonder why he doesn't move. Why he'd want to live in a place that must hold such painful memories for him.

My phone lights up from the passenger seat and I reach out from under the blanket and grab at it.

"Chief?" Steve says down the line when I answer. "We're all good on Sheridan's computer here."

I keep my eyes on Hennessy's window. "Give me something, anything, from that computer."

"Thought you'd never ask." I imagine him holding his numb jaw as he speaks. He lowers his voice. "Our Sheridan was getting hate mail on the Hennessy article. Starting years back. He kept all of it, scanned it into a file on his desktop." I hear the click of the mouse. "Every one arrives around the anniversary of the Hennessy murders, the week he wrote that article." Another few clicks. "I've sent the details to your email."

I hear him tap on the keyboard, Sheridan's history flickering on Steve's screen.

I put him on speaker and click through the screen on my phone. A scanned image appears. It's a letter, handwritten, block capitals, short but the last line is chilling.

YOU DID THIS. I WON'T FORGET. YOU WILL ALL PAY. I CAN WAIT.

"That's the common theme," Steve says. "But despite the personal tone, the letters don't suggest a personal attack. I mean, like, not specific to him."

"You might want to tell that to Conor Sheridan's very specifically dead body in Whitehall."

"No, I mean, the target is not so much only Sheridan but talks as if Sheridan represents the media."

I sit up; the blanket slides down onto my lap. "The media?"

"Whoever was sending Conor Sheridan these letters refers to 'them' and 'youse' or 'you lot,' says 'you'll all pay.' There's a few clippings pasted into the letters. Newspaper clippings of cases where people were wrongly accused, you know, trial by media kind of thing."

I shift my weight, an ache spreading down my leg; the scar on my temple begins to itch. Both reminders of the past. Reminders of what happens when you get too close. I rub the ache away, pull the lever under my seat, let my right leg stretch out under the dash.

"More?" Steve asks.

"Go on."

"Sheridan visited a few dating sites about five months ago. Here's his profile."

Another email expands in my inbox. I tap the phone and it opens.

Conor Sheridan's smiling picture appears and a paragraph about himself in his own words.

Steve continues. "He had a couple of hits. Nothing that stuck. We can't find anything on his computers saying he was sparking with anyone, so whatever he was telling Lynch about an online girlfriend doesn't ring true. We do have his calendar though, and on the night he went missing he had attended an AA meeting. The meeting was in Tallaght town center and we've now got his car leaving the community hall grounds where it was held and heading north to Clontarf."

"So we've got shot of those dark hours. Anything on who Conor was on the phone to that night?"

"No, and there's nothing I can find that indicates why he was heading to Clontarf. Although, there's one obvious reason."

"Jane Brennan."

"Yeah, I'm thinking that's where he was heading and then for whatever reason it was called off. But this is the most damning thing we've gathered from the computer—"

I press the phone closer to my ear.

"—Conor Sheridan had spent years researching the Hennessy case. He has folders and folders of scanned news articles. Transcripts of the court case. Photographs of the crime scene gathered from the press, even the funeral. Pages of notes, journals on his findings. The works. It's clear that the hate mail got to him. That he wasn't able to let the case go."

I remember Jane Brennan telling me how Conor was plagued by guilt after Hennessy's arrest.

"Ultimately," Steve goes on, "the guy was doing a better job at unraveling this case than the guards were. It's like he felt bad about the article and wanted to put things right. Over the last few months, he tried to contact Seán Hennessy himself."

The breath catches in my throat. "What was the angle?"

"He wanted to apologize."

I peer into the rearview. Look back out at the black street.

"The content?"

"A long letter. Again scanned into this file. The brunt of it was how sorry he was if he'd gotten the sitch wrong in the Hennessy family followed by a suggestion that they could meet up to clear the air."

"Any response from Hennessy?"

"Yes. Hennessy's response was: 'Fuck you. I hope you rot in hell.'"

I look out at Hennessy's place. The curtains drawn on the single lit window on the third floor. Occasionally I think I see his shadow cross the room. "That's something all right," I say.

"I thought so," Steve says.

"Thanks. Feed back with anything else," I say, and hang up.

Time is ticking on, ten P.M. on a Saturday night and not a wink of movement from Hennessy's place. A swell of chatter and laughter grows from behind me then passes on down the street. A few cars turn into the nearby hotel, people in their fancy gear out for the night and returning to the hotel for a nightcap and then bed.

I pull the blanket back up around my neck and settle down to wait. But suddenly he's there. Stepping out onto the low concrete step in front of the block of flats. He's wearing a baseball cap, pulled down over his eyes. The security light thrusts a halo over his head. He's looking into his phone.

He laughs at something on the screen. He takes his time, responds to whoever is on the other side of that laughter. Then, pocketing the phone, he strikes out from the flat, away from me, toward Strand Road. I wait awhile. Try to count out a minute but I don't want to lose him. Reaching out, I start the engine and pull on to the road, keeping my speed low. I pass him, just as he turns into Smith's bar.

CHAPTER 20

THERE'S A SIDE ENTRANCE to Smith's, always another door to an Irish pub should you need it. It leads to a lounge. I step up and push the door open. The bar area is long, people packed like cattle along it, all baying for a pint or a chat. I see Seán Hennessy at the far end; he keeps his eyes and space to himself. Baseball cap pulled down low. No one bothers him. The barman nods when he gives his order and shortly a pint of lager is deposited in front of him, his change already counted out on the bar.

I order a glass of wine, sit down near the front of the room. I wish I had a book. A prop. I take out my phone, scroll through the messages, take a few sips of wine. My heart in my mouth. Excitement. I'm this close. When he sees me, he'll come over. He can resist it as much as I can.

He turns, casts around for a seat. Spots me. His expression lifts. He approaches, his chest high, steady footsteps through the shouts and laughter.

"Frankie," he says. Then shakes his head. "Is that okay? I mean, you're off duty, no?"

I nod to the glass of wine. "Sure."

He motions to the empty seat across from me. "You mind if I sit?"

"Help yourself."

He sits. Adjusts his cap over his eyes. The free man hiding in plain sight. "You visiting family?"

"Something like that."

Eyes narrow around a cutting blue. "How is everyone?"

"Great."

"Someone once told me that a good detective never clocks out."

I force a laugh. "I guess there's some truth in that. You meeting friends?"

He lifts the brim of his cap, wipes a hand over his head, replaces the hat. "If only. I'm still working on my popularity. Turns out small towns have long memories." He takes a drink, leans in, lowers his voice. "I was going grand, you know. People were edgy, sure, they didn't know how to take me, but they were coming around. The documentary was helping and reading the papers you'd think that people might be more sympathetic, you know. But these new murders and that press conference, it's stirring shit up again."

"I'm sorry. That must be hard for you."

He looks down, lifts one shoulder in a shrug. "It's raking through old coals, you know."

"People say stuff to you?"

A sharp exhale through tight lips. "A bit." He reaches for his drink and I see a tremble in his hand. "I've had some trouble with a few neighbors. But mostly I can feel it. Eyes"—he looks around—"as sure as hands on my back. They're watching me. I keep myself covered up, stay inside like, but a man who's free should be able to walk down the streets of his hometown."

"That's true."

"Maybe when they've seen the whole documentary or when Tanya gets her case together"—he sighs, a tail of longing on his breath—"maybe then they'll see."

I ask him about Rona O'Sullivan, or Rona Clancy as he would have known her. He looks pained, but when he answers he surprises me with his honesty. He doesn't deny that he had lied about being with her when his family was attacked, killed. "I don't feel bad about that."

"No?"

"I mean, yes, she was right, I didn't stay the whole day with her but I *did* stay. At least if she'd told the truth, even if it didn't help me, it would have went some way toward making me look human. Someone's boyfriend. As it was, to the public, to the guards, I looked incapable of keeping my family or my friends. She dropped me to one side like I was a stinking turd. And when the public thinks you stink, they back off too. She left me with no one."

I peer into the red glow of my wine. "How about your sister? Have you tried reaching out to her?"

"I wouldn't know where to start. Do you . . . You know where she is, right?"

I take up the glass, feel the tang of the wine on my tongue. "It would be difficult, even for me, to get that paperwork through the red tape."

His mouth turns down. "What am I doing?" He drops his head, cradles it in his hands.

And I feel a stirring of pity for him. Seán Hennessy is a stranger in his own home. He doesn't fit. His darkness has followed him and I know what that feels like. "You must've suspected she might not want a relationship with you?"

"If she knows I didn't do it, why wouldn't she want to reconnect?" When I don't reply he continues: "The evidence? Did Tanya fill you in? They really fluffed that, didn't they? Cross-contamination. Even Cara's testimony. She was so young. How'd she remember what happened?"

"You remembered Lola."

"Sorry?"

"You were what? Twelve when you had to kill those pups? That's only two years older than Cara when your parents were killed, and you remembered that in great detail."

His mouth works, jaw tenses. He drags a hand down the side of his face. His fingers rest at his ear. "I know what I look like to you. I know you can't see me, you see only a killer." He glances out at the full room from beneath his cap. "That's all they see. Why would you be any different?"

"Maybe I'm not so different," I say, and watch the frustration creep up his neck.

After a moment he lets his hands fall to the table, settles them round the base of his pint. "You want me to tell you what you want to hear? Is that it? Make it so you can sleep easier at night because the thought that they put away the wrong person is too troubling for you?"

I don't answer and he pulls back, just a little, his shoulders straightening.

His lips tighten as he speaks. "It only took a few months inside before I remembered that evening. The knife in my hand. The heat of the day, the sun spinning white orbs from the windows into my eyes. The stillness. The fizz of the hedgerows, alive with the sounds of parched insects. The crazy whoop of a blackbird in the garden." The pint rotates between his fingertips, a slow grind on the table. Gold-tipped lashes drawn down over his eyes.

"I waited in the kitchen for a while. Just watching them. I was calm, like really calm. Not myself, I don't think. They were just there, a few feet away, but it could have been another galaxy for how close it felt. Dad was in and out of the garage, something wrong with the mower, bottle in his hand, giving the thing a kick every now and then. Mam pulling weeds on the other side, the sun slowly burning the back of her neck. Cara reading, cross-legged on the lawn.

"I thought there'd be screaming. But there wasn't much. The hardest first. Get it over with. Cara. Mam, she turned, ran to her, shouted my name. Just once. I thought he'd come at me then but he didn't. Frozen he was, on the other side of the lawn. A big fucking coward. Every drive of the knife added to the frenzy. The madness. I felt indestructible. For the first time. The first time ever. Ten feet tall. The man of the house.

"When he came for me, he was blustering with rage, spittle flying from his lips. Tears of horror. I remembered enjoying that, however long that moment was, seconds, less, more. I held on to that look. It felt like redemption. It was the sweetest thing. His anger, his grief, his desire to control made him clumsy. Helped me win. All those years, terrified of this man. And there he was, panting like a dying dog against the back wall, begging for death to bend down and kiss his drunken mouth. All those years, terrified of this man," he says again, "this monster, and he was only made of flesh and blood. Flesh and blood like us all."

I'm pinned to the seat. My mind catches on the imagery he uses. The lawn mower. Where was that? It wasn't at the crime scene. *Cara reading*. There was no book. "Are you confessing?"

Disappointment grows on his face, a sad, retired look in his eyes that I don't seem to be getting what he's trying to say. "I was in that cell, alone with what had happened. It pressed in on me, those walls. Those fucking walls. Pressing in. And I was trying to make sense of it. I thought if everyone believes I did this, I must have, right?" When he looks up, there are tears in his eyes. He wipes them away quickly with the back of his hand. "My lawyers! My own sister! I began to believe it, you know. Fuck. I began to think this is what must've happened. But it didn't. It didn't." He pulls back, shakes his head. "It fucking didn't."

He lifts his pint, drinks. "The system only picks the evidence it wants," and there's a flinty bitter edge to his voice. After a moment, he clears his throat. "What happens to the rest?"

"That's up to your defense."

He nods slowly and shrugs. "I had no defense."

There's silence then he says: "You're here. I'm here. You're working on a case. My experience with the law says this was no accidental meeting."

"No."

He laughs. "Well, why is that not surprising." He lifts cautious eyes to mine. "What is it?" he asks, and I hear fear shaking in his voice.

"Conor Sheridan."

"What about him?"

A shout goes up from the bar. A group of thick-waisted blokes, packed into Levi's and faded rugby shirts, chant some god-awful drinking game while one of them downs a pint of slop. The drinker smacks the glass onto the bar amid heavy back-slapping and nods of pride. When I look back at Seán, I see him watching them; envy huddles in his eyes.

"I think you know," I say, bringing his attention back to me.

"I never met him. I only know about his stupid piece for the local paper. What?" he says, catching judgment on my face. "You expect me to feel sorry for him?"

"He was a human being. He died a terrible death."

He grips the front of his shirt, leans close. His voice rattles with intensity when he speaks. "I don't have room to feel sorry for Conor fucking Sheridan. I don't have any more fucking sorrys left in me. I've spent seventeen years saying sorry for something I didn't fucking do, and now you expect me to say it for a guy who helped ruin my life?" He lets go of his shirt, the furnace of his anger red on his face. But he gets himself under control, takes a few deep breaths. "It's sad that a man lost his life. Another one. All of it's fucking sad. That's all I've got to say."

The fury of his words scrapes back my doubts and rings the bell of truth. Here is real emotion. Not rehearsed. Not staged or played out nicely for a camera. And I believe what he's saying. But my mind is caught on his accusation that Sheridan ruined his life. "Conor Sheridan was hardly responsible for your conviction. What's one journalist's opinion?"

His bottom lip comes up in distaste. "It has to start somewhere. He believed his occasional meet-ups with my dad through Gaelic football gave him insight into the type of man he was." He gives a short laugh, leans in. "This is a small town, and he took the line people wanted to hear. That John Hennessy, salt of the fucking earth, could not have attacked his family. But the young brat coming in his wake, who gardaí were holding for questioning, who had no alibi and a criminal record. He had killer written all over him." He gives me a pleading look. "Aren't you sick of seeing headlines describing perfect husbands, perfect fathers murdering their perfect families?"

He snatches a quick breath, goes on: "Conor Sheridan gave me a trial by media and left me to hang by the end of a rope. Every paper in the country went with it then, and he was quoted in almost all of the press. He became the go-to character witness on what a grand man my da was, and he rode my fucking conviction until it smashed up against the prison gates."

I take another drink of wine. Feel the tension ratchet up and down my spine. "Have you ever gotten in touch with Conor Sheridan?"

"No." He throws the answer out the side of his mouth. Doesn't meet my eyes. Then he sighs. "There might have been a letter, well not so much a letter, a note."

I feel the tension peel away from my shoulders. Relief that he's admitted replying to Sheridan's letter. No lies, no guilt. "What did it say?"

"He wrote to me when I was inside. Wanted to meet up. I sent back my reply, which was the longer version of fuck off."

"Do you have an alibi for Tuesday evening and Wednesday morning? When we believe Sheridan's body was left on Clontarf beach."

He swallows. "Seriously? No. I'm on my own here."

"Do you have a neighbor? Someone who might be able to say they saw you on Tuesday night?"

"I don't know; it's an old guy, off his head most of the time. I'm pretty sure he pushed dog shit under my door a couple of days ago." There's a desperate look growing on his face. He turns a finger in on himself. "Am I a suspect? Is all that I'm reading in the press true? You're gunning for me?"

"There are connections to your case and these murders, the Shine murders and Conor Sheridan's. I need to follow up on all leads."

He throws himself back on the seat, closes his eyes, and I wait for him to offer his alibi, wait for him to reveal himself as the organized killer behind these crimes. An organized killer would have his alibi solid. Offer it up smooth as you like. To an organized killer, their story is important. The lie requires embellishment, swathes of detail to convince, and plenty of imagery, feeling, and padding to cover the little black vein of truth that hides the heart of their tale. I wait for Seán to give me his.

After a moment, he leans in, a desperate note to his voice. "I don't have an alibi for that night. Please, this can't happen again, Frankie. You have my DNA on file. Run it against this guy; do whatever you do to link people to crimes. Rule me out."

I sink back against the seat. "That's what I'm doing." And I realize that's exactly what I'm doing. I'm no longer hunting Seán Hennessy; I'm ruling him out.

CHAPTER 21

STEVE DRAINS THE LAST of his power drink. A sickly looking orange concoction that near on rots my teeth just looking at it.

"You need to ease up on the sugar addiction, Detective."

He puts down the bottle quickly. Surprised to see me. He picks up a file, hands it to me. "All the letters that we found on Sheridan's computer," he says.

"Thanks."

I go to the coffee machine, set down the file, and select an espresso. Outside the sky is closing over. Full dark clouds gather over the city. The moon a hidden orb of white in the evening sky. The day is seeping away, lights from the traffic below throw yellow beams across the window.

The office is quiet. Too quiet. The phones have died down. There is little exchange between staff members, no rumbles of excitement at the coffee machine. The team is edging on confusion. All working the scatter of this murder. The only cohesive element is the cluster of victims pressed to our case board. Helen's just about visible behind the partition of her desk, pen tucked behind her ear, brows drawn together in concentration. Paul is the only one who seems happy with the change of pace. It's the first time I've seen his back touch his chair since the case opened. He clicks slowly over his keyboard with one hand, a sandwich poised in the other, his mouth working contently. Out of everything, this alarms me the most.

I rap on the desk, capture their attention. "Let's have a quick debrief."

I see Paul give the sandwich a longing look and think he might cram the entire thing in his mouth before he comes over. With some reluctance, he wraps it up and leaves it on his desk. They gather, Ryan in the front row. Helen gets up from her desk, sits next to him, and Ryan leans away slightly. Baz folds his long limbs, hooks his foot over his knee. His laces have come undone but he doesn't notice. He reaches for his notebook, balances it on his lap.

"The killer is ticking off a sequence of murders that fit the normal pattern of crime," I say. "Victim, weapon, and killer. Now he's come to the end of that pattern, we'll likely have a cooling-off period before he attempts to kill again."

I start at the middle of the case board. Work outwards, use the photos as a guide.

"Victim one: Alan Shine, forty-five years old. Electrician. Murdered by strangulation between the fourteenth and seventeenth of August. Body recovered next to his wife at St. Catherine's, Clontarf Road, on Sunday the nineteenth of August. We believe he was killed elsewhere then dressed in priest's vestments before being positioned in the church by the killer. Alan Shine was murdered as part of an elaborate display by the killer. In the killer's eyes and in our case we have named him Weapon.

"Victim two: Geraldine Shine, forty-two years old. Online beauty salesperson. Worked from home. Stabbed to death in St. Catherine's church on Clontarf Road on the nineteenth of August between the hours of two P.M. and six thirty P.M. She was stripped naked to the waist at the scene, laid prone next to her husband. The murder weapon was located in her husband's hand, although we know that Alan Shine could not have killed his wife as he was already dead. There were eleven stab wounds inflicted on her back postmortem. These are significant. They mimic the injuries sustained by Bríd Hennessy on August 13, 1995. The killer has labeled Geraldine Shine, Victim.

"Victim three: Conor Sheridan, forty years old. Father of two and ex-husband of Jane Brennan. He's been paying his bills with intermittent contract work over the last few years. An alcoholic but toxicology and witnesses say that he's been sober for the last five months. We believe that Conor felt under threat. He'd been receiving hate mail from an unknown sender. At his home in Tallaght, we discovered his room was tightly bolted. It might've been he knew or suspected his life was in danger.

"Conor was murdered at an unknown location and brought to Clontarf beach, probably via boat, in the early hours of the twenty-second of August 2012. His body had been cleaned, dressed in a new suit, and posed against the seawall at Dollymount Avenue. The word KILLER was written in the sand at his feet, suggesting not only that our perp was determined to leave a message but that he understood the tides well enough to know his message would remain at Sheridan's feet until his body was discovered.

"During postmortem the cause of death was found to be a gunshot through the heart. Conor was stored in refrigeration for at least five days before the killer moved him to the beach.

"We've been following a lot of leads to no avail, so now our primary objective is to find where Conor Sheridan and Alan Shine were murdered, where their bodies were kept. We do that, I've no doubt we'll find this murderer. These types of killers can't ever let go of their crimes. They store their kill kits, tokens from their victims; they revisit crime scenes. If we can find where he's based, or where he murders his victims, we'll have a nest of evidence at our disposal."

Baz adds, "A reminder: We're looking at fridges or locations large enough to store bodies for days at a time. We're looking for the boat that may have transported Conor Sheridan's body to shore."

"Update on Robbie McDonagh?"

Ryan shifts on his seat. "He's been quiet lately. Quality time with his ma, looks like. Hits the corner store most evenings for a six-pack. But all in all he's been lying low."

"No visits with Jimmy Lynch?"

"Nothing. Local gardaí are finding it very unusual that Robbie's not at his local hangouts," he adds.

Baz is the first to get up. He slots his notebook into his back pocket and catches my eye.

"Good work, everyone. Who's on late tonight?" I ask. By late I mean through the night. Helen and Ryan put up their hands.

Steve returns to his desk, gathers up his coat, a worn black denim jacket. "Emer's due in." He looks pointedly at the clock, which shows five after nine. "I tried to clean up the CCTV footage with Sheridan at the shop but all I can get from the reflection in the shop window is a shadow. We've still not been able to get who he was calling but we ran through Jane Brennan's records and as suspected, we discovered that she did receive a call from him around that time. The call lasted under thirty seconds and Jane says he was canceling a visit with the kids the following day."

"Right, can't you hold off until Emer gets here? Keep working on the footage?"

He removes a packet of gum from the top pocket of his jacket, pops one in his mouth, already shaking his narrow head. "No can do, Chief. Got band practice tonight."

Baz follows me into my office, sits down at the desk, lowers the chair, and stretches out. It's dark and stuffy, and I go to the window and push it open the couple of inches it allows. I stand there for a while, breathing in the cool air, the grime and sweat of the case thick on my skin and the taste of failure sour in my mouth. At the beginning of a case, it's easy to keep energy high and convince yourself you've got the upper hand, and some cases work like that, under every rock you kick up, a microcosm of evidence, but not this one. Not this time. Clancy used to say that there's a moment in every case when you know you're not going to win. When you realize that all the shreds of evidence you've at your disposal are never going to stitch together. For some cases you know immediately. For others it can take months before that moment comes. And now I think I know what he meant by that.

Baz stifles a yawn with his hand. "What's that you always say? The answers lie with the victims. Don't forget them," he says.

I sit down at the desk and move the mouse of my computer to wake the screen. I see two emails from Donna Hegarty. One about the case budget and the other asking me for a detailed report on what Jack Clancy has told me about his daughter and Seán Hennessy.

"That sounds like good advice."

"Well, maybe we've lost focus a bit. Forgotten them. If we look at what links them . . ." He rubs a palm over his face as if to wake himself up. "Alan, he was dressed as the priest; he was also a lay minister. That says someone local, right?"

I move the cursor over the emails. Click *delete*. "We know it's someone local."

"But someone who went to Mass occasionally. And not just any Mass but the service at St. Catherine's."

I look round the computer at him. "Did we get a list of the congregation?"

Baz reaches forward, picks up the phone, puts it on speaker. "Helen, do we have a list of the congregation at St. Catherine's?"

"No. Healy said he couldn't possibly name everyone who attended services."

I recall Mrs. Berry's testimony that there'd been only twenty in the church that afternoon.

"Well, why is that not surprising," Baz says, the eye roll clear in his voice. "Get on the phone to Healy. Tell him we want the names of the regulars at his Sunday service. If he doesn't cough up, tell him to put the kettle on because I'll be round within the hour."

"It's quite late."

"Keep ringing until he answers," Baz says firmly.

"Okay, also Emer's just in and she says she's got a rough view of the vehicle in the Sheridan footage."

Baz puts down the phone and pulls himself out of the chair. He shakes out his hands and I can see a flash of satisfaction in his eyes at the thought of putting Healy out.

I smile at him. "Don't be too smug."

He spreads his hands in a show of innocence. "What?"

I shake my head and leave the office, Baz at my side, the bounce back in his step.

Emer is hunched over Steve's desk again and I'm glad he's not here to see the order she's restored to it, files and notes neatly stacked. Not a sign of Coke can. It's close to a violation.

"What have we got?" I try to keep my excitement in check. The image we'll get, if any, might just be a passerby. Someone slowing to ask for directions maybe. It could be nothing, another stray lead to follow to a nothing end. Emer clicks on a tab and the screenshot appears, displaying a murky photo of shadow and light. I look down at the dark reflection of the vehicle and remind myself that cases often hinge on the smallest of offerings, even the shadow of a car.

"Steve attempted to resize it but it scrambled the image so it's taken me a while to get back to where I was yesterday," she grumbles.

I suppress a smile. She can't have been in the office more than ten minutes.

"The vehicle is substantial enough," she continues, "the height of the lights off the ground, not quite SUV territory, but comparable to a sedan model." She clicks the cursor over the image, draws in the shape of the lights. "Considering the height of the vehicle, length, the angle, length of the hood, and position of the wheel hubs"—she adds more shape to the image—"the model of the vehicle reflected in the window is likely similar to—"

"It's a Beemer," Baz says from over my shoulder. Emer shoots him an irritated look that he's jumped all over her discovery. "Sorry. Go on," he murmurs.

She clicks another minimized tab on the computer and the

screen unfolds, spreads out to reveal a blue BMW saloon car. "As I was saying, it's similar to a vehicle in this series. It ran in variations of black, red, blue, gray, white, silver, and metallic versions of these colors so I reckon either a charcoal gray, blue, or black here."

"The year?" I ask.

She pulls up two photos of the car. She hovers the cursor over the first photo. "This is the 2011 model, the trunk, there's a lip on the edge, it's a little stylized. But in the 2012 model"—she clicks on the other photo—"you can see they've smoothed out that ridge. The car in the CCTV appears to hold a similar shape at the rear. So I'd say, new. A 2012 BMW saloon in blue, black, or charcoal gray."

I can see it, see that the trunk appears to slope downwards. I imagine streetlights skimming over the smooth paintwork as it moved down the road, out of sight, into the darkness.

My heart picks up. I can feel the plates of the case groan beneath my feet, begin to align. "David Brennan, Jane's husband. He collected the kids in a car like that, the morning I spoke to her."

She opens up the National Vehicle and Driver File, types in David Brennan's name, address. Looks up his birth date, then enters that too. In a few seconds she has his car details.

"That's a match. Similar car," she says. She writes down the registration number and passes it to me.

"Expensive car for a crane driver." Baz remarks.

"I think David Brennan likes to top up his income by other means. Thanks," I say to Emer. "If David Brennan was the last person to see Conor Sheridan, he's either involved in this somehow or at the least, he might've seen someone."

"Can we check his working hours against the timeline for the Shine murders?" Baz asks.

Emer searches for Dublin Port, brings up the staff page, scrolls through the departments. "He's in cargo, right?"

Cargo. The image of Dublin Port rises in my head. A dark, echoing landscape, the sounds of metal groaning against the crash of the Irish Sea. The busy turn of cranes, loading and unloading containers onto ferries, and the trundle of lorries waiting to move their containers aboard.

"Containers," I murmur.

Baz and Emer glance at each other, a confused kind of worry widening their gazes.

"Containers," I say again. "Could you hide a body in one? A fridge or freezer even?"

Baz gives a slow nod. "I guess, if you knew which ones weren't in use."

"And worked somewhere where you wouldn't necessarily draw attention going to and from one." I can see the excitement light in Baz's eyes.

"What do we do about Brennan?"

"If we can get evidence first, find that crime scene, we'll have a stronger interview. But fill the team in; I want a close eye on him. Contact me if there's any movement. We need to find that container now."

I return to my office, pull on the holster, and throw my coat over my shoulders.

Baz meets me on the floor. "What's our move?"

THE BUSTLE AND BEEP of the port bleats out into the dark night. A few voices shout into the wind along the dock. The clunk and bang of hatches opening, the rattle of semitrucks easing closer to the dock.

Baz gets out of the passenger seat and walks to my side. "Jesus, it's fucking freezing. Where to?"

We're close. I can feel it. The answer to this case is a step away.

"Over there." I point across the terminal to a chain-link fence.

Even from this distance, I can see it's broken down in places, and beyond it is a scrapyard of sorts. Mounds of rusting metal pipes; an old digger, grass growing up around its runners. And windowless houses, old containers, gathered up against a high concrete wall. A mini-city of steel.

"How many are there, do you reckon? Seventy odd?" I open the back door of the car, remove a couple of stab vests, pass one to Baz. He shakes the cold from his fingers, then shrugs out of his jacket, hooking the vest over his head and securing the Velcro straps at his chest then he pulls his jacket back on quickly. I do the same, my coat uncomfortably tight over the extra bulk of the vest and the weight of the gun at my shoulder.

"We'll be through it in no time," he says, and jogs his body up and down on the spot, like an athlete ready to run.

I shove some plastic gloves in my pocket, should we strike it lucky. Determination to pick up this lead rises through me. Baz heaves a crowbar out of the trunk. "Let's go find us a crime scene."

We move forward into the darkness. There are rows of containers, stacked high like forgotten Lego bricks. I shine the torch over the uneven ground. The wind screams through the narrow passages created by the containers. My feet catch on gravel and metal. But once we get in the thick of it, the wind drops, held back by the walls of metal around us. The safe sound of activity on the port becomes muffled, and we both stand for a moment to work out our movements.

"I'll go this way." Baz points the crowbar to the right. "Keep your radio on three."

I turn the dial of my radio. "There'll be a generator, for the freezer, listen for it."

"If the wind bloody stays down. Hopefully we'll make light work of this. It's not the kind of night for a jaunt along the fucking seafront." He walks away and in seconds he's gone, invisible in the night.

I move on through the maze but I can hear Baz tapping the sides of a few of the containers, the clang of metal on metal. I keep my torch low, scan the sides, the levers that open the containers. Deep in the center, I see one, slightly off at a distance, long side facing out, not in line with the rest. I move toward it and slowly I pick up a track in the gravel, the suggestion of a path, the odd footprint in the mud beneath the gravel. And then there are footsteps, a skitter of stones behind me and the crunch of gravel. I stop. And the footsteps stop.

I turn off the torch, slide it into my pocket. Move slowly; my hand reaches for the Sig Sauer at my shoulder. My palm welcomes it. My breath settles. I wait. Ear cocked, hearing nothing but the persistent roar of the Irish Sea. Then a figure, tall and swift, crouched over, speeds ahead of me, disappears into the maze. And I chase after it. Through the network of containers further into the darkness.

CHAPTER 22

"FREEZE! GARDAÍ." But whoever it is does not stop. He goes deeper into the maze of containers.

"Harwood!" I shout.

My voice bounces back and in moments there is silence, broken only by the cold hiss of the wind beyond the walls of the containers, the distant drone of traffic and lorries easing away from the port toward the city. I try his radio but am met with static. I fight to control my breathing. Feel that old panic rise, feel it creeping around my chest; sweat gathers along my hairline. I turn the torch on again and move slowly after the shadowly figure.

The beam from the torch slices through the darkness. I round the corner of a container. Ahead a narrow path. More containers, rusted yellows and oranges. He can't be far. Baz can't be far. And then on the other side, the scuffle of feet. A groan. I hear Baz swear then a loud crash; the dull thud of thick metal. I hurry toward the sound. Find Baz on the ground. I scan the area, look for our hostile. But he's gone. Run off into the darkness.

I squat down. Move the light over Baz's face. "Who?"

"I didn't see," he pants. "He hit me from behind." He raises a hand, rubs the back of his head. When he brings his hand away it's bright with blood. "Looks worse than it is; gave my ribs a good kicking though." He doesn't look up at me, his eyes down. In the torchlight I can see the pallor of his face. Lips dry. Eyes tight with pain. "Do you mind not shining that fucking thing in my eye," he snaps.

I lower the torch. "Sorry."

He tucks a foot under him, pushes upright, his hand pitched against his side. A low groan squeezes out from his throat. He stands for a moment, testing his breathing, his head down. Finally, he glances up, looks at me. "Sorry. I didn't mean to snap."

"I'll live," I reply.

His mouth lifts into what could be a smile but looks like a grimace. "Fucking fucker," he says, limps sorely toward the fallen crowbar, then with some effort reaches down and takes it up.

"He came from back there." I indicate over my shoulder.

I lead us back. Watchful for any movement among the corridors of containers. Not wanting to be hit again. Baz was lucky to get away with a few slaps. And our assailant is lucky our trigger fingers are out of practice. We find a container on the perimeter of the yard. It stands alone. A generator at the back end hums quietly into the night, the sound easily swallowed up by the thrum of the port. A stiff breeze lifts the hair from my forehead, sends cold down my neck.

"This has to be it. I'll call it in, get a cordon set up," I say to

Baz. His head wound is bleeding into his shirt. Hand gripping his side. "You need to get seen by a doctor."

"No way." He tries to straighten but only manages a pathetic lift of his left shoulder. "I'm not leaving until I see the inside of this thing." He leans down on his knees, looks up at me. "He could still be here."

I look out into the darkness. "He's gone and I'm not having you bleed all over my crime scene. As soon as a vehicle arrives, I'm sending you back with them."

I make the call and we wait for the team to arrive. Baz eases down onto the damp ground against one of the containers, draws his knees up, and rests his head on his arms.

The first gardaí cars arrive within the half hour, by which time I'm pacing over and back to keep warm. Baz gets up, but despite the cold, he seems to move easier.

"I'll see you back at the office," he says, the sulk pulling on his face and thick in his voice. He follows a guard back out through the containers.

KEITH'S BLUE BERLINGO pulls up at the edge of the cordon. He gets out of the van and opens the back. I hold on to my patience. Hand tight around the crowbar. I'm desperate to get into the container but we can't compromise the process of collecting evidence. So I wait, wait while Keith chats to every uniform about. Wait for him to collect his tools. He pulls on his suit; the SOCO with him does the same. Then finally taking two holdalls of equipment from the front seat, they duck beneath the outer garda cordon and step through the wire fence.

"Detective Sheehan," he calls out a few feet from me. "We got some goods here then? You thinking a body?"

"Murder scene. No body. I hope."

He stops when he reaches me, turns to the SOCO trailing in his wake. A young one, fresh out of training, full cheeks hamster-like beneath the white hood of her protective clothing. The bags of equipment pull on her shoulders. "Get the tent up there, Theresa, and set up the log."

"Yes, boss." She sets down the bags and bends over them, removes a spare pair of gloves, which she offers to me.

"Thanks, I have some," I say, removing the gloves from my pocket and pulling them on. I move to the lock on the container. "Ready?"

He bounces on his heels. "It's too cold of a night to be hanging around, that's for sure."

I put the crowbar through the lock and lever downwards. The mechanism slips but doesn't budge.

"Theresa, bolt-cutters."

The SOCO passes them over.

"That's the business," Keith says. He places the mouth of the cutters on the bolt, tongue down against his bottom lip. He has to reach upward to get level but he persists and with a loud metal groan, the sharp edges come together and snap through the container lock. He passes the cutters back as if he was a surgeon and Theresa his surgical assistant.

"Right, after you." He makes a sweeping gesture with his hand.

Reaching out, I pull the bolt away from the door and it swings open on blackness. Keith's shouting at one of the uniforms for lights. I peer into the gloomy darkness of the container. The smell comes first. Stale blood and the musky scent of damp air swirls out around me but inside I can pick out the white, hard edge of a freezer. Theresa passes me a torch, and I point the beam inside the container.

The container is a pit of evidence. One man-sized freezer, connected to a generator. Hanging inside the door, two green plastic suits.

I point them out to Theresa. "We'll need those processed immediately."

"Yes, ma'am."

The heat is on me, over my skin, along my hairline. Excitement. Rabid. I swallow. The lights go up outside and the container transforms under the steady beam. It takes on an almost homey look. Thin, dark carpet with a snaking cream pattern has been laid over the walls and the floor. An attempt at soundproofing is my guess.

Along the back wall I see an upturned wooden crate. A black nylon bag slumped like a dead animal on top of it.

Theresa waits beside me. "There." I point the light toward the crate. "What's in that?"

She pales and I know what's wrong. I remember that feeling, early on in my career, stepping into a killer's lair. Some primitive part of your brain tells you to walk the other way. The smell, the remnants of death, the sad echo of the victim calling out for eternity in the air. But whatever she's feeling, she pulls back her shoulders and steps inside.

She stands over the crate, carefully opens the bag. Takes up a camera from around her neck, photographs the contents. "It looks like a kill kit," she says, and takes more shots. "Rope. Tape. Plastic. Gloves."

"Weapons?"

"No."

"No gun?"

"No."

I push away frustration. I hold the torch up, cast the beam along the carpet. It's dark, dirty, but the cream pattern is almost obliterated at the center of the container.

I nod to the stain. "Blood?"

Suddenly she's unsure, a flash of fear crosses her face, and she peers out beyond me as if she could conjure Keith. And as if on cue, the ground crunches and then his voice booms next to my ear.

"Well, well. What have we got here then?" He squints into the container.

I nod to the floor. "Does that look like blood to you?"

He turns, puts his foot up on the ledge, and levers his short body inside. "Oh yeah. That's a pretty big wound that caused that." He squats down. "Old though. Someone's done a poor job mopping it up. And a nice little bullet hole here." The tip of his finger hovers over the floor. He glances up at Theresa, who already has the camera aimed down at the spot. "Get that marked up there, Theresa. Let's see what we've got in the big box then," he says, referring to the freezer. "Are we letting hope out or something else, do you think?" He gives a chuckle at his reference to Pandora's box, and I hear Seán Hennessy's voice in my head: *Here I was, inside Pandora's box. And no one was going to lift the lid.*

"Just open the fucking freezer, Keith."

"Miss your coffee break, Detective?" he snarks back. But he goes to the freezer and, without so much as a breath, lifts the door.

"Kind of disappointed there's no body," he says. He waves his hand, and Theresa passes him a torch. "But we've been left something, all right." He bends over and reaches down into the trunk of the freezer; white clouds of cold vapor billow out around him. When he straightens his face has reddened but he looks triumphant. In his hand there's a book, wrapped in clear plastic. He hands the torch back to the SOCO and moves toward me, unpeeling the plastic from around the book.

Reaching out a gloved hand, I take it, look over the worn cover then turn the pages slowly. Pictures of all the victims. The original article from Conor Sheridan, photos of the final crime scene at the Hennessys'. Notes outlining plans. Careful. Notes on cleanup. Timed and dated. I come to a page marked with the Shines' names. It details Geraldine Shine's movements over the course of three weeks. Her morning runs, how long it takes her to complete her 5k circuit. The frequency of her deliveries. Her visits to the church, her meetings with Father Healy. Notes on Alan Shine's preference of the pub ahead of his wife. The nights he returned drunk, the nights he beat Geraldine. Conor Sheridan's address, his work hours, his commute, photographs of him leaving Jane Brennan's, kissing his young kids good-bye. The writing is slow, precise. All capitals. All between the lines. Someone has labored over this, treasured it.

On one page is the image of Bríd Hennessy facedown on the lawn, red wounds down her back, and overleaf, Geraldine Shine in the same resting pose. Pages of detail into the capture and kill of all three victims. I turn more pages and stop when my own face looks back. I'm standing on the wooden bridge looking back over Dublin Bay, toward Clontarf. I remember that day, the damp air, the sharp sea wind, and what was filling up my head:

the hot sun on Bríd Hennessy's face as I recalled her passing me on the path, seventeen years previous. I feel my tongue grow thick in my mouth, bile rises in my throat. He was watching me.

I turn the page. Photos of the team, my work colleagues. Jack Clancy, in his car, window down, his elbow propped on the ledge, cigarette in one hand, phone held to his ear with the other. Baz mid-stride, two coffees stacked on top of each other, a brown bag dangling at his side that I know contained two stodgy bagels. I feel the whole night close in around me, the victims peering over my shoulder. While we were stalking the killer, he was stalking us.

On the final page, there's a grainy photo of a young Seán Hennessy standing in his childhood back garden. Above his image, one word in large letters, like an angry threat overhead: JUSTICE.

I glance at Keith, fear tight on his face. His eyes, small and round, look out into the port, search the darkness.

"He's not here," I say. "Whoever did this."

He draws his gaze back. Gives a short, trembling laugh. "Oh. No. I was just seeing what the weather was at. Could probably do with the tent up around here, get the car closer. Maybe ring in a few more SOCOs."

I close the journal. "We need this whole container pulled apart. Wrap and seal the journal for me, send it to Forensics. I want a copy back at the Bureau within the hour."

WHEN I GET BACK to the office, Steve is dancing as if he's on hot coals.

"Paul's had a call from a Mr. Charles Derry, off the back of the press conference. Mr. Derry has a boat that was borrowed a day before we think Sheridan went missing. He frequently rents it out in the summer months."

"Type of boat?"

"Small RIB. It's a rigid inflatable dinghy."

"He have the name for us?"

Steve smiles, his thin face taking on a ghoulish appearance. "David Brennan. Two uniforms were sent out fifteen minutes ago to pick him up."

"Get CSI out to his house while he's here. Clear out the missus and the kids. A basic sweep and seize his car. Is Baz here?"

"He's waiting in your office."

"How is he?"

"Nursing his ego more than his bruises. He's grand."

"You've sent the retrieval team for the boat?"

"They should have it at Forensics in about an hour."

"I want prints, DNA, and a detailed search for blood samples. Compare them with every name that's been linked to this case."

"Copy that, Chief."

I make my way to the office. When I step inside, Baz closes the door behind me. I look him over. He's changed his shirt. His hair and face are clean. He looks agitated but it's not pain I see tightening on his face; it's anger.

"You sure you're up to this?" I ask.

The muscles over his jaw give a little pulse of movement. He crosses his legs. "Of course."

"You seem tense."

"I just got jumped by some shit. How should I seem?"

I lean up against the wall of the office, watch the stiff set of his face. The unfamiliar pinch of skin between his eyebrows and the white flare of his nostrils. And I feel for him. I understand his anger but he can't allow it to spill over into an interview. And I won't have a detective throwing a fit at a suspect because they can't keep their mood in check.

"You hear about the boat hire?"

"Yeah."

"We've David Brennan coming in now for questioning. Two strikes for him," I say, hoping to engage him in something other than the storm of his thoughts. When he continues to glower, I say, "Can you put it to the side?"

He looks up at me from beneath lowered brows. "What?"

"You look about fit to drive your fist through a wall, and I'm worried a man like Brennan will smell that on you a mile away and invite you to try your fist on his face, rather than a wall, thus fucking over my investigation. *Our* investigation."

He pushes back into the seat. There's no wince but I see the slight paling of the skin around his temple and know that he's feeling more than a sting in his ribs. "I can put it aside when I need to. Clancy's not the only one in here with two faces."

"That's a bit low."

"Is it? The commissioner is right, fair enough, he covered up some shit back in the day, but he lied to us. Why's that okay? Why does he get to decide who knows what and when?"

"Rona's testimony has nothing to do with these cases and you know that."

"It was a time suck. You dancing around looking for answers to Hennessy's past—"

"You're saying I missed something related to these cases because of Clancy's secrecy on something that happened years ago?"

"His silence on this created a link between the cases. Made Hennessy look like he might have it in him. Made a shitty link look stronger than it was."

I drag in a lungful of air. He's angry. Unreasonable. And he's looking for someone to blame for his bruises.

"There was a link," I say, trying to keep my voice low. Calm. "There is a link. The bodies were arranged as the Hennessys were, remember? And there's the Sheridan article. The hate mail related to that too."

He scrunches up his eyes as if he doesn't want to hear. "Clancy's silence threw another log on the fire though, didn't it? And now it's given the media everything they want, and we're tiptoeing around a serious investigation afraid to take a fucking dump in case it's the wrong shape and we'll be laughed at for it."

"We're no further back nor forward with or without Rona O'Sullivan's alibi for Seán Hennessy. It was seventeen years ago." But I can see my words are having little effect on him. His head is down, shoulders up, the pads of his jacket high against his neck. I try a different tack. "Clancy's secrets have hurt no one but himself. He's not responsible for what happened to you tonight, and you know he'd be the first one at your back if he'd been there."

He glances upward briefly, his expression one of cynicism. He's silent for a moment, then he directs his gaze back to the floor.

Eventually, he says, "I should've paid more attention at the port. Should've grabbed that fucker but he caught me off guard." He looks up at me, meets my eyes. "That shouldn't have happened. Next time I'll be ready."

"There won't be a next time," I say.

"Too fucking right. Next time I'll take the first shot." He gets up, walks to the door then looks back expectantly. "Are we going to question this fella anytime soon?"

I nod slowly, feeling a stab of concern over the tone in his voice. Everything turning gray around me, my work, my colleagues, myself. "I'll be there in a minute," I reply.

He leaves, the door closing quietly behind him. I sit at the desk, push my fingers against closed eyes. I resurrect the faces of the killer's victims: Geraldine Shine, Alan, Conor, and somewhere in the mix, Bríd and Cara Hennessy; John Hennessy a gloomy, faceless figure in the background of my mind. I remind myself that what matters is I bring home justice for those victims.

If our killer is obsessed with Hennessy, then that's who we need to be obsessed with too. Waking my computer, I search for my place in the Hennessy footage and click the next clip. Seán Hennessy sits on his stool. Hands clasped between his knees.

"Inside, innocent or not, people are their crimes," he begins. "At first, you're just you, you know. That youngster thrown into the darkest of places among the darkest of people. But at some stage, you got to live, you know. You got to find a way. And when that realization comes on you, the whole place opens up. You get used to the rhythms of the day. You become an expert at spending time. Play cards, exercise, read, paint, write. And you walk into your role as a criminal. For me, as a murderer. I wasn't a murderer when they locked me up but after a few months I began to move like one, talk like one.

"I made friends. There was a group of us, we'd sit together. Share our stories, jokes, united in our hatred of the system. Those friends, in any other walk of life you'd move away from but inside they felt like family. And as I got to know them, I saw how common my life was, a dad absent or abusive. With only a stern hand to guide my youth, how could I help but slip out from under it? These guys knew that life well. It was like talking into a mirror."

CHAPTER 23

I STEP OUT ONTO THE FLOOR, and Helen is up from her desk immediately. "We've got some prints from the container."

"Go."

"Brennan's prints were found on the lock outside the container. A further two sets of prints from inside and hair from two of our victims, Sheridan and Alan Shine."

"Any match on the prints from inside the container?"

"Yes. Jimmy Lynch. Both on the lock and on the freezer door."

And I thank fuck that finally the ball is rolling. "The other set?"

"Not on record. Ryan's gone to pick Lynch up now with a couple of uniforms."

"Getting crowded in here. He won't come easy. Again, organize a CSI sweep on Lynch's flat while he's in for questioning."

"Right away, Chief. Also, Abigail has confirmed that the fiber taken from Conor Sheridan's cheek during autopsy is a match to the carpet inside the container."

"Great. We can use that during interview. Thanks, Helen."

I meet Baz in the viewing area outside interview room one where David Brennan is waiting for our questions. I fill Baz in on Jimmy Lynch.

"The fuck? So Jimmy Lynch is living with Conor Sheridan, his housemate for five years, and now he's involved in his murder? These assholes." He presses a hand against his ribs and winces. "So is his mate McDonagh featuring here?"

"Not sure. The plainclothes we've put on his house say he's still spending all his time with his ma. Not moved much since we let him out."

"Well, he's been awfully fucking quiet."

"Something tells me his ma is prison guard enough for him."

I peer through the window at David Brennan. He's vacated the interview chair. Stretched out he is, on the floor, as if he was on the fucking Côte d'Azur sunning himself. Sleeves of his lemon-colored shirt rolled up, his arms clasped lightly across his stomach. He's removed a white trainer, pitched it under his head to act as a pillow. His mouth gapes open, his eyes closed.

"Bet he snores," Baz says.

"No need to bet. Come on, let's wake Sleeping Beauty."

I rap hard on the door and walk in. His eyelids lift, lazy and slow. He doesn't move.

"You comfortable, Mr. Brennan?"

He stretches his arms above his head, thick muscles packed tight beneath his thin shirt. "Could be better," he says.

"This is Detective Barry Harwood. He'll be joining us for this interview."

Baz pulls up another chair, sits down. And David Brennan peels himself off the ground. Runs a hand over his hair.

"Howya."

"Not so bad, my friend. Not so bad," Baz answers. He nods to the chair. "Would ye take a seat for us, David? We've a few questions for you."

Brennan drags the chair back, sits down, crosses his legs, cups his hands around his knee. Yawns.

Baz gives him a wide smile, drops Brennan's file down onto the table, and then settles into the seat across from him. He rests a foot on his knee, matches Brennan's chilled posture. And I relax, whatever bad thoughts were twitching away in him earlier are gone. You'd not think for one moment that Baz had anything but the easiest of nights. His eyes are alert and direct, his hand, pen ready, taps once on the cover of the file. "Can I get you a coffee, mate?"

"I'm grand," Brennan replies. "Caffeine gives me shocking heartburn." He beats his chest with his fist, burps into his hand as if to prove a point.

"We'll get started then so," Baz says with another smile.

I don't sit but stand just inside the door, facing the table. Waiting for Brennan to settle. See what face he's playing with. He's got an air of control about him. He's feeling comfortable.

Baz turns on the recorder. "Interview with David Brennan, conducted by Detective Barry Harwood and Detective Chief Superintendent Frankie Sheehan." Then he sits back, rests his hands on the table. "Let us tell you how we got here, Mr. Brennan." A patient smile. "We've been tracing the last known movements of your wife's ex-husband, Conor Sheridan. You know who we're talking about?"

"Of course I bloody do."

"Okay. We've footage of him in Fairview car park on Wednesday the fifteenth of August at approximately ten P.M., doing a bit of late-night shopping. He exits the shop and his attention is drawn to the road. He walks up to the car park entrance and appears to have a brief interaction with someone driving past. Do you know who that could be?"

"No."

"Where were you on the night of the fifteenth of August between ten and ten forty-five P.M.?

"I was at home."

"Do you have someone who can verify that?"

He glances over at me. "My wife, Jane."

"This is Jane Brennan, Conor Sheridan's ex-wife?" Baz asks.

"That's correct."

"So you did not have a run-in or meet or see Conor Sheridan that evening? You were at home?"

"That's correct."

Baz pulls out a photograph of the footage. "This is an image of Conor Sheridan and beyond him that of a vehicle that slowed and stopped before driving off on the night Mr. Sheridan was last seen. Do you recognize the vehicle in this photograph?"

Brennan studies the photograph for a few seconds. "No, it's blurry."

"We've been able to identify it as a BMW sedan, 2012. Nice and new."

Silence.

"What vehicle do you drive, Mr. Brennan?" Baz continues.

"Similar, I suppose."

"Okay. So a person driving this vehicle slows and speaks to our victim on the evening we suppose he went missing, possibly murdered. And you, who live in the area, drive a similar vehicle, and not only that but the victim is your wife's ex?" Baz blows air through his lips. "You see how this looks for you?"

The color drops from Brennan's face.

Baz smiles at him. "Can you take us through your movements on Sunday the nineteenth of August?"

He looks over at me again. "I was working. My shift started at five."

Baz scratches his ear. "Right so, right so. How long did your shift last?"

"It's an eight-hour shift, until one A.M."

"And did you visit the container that held Alan Shine's body in that time?"

David Brennan's mouth opens. He looks to me then to Baz then back again. Then he tucks his hands between his thighs like a child ready for scolding. "What are you talking about?"

My cue. I move to the table. Sit down. "Mr. Brennan, we've found the container. One of your colleagues has already verified that you've been seen heading in the direction of the . . . what did he call it?" I look to Baz.

"The container graveyard," Baz offers.

"That's right. The container graveyard. And you know what we found there. Our murder scene."

He swallows, his eyes widening. "No. That's got nothing to do with me."

"Your prints were on the lock of a container at the port. Can you explain that?"

His hands have moved to the table, palms down, fingers spread. He stares down at them and then shakes his head.

"We recovered from this container hair strands from two of our victims, Alan Shine and Conor Sheridan. During postmortem examination we recovered fibers that came from the inside of the container on Conor Sheridan's body."

His neck snaps up. "I don't know what this is but I've nothing to do with that."

"Tell me what you know about this container, Mr. Brennan?"

"I don't know anything."

"We want to help you out of this mess, but to do that we need you to tell us the truth. This is your chance. You've already lied to us and we found you out."

"I swear to you. All I was told was to check over the generator. I had no idea what was inside. Wasn't it drugs?"

"No."

He swallows.

"It was used to store bodies. Murder victims, Mr. Brennan."

He pales. "I don't know anything."

"Who told you to keep an eye on the container?"

"A bloke. Someone I met inside a few years ago, we do a bit of work for one another from time to time."

"His name."

"Jimmy. Jimmy Lynch." He continues in a rush, "I just found the location for him. Kept an eye on it from time to time. That was all. I was never inside it. The generator was just to the back, on the outside, covered in black tarpaulin."

BY THE TIME the interview finishes, there are circles of sweat darkening the soft lemon of Brennan's shirt. His hand goes to his temple often to scoop away droplets of moisture. His eyes are round with fear. We leave him bent into his arms, and Ryan enters the room to take his statement.

"What are you thinking?" Baz asks when we step onto the office floor.

"I think he's telling the truth. His prints weren't inside. He's just about thick enough to take money for this and not ask questions."

"I agree. I can see him getting caught up in this mess all right but murdering Geraldine Shine, putting a bullet through his wife's ex, strangling Alan Shine." He shivers. "And the whole way the bodies were laid out. I dunno."

"Exactly. Don't think Brennan has the gray matter to put this together." I take up the file.

Lynch is settled in our second interview room, and we go straight for him. Baz follows me down the short hallway into the viewing room. Someone has left some boxed sandwiches on the small round table in the center of the tiny viewing room and a couple of coffees. Baz dives on them like a red kite on prey. He splits a packet open and offers me one. "No thanks," I say, trying to hide the grimace. Food is the last thing I can think about right now. Taking up a coffee, I turn to the window and look in at Jimmy Lynch's bulk.

Lynch is motionless in the chair. I get the image of a crocodile in water when I look at him. Eyes pinned to the wall across from him. Breath so even, it's impossible to pick out the rise and fall of his chest. His hands are cupped into each other on his lap. The only movement that betrays him is the slow beat of his index finger against the back of his hand. I let out a long breath, remind myself to stick to the right questions, wrap this fuck's answers around his own neck so my victims get their justice. I throw an impatient glance at Baz.

"All right, all right," he says, and puts down the sandwich. "I can see you're about ready to jump through the fucking glass." He takes a swig of the coffee then pulls a face. "No sugar."

I open the door and greet our latest suspect with a sure smile.

"Jimmy, how's it going?"

"Fuck off."

I wait for Baz to sit next to me.

"Interview with Jimmy Lynch of 9b Beagan Heights, Tallaght. Present are Detective Chief Superintendent Frankie Sheehan and Detective Barry Harwood."

"Mr. Lynch, have you been read your rights?"

"Fuck off."

"You've turned down an offer of legal representation. That right?"

"Don't need a fucking lawyer. Bloody blood-sucking layabouts."

"Right. Let's start then." I look to Baz.

Baz looks briefly through the report in his hand. "Mr. Lynch, did you meet or know Alan and Geraldine Shine of One Kincora Drive?"

Jimmy brings up his big knucklehead. Sets those beady brown eyes on Baz. Folds his arms. He doesn't even give us a *no comment* answer.

"Mr. Lynch, can you answer the question?"

"No, I can't."

I look down at the table, nod. "Okay." When I lift my eyes, he's watching me, his eyes hard, his body still locked tight to the chair, his breath controlled. And I get the impression that he's waiting for something. Like he's built up all his defenses because he suspects what might be coming.

I fix my gaze on his. "Tell us what you know about the container at Dublin Port."

He looks out from the thick ledge of his forehead. "What container?"

"We already know all about the container."

The muscles at the tops of his arms tense beneath the thin T-shirt he's wearing, and he gives a stiff shrug. "Well, then you know more than me, don't ye."

I change tack. "Are you familiar with the Hennessy case, Mr. Lynch?"

"No." You could miss it, the tiny flicker that crosses his face. But I see it, a little spark of emotion at the mention of the Hennessys.

"It's been all over the news."

He sighs. "Well yeah, I'd heard of it, but I don't know either of them."

I straighten. "Either of them?"

"Seán or the sister," he adds.

I give him a moment, watch the movement of his thick neck, the muscles convulsing as he swallows. He throws his head to the side and his neck pops. Cracks each of his knuckles in against his palm.

"Let's go back to the container, shall we? We located it in Dublin Port and we believe it was used to store Alan Shine's and Conor Sheridan's corpses. Mr. Brennan has kindly let us know that you were the one who used it most. He says you instructed him to look out for it."

He draws his chin in. "Is that so?"

"Your prints were found inside this container."

He glances at the camera again. Sighs. And I can feel the change in him, and it makes me nervous. Like someone's flicked a switch. He looks down at his hands.

"Okay," he says.

I glance at Baz. Surprised at the change in Lynch's tone. "Why were your prints found inside this container?"

He looks up at me, a curl of a smile on his mouth. "I'd say that'd be from when I packed Alan Shine's cunting body into the freezer. And Sheridan's too, for that matter. Forgot to wear gloves on one of them, can't remember which though."

In my mind I'm running backward, trying to correct the pace of this interview where we are suddenly playing catch-up. Baz is choking, flicking through his notes like a newbie.

"When was the last time you saw Alan Shine alive, Mr. Lynch?"

"Must be up on three weeks ago now. Yeah. Was a pisser of a day. I remember the rain beatin' down on the metal roof of the container."

"You killed Alan Shine?"

He grins. "Yeah." He takes a deep breath and the playing field of his chest swells.

"Why?"

He shrugs. "Why not."

"And Conor Sheridan?"

He lifts his chin. "Him too."

"You strangled him?"

He lifts both his hands, holds them up at the level of my neck, squeezes the air in front of me. "Wouldn't have taken long but no, I shot him."

"Where is the gun now, Mr. Lynch?"

"The sea."

"Right, so you shot Conor Sheridan, your housemate of five years; what did you do then?"

"Put him in the freezer 'til the right tide came up. Then dressed him up nice and clean and laid him out on Clontarf beach."

It should feel good to get his confession but it reeks of lies. "Did you carry him down? To the beach?"

"No, came in by water."

"By boat?"

"No, I fucking swam. Of course by boat. A friend of mine owns one. I asked if I could borrow it. Has a nice wee inflatable he didn't mind me taking out as long as I put fuel in the engine."

I remember that the boat information is up for grabs. That it's public knowledge.

"So you left Conor Sheridan on the beach. Then what?"

"Then I left."

"You wrote something in the sand?"

He looks down at his hands, and for the first time, he seems uncertain. "Dunno. Maybe. I was in a bit of a rush."

I straighten. Test his story. This killer will not have forgotten a single aspect of Sheridan's death. Particularly the one-word label he left at his victim's feet for us to find.

I take a drink of coffee. Nod. Keep my tone light. "What did you write?"

His hands come up, move over the top of his hairless head. He doesn't meet my eyes. "I don't remember."

"We found a knife in Alan Shine's hand. There was something written on that too. What was it?"

He leans forward, irritation knitting his brows together. "Who cares? I killed them both."

Baz looks up from his notes. He takes up the thread, catching on quickly to the problem Lynch is building around this interview. "Can you describe the inside of the container, Mr. Lynch?"

"It has carpet on the floor, dark. A big fuck-off freezer hooked up to a generator."

"Anything else kept in the freezer apart from your victims?"

"Nope."

"Are you sure? Nothing important to you, perhaps?"

Lynch's narrow eyes glare at Baz. His jaw thrusts out so that his bottom lip rests in a stubborn pout over the top. "Nope," he answers.

No journal.

"Did you set it up?" Baz asks.

"I did, yeah."

"And what about Brennan? What has he got to do with it?"

He looks at Baz. "Paid Brennan to keep the area clear and keep an eye on it. He works there. Could come and go without much bother."

Baz pushes him further. "Can you give us some more detail about the contents of the container, Mr. Lynch?"

"I don't fucking know. I wasn't eating my meals there or nothing."

"Right." I stand. And he looks panicked and relieved all at once. He holds out his hands.

"You charging me now?"

"We've a few things to check out first."

He gets up and his chair tips over. "I fucking confessed. It was me; I did it."

"Thank you, Mr. Lynch."

He moves out from behind the table, steps toward me. "Do you need me to give you a demo, Detective?"

Baz is on his feet, fists clenched. "Calm down, Jimmy. These things take time."

I move to the door. "Put your feet up," I say, and watch the red rage descend over his face. "We'll be back soon enough."

Baz follows me out of the room. I close the door on our suspect, and both of us pause. Clancy is standing at the viewing window. Eyes on Lynch.

"That was something." He gives us both a sheepish smile.

Silence draws out across the small room. I look to Baz. He tucks his notes under his arm, then pushes both hands into his pockets. "Well, I wasn't expecting a bloody confession, that's for sure."

More silence. Finally Jack looks between us. "I'm sorry," he says.

I nod. Make my way into the hallway. "Lynch is lying," I say over my shoulder.

Jack gives a short laugh. "No doubt about it."

I wave them out of the room toward the main floor. Jack draws the staff's attention; eyes peek out round partitions. Helen on a call, half-listening, tracks our progress to the case board.

He stands in front of the board, tips his head back, takes in the width of the case. "The suit," he says. "That's important."

"Sheridan's suit?" Baz asks.

"Yes," I say. "The suit looks increasingly like a remorse thing. I thought it was part of the killer's signature maybe, an extra little flourish to add to his titillation but, after Lynch's account, I think dressing Sheridan in the suit was Lynch."

I scan the array of photos. The Hennessys. Sheridan. The Shines. Our line of suspects, major and minor: McDonagh, Brennan, Lynch. "Maybe he's developed a relationship with the killer. A closeness. Neither of the Shines was dressed with such care. The priest's vestments were clearly part of the killer's signature. A two fingers up at hypocrisy, Alan Shine the church volunteer who then went home to terrorize his wife. Geraldine Shine was left naked from the waist up. But Conor was dressed well enough for his own funeral. It's common among killers who know their victims to cover the bodies up afterward. Conor Sheridan's clothes might have been a display of remorse that came from someone who knew the victim. And as you said"—I glance back at Baz—"Jimmy Lynch was his flatmate of five years."

Baz shakes his head slowly. "But he was happy enough to stand by and let him be murdered. At least we now know why Conor's room was bolted. He probably suspected something was going on with his housemate."

I give him a smile, nod. "I don't think Jimmy Lynch killed Conor Sheridan, but he was definitely there when his flatmate murdered, or soon after, and dressed him in that suit."

Baz lets out a long breath; his shoulders sag. "He got the crime scenes all wrong too. No mention of the journal in the freezer. Not able to remember he'd written KILLER in the sand at Sheridan's feet. Or recall that WEAPON had been etched on the knife."

"I would think he was on a need-to-know basis."

Clancy is still studying the wall. "So he's protecting someone, or he's more afraid of the killer than a prison sentence," he murmurs to no one in particular.

"Helen?" I call out. She puts down the phone and approaches. I see her arms twitching at her sides and for a moment I think she might just hug Jack Clancy.

"Hi, sir, just wanted to say how good it is to see you back." A well-restrained smile tugging at the corners of her mouth.

Clancy doesn't lift his gaze from the case board when he replies. "I'm not back."

Her smile widens. "Yes, sir."

I bring her attention back to me. "Helen, have you got the copy of the journal?"

"Yes, Chief." She goes to her desk, collects it, and brings it over. "We've been working with a hand-writing expert. Nothing to name the writer but the samples match the letters to Sheridan, also the message written on the brick that was thrown through Tanya's window." I feel a gut-punch of anxiety at the mention of Tanya's name. The case reaching out, someone's hands grasping at my home, my family. I cough to clear the tightness in my throat. "However." Helen hands me the journal. I open it and she continues. "I did notice something about the picture of Seán Hennessy. It wasn't one that has been circulated in the press. I'm guessing it must be from the family's collection?"

I turn to the image of Seán Hennessy at the back of the journal, pass it to Jack. Then look over his arm at the photo.

Jack taps the photo as if to bring forth the memory. "You're right. He's much younger here, hair not as long as when—" He stops and I reckon he was about to say *when he was with Rona* but he catches himself. "—when he was arrested," he finishes.

I take the journal from Clancy. It's still open on the last page. The image of Seán, pigeon-toed and skinny, standing in his garden. Along the side of the photo where it has been cut, the edge of a green sleeve. Another person standing out of shot. Something stirs in my memory. For some reason, I know it to be the sleeve of Bríd Hennessy's coat. A green wool coat. A bright color. I hunt for why I know this.

"You all right?" Clancy asks.

"The photo," I say. "Cara Hennessy. I visited her a few days ago. She was wearing a locket. Inside was a picture of her and her mother, Bríd. This looks like it was cut from same image."

I remember the small picture enclosed in Cara's locket and can easily imagine what the whole would've looked like. A family portrait. The sky scrubbed gray, like it might be drizzling. The family under the sycamore in their backyard. A formal presentation for an important day. Bríd's hand resting on Cara's shoulder. Cara is in her Communion dress. Her dress is grand. Startling white. Neat white slip-ons encase her feet, her hands are pointed in prayer.

Baz leans in. "*Justice*," he says, reaching across and pointing at the label over Seán Hennessy's image. "The final stage in the criminal sequence. Victim, weapon, killer, *and* justice."

"Seán's the final victim?" I ask.

Immediately Baz asks another question. "So that's who Lynch is protecting? Cara Hennessy. She's directing and he's doing the heavy lifting."

I share a worried glance with Baz. My mouth becoming dry at the thought that Cara has been pulling the strings of these murders all along. Seventeen years in the making. A grand tapestry of death, mimicking the murders of her parents. Her victims chosen carefully, all symbolic of the slow, winding path that led to her own family's destruction. The victim of domestic abuse, the abuser, the killer who wrote up the story, selling the lie that an abuser was a good man and therefore leaving more victims vulnerable. And now, finally, justice for what happened to a ten-year-old girl on the back lawn of her home. "She blames Seán for what happened." I taste acid on the back of my tongue. "If she got close to Lynch, she could get close to Sheridan," I reply. "Maybe she convinced Lynch this had to happen until his belief matched hers."

Clancy looks down at Hennessy's picture. "If Cara Hennessy is after justice who else could be on her list?"

Baz is leafing through the journal. He lingers over the pages with his image, Clancy's. "I think if she's looking for justice, there are many who could fit that bill. The law, for example." He glances quickly at Clancy then at me. "All of us here, Tanya, the lawyer who is trying to overturn her brother's conviction . . ." He pauses, glances at Jack. "Even Rona could be a possible target."

Clancy shifts his weight. "Someone should get Hennessy to a safe house. Get armed officers out to Tanya and"—he clears his throat—"Rona. The rest of us, stay armed and stay in touch."

Baz hands me the journal, points to the picture of Bríd Hennessy facedown on the lawn. There is a large circle drawn in red over the top half of Bríd's body; I'd thought it was the killer's way to focus their attention on the pattern of stab wounds but now I see what's caught Baz's eye.

"The blouse," I say.

"Makes some sense now," he says. "If Bríd was found like this, with her top torn off, Geraldine had to be found like this also but"—he peers back into the journal—"perhaps returning the blouse to the house was all about a longing to bring her mother some respect. If she couldn't cover up her mother's nakedness, she would return her clothing to a symbol of their home." When he looks up, there's a heavy kind of sadness in his eyes. "You said a deep psychological need, didn't you?"

"But the partial footprint?"

"Jimmy's." He straightens, nods to Helen. "Helen, put an alert out on the system. She could be armed. What's her address, Frankie?"

I take a deep breath, pull back the curtain, and let Cara Hennessy out from behind Eva Moran's shadow. "Milfield Road, Athlone."

"I've no doubt Lynch will have sent her word before we brought him in, but maybe luck is on our side," Baz says.

I picture Seán Hennessy. A sitting duck in his flat. How delighted he'll be when his sister turns up on his doorstep. All full of the hope of reconciliation. Would she kill him immediately, or would she crush that hope first?

Helen raises her pencil in the air. "How about her phone? Could we use that to trace her? Site Analysis might at least give us a county to start with."

In my mind's eye, I see the picture of Seán Hennessy, the word JUSTICE hanging over his head like a guillotine. "I don't think there's much doubt about where she's heading but yes, try it." I grab my coat. "I'll get Seán to a safe house."

During the interchange, Clancy has gone quiet.

"Okay?" I ask.

I can see the worry shifting beneath Jack's thick brows. Rona.

"I—" he starts.

"You should go to Rona's."

He draws in a breath, his head bobbing in agreement. Then he's gone, a desperate stumble in his step as he hurries to get to his daughter.

Baz has already taken over a desk. Phone against his ear, Athlone garda station on the other end. I take a last look at the wandering case on the wall. Seventeen years in the making. A grand tapestry of death, mimicking the murders of her parents. How long has Cara been planning this?

I think of that little spider hidden under its roof of silver. Waiting. So patient. And I know the answer. She's waited a long time to come out of hiding. And all the while she's been laying out her web, waiting for her prey to hit the sticky tendrils.

CHAPTER 24

BY THE TIME we get out to Seán Hennessy's, dawn is reaching across the sky, gray clouds softening the light. I park a little way down the street. It's raining. A soft swirl on an icy breeze. Baz sits tense beside me, his eyes searching the front of Hennessy's building. I turn off the ignition. The streets are pretty empty. No dog walkers but a couple of cars pass, early commuters determined to beat the city traffic into work. The silhouette of a jogger disappears down the promenade, sending a flock of seagulls into the damp air; their screeches echo across the quiet bay.

It's not that I expected Cara to be walking the streets of Clontarf but all the same I can't help looking out for her quick stride, her head bent to her chest, her hands in pockets, doing her best to remain unseen. But if she is here, I can't see her, although I know she won't be waiting for us.

"Ready?" I look to Baz.

He nods, checks his holster. "Why do I feel like we're walking into something bad here?"

"We just need to get Seán to safety and then we'll regroup. Keep watchful."

He reaches into the backseat and grabs the enforcer. "Just in case," he says, and I nod in agreement.

He pushes the door open, and I follow suit. We meet round the front of the car then with another glance up and down the road, we cross and walk briskly toward Hennessy's building. There's a nervous kind of anticipation emanating from Baz. His hand goes to his ribs too often, and I worry that he might still be harboring bad feelings about the beating.

We've sent uniforms out to the old Hennessy house, or where it once stood, although I know they'll find nothing there. This is not the movies. We won't find our killer sitting in their favorite childhood spot, bathed in a sepia light and contemplating the path that led them there. No, we find our perps in one of two places, either running from us or toward us.

When we get to the building door, we try Hennessy's doorbell and wait for an answer. When none comes I press the doorbell of the flat opposite. Seán had mentioned an aged neighbor, and I hope whoever it is will let us into the building. After a few moments, a shaky voice crackles through the intercom.

"Hello?"

I lean close to the speaker to overcome the sound of the wind coming in from the sea. "Hello, this is Detective Frankie Sheehan. We're trying to access flat six; could you let us in, please?"

There's no reply but shortly after the door buzzes and we push inside. I make my way up the stairs in silence, Baz trailing after me. I can feel his watchful eyes on my back. When we arrive on the right floor, the neighbor's door is ajar and I see the old man, wearing a pressed light gray shirt, his white snowy hair and soft eyes peeking through the few inches that his door chain allows.

"You looking for Seán?" he asks. His voice quiet and hesitant. Not quite what I was expecting given Seán's description of him.

"Yes," I say, and hold up my badge. "Is he in?"

The man's eyes widen a little in what could be fear or understanding. He purses his lips slightly as if he's about to tell us something then shakes his head. "I couldn't say." And he shuts the door and I hear the sound of the lock turning.

Baz doesn't wait much longer; he raps on Seán's door. "Mr. Hennessy, it's Detective Harwood and DCS Sheehan. Could you open up, please."

There's no answer but I can hear movement beyond the door, the gentle pad of footsteps across the floor. Baz glances at me; he hears it too. He tries again. "Seán?" Another rap.

And for the first time since leaving the Bureau, I feel a real twist of discomfort in my gut. A fear that pulls on my breath. I have an image of Seán taking up those pups, submerging them in the bucket of cold water, then Cara spinning the locket at her throat. I blink, inhale the stiff air of the stairwell and try to focus. Baz looks back at me, nods, an understanding that we're going in. I unclip my gun and suddenly I'm unsure about what we're going to find on the other side of the door. Seán, confused but alive, well and muttering about being woken so early—or something else.

Baz stands a little back from the door and widens his stance; he takes a second to brace himself then drives the enforcer at the door. The wood of the door splinters and the sound of the impact crashes through the building. Another swing and the lock gives. He steps aside, puts down the enforcer, and removes his weapon. I've already moved forward, my hand out on the edge of the door. I push it all the way open, into Seán's flat and a cold dread washes through me.

"Don't move," I hear Baz command from over my shoulder. His voice is hard but it has little effect on our suspect.

Cara Hennessy sits at a table by the single window in the flat. Her small hands rest over a gun. She's wearing the same blue hoodie she had on when I met her, her brown hair loose around her face. She's looking right at us but makes no move when we step inside.

"Where's Seán?" I ask.

She fixes me with a dull look. "He said you'd come here." Her voice is small and calm. She lifts the gun and holds it out. "Don't worry; it's not loaded."

Baz keeps his weapon trained on her. "Drop it to the floor and slide it toward us."

She does as she's asked, lays the gun on the bare boards of the floor and pushes it away with her foot. Baz removes a plastic bag from his pocket, takes the gun up, checks the chamber. Satisfied it's not loaded, he drops it inside the bag and puts it in his pocket. I walk toward Cara Hennessy, cuffs ready. She holds out her hands.

"Against the wall," I say.

She moves, faces the wall next to the window.

"Wrists together at your back." She does as instructed. I close the cuffs around her narrow wrists, give them a tug to check they're secure then turn her to face me. "Where is he?"

She keeps her mouth tightly closed as if parting her lips even for breath might cause the answer to spill out.

"Cara Hennessy, I'm arresting you for the murders of Alan Shine, Geraldine Shine, and Conor Sheridan. You do not need to say anything but anything you do say may be taken down as evidence and used against you in a court of law. Do you understand?"

She doesn't answer but looks at me as if she can see right through my being, the expression on her face calm but there's a defiant spark in her eyes. Baz is checking through the other rooms in the flat. He emerges from the bedroom, a pair of trainers in his hands; he holds them out toward me. "I don't think Seán is the one in danger here," he says. The trainers are black and are the same brand as those that left the impression on Geraldine Shine's kitchen floor. The house is around me again. That soured place. The smell of the blackened roast in my nostrils, the piercing speck of blood lit up by the luminol and beside it a shoe print. My throat closes over. And I see him. Seán Hennessy. A dark figure against the orange evening. He's at the back of the Shine house. His hand, gloved, pries open the window. It's easy to slip inside but not so easy on a wet day to not leave something behind. The edge of a footprint as he steps across the kitchen floor, the impact shakes a mist of blood from his sleeve. It's a risk but the desire is great. How perfect to invade his victim's life with such thoroughness, to violate the haven of her home with a token of her death.

Baz directs Cara to the car, and I wait for him to disappear down the stairwell and then phone Tanya. There's no answer. Heat gathers around my neck and I feel panic beating against my temples. With shaking fingers I call Helen and ask her to patch me through to the uniforms that were sent out to Tanya's house. When the officer connects, he tells me they're at the property and all is safe and secure. I can hear Tanya in the background, her voice high with anger at being woken at an *ungodly hour*.

Then, "Give me the phone," I hear her demand, and the officer's voice grows distant.

"What's this about, Frankie? They won't tell us anything here." Her voice is urgent down the line.

"Our suspect, the killer, he's on the run and we have reason to believe that you are a possible target."

She clicks her tongue in annoyance. "Give up the police speak. Who?"

"We thought first Cara Hennessy but now"—I take a shaky breath—"now it's looking like Seán."

She's silent, then, "And you think he could come here?"

"We don't know. We don't know where he is; all we know is he's not finished and he's dangerous."

"Okay." She sounds stunned or stung, I'm not sure which.

"I've got to go. Please stay where you are until we apprehend him."

"Yes," she murmurs.

I hang up, run down the stairs. CSI is pulling up. Keith climbs out of the front of the van. "Third floor, flat six," I say. He nods and begins setting up.

I go to my car, where I can just make out the crown of Cara Hennessy's head through the back window. I get into the driver's seat, clip on the belt.

"Back to process her?"

"Yes." I turn the car around, head back down Strand Road, Dublin city in the distance. The traffic now heavier, commuters, tourist buses, and lorries trundling toward the motorways and city. "Tanya's safe," I say to Baz.

"As are Clancy and Rona, he's just texted." He holds up his phone. "And I've put in an alert for Seán Hennessy's whereabouts."

My hands tighten on the steering wheel. "Who else? Who else are we missing?"

"Could he have just taken off?" Baz asks.

This wins a sound from Cara, a sudden hissing snort. I study her face in the rearview. She's staring out the window, watching the gray, flat sea pass beyond the seawall.

"Do you know?" I direct the question to her reflection in the mirror but she doesn't turn. Her chin juts in a display of stubbornness. I drive slowly; something tells me that if Cara is going to talk it's here where the walls of the Bureau aren't tight around her and the question of her freedom is not so definite.

"Is it someone in law enforcement? Is that the justice he wants? Was it Tanya? Is that it?"

I can see the small muscles in her neck tighten and relax as she swallows down a response.

"Who is Justice, Cara?" She doesn't answer. A cool smile growing on her lips. The blank sea passes to my left. Ahead, St. Catherine's is tucked away behind the iron railings, bathed in the frigid dawn light. The church where the Shines were found, where Cara once bounced a dry stick on a dry day. Where Bríd Hennessy first approached my mum for help.

I slow to a stop at the pedestrian crossing, let a woman and child cross. In the middle of the road the child bends, scoops up some precious find but the woman shakes her finger, her face glowering with a reprimand. The child throws her treasure down, glares at it for a moment, then strikes out with a small foot, against the woman, in retaliation.

And suddenly, Cara's voice comes from the back, chilled and steady. "You're looking at justice with the eyes of the law; you should look at it through the eyes of the wronged."

I drive on. She's right. From Cara and Seán's perspective, they're not interested in the justice that I serve. They are interested in the opposite.

"Revenge," I whisper.

Then Cara, not quite able to contain her gloat, continues through taut lips. I watch her tiny teeth flash as she speaks. "She could've stopped it all if she'd taken the time to help my mum. She said she'd help. We waited and all we got was a stinking pamphlet. A pamphlet that my da found. Your ma turned her back, like everyone else, decided it wasn't her problem. Wiped her hands clean of our dirt."

A terrific fear drops through me and my hands tighten on the steering wheel. I look to Baz; he already has the radio in his band.

"Dispatch," a voice says.

"Armed unit to 43 Conquer Hill. Immediately," he orders.

Swallowing, I turn the car around, the hollow ring of dread in my ears. I reach for the lights. The dash and rear window bubble up in neon blues. The siren, sound unfolding, spiraling down. Cars and vans choke up the route, and I turn up a side road, navigate my way across the back streets of Clontarf, sirens raging.

CHAPTER 25

I PULL TO A STOP on my parents' street and push out of the car. The street is still full with parked cars, curtains drawn on all the houses. The wind is damp and cold. It blows over my face, snakes round my neck, where it feels like a hand is gripping my throat. Looking at the house, at first it appears as if nothing is amiss and I have a stupid thought that maybe Cara has got her brother wrong. But then I see that the door is open, just a fraction, an inch or two. It creaks inwards then back again, sucked to and fro by the wind.

I must move quickly because I'm at the gate. Baz is somewhere close, behind me, beside me, I'm not wholly aware but I know he's here. The gate opens, groans beneath my palm. Then, fear stiffening my movements, I walk up the short path, put a hand on the shining varnished wood of the front door, hear the familiar sigh of the hinges, the drag of the doormat. I step into the hallway and the soft scent of the polish my mam uses drifts up around me but beneath the warm familiarity of the house there's an unsettling silence. No sound of a kettle bubbling from the kitchen, no clink of cutlery, no murmur of the television from the living room or the crackle of a newspaper as Dad turns the pages.

I sense Baz move in behind me, his presence swallowing up the light. I'm halfway down the hall when I feel the breeze. It threads up through the narrow corridor of family photos and lifts the hair from my forehead. I walk into the kitchen. The table is clear, no breakfast utensils out yet but the window is wide open. The blind, torn from its runners, is hanging partway down the pane. The stiff material puffs and flattens in the breeze. The back door is wide open. Finally, I look back at Baz; his eyes are on the back door. He moves to the other side of the room, prepares his firearm. Hands shaking, I do the same, then taking a big lungful of air, I step out into the garden.

The breath leaves me, and for a moment I feel my legs want to fold, to drop me into nothingness. I take in a long breath and lock my elbows, keep my gun high and aimed at our target. Seán is sitting on the swing. One hand curled round the chain, the other bloody and resting in his lap, a knife gripped casually in his fingers. He's breathing fast and even from the short distance between us I can see the wildness in his eyes. The excitement at what he's just done.

At his feet, my mum. I'm afraid to look but already I can feel the cry ripping up my throat. Tears blur my vision. My dad lies some way off to the left. I allow myself a quick glance at him. I can't see any blood, and I'm not sure if I imagine the rise and fall of his chest. Baz moves slowly toward him, and Seán turns his head to watch.

"Don't move." I hear the growling order come from between my teeth and it surprises me.

Baz squats down, his hand going to my dad's neck, searching for a pulse. After a moment, he glances over at me and nods.

I take a tremulous breath and look properly at Mam. She's in her nightdress, her slippers still warming her feet. She lies partly on her front as if Seán has just dropped her by accident. Her face is relaxed, her mouth slightly open. I could convince myself she was okay if it weren't for the bright red staining her front. Pain explodes inside me, sends spikes of agony through my being, and the gun shakes in my outstretched hands. I can feel my mouth moving, opening, closing, dragging in air, my pulse thrumming in my ears. I have the sense that if I blink hard enough, look fast enough to the side, to another place, all of this will disappear, I'd sidestep it or rewind time and none of this would be happening.

Then he moves and reality snaps around me. He lets go of the swing and draws the bloody knife higher onto his lap. I point the gun. The trigger hot beneath my finger. He looks right at me, and I see that he knows what I'm about to do. Knows that I mean to kill him. Acceptance is written over his face. I fix the gun more firmly in my hand. Cup my other hand beneath to steady the shaking.

I hear the click of Baz's gun, the safety released, and then the warning in his voice, telling me to stand down. "Frankie."

But all I can see are Seán's eyes, intense and victorious, at the end of the chamber. And all I want to do is tear him down. Throw away gun and knife, go at him, fingernails and clawing hands until he is crying out in agony, until he can feel something of what I'm feeling. Then she moves, my mum, a little heave of her back followed by a weak, choking cough. And relief splinters through my insides, a huge breath of it rushing in so quickly it could split me open. Seán's eyes go to her then back to mine in a second. Confusion and anger on his face. He hadn't meant to leave her alive. His eyes narrow, darken on her prone form.

"Don't move!" I shout.

But even as I scream, he's tightening his grip on the knife, moving over her. His arm is a blur as it descends but it never reaches its target.

The sound of the shot cracks against my ear, and Seán's body gives a sudden lurch as if he'd been punched in the throat by some invisible force. His face registers a brief moment of surprise and the knife slips free of his sticky grasp. He tries to reach for the swing but his hands flutter blindly in front of him and he slumps down onto the lawn.

I pull back my weapon. Unsure about what's just happened. I look to Baz. He's still in a firing stance, the gun trained at Seán as if he was fighting some battle not to shoot again.

I run to Mam, crouch at her head; my fingers looking for the pulse along her neck, my ear low to catch her breath. I find it, a quick flicker of life just above her collarbone, and I grip her hand in relief. Tell her to hold on, that I'm here. Baz is kneeling at my dad's side, phone to his ear, already calling in paramedics. They arrive swiftly, swarm in through the house, lay down stretchers and equipment over the lawn. They take away both my parents, shouting instructions as they go, and I follow them back into the house but at the door, I pause, look back. Baz is standing watchful to the side of the garden. Seán laid out in the middle of the lawn, his limbs spread and unmoving. Two medics are working a tube down his throat, working to save his life.

CHAPTER 26

THEY PLAY CLIPS from the documentary between the news segments.

"Did I feel sad that my dad was gone?" Seán Hennessy asks. "No. I didn't. The only emotion I felt was anger. Anger at what had happened to me. Anger that he'd gotten away with it. He'd escaped. He succeeded in screwing me over. Ma, she planned to leave him. I saw her try but she couldn't quite do it. Even for us. That made me angry too.

"Inside, I learned all I could about the little cogs of psychology that left us imprisoned in a childhood of terror. I learned that I should have felt sorry for my ma. I learned about the terror that reigned over our lives, infused by the mundaneness of domesticity, having breakfast together while nursing bruises. Ironing school uniforms, polishing shoes among the mayhem. All the small events that told us that we were normal. But we weren't.

"That is how it happens. And another hour, another day slips by and into that web you go, deeper until you wake one day and realize you don't have what it takes to extricate yourself. The hurdles have risen when you weren't looking and now you can't get over them. The only way out for my parents was death. Isn't that the way out for us all."

The hospital café is quiet. Relatives asking to be distracted from their individual crises. Eyes trained on the TV in the corner of the room. And Hennessy is a good distraction. Completely absorbing. They are looking for the signs of a killer and finally they're visible. He's visible. Occasionally, a doctor, a cleaner steps away from their work to eat, chew through a stale sandwich.

In the end we discovered Cara Hennessy's isolation in Athlone was not as isolated as it should have been. The search of her house turned up a suitcase filled with letters, the envelopes showing the sender's address as Bríd Hennessy's sister, Cara's aunt, Irene Duffy.

Cara Hennessy has refused to speak since her arrest but her aunt gave us the background we needed. Irene is a shy woman. From the moment she opened her front door to us, she half-hid behind it, then after inviting Clancy and me in, she retreated back into her home as if she were the one who didn't belong there. She lives alone and when she spoke her face took on a startled expression as if unused to the sound of her own voice. I liked her. Sometimes you get a sense of the goodness in people and to me, it was clear Irene Duffy's involvement in this case was down to misguided good intention.

"I've let her down," she said. Quiet. Referring to Bríd. "I should have pushed more, insisted that Cara stayed with me but social services, the guards they thought I wouldn't handle it so well. They did tests." She touched the side of her head then looked to the floor, hair all thick fuzz, still dark despite her age.

Her mouth had puckered a bit, and she rolled her lips one over the other before she spoke again. "But I couldn't go without trying to reach out to Cara. To let her know that her family was still here. I know Bríd wouldn't have wanted her to be alone. She was the baby. I gave her the locket and asked her to write to me. That it would be a secret."

It was seven years before Cara wrote that first letter. And she had one request for her aunt. To contact her brother. She wanted to know why he'd killed their parents.

But Irene had never believed her nephew killed his parents. "John." She had pressed her lips then, as if she'd just uttered a swear word, her eyes taking on a brittle hardness. "I knew it'd been him. Poor Seán." She looked up at me then, testing my reaction. "He must have been very frightened. He was just a child really."

She hadn't visited Seán though, which said something behind all her regret. Perhaps it was her natural shyness that kept her away, perhaps guilt at not helping her sister sooner, or maybe she'd sensed that badness, saw it had been cracked open and was already leaking into the future.

Then came the complex exchange of mail. Seán sending his letters to Irene, who would then send them to Cara, ensuring their correspondence went unnoticed by authorities. Unchecked. Until it was too late.

"I thought I was doing something for Bríd; she would've wanted them to know one another."

Shortly before Seán's release, Irene had written to Cara, suggesting they should all meet up. But no reply came. After a month, she wrote again and was met with more silence. She could've visited her, she supposed, but she knew her niece wouldn't have welcomed an intrusion, so she didn't.

Clancy and I gathered up all the correspondence between Seán and Cara and then the texts and emails that had continued between the siblings after Seán's release. Finally I could hear Seán Hennessy's true voice. Could see the killer in the man, clear as morning dew. Seven years of preparation and careful manipulation.

I read through the correspondence, saw the new narrative that he drip-fed patiently into a vulnerable ear. How wronged they were. How alone. They owed it to themselves to act, to do something grand that would finally allow their story and the many like theirs to be heard. A slow coercion of his sister until she saw their past, saw their future as he did. Saw that someone needed to pay. Eventually, Cara began to offer up ideas on how they could take revenge. Her courtship of Jimmy Lynch. Her excitement at the progression of their relationship. *He'll do it*, she wrote. *He'll do anything for me.* Then the letters grew longer. More hatred of the system, of those responsible. As Baz said, seventeen years is enough time to cultivate hatred. They took their time stalking potential victims. It was at a pub that Seán heard about the Shines, McDonagh mouthing off about his affair with a battered wife.

Geraldine Shine, an innocent who did nothing to deserve her end, only that the abusive marriage she found herself in had awakened some slumbering anger Seán had at his mother. The blouse returned to the house may be one of those things that will remain elusive to us, the reason never fully accessible. But Baz's comments on a deeper psychological need ring true.

Maybe it was some odd attempt at restoring his mother's dignity. Or maybe, there was some part of Seán and Cara that wanted to make a point about her partial nakedness, wanted to show how their mother's clothes were never straightened, that Seán was swept away or wasn't allowed near her to cover her up, not before all those medics and forensic examiners had photographed and pawed at her body. Something they both know she would have hated.

Alan Shine, the church worker, wife beater, was everything that Seán despised about his own father, and Conor Sheridan had never left Seán's sights, his anger further fanned when Conor wrote to him suggesting that they should meet.

I get up from the table, go to the coffee machine, place a paper cup under the spout. Select espresso. When the cup fills, I take it and move out of the café. My dad is recovering from a concussion at home, but it will be days, if not weeks, before I can take Mam home. Every time I visit her, I feel anger build at what Seán did, what he took from us; the sanctuary of our home forever scarred by his violence.

The squeaking polish of the hospital floor clicks under my heels. He's been moved from intensive care. *Stable.* That's the word they've used.

I pass the uniform at the door. Give him the espresso.

"Thanks, Chief," he says.

I nod. Then, taking a deep breath, I open the door.

He's awake. Frigid eyes looking out from a white face. The nurse orbits him, checking machines, tapping the bag of fluid on an IV stand. I wait by the window. The blind is rolled up and the view looks down on a full car park. Sheets of rain descend from gray heavens. The nurse makes a mark on a clipboard then returns it to a holder on the wall. She nods at me before she leaves and I nod back. The door closes and finally, I turn to him.

He speaks immediately: "I asked my mother once why she couldn't leave him." His eyes on the ceiling. "Your dad, she said, he was the monster but sometimes, sometimes he was the hero."

I take out my notebook. "I need the names of who you worked with."

He turns his face toward the window and I can see the clench of his jaw, the smooth columns of muscle along his neck.

"I didn't attack my family, kill my parents. I wish I fucking had, but I don't regret what happened to them. What happened to me. All that"—he turns his face back to me, smiles—"made me the man I am today." He lets out a long, slow breath. Winces and the round caps of his shoulders tense against pain.

"You'd just murdered Geraldine Shine when you met with Tanya West and me," I state.

He gives a little burst of laughter, his eyes dancing in his devil face. Hand braced on his chest. "That was a rush, I tell you. Thought it would be written all over me, for sure." His expression seems to soften in remembrance. "Had only time to change my clothes. Can you imagine? I could smell her death all over me that evening. And you sitting right there."

There's a knock on the door and Baz enters. Clancy on his heels.

"Seán Hennessy," I begin, "you are charged with four counts of murder. On the nineteenth of August 2012, you attacked Geraldine Shine with a knife with the intent to kill. The injuries she sustained resulted in the loss of her life. Somewhere between the dates of the fourteenth of August and the seventeenth of August, you abducted and strangled Alan Shine until he was dead. You are further charged with denying the victim the right to burial. On the fifteenth of August, you assaulted and abducted Conor Sheridan. You are charged with being complicit in his murder. You are further charged with denying the victim the right to burial." I swallow. "You are charged with the attempted murder of Sharon Sheehan and the assault of Martin Sheehan on the twenty-seventh of August. Do you have anything to say?"

He takes his time. Looks at each of us individually, his eyes sparking with satisfaction. "You made me."

I SIT IN THE DARK of my office, my eyes on the CCTV footage on my computer screen. I replay the film again. Watch Seán Hennessy appear on the camera outside Tony's chip shop. He's wearing his baseball cap. Navy blue, silver buckle at the back and his windbreaker is done up, collar so high around his throat it reaches his ears. His head is down, his face concealed from the camera. He deposits the outer paper wrapping from a bag of chips in a trash bin, then steps off the pavement, walks across the street toward a bench on the promenade.

I rewind the last few seconds, his long limbs, perhaps a little too thin, walk stiffly backward until I let the film play again. Now I see it, the right foot. A little quirk in his step. A bob at the knee. And I know that walk. I watched it on the footage taken of the street leading to the Shine house. I replay it again, watch the moment we made the mistake, where we failed to see that although Seán entered the shop for takeaway that evening, he was not the figure who made his way to a bench on the promenade. They'd switched. Robbie McDonagh, wearing a cap and clothing similar to Seán. Robbie was paid for this little stunt. Probably just enough to buy a few grams of weed. But it cost us another two victims. Not that he'll admit to any of it. *A bloke can buy chips, can't he,* he'd said, a dirty little grin pinching the corner of his mouth.

Baz steps into my office and stops. He reaches for the light, flicks it on. "Mood-lighting?" He closes the door then places a coffee on the desk.

I take it up, smile my thanks.

"Cara's fingerprints were the unknown in the container," he says.

I nod.

"You okay?"

"Yes. You?"

He pulls back a chair, flops down into it, rubs his face. "I don't fucking know."

Jimmy Lynch finally spilled when he was told of Cara's arrest. He didn't see manipulation. He saw love. I could've laughed, only I'd missed it. Missed the signs of Cara's involvement. He told us of their eight-month-long affair. How he'd met her on-line, that Conor's phantom girlfriend had really been his. He told us of how a couple of months into the relationship she told him who she really was, how her brother had been wronged. When he'd mentioned Conor's name, she knew it, straight off. He told us she'd seemed obsessed with him. At first, he'd thought it would blow over but then she wanted Conor to pay. He said how she was going to get a gun. She convinced him to help her brother enact his revenge. If he loved her, he would. Jimmy was all she had.

Lynch was the muscle. The man with a van. He didn't kill but he watched when Conor Sheridan was dragged blindfolded into that container. He watched as Conor was forced to his knees. And he watched Cara shoot Conor through the chest. And it made sense to me. Cara had the stomach for revenge, but not for the head shot. The last time Lynch had visited the container had been the same night Baz and I discovered it. Our assailant unmasked at least.

Hennessy had left the journal in the freezer. He knew we'd find it. Hoped it would bring me close to him. Revenge is all the sweeter with an audience.

My report for the commissioner is thesis length. I bundle the interview summaries to one side and then shuffle through the crime scene photos. I stop at a picture of the slipway. It's dark but morning light is stealing out over the sky. Conor Sheridan's body a dark slump against the seawall.

I imagine the boat that carried him drawing close to the slipway. The moon, full that night, rolls on the black sea. The strand is empty. The promenade is clear of people. I picture Jimmy turning off the engine, throwing a rope around the wet wooden leg of the slipway. Then he eases into the water. It's only to his knees and he knows they won't have long before the water pulls away and the boat is left stranded.

He reaches back into the boat. Pushes his hands beneath the man's shoulders. It's pointless but he holds his breath anyway. The man stinks. He tries not to think about what he's doing. He focuses on Cara, her small face, her eyes full of need for him. No one has ever needed him before. He heaves the upper body against his chest. The boat rocks as Seán Hennessy stands. He lifts the legs, holds one on either side of his waist.

"Don't drop him," he says to Jimmy. His voice is low but it slices across Jimmy's nerves. It takes a lot to frighten Jimmy Lynch but there's something about his girlfriend's brother that could make a grown man piss down his own leg.

"I won't," he replies.

They maneuver the corpse toward the beach. Between the breath-holding and the weight, Jimmy is sweating and gasping by the time they set Conor Sheridan down. Jimmy looks at his flatmate. He's pleased he'd gotten him the new suit. A dead man should have a suit.

"Leave," Seán says.

"You're just gonna dump him here?"

"Leave."

Jimmy doesn't need to be told a third time. He'd walk to the ends of the earth for Cara but he wasn't going to challenge this fucker. There was a look to his eyes. Jimmy couldn't quite describe it, but he'd seen the same look on some of the more creative criminals inside. A living deadness.

He turns, wades back out to the boat, unhooks the rope from the wooden pier, and pushes away. He sniffs the sleeve of his sweater. The dead man's stink is stuck to him. He'd have to burn his clothes. Cara had been impressed with him when he'd told her that Conor Sheridan was his flatmate. For a short while, he'd suspected that she'd singled him out for that reason. But in the end, he thought, it didn't matter. Besides, she'd told him often enough. Apart from her brother, Jimmy was the only other man she'd ever trusted. And that was something to Jimmy. Women rarely fell for him, that's for sure.

Baz breaks through my thoughts. He's moved to the window and is looking pityingly at the well-clipped bonsai on the sill. He picks up a shorn branch. "You've fair gone after it here."

I don't say anything but I can see he's struggling. He almost killed a man. But I don't know which part of that sentence haunts him more, the killed or the almost.

"I wish I'd done it," he says suddenly, as if reading my mind. "Killed him."

I think of my hands round the gun. How ready I was to fire. To extinguish Seán Hennessy's life. I think of my dad that day in my parents' bedroom, how I almost walked away, let him die. We are none of us far from the killer inside us.

I look at Baz. "No, you don't."

He pushes his hands back on his hips, nods, a strained expression on his face. "It feels wrong, you know. Like the stain of his crimes can't ever be washed out. Maybe if he was gone, he'd take all of it with him."

I slide the photos back into the folder. They're copies. Along with a summary. "You know that's not how it works."

Seán Hennessy's documentary footage is stored on a USB. I take up my review on the old Hennessy case, slide both items into an evidence bag. Then add them to the case folder. I put the folder into an envelope, peel away the adhesive. Seal it closed then check the address. *Donna Hegarty, Commissioner.* I push the envelope to the edge of the desk.

Baz turns away from the window. "Do you think he had a point? That the system made him?"

I don't get a chance to answer. A timid knock sounds at the door and Helen steps inside. "Sorry to disturb you," she whispers. "Only, the assistant commissioner is waiting outside."

I throw Baz an apologetic look and he nods. I get up, follow Helen out of the room to where Jack Clancy is standing next to her desk. He holds a large bouquet of lavender. The sight of the flowers is so incongruous in Clancy's hand that despite how I'm feeling, I could laugh.

He throws a miserable glance down at them when I appear. "Helen said they mean serenity, peace, or something. She thought we could take them there."

"That sounds . . . very Helen," I reply, and he gives me a pained grin.

THE HENNESSY HOUSE no longer exists. The site where it once stood holds only an outline of concrete in memory. I sit in the car, peer out the window. The hedgerow has grown, green and high. It looks impenetrable, like something from the fable of Sleeping Beauty, shielding a home that no longer exists. A little way down the street, the other houses are all turned away as if in the aftermath of tragedy, like bricks and mortar could shift perspective with the sheer horror of what they've witnessed. Behind me, a new overpass trembles overhead, ensuring that this plot won't become home to another family. There's no second chance here.

Clancy sits in the driver's seat next to me, the bouquet resting on his knee. "Ye all right?"

I open the door. "Come on."

I get out of the car, walk toward the hedge, find a gate at the side. Someone has trimmed back the shrubbery so the entrance is clear. I lift the latch, push the gate open, and we step into the Hennessys' yard. The lawn has been cut recently, and the foundations of the house are bare apart from a few determined thistles growing up between cracks in the concrete.

We move toward a large sycamore in what would have been the back garden, neither of us wanting to traverse the area where the home once stood. We stand beneath the tree in silence and survey the site, the mean sky looking down, a soft drizzle blowing in our faces.

The patio still skirts the house and gives the area a sense of geography. From my position, I can imagine easily where the back door stood, wide and open. The kitchen window, Bríd Hennessy's face, white and worried, looking out at her family in the garden. To the right, the crooked shed where John once locked the dog. To the left, the corner where Seán drowned four pups in a bucket.

Clancy holds up the flowers. "For Bríd," he says, and I nod.

He locates the patch of lawn where she was found. Bends with a huff and lays them down.

He straightens with a quick brush of his palms, relieved. "We should go," he says.

I look back at the sycamore. And picture Bríd in that ridiculous green coat, her hands resting on Cara's tiny shoulders. Cara in her Communion dress, all lace and tulle, a white rosary dangling from her fingers, a prayer book suspended at her elbow by a white ribbon. Cara Hennessy grew into her role as killer but I can't quite see her as bad. Seán Hennessy's grip was so tight on her broken heart, she ceased existing long ago.

Taking a deep breath, I start back across the garden. "Yeah," I say to Clancy as I pass, "let's get out of here."

Sitting in the passenger seat, I wait for Clancy to start the car, my eyes still lingering on the thick hedgerow, seventeen years of growth blocking out the Hennessy home. Time consuming everything but grief.

"We didn't create Seán Hennessy," I say. More to myself than to Clancy. "He was made in the home. He was made right here."

ACKNOWLEDGMENTS

THERE ARE A FEW PEOPLE I'd like to thank for their support and help during the writing of *The Killer in Me*.

At riverrun, I'd like to thank my incredible editor, Richard Arcus, for his detailed reading, enthusiasm, and brilliant editorial advice. My heartfelt gratitude to all the team at riverrun, to my copy editor, the design team, and everyone who has helped get this novel "out there" and into the hands of readers.

Thank you to all the publishing team at Dutton, in particular my wonderful editor, Stephanie Kelly, whose patience and editorial excellence have been invaluable.

Huge thanks to my fantastic agent, Susan Armstrong, and to all the rights team at C&W Agency, and to Zoe Sandler at ICM. Special thanks to my sister, Ann Kiernan, to whom this book is dedicated, for her friendship and for making me laugh (at myself). Thank you to all the friends and writing groups, especially the LadyKillers, who continue to support, read, and shout about my books.

For research, thank you to those members of the Thames Valley Police and An Garda Síochána who patiently answered my queries on police procedure, and to solicitor Brian P. Doyle for talking me through some of the more technical legal subjects in this novel; any errors or bending of reality are my own.

Finally, thank you to Matthew for his encouragement, belief, and love—and to my daughter, Grace, who inspires me to do better every day.

ABOUT THE AUTHOR

Olivia Kiernan grew up in the Irish countryside, a background that left her with a great appreciation of storytelling. Being almost sensible, she shelved aspirations of becoming a writer and embarked on a career in science, spending six years in university studying anatomy and physiology before receiving a BSc in Chiropractic in 2003. She worked in this vein for more than a decade, always writing in the evenings after work and completing an MA in Creative Writing through part-time study in 2012.

In 2015, she began writing her debut novel, *Too Close to Breathe*, the first in a crime thriller series featuring Detective Frankie Sheehan, which published in 2017. *The Killer in Me* is her second novel.